Belladonna

ANNE BISHOP

Belladonna

RoC

A ROC BOOK

ROC
Published by New American Library, a division of
Penguin Group (USA) Inc., 375 Hudson Street,
New York, New York 10014, USA
Penguin Group (Canada), 90 Eglinton Avenue East, Suite 700, Toronto,
Ontario M4P 2Y3, Canada (a division of Pearson Penguin Canada Inc.)
Penguin Books Ltd., 80 Strand, London WC2R 0RL, England
Penguin Ireland, 25 St. Stephen's Green, Dublin 2,
Ireland (a division of Penguin Books Ltd.)
Penguin Group (Australia), 250 Camberwell Road, Camberwell, Victoria 3124,
Australia (a division of Pearson Australia Group Pty. Ltd.)
Penguin Books India Pvt. Ltd., 11 Community Centre, Panchsheel Park,
New Delhi - 110 017, India
Penguin Group (NZ), 67 Apollo Drive, Mairangi Bay,
Auckland 1311, New Zealand (a division of Pearson New Zealand Ltd.)
Penguin Books (South Africa) (Pty.) Ltd., 24 Sturdee Avenue,
Rosebank, Johannesburg 2196, South Africa

Penguin Books Ltd., Registered Offices:
80 Strand, London WC2R 0RL, England

First published by Roc, an imprint of New American Library,
a division of Penguin Group (USA) Inc.

First Printing, March 2007
10   9   8   7   6   5   4   3   2   1

 REGISTERED TRADEMARK—MARCA REGISTRADA

LIBRARY OF CONGRESS CATALOGING-IN-PUBLICATION DATA:

Bishop, Anne.
Belladonna/Anne Bishop.
p. cm.
ISBN-13: 978-0-451-46126-1
ISBN-10: 0-451-46126-6
I. Title.
PS3552.I7594B45 2007
813'.6—dc22   2006021515

Set in Centaur MT
Designed by Ginger Legato

Printed in the United States of America

For
Mia Qian Lee Debany.
Welcome to our landscapes.

And for the
Magicians, who understand that
love is the real magic.

ACKNOWLEDGMENTS

My thanks to Blair Boone for continuing to be my first reader, to Debra Dixon for being second reader, to Doranna Durgin for maintaining the Web site, to Dirk Flinthart for answering questions about the Irish whistle, to Nadine and Danny Fallacaro for information about things nautical, and to Pat Feidner for sharing the joys and sorrows of the journey.

Chapter One

present

In the pale gray light, that herald of the dawn, Glorianna followed the path through the woods until she reached the two-story cottage. The shutters had been painted recently, she noted as she skirted the building. In fact, the whole place looked like it had been turned out for a thorough cleaning. Even the surrounding land showed signs of being brought to order.

Good thing her cousin Sebastian and Lynnea, his heart's desire, had married at the end of summer. If Lynnea had been able to plant the gardens she wanted as well as tidy up the cottage, it was doubtful Sebastian would have had enough energy left to fulfill his duties as a married man once he fell into bed at night. Since Sebastian was an incubus and thought breathing was the only activity more necessary than sex, that was saying something about Lynnea's ambitions.

Amused by the thought, Glorianna grinned when she spotted her cousin. He stood on the other side of the lane that ran past the cottage, where a break in the trees gave him a clear view of the sky and the lake beyond the cliff.

The grin warmed to a smile that held all the love she felt for him.

His head turned a little, the only sign that he heard her approaching, but he didn't take his eyes off the sky as the sun rose.

"Will I become like other people?" Sebastian asked quietly as she slipped her arm companionably through his. "Will I start seeing the sunrise as a commonplace thing and no longer feel the wonder of it? Will I reach the point where I look at the first light of the day and see it as nothing more than a way of marking time?"

"You had to earn your sunrises," she replied, blinking away the tears that suddenly stung her eyes. "So, no, Sebastian, I don't think you'll ever take them for granted."

She could have lost him. When she'd gone to Wizard City to trap the Dark Guides, who were the most insidious allies of the Eater of the World, she had gambled on Lynnea's love and courage to keep Sebastian safe when she unleashed Heart's Justice. If Lynnea had faltered, Sebastian would have been drawn into a dark, twisted landscape that resonated with the bleak life the Dark Guides had made him believe was all he deserved.

But Lynnea hadn't faltered, and Sebastian had followed his heart, bringing them to the cottage. During the years he had lived there alone, the cottage had existed within the boundaries of the dark landscape known as the Den of Iniquity. Now it stood in the daylight landscape of Aurora, her mother Nadia's home village.

Sebastian sighed with pleasure, then looked at her. "Want some koffee?"

"Sure." But she made no move to go back to the cottage. A wistfulness floated on the new day's light, making her heart ache. Sebastian's marriage to Lynnea—followed a week later by her mother's marriage to Jeb, a woodworker who had been Nadia's neighbor and lover—had been a joyous celebration. But it had also been a sharp reminder that she'd never known a man who had loved her that way. She'd had sex partners, but no one she would have called a lover.

Well, no *real* lover. There had been times over the past month, as she drifted off to sleep, when she could have sworn she felt the heat of a man's body, felt the comforting weight of his arms around her.

Should she mention those wisps of dream to Sebastian? An incubus could create the feel of a tangible lover by connecting with a woman through the twilight of waking dreams, and the pureblood incubi, who had escaped the dark landscapes that had been sealed up with the Eater centuries ago, were deadly. But she didn't think any incubi, pureblood or otherwise, would stay around for a dream that had the warmth of romance but no sexual fire.

She looked up and forgot what she was about to say. The peculiar expression on Sebastian's face made her wonder how long she'd been drifting in her own thoughts—and made her wonder if the birthday gift he'd given her was created from a little more than just his imagination.

"Your birthday was last week," Sebastian said, brushing the subject of her thoughts a little too closely for comfort. "So now you're older than me."

The subject might have been close, but the content was not. "I'm always older than you," she replied, trying not to sound sour about it. After all, it wasn't like she was *old*.

"Yes, but there will be months and months when I can say I'm thirty and you have to say you're thirty-one, and it will be obvious to *everyone* which of us is older."

The temptation to pout embarrassed her, so she stepped away from him. "I'll get my own damn koffee." She turned on her heel and stomped toward the cottage. Right now, adulthood was a frayed scarf, and the harder she tried to hold on to it, the faster it frayed. In another minute she was going to resort to childish name-calling and shin-kicking. Well, not name-calling. She'd never indulged in name-calling. That would have hurt Sebastian too much. But when they were eight years old, she'd done her share of shin-kicking.

As she reached the lane, his hand gripped her shoulder, stopping her. She considered giving him one little shin-kick as a present to herself, but his expression warned her that he wasn't above retaliating. So she grabbed the frayed ends of adulthood and wrapped them around herself—and realized being annoyed with him had eased the wistfulness that had made her heart ache. Which, she was sure, had been his intention. Even when he wasn't slipping into someone's dreams, sometimes Sebastian read emotions much too well.

"So," Sebastian said, tipping his head to indicate the break in the trees. "I know why I'm up at this time of day. Why are you?"

Now that the question had been asked, she really didn't want to talk about the reason she had sought him out so early in the morning. "Lee snores."

"Uh-huh."

"Well, he does."

"Tell that to someone who hasn't slept in the same room as Lee on occasion. Unless there's something unusual about the acoustics in Jeb's old cottage, Lee doesn't snore loud enough to keep someone awake—especially someone in another room." Sebastian gave her an astute look. "Unless you were having trouble sleeping to start with, and you're dumping the blame on him."

Caught. What excuse could she give that Sebastian would believe—or, at least, accept instead of pushing?

There wasn't one. Her brother Lee, feeling the weight of his own efforts to protect Ephemera's shattered landscapes from the Eater of the World, wouldn't push. Sebastian would.

She looked at her cousin. His hair was dark brown instead of a true black, but he had green eyes like she and Lee did, and in build and face he and Lee were similar enough to be mistaken for brothers. But where Lee's handsomeness was tempered by a natural friendliness, Sebastian was all dangerous sensuality. Now that the wizard side of his heritage had manifested, he was not only an incubus but the Justice Maker for the Den of Iniquity.

Despite his gifts and his new role as the Den's protector, Sebastian didn't have the responsibility for so many lives as she did, being a Landscaper, or as Lee did, being the Bridge who kept her pieces of Ephemera connected. Maybe because he wasn't directly involved with the gift that had given her too many sleepless nights lately, she gave in to voicing her fears.

"It's been over a month since I stood outside Wizard City and performed Heart's Justice, depriving the Eater of the World of some of Its strongest allies," she said, looking away from him. "There's been no sign of It since then. At least, not in the landscapes under my control or in Mother's care. But after It killed the Landscapers at the school, It had access to all the pieces of the world anchored in all those gardens. It could be anywhere at this point, sowing fear in people's hearts, nurturing feelings that feed the Dark currents. Without realizing it, people will diminish the currents of Light that would have given them the hope and strength to turn aside the Dark. In the end, if there is no Landscaper to impose her will on the world, Ephemera will reshape pieces of itself to resonate with those darkened hearts—and other nightmare landscapes will be born."

"Could the Eater have been destroyed when you took the Dark Guides out of the world?" Sebastian asked.

She shook her head. "It was formed from the dark side of the human heart. As long as the heart is capable of those feelings, It will continue to exist."

"Then how can we destroy It?"

"Not 'we.' Me. I'm the only Landscaper strong enough to fight It. And I'm not sure I'm strong enough to defeat It." There. *That* was the fear that plagued her nights. If she couldn't find a way to contain the Eater of the World as the first Landscapers had so long ago, nothing would stop It from changing the world into manifestations of humans' deepest fears. Those first Landscapers, the Guides of the Heart, had shattered Ephemera during their battle against the Eater. That had worked to their advantage, since they were finally able to isolate It and take It and Its dark landscapes out of the world. But what had worked to their advantage now worked against her. She could only reach the landscapes that resonated with her, while the Eater, if It found a way to cross over, could prey on the rest of the world, out of her reach.

"You're not alone, Glorianna," Sebastian said, running his hand down her arm to soothe and comfort. "You have to be the leader, but you won't be fighting alone."

Yes, I will. "You offered me koffee, remember?"

He studied her long enough to make her wonder what he might be picking up from her feelings that she didn't want to share. Then he took her hand as they crossed the lane and led her to the back of the cottage.

When they reached the kitchen door, he hesitated and said, "Best to keep things quiet."

"Lynnea is still asleep?"

"Yes, but she'll sleep through the sound of people talking. Bop won't."

Glorianna's eyebrows lifted. "Bop?"

"The keet."

Since they were supposed to be quiet once they got inside, she tugged Sebastian back a step to stop him from opening the door. "Why did you name him Bop?"

"Has something to do with him smacking into my forehead every time we let him out."

Glorianna frowned. Lynnea had gotten the baby keet from Nadia, who should have noticed if there was a problem with the bird. "Is there something wrong with his wings that he can't fly well enough to avoid colliding with you?"

"He has no problem flying in circles around Lynnea or following her from room to room," Sebastian grumbled. "He has no problem flying up to the sills above the doors and windows when he wants to play 'catch the keet.' But me? Standing, sitting, makes no difference. He flies straight at me and—" He smacked his fingers against his forehead.

"Oh, dear."

"Then, of course, he gets upset because there's no place to perch, so he slides down my face and grabs my nose."

She winced.

Sebastian nodded. "Do you know what it feels like to have those sharp little nails digging into the end of your nose? So he's there, flapping his wings to keep from falling off and making scoldy noises at the top of his little lungs, while Lynnea stands there and says, 'Don't scare him, Sebastian. He's just a baby.' "

Wondering how Lynnea managed to keep a straight face while watching man and bird, Glorianna clamped a hand over her mouth to muffle her laughter. "Oh, I know it must hurt, but what a picture!"

"Uh-huh."

Something in his eyes made her take a step back. "Is any of that true?"

"All of it."

He'd known what he was doing. For a few moments, while picturing Sebastian trying to deal with Bop, the worries that had plagued her had vanished in the brightness of laughter, like sunlight burning off fog.

But the laughter was also a reminder of why she had to face the Eater of the World and win the battle. She wasn't preparing for this fight just to protect the great Places of Light, but also to prevent these little pieces of brightness from being snuffed out of existence.

"Am I ever going to get any koffee?" Glorianna asked.

Smiling, Sebastian slipped an arm around her shoulders and opened the kitchen door. "Sure. Why don't you make the koffee while I toast some bread for Bop?"

"He gets toast?"

"He doesn't get a whole piece," Sebastian replied, sounding defensive. "He's little. He has to share."

Glorianna glanced at the covered cage that sat at one end of the dining table. Then she followed Sebastian to the counter, where he'd set out the bag of koffea beans and the grinder. "You don't think he'll get spoiled by getting a treat every morning?"

Sebastian snorted. "It's just toast. It's not like he gets butter or jelly on his part of it."

"Of course. How silly of me not to see the difference."

He gave her a long look, then said, "Grind the beans."

She had to admit that Sebastian and Bop put on an entertaining show, especially when the bird made it clear that he was *not* used to having his treat dumped in the food dish and expected it to be held so he could sit on Sebastian's fingers and eat his toast properly. Bop's training was a little iffy, since it seemed to consist of the bird learning what he wanted to learn. However, Sebastian's training as playmate and servant to a little feathered tyrant was coming along quite nicely.

The glow of amusement that filled her when she left the cottage stayed with her for the rest of the day.

two weeks earlier

Erinn shoved her hands in her coat pockets as she stopped beneath one of the lit streetlamps. What had Tommy Lamplighter been thinking to be lighting every fourth lamp? Granted, it wasn't a busy street since there was nothing on one side but the back entrances of the shops that ran along Dunberry's main street, and the other side had little row houses that belonged to working folk who couldn't afford better. But it was still early enough that people would be making their way home from an evening out, and they shouldn't have to be walking in the dark.

Which you wouldn't be, Erinn Mary, if you'd taken the main street like you'd promised Kaelie's father you would. Or you should have taken him up on his offer to hitch up the horse and drive you home. There have been enough bad-luck things happening around the village lately to make anyone uneasy, not to mention the two boys who went missing last week.

But walking down the main street would have taken her past Donovan's Pub, and she hadn't wanted Torry or his friends to see her and think she'd passed by to check up on him.

A sudden gust of wind made her coat flap around her, and there was now a sharp bite of winter hidden within the unseasonably crisp autumn night—as if the wind itself was urging folks to get indoors.

A fanciful thought, to be sure. But fanciful or not, the thought made her shiver.

Erinn hurried toward the next lit streetlamp.

When next she saw Tommy Lamplighter, she'd give him a piece of her mind—and maybe a thump on the head to go with it. Dunberry was big enough to need more than one lamplighter, but each man had his assigned streets, and their wages came from the taxes that were collected for the village's upkeep, so Tommy shouldn't be neglecting his duty.

Just like Torry shouldn't be neglecting *his* duty. No. It should never be duty. He should *want* to spend time with the woman he was going to marry at the end of harvest. But he was down at the pub, drinking ale with his friends and playing darts. . . .

And flirting with the girls? a soft voice whispered in her head.

No. Torry didn't flirt. Not much anyway. Just enough to be friendly. And he certainly wouldn't be flirting with other girls *now*, not after she and Torry had . . .

Why not? the voice asked. *How much pleasure could he have gotten with a girl who can't say what she's done, not even in her own head?*

Sex. They'd had sex, Erinn thought fiercely as she stopped beneath the next lit streetlamp. It had been nice enough after the first time, and Torry had said it would get better as they got to know each other in that sense, so he had nothing to complain about.

Not complaining doesn't mean he wasn't disappointed, isn't wondering what other girls will offer that you can't—or won't. And how does he know it will get better unless he's already done these things with another girl? A girl he left behind. Just like he'll leave you.

No. Torry wasn't like that.

A glass of ale and time with his friends. Are you sure that's all he wanted at the pub? Maybe he was looking for something more. Or someone like . . .

Shauna? Everyone knew Shauna was a bit wild, and willing to give the lads more than a few kisses. And she'd had her eye on Torry, even though he'd never noticed.

Oh, he noticed. You're the one who can't see.

A dark, bitter feeling rolled through Erinn, followed by a shivery pleasure at the thought of scratching Shauna's pretty face. No, better than that. She'd scratch the bitch's eyes out. *Then* Shauna wouldn't look so pretty. *Then* the bitch wouldn't be casting out lures and spoiling things for decent girls. *Then . . .*

Gasping for air, Erinn shook her head. Why was she thinking these things? It was like someone else was inside her head, whispering every uneasy thought that had lodged in her heart since feelings had overruled prudence and she'd let Torry talk her into doing the man-and-woman part of the wedding before making the husband-and-wife vows.

But she loved Torry. And he loved her. And she *wasn't* going to listen to these foolish whispers anymore.

Erinn's hands lifted, closing into fists that gripped the front of her coat as she stared at the dark street. No more streetlamps were lit. There were no lights on in the houses. There was nothing but the dark, which suddenly felt thick, almost smothering—and aware of her.

Nearby, a dog began barking, startling her. Maybe it had caught her scent. The wind was in the right direction.

Or maybe it had caught the scent of something else.

She looked to her right. A service way ran between the buildings. Not wide enough for wagons or carriages, it still provided a cut-through for delivery boys on bicycles and for people who didn't want to go the long way round in order to reach the main street to do their shopping and such.

Donovan's Pub wasn't far from there. She'd go in and ask Torry to walk her home. She didn't care if he thought she'd come to check up on him. She didn't care if he thought she was foolish to be afraid of the dark when she'd never been afraid before. Tonight, she *was* afraid of the dark.

Taking a deep breath that shuddered out of her in something close to a sob, she entered the service way and hurried toward the light at the other end, whispering, "Ladies of the White Isle, hold me in the Light. Ladies of the White Isle, hold me in the Light."

Halfway through the service way, just beyond the lamplight's reach, she heard something move. Before she could run, before she could scream, something grabbed her, swung her around, and pinned her against the brick wall of the building. A hand clamped over her mouth.

A fast movement. A ripping sound followed by the feel of chilly air where the coat had suddenly parted. Followed by an odd, shivery feeling as the skin and muscles in her side opened up.

Lady of Light, protect me. Help me.

In the few seconds it took for her body to recognize pain, the knife had moved. Was now resting on her cheekbone, its tip pricking just beneath her left eye.

"Scream," a smooth voice whispered, "and I'll take your eye. Tell me what I want to know, and I'll let you keep your pretty face."

The hand clamped over her mouth moved. Curled around her throat.

"Please don't hurt me," Erinn said, too afraid to do more than whisper.

A man. She could tell that much, but there wasn't enough light for her to see his face.

"Tell me what you whispered," he said. "About the White Isle. About the Light."

"Please let me go. Please don't—"

"Tell me."

"T-the White Isle is the Light's haven. All the Light that keeps Elandar safe from the Dark has its roots there."

"And where is the White Isle?"

She hesitated a moment—and felt the knife prick the tender skin beneath her eye. "N-north. It's an island off the eastern coast. Up north."

The hand around her throat loosened. The knife caressed her cheek but didn't cut her as he took a step back.

"Who are you?" Foolish question. The less she could tell anyone about him, the safer she would be.

He smiled. She still couldn't see his face, but she knew he smiled.

"The Eater of the World."

So he wasn't going to tell her. That was good. He would go away, and she would be safe. She was hurt bad. She knew that. But it was only one step, maybe two, and she'd be in the light, the glorious light. Her legs felt cold and weak, but she could get to the end of the service way, could get to the main street. Someone would see her and help her. Someone would fetch Torry, and everything would be all right. They would be married at the end of harvest and—

She saw him raise the knife. And she screamed.

Then he rammed the knife into her chest, cutting off the scream. Cutting off hope. Cutting off life.

Voices shouted and boots pounded the cobblestones as men ran toward the service way.

The Eater of the World shifted to Its natural form and flowed beneath the stones, nothing more than a rippling shadow moving toward the main street. One man stumbled as It flowed beneath his feet, and It left a stain on his heart as It passed.

Then It paused as the first man to reach the girl screamed, "Erinn! No!"

Following the channel cut deep into the man's heart by grief and the shock of seeing his hands covered in the girl's blood, It stretched out a mental tentacle, slipped into the man's mind, and whispered, *She was here in the service way because of you. This happened because of you.*

"No!" But there was something—a tiny seed of doubt, a hint of innocent guilt. Just enough soil for the planting.

Yes, It whispered, putting all of Its dark conviction into the word. *This happened because of you.*

It retreated, certain Its words would take root and fester, dimming the man's Light, maybe curdling that Light enough that it would never fully bloom again, scarring the heart enough that the man would never fully love again.

And the Dark currents that flowed in this village would become a little stronger because of that—just as the Dark currents had grown stronger every day since those two boys disappeared. There had been so many hearts eager to hear Its whispers about the boys going into the woods with a man they knew well enough not to fear.

Until the seasons changed, Its death rollers would remain in the sun-warmed river of their own landscape rather than hunt in the cold water of the pond located at the edge of the village's common pasture. By the time Its creatures came to this landscape, no one would remember the story those boys were telling about a big log that had come alive and pulled a half-grown steer into the water. And by the time the next boy, or man, wandered too close to the pond and died, the fear that lived in these people would be that much riper, that much sweeter. Would resonate with Itself that much better.

It flowed beneath the main street, heading out of the village. People shuddered as It passed unseen, unrecognized for what It was. Its resonance would lodge in their hearts as uneasiness and distrust, making them wonder which of their neighbors had been the person who had held the knife. When they found the body of the lamplighter . . .

It had been so satisfying to change into a shape with jaws powerful enough to crush bone. So It had crushed the lamplighter, piece by piece. When It tired of playing with Its prey, It had dragged the body into a dark space and fed while the flesh was still succulent . . . and alive.

Of course, by the time the other humans found the body, the rats would have had their feast as well.

It would return to this place called Dunberry, and when It did, the people would be even more vulnerable to the whispers and seeds It would plant in the dark side of the human heart—the same side that had brought It into being so long ago.

But first, It needed to reach the sea and head north. The hunting in this landscape would be sweeter once It destroyed the Place of Light.

present

Michael paused outside the door of Shaney's Tavern and fiercely wished he'd already downed a long glass of whiskey. The music was out of tune here. Off rhythm. *Wrong.* Not as bad as Dunberry, but . . .

Dunberry. What had gone wrong *there?* All right, so he'd done a little ill-wishing the last time he'd passed through, but the ripe bastard had been cheating at cards and deserved to have some bad luck. It wasn't as if *he'd* prospered from it. He just didn't think it was fair for Torry to lose his stake simply because the boy had had the poor judgment to try to plump up his wedding purse by playing a few hands of cards. And didn't Torry find a small bag of gold a few days later—gold his grandfather had hidden in the barn and forgotten years ago? That bit of luck-bringing had balanced out the ill-wishing, hadn't it?

But the girl Torry was going to marry . . . Stabbed to death, wasn't she, and so close to help that Torry and his friends had heard her scream.

He'd heard about it fast enough when he came into the village. Just as he heard what wasn't quite being said. Not about the girl, Erinn, but about two boys who disappeared a few days before she was killed. Someone had seen them going off with a man who wasn't from Dunberry but was familiar enough to be trusted. What would a man be doing with two young boys that they would need to disappear after he was done with them?

He hadn't been in Dunberry for weeks, but sooner or later someone would put his face or his clothes on that "familiar enough" man, and it wouldn't matter that he'd been in another village when those boys had disappeared. Once the villagers decided he *was* the man, he wouldn't survive long enough to get a formal hearing.

So he'd snuck away in the wee hours of the morning, putting as much distance between himself and Dunberry as he could before the people began to stir.

He no longer fit the tune of that village. It had turned dark, sharp-edged, sour.

That's how he heard places and people. They were melodies, harmonies, songs that fit together and gave a village a certain texture and sound. When he fit in with a place, he was another melody, another harmony. And he was the drum that settled the rhythm, fixed the beat.

But not in Dunberry. Not anymore.

The bang of a door or a shutter made him jump, which jangled the pots and pans tied to the outside of his heavy backpack. The sounds scraped nerves that were already raw, and his pounding heart was another thumping rhythm he was sure could be heard by . . . whatever was out there.

Tucking his walking stick under the arm holding the lantern, he wrapped his fingers around the handle on the tavern's door. Then he twisted around to look at the thick fog that had turned familiar land into some unnatural place that had no beginning or end.

Didn't matter if the music was wrong here. He'd beg or barter whatever he had to in order to get out of that fog for a few hours.

Giving the door a tug, he went inside the tavern, pulling off his brown, shapeless hat as he strode to the bar. The pots and pans clattered with each step. Normally he found it a comforting sound, but when he'd been walking toward the village that lay in the center of Foggy Downs, a lantern in one hand and his walking stick in the other, feeling his way like a blind man . . . The ordinary sound had seemed too loud in that gray world, as if he were calling something toward him that he did not want to see.

"Well, look what stumbled out of the forsaken land," Shaney said, bracing his hands on the bar.

"Lady of Light," Michael muttered as he set his hat and lantern on the bar. "I've seen fog roll in thick before, but never as bad as this." Leaning his walking stick against the bar, he shrugged off the straps of the pack, glad to be rid of the weight.

Then he looked around the empty tavern. He could barely make out the tables on the other side of the room since Shaney hadn't lit any of the lamps except around the bar.

"Is everyone laying low until this blows past?" he asked, rubbing his hand over one bristly cheek. If business was slow and the rooms Shaney rented to travelers were empty, maybe he could barter his way to a bath, or at least enough hot water for a good wash and a shave, as well as a bed for the night.

Shaney put two whiskey glasses on the bar, then reached for a bottle. He poured two shots.

Michael looked at the whiskey, craving the fire that would ease the chill in his bones. But he shook his head. "Since I'm hoping for a meal and a bed tonight, whiskey is a little too rich for my pocket just now."

"On the house," Shaney said, sounding as gloomy as the fog. "And you're welcome to a bed and a share of whatever the Missus is making for the evening meal."

"That's generous of you, Shaney," Michael said, knowing he should be grateful but feeling as if the ground had suddenly turned soft under his feet and a wrong step would sink him.

"Well, maybe you'd be willing to play a bit this evening. I could spread the word that you're here."

Picking up a glass of whiskey, Michael took a sip. "I'm flattered you think so highly of my music, but do you really expect people to come out in this for a drink and a few tunes?"

"They'll come to play a few tunes with you."

A chill went through him. *The music is wrong here, Michael, my lad. Don't be forgetting that, or what you are, and lower your guard.*

He'd been shy of seventeen the first time he'd come to Foggy Downs, and had been on the road and making his own way for almost a year. Over the years since, he'd come to depend on this being a friendly, safe place to stay. If people realized what he was, Foggy Downs would no longer be as safe—or as friendly.

Shaney downed his whiskey, then pulled a rag from under the bar and began polishing the wood. "Do you remember old Bridie?"

Michael rubbed a finger around the rim of his glass. "I remember her. She smoked a pipe, had a laugh that could put sparkle on the sun, and, even at her age, could dance the legs off any man."

"That pipe," Shaney murmured, smiling. "She never ran out of leaf for that pipe. She'd be down to her last smoke, and something or someone would always come along to provide her with a new supply of leaf. People would ask her if she had some lucky piece hidden away because, even when bad things happened, some good would come from it. And she always said currents of luck ran through the world, and a light heart and laughter brought her all the good luck she needed."

A silence fell between them, but it wasn't the easy breathing space it usually was when neither felt like talking.

Finally, Shaney said, "The first time you came to Foggy Downs, Bridie saw you, heard you play. She took my father aside after you'd gone on down the road, and she told him to look after you whenever you came to our village. Said she had a feeling that we'd be putting her to ground by the spring, and even though she didn't think you were ready to give up your wandering to put down roots, you were the best chance Foggy Downs had of having a lucky piece once she passed on. So some of us have known what you are—just as we knew what she was."

Michael downed the rest of the whiskey, wishing it would ease the despair growing inside him. He truly didn't want to go out in that fog, but he didn't want to end up being accused of something he didn't do and die at the hands of a mob either. "I guess I'll be on my way then."

Shaney tossed his rag on the bar and gave Michael a look that was equal parts disbelief and annoyance. "Now what part of what I was saying made that pea-sized brain of yours figure we wanted to see the back of you? And what makes you think so little of me that you'd figure I'd ask any man to walk back out in a fog that someone can get lost in when he's still within reach of his own door?"

Michael said nothing, surprised at how much Shaney's annoyance gave his heart a scratchy comfort.

"I can't change what I am," he said softly.

"No one is asking you to." Shaney scrubbed his head with his fingers, then smoothed back his hair and sighed. "Something evil passed through Foggy Downs a few days ago. The whole village had a bad night of it. Children waking up screaming from the nightmares. Babes too young to say what gave them a fright wailing for hours. And the rest of us . . . It's a strange feeling to have an old fear come up and grab you by the throat so you come awake with your heart pounding and you don't quite know where you are. 'Twas a hard night, Michael, and the next morning . . ." He looked at the fog-shrouded windows.

Michael stared at the windows before turning back to Shaney. "It's been like that for *days?*"

"First couple of days, folks went about their business as best they could, taking care of only what was needed, sure the fog would burn off to what we're used to having here. The Missus and I even had folks gather here that first night. Had us a grand party, with music and dancing, while we all tried to put aside the bad dreams of the night before. But the fog didn't lift. Hasn't lifted. And I'm thinking this fog is more than fog, and if evil used some kind of . . . magic . . . to create it, then it's going to take another kind of magic to put things back the way they were."

The two men studied each other. Then Michael pressed his hands on the bar and closed his eyes.

He had no words for what he sensed, what he could feel. But the *sound* that filled his mind was a grating, creaking, sloshing, oozing, tearing. The sound of poison. The sound of old hurts, painful memories, deeply buried fears.

Then he imagined his music filling Shaney's Tavern, the bright notes of the tin whistle shining in the night like sparkles of sunlight. Certainty shivered through him. His music would shift the balance enough so the people here would be able to heal Foggy Downs. He could reestablish the beat. Fix the rhythm. Restore the balance enough to still belong.

He opened his eyes and looked at Shaney. "You put out the word, and I'll provide the music."

Shaney put out the word, and the people gathered. No one from the outlying farms, to be sure, but the families who lived close enough to the tavern to brave the fog came with a covered dish to pass around and children in tow. So Michael listened to gossip and passed along news from the other villages he'd visited during this circuit of wandering. He ate a bit of everything so no lady would be offended and pretended not to notice the speculative looks a few of the young women were giving him. He was used to those looks. Since he was a healthy, fit man who rarely stayed more than a few days in a place, certain kinds of women often looked at him like a savory dish that was only available a few times a year, which enhanced the appeal, and there were a few young widows who were willing to offer him more than just lodging when he came to their town.

While he looked like a scruffy ne'er-do-well most of the time, he cleaned up well enough when he got the chance, and the smoky blue eyes and brown hair that was always a bit shaggy went with the face that was handsome enough to attract the ladies but not so handsome it made people uneasy.

Until they found out what he was.

As the rhythm of the gathering shifted from gossip and food to unspoken hopes and expectations, he fetched his tin whistle, nodded to the other men who had brought instruments, and shooed the children out of the small space that had been cleared for the musicians.

Michael closed his eyes and let himself drift on the feel of the room. Ah. There was that odd sensation he sometimes felt when he was deliberately trying to change the feel of a place. A *presence*, like a child too shy to come forward where it might be noticed, but too intrigued by the things and people around it to go away. More than that. This wild child, as he thought of it, was intrigued by *him*. He had the feeling that it could hear the music in *his* heart in the same way he could hear the music in other hearts, and *that's* what intrigued it enough to come to a gathering. The reason didn't matter. What mattered was that when he felt the wild child's presence, sometimes he could make things happen that were more than a little luck-bringing or ill-wishing directed at a specific person.

Lifting the tin whistle to his lips, he let the first notes float through the air, soft and bittersweet . . . and hopeful. Little by little, conversations faded—or maybe he no longer heard them. The fiddler joined him, slow and easy.

There was nothing but the music, and he wasn't playing for the people in the room. Not yet. This song was for the wild child. To catch its interest, its attention. Its heart.

With his eyes still closed, he slipped into the next tune. More energy. Drum added to the fiddle and whistle. A sparkle of notes drifting out into the night, dancing in the fog, glistening with the energy and good spirits of the people like dew glistened on a web when touched by the morning sun.

Yes, he thought as he opened his eyes and watched the dancers, these were good people who welcomed the Light, who deserved the Light.

Musicians came and went, taking their turn for a few songs, then stepping back for someone else. When he was given a shove and told to take his turn on the dance floor, he ignored the bold, silent invitations—especially the one from Doreen, who worked for Shaney and always made him think of the fate of the mouse caught under the cat's paw—and chose a girl who was old enough to be flattered by his asking to be her partner and young enough that she wouldn't expect him to be any other kind of partner.

Not that he didn't want to take hold of a woman and kiss her senseless. The music was hot. The energy was hot. And he wanted with a need that chewed at his bones.

But what he hungered for wasn't here, so he gave himself to the music.

Food was reheated. People drifted to corners farthest away from the music in order to talk. Shaney opened up a few of the upstairs rooms, where children were tucked up in beds, cuddling together like puppies.

Michael talked. He danced. He ate. He played. And always, he held in his mind and heart the image of the notes sparkling in the night.

As her mind rose to that twilight place that was neither true waking nor sleeping, Glorianna dreamed of music. Folksy, but like nothing she'd heard before. Slightly different sound to the drum and the violin—at least, she thought it was a violin. But it was the bright notes of the whistle that made her smile, that had her feet twitching as if they wanted to dance, and the drum heated her blood until her heart pounded with the rhythm.

The music dimmed, as if someone had shut a door, and she stood outside in a fog as thick as a soft blanket. She wasn't surprised when his arms closed around her, pulling her back against the warmth of his chest. Then . . .

She heard the drum in the beat of his heart, heard the long sigh of the violin in his breath. Knew the bright notes of the whistle would be in his voice, in his laugh.

"There is music inside you," she said. "I can hear the music inside you."

His smile, that curving of lips against her cheek, was his only answer.

Hours later, drained in body, mind, and heart, Michael lowered his whistle and looked at the men slumped in the chairs around him. "Well, lads, looks like we're done here."

One of the men looked at the people asleep at the tables and grinned. "I'd say we are."

Wanting some fresh air, Michael wove his way through the tables until he reached the tavern door and pushed it open.

"Lady of Light," Shaney whispered behind him. "Look at that."

Oh, he was looking—and he was stunned by what the dawn light revealed. Thick strands and knots of that heavy fog clotted the street, but it was broken up by a thin mist—the kind of mist that softened sunlight and created rainbows.

"You did it, Michael," Shaney said, resting a hand on Michael's shoulders.

"We all did," he replied. He'd never influenced a place so much, so obviously. He wasn't sure what to do about it, what to think about it.

"Wouldn't have happened without you, though. You're a fine musician. The best I've ever seen."

"And you've seen the last of me for the next few hours."

"You've earned your rest and more. If the Missus and I aren't around when you wake, just help yourself to whatever you find in the kitchen, and she'll fix you up with a proper meal later."

Michael just nodded and headed for the stairs at the back of the tavern that led up to the rooms Shaney rented. He felt drained, hollowed out. But it was a good feeling that left him looking forward to the pleasure of stretching out on a bed with clean sheets and sleeping through the day.

He didn't see Doreen until he was at the top of the stairs. By then it was too late to fix the tactical error of coming up to his room alone.

"Took you long enough," Doreen said, giving him a smile that was meant to be enticing.

"It's a proven fact that the number of stairs increases in direct proportion to the amount of drink that is consumed or the amount of sleep that was lost," Michael said lightly.

Doreen shrugged, clearly not interested in anything but what she'd planned. "I figured, after playing all that fine music, you'd be wanting a bit of company about now. Private company."

You figured wrong. There was a meanness in Doreen. She hid it well, most of the time, but he heard sharp notes every time he was near her. He didn't like her, and yet despite those sharp notes, she *had* fit into the music that was Foggy Downs. Right now, however, even if he had wanted her, he wouldn't have done either of them any good. At least he could be honest about that much.

"I thank you for the offer, Doreen, but I'm too tired to be good company—or any kind of company if it comes to that."

Her smile faded. "You think you're better than me, don't you? I know you've pleasured other women, but because I wait tables in a tavern, that puts me beneath men of good reputation."

Michael shivered. He wasn't sure if it was due to fatigue or the other meaning beneath Doreen's words. And maybe he was just too muzzy-headed and tired to hear it clearly, but her tune didn't seem to fit the village anymore. It was *too* sharp, too . . . dark. Wrong.

"But you're not a man of good reputation, are you, Michael? You're nothing but a drifter, a wanderer, a—"

The word she spoke struck him like a blow to the heart.

"What's that you called him?"

Michael jumped, startled by the voice on the stairs behind him. He stepped aside to let Maeve, the village postmistress and owner of Foggy Downs's lending library, pass by.

"Musician?" Maeve said, touching fingers delicately to one ear. "Well, there's no need to be sounding all dramatic about it. Of course he's a musician, girl! Are your ears so stopped up with wax that you couldn't hear him playing all night?"

Doreen's eyes flashed with anger, but she didn't reply.

Smart girl, Michael thought. Maeve might have a thinning head of white hair and a wrinkled face, but there was nothing wrong with her mind or her hearing. And since she was responsible for obtaining the magazines published in the big city that informed young ladies about the latest fashions and young wives about household tips, even the sassiest woman understood the value of being respectful to Maeve.

The postmistress shook her head and let out an exasperated sigh. "Leave the boy in peace, Doreen, and let him get some sleep. Any woman worth her salt knows a man that tired hasn't the wit for romance."

He wasn't sure he appreciated Maeve's way of helping him escape, but he wasn't going to ignore the opportunity.

"Good night, ladies," he said, slipping past both women to reach his room. Once inside, he slid the bolt home as quietly as possible. No point insulting Doreen into doing something foolish by letting her hear him lock the door. But he wouldn't rest easy without the lock, especially since she seemed determined to have him.

He couldn't imagine why. Doreen enjoyed men for what she could get from them, and he didn't have much to offer in terms of providing a woman with material things. Wary of her interest, he'd always found an excuse not to be one of her men—and now it was going to cost him. Even if Shaney and Maeve stood by him, it was still going to cost him sooner or later.

He walked toward the washstand, intending to rinse a bit of the fatigue and grittiness from his face. But he ended up staring in the mirror above the dresser.

He was twenty-eight years old. The last twelve years hadn't been easy. He missed his sister Caitlin and his friend Nathan. Even missed his aunt Brighid on occasion. Missed the feeling of having a home and roots, even though he hadn't felt like he'd had either when he lived in Raven's Hill. But his continued presence would have made things harder for his family. Brighid had been a Lady of Light and still commanded respect because of that, but Caitlin Marie was whispered to be odd, strange . . . unnatural. A young girl who had found the walled garden hidden somewhere on the hill behind the family's cottage. Caitlin would never be offered the things most young women dreamed of—a home, a husband, children—and his heart ached for her.

Until people discovered Caitlin's link to the hidden garden, he had been the one the villagers didn't want around because he had a power no one understood. But everyone knew what it did and what the person who wielded that power was.

A luck-bringer. An ill-wisher.

A Magician.

There was nothing wrong with Maeve's hearing. And there would be nothing anyone could do to curb Doreen's spiteful tongue. It wouldn't matter if Maeve tried to soften the gossip. The damage would be done. By the time the next market day ended, everyone in Foggy Downs would know he was a Magician.

Some would hate him for it, and would blame him for any bit of trouble that came their way. And, in truth, he would deserve some of that blame. But he had heard of Magicians who had been killed in other parts of Elandar because it was so easy to bury them in the blame.

So he would leave Foggy Downs while the people still thought kindly of him. He needed to get back to Raven's Hill anyway, needed to talk to his aunt as soon as he could.

Because of the dreams. Because of *her*.

That was the real reason he wouldn't have been of any use to Doreen, even if he'd been willing. He didn't want any other woman since he'd begun dreaming about her.

Long black hair. Green eyes. A beautiful face that he had never seen in the flesh. But he could feel the shape of her in his arms, breathe in the scent of her, taste the warmth of her. Hear the music of her heart.

That, more than anything, seduced him. He could hear the music of her heart. And it made him yearn for things he couldn't put into words, except one: *home*.

Night after night, she filled him with hungers he thought would kill him if he didn't satisfy them soon. And there was always someone or something whispering in his ear, "This is what you've searched for. This is *who* you've searched for."

Deny it, defy it, reject it during every waking moment. It didn't matter. Somehow he had fallen in love with the woman who haunted his dreams—a woman he'd never met and wasn't certain even existed.

His aunt was the only person he knew whose training might provide him with an answer about the nature of these dreams, so he was going back to Raven's Hill.

Stripping down to his drawers, Michael got into bed and was asleep within minutes. He didn't dream about the woman; he dreamed about his aunt. She stood in front of the family's cottage, holding out two plants.

One was called heart's hope. The other was belladonna.

Chapter Four

It found Its way to the sea. Taking the form of the well-to-do, middle-aged gentleman that had served It so well in other places, It spent a few days hunting around the docks and alleyways of the seaport. To Its delight, the brutal killings nurtured seeds of distrust and fear that sprang up whenever humans encountered someone who wasn't exactly like themselves. Easy enough to hunt and then feast on the dark feelings shaped by terror—and then be the whisper in the back of the crowd, assuring people that anyone who wasn't them *must* be evil.

Easy enough. But not as easy as It expected. There was strong bedrock around the docks of this seaport—a heart and will through which Ephemera manifested the emotions and wishes of other human hearts.

But what bedrock, what heart? It had destroyed most of the lesser enemies, the females called Landscapers and the males called Bridges. Through Its creatures, It controlled the school where the enemies had gathered, turning their place into one of Its own landscapes. Now the few Landscapers who had survived were contained in whichever landscapes they had fled to, leaving all the other landscapes in their care vulnerable to Its influence.

But this bedrock did not have the resonance of a lesser enemy. And it didn't feel like the True Enemy, the one called Belladonna. This was something *other*, something different.

A new kind of Enemy.

It had touched the resonance of this Enemy in two other places in this part of the world. It would recognize that heart now if It found the resonance in another place.

But if *It* could recognize the Enemy, could the Enemy recognize *It*, find *It*?

As that thought took shape and grew stronger, It lost Its pleasure in the hunt. It didn't want to be found until It was ready to be found—until It had destroyed the Place of Light the True Enemy hadn't yet hidden within her landscapes.

It left the seaport and flowed steadily north, a shadow beneath the waves. When It wanted to feed, It changed into the form that belonged to the sea, swelling Its size to be able to hunt whatever creatures were available.

Then It stopped at a fishing village, hungry for more than the flesh It could find in the sea. Slipping into the human minds through the twilight of waking dreams, It found a fear that matched Its sea shape. A diminished fear; a safe fear that produced no more than a delicious shiver. Because the thing that was feared was nothing more than a story now, wasn't believed to be real.

Pleased by the discovery, It followed the fishing boats the next day, causing no more than ripples of uneasiness as It flowed around and beneath the boats. But It also herded schools of fish into the nets, so the uneasiness that might have kept the fishermen away from that spot was drowned by their excitement in hauling in such a good catch.

It watched the fishing boats head back to the village at the end of the day, felt the swell of happiness in the hearts of the men—and the hope that the catch would be as good tomorrow.

The catch would be as good. But not for them.

While the hope and happiness of the fishermen and their families fed the currents of Light, the Eater of the World floated in the water—and waited.

Ten fishing boats went out the next morning. Five returned home.

Fathers, sons, brothers. Dead.

The older men said they should have known something was wrong, with fish practically leaping into the boats to escape some danger hidden in the sea. But no one had imagined something out of the old stories coming to life. No one had considered the terror that would fill a man's heart when he saw tentacles as thick as masts and twice the length rise up out of the water and smash a boat into kindling. No one had considered the anguish of hearing a friend, wrapped in one of those tentacles, screaming as the life was crushed out of him. Or, worse, hearing bones snap before a man was flung into the sea, too injured to stay afloat for long or even swim toward another ship, but too close to the tentacles for anyone to risk trying to save him.

Because every time they had tried to save a man, another ship was lost.

So the survivors sailed back to the village, knowing they were leaving men to die. And the pain of that, the shame of it, smeared their hearts with so much hurt that the darkness of their grief seeped through the bedrock that protected their village, staining everything until a man only had to think of the possibility of bad luck to have it come true.

Chapter Five

Merrill fingered the silver cuff bracelet on her wrist as she stared at the stone that formed a natural, shallow basin. The Sisters filled the basin with water every morning for the birds. Brighid, their leader until she had abandoned them sixteen years ago, had found the stone and designed this little contemplation corner around it.

But Merrill hadn't come for contemplation this morning. She had come to let her heart speak to the Light as eloquently as it could. She needed help. They *all* needed help.

Help me find a way to protect the Light. Please, help me find a way.

Pulling the cuff bracelet off her wrist, she placed it in the shallow basin. Since it had been a gift from Brighid, she valued it more than any other possession. Giving it up seemed a sacrifice worthy of the help she sought.

Not that she really believed her prayers or a bracelet would make any difference.

Turning away from the basin before she changed her mind and took back the bracelet, she returned to the terrace that overlooked the gardens behind Lighthaven's sprawling manor. For forty years she had lived in the manor and walked through these gardens. She had been born here on the White Isle, had spent the first years of her life in Atwater, the seaport village that acted as a portal to the rest of the world. The day after her tenth birthday, her father brought her to Lighthaven and left her with the Sisters of Light in the hopes that she would become one of them.

She had lived nowhere else since, had known no other place. She had rarely traveled beyond the boundaries of Lighthaven in all the years that had passed since that girl had stood at the visitors' gate and felt her heart soar at the sound of women's voices raised in a ritual song. She didn't regret the innocence that came from the lack of worldly experience. She wasn't completely ignorant of what lay beyond the shores of this island—the world brushed against the White Isle often enough—but those things had never touched her, leaving her heart a pure vessel for the Light.

Now she wondered if that ignorance would doom everyone and everything she cared about.

"If the gardens give you no peace," said a voice behind her, "do they give you answers?"

Merrill turned to look at her closest friend. Shaela never spoke of her life before coming to Lighthaven, had never once revealed what had driven a girl on the cusp of womanhood to steal a rowboat and try to make her way across the strait that separated the White Isle from Elandar. She had never said what had caused the blindness in her left eye or the slight paralysis of the left side of her face or the lameness in one leg.

There were scars on Shaela's body that the years had faded but couldn't erase completely. And there were scars on her heart that would never fade.

Because of that, there was always a shadow of Dark inside Shaela, but that shadow made her value the Light even more than the Sisters who had never been touched by evil.

"I feel the chill of winter," Merrill said, turning back to look at the garden. "I dread the cold days and long nights that are coming because I can't stop wondering if we'll ever see the spring."

Shaela sighed, an exasperated sound. "You've been chewing on this for over a month. You've been over the old records again and again and found nothing."

"I found the old stories. They support the warning we heard."

"That the Destroyer of Light, the Well of All Evil, has returned? You've been wearing yourself out because a voice—a *man's* voice— came to you in a dream."

"A warning," Merrill insisted. "And a riddle." She wrapped her arms around herself, adding quietly, "And we aren't the only ones who heard the warning."

"Can Brighid be trusted?" Shaela asked just as quietly.

"She was a Sister. Is still a Sister, even though she hasn't lived with us since—" Sorrow welled up in her, as sharp as it had been sixteen years ago when she'd helped Brighid pack a trunk and leave Lighthaven in response to a young boy's desperate plea for help.

"Since her sister, Maureen, sick in mind and heart, walked into the sea," Shaela said.

"Yes."

Brighid had walked in the Light, a shining beacon. But Maureen had been a bit wild, even as a girl. Instead of settling down with her man once she'd become a wife and mother, she got stranger, more twisted—until something inside her finally broke so much that she chose the sea's cradle over her own children, leaving Brighid with the task of raising two children who had in them some Dark blood that gave them unnatural abilities to make things happen.

"Heart's hope lies within belladonna," Merrill said. "That's what the voice said."

"Belladonna is a poison," Shaela replied. "What hope can be found in something rooted in the Dark?"

"I don't know, but I can think of only one way to find out."

Shaela remained silent for a long time. Then she lightly touched Merrill's shoulder. "Writing to Brighid was one thing. But if you go to Raven's Hill, you'll open old hurts and leave fresh wounds."

"I know." The thought of it made her ache. "But if this danger is real, there is no one else I trust enough to ask for this kind of help."

"When are you leaving?"

"There's a ship leaving Atwater tomorrow morning. The captain has agreed to take me to Raven's Hill."

"You haven't the skills to deal with the outside world."

"Two men from the village are coming with me as escorts. They're worldly enough, I think."

Shaela sighed. "I'd better take care of the packing for the both of us. It's not a long journey by sea, but you still won't consider half of what you'll need."

An odd blend of alarm and relief flooded through Merrill. "You don't have to leave the White Isle."

Shaela spoke slowly, as if picking each word with care. "It's best if I make this journey with you. Yes, I think it's best."

Merrill stared at her friend. "You believe the warning, don't you?"

Shaela hesitated. "No, I didn't. I *didn't*—until you said you were leaving. Then I imagined you traveling by sea, and a sense of foreboding came over me. The Light within you will be a beacon in the dark. If you leave, you *must* succeed—and you must return or everything will be lost. I can't shake the feeling that something will stop you from returning unless I'm with you."

"Something's coming," Merrill whispered.

"Yes."

"Something that can destroy the White Isle."

"Yes."

She squared her shoulders. "Then let's make this journey—and hope the answer to this riddle is what we need to save the Light."

Chapter Six

Merrill watched the shoreline as the sailors worked to bring the ship within the shelter of Darling's Cove. An odd name for such a practical-minded village of people, but it was said that the man who first settled there adored his beautiful wife. Fearful that water demons would become enamored with her and try to lure her too far into the water whenever she walked along the beach, he never called her by name when they were near the sea, only darling. Always darling.

But it was his darling who, it was said, had an unusual connection to the land and had created the secret place Merrill hoped would have what they needed.

"It's not too late," Shaela said, coming to stand beside Merrill. "We can still turn back, find another way to do this."

"We can't turn back," Merrill replied. "And it is too late—was already too late before we set foot on the ship. We're running out of time. I can feel it. If we don't find what we seek here . . ."

What happens then? she wondered. *Nothing? Everything? Are we set free by our failure, or are we doomed because we failed to find the answer that would have saved us? And how am I supposed to know the difference?*

"I'll be glad to get off the water," Shaela said. "The further south we've come, the more uneasy I feel."

"I know," Merrill whispered. "I feel it too. Like something knows we're out here." *Like there's a stain of evil on the water. It's not here, not yet, but it's getting closer. Whenever I enter that still place where the Light within me dwells, all I have to do is think about the sea, and the Light is diminished. Surely that's a warning.*

"Getting into port this early in the morning, we'll have the whole day," Shaela said. "If the girl can provide us with what we need quickly enough, we can be sailing home with the evening tide." She slanted a glance at Merrill. "Unless you want to stay overnight."

"We won't be welcomed as guests," Merrill snapped, lashing out in response to the pain held in that truth.

"No," Shaela said quietly, "we won't. We're going to hurt both of them by coming here." She lifted Merrill's left wrist. "Maybe you should have offered the bracelet as a gift instead of leaving it on a rock for a raven to snatch and take back to its nest."

"It felt like the right thing to do," Merrill said, as troubled now by the impulse to leave the bracelet as an offering to . . . something . . . as she had been at the time she'd done it. But it wouldn't have been an appropriate gift since Brighid had given it to her in the first place. Had Shaela forgotten that? Or did she not realize what the return of a heart-friend's gift meant, that it was a permanent severing of a friendship?

She turned away from Shaela, wishing the task was behind them instead of something yet to be faced.

The ship anchored within easy distance of the cove's southern arm. The northern arm had wharves for merchant ships and fishing vessels; the southern arm grudgingly accommodated visitors. Piers jutted out from the land in such a way that rowed boats sent out from larger ships could discharge their passengers, but the stairs that connected the piers to the land above made use of what nature had provided, and the uneven lengths and heights of the steps were a punishment for anyone with a weak leg.

Shaela said nothing as they climbed the stairs, but it was clear her bad leg wouldn't hold up to the strain if they had to scramble around a hillside with the girl.

Maybe I could suggest she remain behind with Brighid, Merrill thought, slipping an arm companionably through Shaela's—an unspoken apology for being snappish earlier and unobtrusive support as they made their way to the stables where a horse and buggy could be rented for the day.

She hadn't told the ship's captain the reason for this visit to Raven's Hill—or who she was visiting—but any man who sailed out of Atwater knew about Brighid—and why she no longer lived on the White Isle. So Merrill wasn't surprised when the men who had accompanied them as far as the stable didn't offer to go farther.

After paying the stable fee, Merrill climbed into the buggy, collected the reins, and made sure Shaela was comfortably settled before giving the horse the command to move forward. The cottage was no more than a mile outside the village proper, nestled at the bottom of the hill. It was in the center of a modest acreage that could have provided the family with a respectable living if there had been more than a girl and a woman to work the land.

She had visited twice before—once shortly after Brighid had settled into the cottage and again three years ago, when Brighid, on behalf of her niece, had requested that a Lady of Light come to Raven's Hill to test the girl.

It had become clear in that brief meeting that becoming a Lady of Light and living on the White Isle was Caitlin Marie's all-consuming dream and ambition. And it was just as painfully clear that something lived inside the girl that was at odds with that dream and ambition. Something that would not be welcome on the White Isle.

The girl was as tainted as her brother. Some things came through the bloodlines and never could be washed away.

Guardian of Light, cleanse my thoughts of such unkindness. The children cannot be blamed for their nature, and they have never used it for harm. But . . . I would not want one of their kind on the White Isle.

"We're here," Shaela said when the cottage came into sight.

As the horse's pace brought them closer and closer to success or failure, Merrill thought about those first two visits. Then, the hill looming behind the cottage had struck her as menacing, as if an ill-spoken word was all that was needed to bring the hillside down on the people living in its shadow. Now that same hill struck her as protective, as if it guarded something precious.

Which impression was closer to the truth? Or had the strain of the journey turned her mind to fanciful imaginings?

When they reached the cottage, Shaela climbed down and attached a lead to the horse's bridle, tying the other end to the hitching post. As Merrill secured the reins and set the brake, she caught the movement of a curtain falling back into place. A moment later, the cottage door opened, and Brighid, looking older and more careworn than Merrill had expected, stepped outside to greet them.

"To what do we owe the pleasure of this visit?" Brighid asked with cold politeness.

You know why we've come. Merrill searched Brighid's face but found no sign of welcome. And that sharpened her sadness over the necessity of coming here. They had been friends once, sisters in the joyous work of nurturing the Light. Now two children, especially the girl, stood between them.

"We need your help," Merrill said. The girl suddenly appeared in the doorway, her blue eyes bright with hope when she caught sight of them. No, not a girl anymore. Eighteen now, wasn't she? A woman come into her power. Whatever it might be.

Pretending she didn't see the hope, she kept her eyes fixed on Brighid. "We need Caitlin's help."

"For what?" Brighid asked warily.

So. Brighid was going to hold a grudge, wasn't going to bend even now.

"There are two plants we need for a . . . prayer . . . circle. They do not grow on the White Isle. We thought Caitlin, with her skills, could acquire them for us."

Hope burned away in Caitlin's eyes, replaced by bitterness. "So the Ladies of Light require the help of a sorceress."

"That is not a word to be bandied about," Shaela said sharply.

"Maybe not," Caitlin replied just as sharply, "but I want to hear *her* say it. She's so good at speaking the truth, let her speak it now."

"I have a name," Merrill said.

Brighid raised a hand, silencing Caitlin before the girl could reply. "What do you want?"

We have no time for a battle of wills. Can't you feel it, Brighid? Evil is already drifting among us.

"Heart's hope—and belladonna," Merrill replied.

The small jerk of Brighid's body gave Merrill hope, but Caitlin's expression showed no sign of yielding.

"Those plants don't grow around here," Caitlin said, as if that ended all possibility.

"But there is a place nearby where unusual plants grow," Merrill insisted. "I could accompany you and help—"

"*You* aren't welcome there."

"Caitlin Marie!" Brighid turned on her niece. "I understand your disappointments and why a wounded heart makes for a bitter tongue, but that is no reason to forget your manners."

"So they should get whatever they want from me just for the asking?"

Girl and aunt stared at each other, and Merrill had the uneasy feeling they were no longer talking about plants.

Then Brighid sighed and rested a hand against Caitlin's cheek. "No," she said. "You should get the Ladies what they need because *I'm* asking. And because this is more important than any one person."

Caitlin hesitated, then bobbed her head once in agreement. "For you, then." She disappeared into the cottage. A few moments later, they all heard the back door slam.

"We came at a difficult time," Merrill said soothingly, wondering if she and Shaela were going to stand outside for however long it took Caitlin to retrieve the plants, or if Brighid would stand by her own words and remember her manners.

"Manure has its uses, Merrill, but it never smells sweet," Brighid replied tartly. "Don't spread it here."

So much for stepping around the point of contention that had bruised their friendship. Not broken it, though. She wouldn't believe it was truly broken. Someday Brighid would be free to come back to the White Isle . . . and Lighthaven. "The girl doesn't belong on the White Isle. I stand by the decision I made three years ago. She isn't one of us, Brighid. She never will be."

Brighid leaned against the door frame. "A young man from the village called last week. Asked Caitlin to go walking in the moonlight—the first who has ever done that since she's considered 'strange.' He made her an offer."

"Oh." Merrill smiled. A wounded heart and an offer? Yes, that could explain the sharpness of Caitlin's temper. "Well, young women are often afflicted with nerves and quarrel with their lover before the wed—"

"He made her the kind of offer no woman with pride or heart would accept."

"Ah." Merrill's face heated with embarrassment, and out of the corner of her eye she saw Shaela turn away, head down, clearly uncomfortable with the turn of the conversation.

"Your presence here today is salt on a fresh wound," Brighid said, her voice sad and quiet. "You come asking for favors from one you turned away and offer nothing in return."

"There's nothing I *can* offer. And you *know* why we've come."

"Yes, I know why. As I said when I answered your letter, I, too, heard the voice in a dream. The words are a riddle, and I have found no answer." Brighid hesitated. "But I think the answer is more than an answer for whoever discovers the meaning of the riddle."

Shaela looked up, alert. "What do you think it is meant to be?"

"A door."

Reaching the spot on the hillside that she had decided years ago was the end of the path, despite the path continuing on up and over the hill, Caitlin closed her eyes and sent out that silent call: *I'm here.*

When she opened her eyes, the path ended at the walled garden that branded her a sorceress and was her only comfort and friend—the walled garden that didn't exist for anyone except her.

Slipping through the rusty gate that never closed properly, she hugged the two pots she'd brought with her and slowly examined the beds. She didn't know what belladonna looked like, but she was certain she'd know the feel of it.

And there it was, tucked in the corner of the garden that never managed to grow anything well. Beside it was a heart's hope plant she *knew* hadn't been there a few days ago.

Kneeling in front of the plants, she put the pots aside, then brushed her fingers over the plants' leaves.

Something here. Something strange.

Her fingers brushed leaves, but she had the sensation of a warm hand clasping hers. An accepting hand.

She understands me.

The thought made no sense. Neither was the certainty that she had almost managed to touch someone who wasn't there.

She sat back on her heels and studied the plants. Aunt Brighid had been acting odd, uneasy. As if she'd had a premonition of bad news and was expecting it to be confirmed every time someone came to the door.

Well, bad news *did* come knocking, didn't it?

"Prayer circle," Caitlin muttered as she pulled a trowel out of her skirt pocket and carefully dug up the heart's hope. "I'll bet it's going to be an interesting *prayer* circle."

An important one, anyway, she thought as she settled the heart's hope into one of the pots. Merrill wouldn't have come to Raven's Hill unless it was important. She didn't think Aunt Brighid had expected Merrill to show up, but Brighid had understood *why* Merrill was asking for these particular plants.

Caitlin transplanted the belladonna—and shivered as if she'd suddenly stepped into a deep, cold shadow.

Something important. *And I'm part of it.*

Following impulse, she loosened her braid of waist-length brown hair. She pulled out two hairs, wrapped one around the base of each stem at the dirt line, then added a little more dirt to hide what she had done.

She wasn't welcome at precious Lighthaven, but she would be part of whatever ceremony the Ladies of Light performed with the plants.

Humming a folk tune that was currently popular in one of her landscapes, Glorianna headed for her walled garden, a basket of gardening tools in one hand and a watering can in the other. When she and her mother, Nadia, had ganged up on her brother Lee to insist that he take one day out of each seven-day for rest and renewal, she hadn't expected him to surrender so quickly—and she hadn't expected the two of them to then turn on her and make the same demand! But, like Lee, she had been working too hard, pushing too hard. That had been understandable when the threat of the Eater of the World finding a way into her landscapes had been so immediate. After all, It *had* found Its way into two of her dark landscapes. But there had been no sign of It for weeks, and while the danger to Ephemera hadn't lessened, there was less she or Lee could do until they found some sign of where It had gone.

So today was for pleasure and, for her, that pleasure meant tending the earth, not as a Landscaper who was always vigilantly aware of the balance of Light and Dark currents that flowed through her landscapes but as a woman performing the simple chore of looking after her plants and cleaning out the weeds.

Even here on her small island, the autumn day was unseasonably—and delightfully—warm, so she wore an old pair of trousers she had cut off just below the knees and one of Lee's old cotton shirts—with the sleeves cut short—that her mother would have thrown in the rag basket if Glorianna hadn't snuck it out of the family home after deciding it was perfect for warm-weather gardening. Her shoes were worn at the heels and so broken-down that her striped sock poked up through a hole in the toe, and her black hair was bundled up under a battered straw hat whose ribbons fluttered in the light breeze. Nadia called it her urchin attire, but the garden—and Ephemera itself—didn't care if she was fashionably dressed and looked pretty.

No one really cared how she dressed or if she ever looked pretty.

If I ever fall in love, she'd told Lee once, *it will be with a man who can see me dressed like this and still think I look beautiful.*

Of course, the man would have to overlook the fact that she was a rogue Landscaper and was feared and reviled by all the other Landscapers who protected their world.

"If you want romance, my girl, read a book," she muttered as she unlatched the gate and gave it a bump with her hip to swing it open enough to slip inside. "That's the only place you'll find a man with enough heart to stand by someone who can control Ephemera like you do." Like no other Landscaper, not even her mother, could do.

Then she froze, all thoughts of a pleasant day in the garden and imagined romance forgotten, as the shock of what brushed against her senses caused her to drop the watering can and basket.

"Guardians and Guides," she whispered.

A dissonance in her garden. Something here that didn't belong. Something that didn't resonate with *her*.

She plucked the short-handled hoe and tines from the basket, wanting something she could use as a weapon. A quick look around convinced her there was nothing out of order in the beds closest to her, so she closed her eyes and steadied her breathing. Her garden covered almost two acres of land, but what it represented was the safety and well-being of thousands of people who lived in the landscapes in her care. She had to find the dissonance and weed out the source before it contaminated everything.

Despite her vigilance, had the Eater of the World found an anchor point in one of her landscapes that connected with this garden? Had It burrowed in somewhere like a dark, malevolent weed, waiting until she got close enough before unleashing one of its nightmarish creatures in hope of destroying her?

Then she felt Ephemera stirring, trying to align itself to the emotions and wishes churning inside her. The world trusted her as it had trusted few others since the time of the first Landscapers, who had been known as Guides of the Heart. It would manifest her emotions, thinking that was what she wanted—even if that meant creating an access point through which the Eater of the World could enter.

She had to regain control of herself. She had to *think* instead of feel. She had to think for both of them, because that was her purpose; that was why the world had shaped her kind in the first place.

Closing her eyes, she focused on the dissonance, and as the first shock that anything could have invaded her garden wore off, she caught the faintest hint of anxiety—rather like a puppy who had caught a small creature and brought it home but wasn't receiving the expected praise.

Ephemera had done this? Why?

She opened her eyes and strode to that unsettling spot. The

placement of the thing, tucked in an empty piece of the garden that connected with Sanctuary, sent a new jolt of uneasiness rushing through her, but she crouched down to study this unasked for "gift."

This particular spot had been filled with nothing but clover to protect the rich soil. Now, in the center of that clover, was a stone shaped like a natural basin shallow enough to provide birds with a place to drink and bathe. In the basin, just beneath the water, was a silver cuff bracelet with an intricate design of knots that flowed one to the next.

She reached out, resting her hand on the stone so her fingertips dipped into the water.

Turmoil. Ambivalence. Need and denial. Powerful emotions that tugged at her and also pushed her away.

This stone didn't come from a place of darkness but a Place of Light. She could feel the Light's currents singing in the stone and the water. There was some comfort in that, but it didn't explain why Ephemera had plunked down an access point to an unknown landscape that was connected to who knew where.

Focus, Glorianna. This wasn't idly done.

Someone had cried out with a heart wish strong enough to produce this response from the world, but bringing this stone here to her was as far as Ephemera could take that heart wish.

At another time, she would have used that access point to cross over to the unknown landscape. Standing in that place would have given her a better feel for what that part of Ephemera needed. Except . . .

This Place of Light resonated with her and yet it didn't. It was tangled up somehow, and the reason for that was outside her experience.

The currents of power that flowed through Ephemera circled around her, anxious, eager.

Sighing, Glorianna rose. "All right. It can stay." *For now.* "Let's see if we can get through the rest of the day without any more excitement, all right?"

The currents of power drifted away from her, making her think, again, of a puppy who had already done the very thing she just told it not to do. Not a good sign.

So she wasn't surprised when she saw Lee hurrying up to the garden's gate.

"This is supposed to be your rest day," she called as she hurried to meet him.

"I know. Yours too."

He looked pale and troubled—and his suppressed anger was strong enough to produce a shimmer in the island's Dark currents.

"What's wrong?" Glorianna asked. "Is everything all right at home?"

"It's fine. Home is fine." Lee raked a hand through his hair.

"*Lee.*"

"A handful of Landscapers and three Bridges have found their way to Sanctuary. They're . . . distraught . . . and a bit too quick to start casting blame when—"

She raised a hand, silencing him. Not a surprise that the others would find a way to blame her for the Eater of the World's escape and the destruction of the Landscapers' School. No, not a surprise. But it still hurt that any of them thought her capable of such a heinous act.

"If their landscapes have been compromised . . ."

"I know, Glorianna. I *know.*" Lee looked away. "We need to find out how they got to Sanctuary: what bridges were created and where."

"We may have to shut them out of Sanctuary in order to protect the Places of Light."

"I know that, too. But Yoshani thinks it's best to let them rest for a day, let their emotions settle a bit. Then he thinks you should talk to them."

Yoshani was a holy man who came from a Place of Light in a distant landscape. She had stumbled into that landscape when she was fifteen, had used the access point Ephemera had created and crossed over to that distant place. That choice had saved her from the Dark Guides and prevented them from walling her up inside her garden at the school. After she brought the Places of Light together and formed Sanctuary, Yoshani began dividing his time between his own community of Light and the part of Sanctuary that was more accessible to visitors. People felt easy around him, so he had become an informal listener and counselor to the weary hearts that reached Sanctuary.

He was one of the few people she trusted without reservation. But . . .

"They don't want to talk to me."

Lee looked at her, his temper shining in his green eyes. "They don't have a choice, Belladonna. The leaders of the Places of Light were very clear about that. *All* the leaders."

You're not without friends, Glorianna thought. *And you're not without family. Those are blessings you need to hold in your heart and remember.*

"Are you going back to the guesthouse in Sanctuary?" Glorianna asked.

"I'd rather not."

She figured as much and would welcome his company, but she was worried about the depth of his anger and bitterness. So the best thing for both of them was to fall back on a simple ploy that had never failed her: treat him like the younger brother he was. "Did you bring something to eat? The last time you were here, you cleaned out the pantry and didn't bother to tell me."

He crossed his arms over his chest and narrowed his eyes. "Yes, I brought something to eat. And I did *not* clean out the pantry, just that last bit of cake Mother had made—which was stale, by the way, since you'd left it so long, so that doesn't count."

"Does too."

"Does not."

"Does too."

"Does—" Lee glared at her.

"Do either of us have to cook this food you brought?"

"We'll have to heat it up and slice the bread and cheese. Even I can manage *that*, Glorianna."

Satisfied that he was now focused on being an annoyed sibling, she smiled sweetly. "In that case, you can stay. Want to make yourself useful and help me weed?"

"Not a chance." He gave her the look that always made her want to smack him. "It's my rest day. Remember?"

Chapter Seven

Caitlin dug her pitchfork into the compost heap that was tucked away in one corner of her secret garden. Pull out the weeds that choke the flowers and form a messy tangle around the bushes, let them simmer in a corner where sun, water, and air turned them into a rotting stew, and gradually they become a rich loam that fed the same flowers and bushes they had tried to usurp.

If only her own life could be that simple. If only the rotting stew of her emotions could be changed into rich loam.

She worked until her muscles ached. Not because the compost heap needed that much work but because she didn't want to touch the rest of the garden while bitter anger churned inside her. When thirst became a torment, she gave the compost heap one last turn, then leaned the pitchfork against the garden wall and walked over to the little pool of water shaded by a willow tree. The ground around one side of the pool rose up chest high and was a tumble of stones and pieces of slate that created a series of small waterfalls. The spring that fed the pool had to start somewhere among the stones since there was no sign of it on the other side of the garden wall, but she had never found the source.

Taking the tin cup she kept tucked among the stones, she filled it under one of the little waterfalls and drank it dry once, twice. When she filled the cup a third time, she settled beside the pool, one hand moving idly through the water as she sipped from the cup and looked around the garden that had provided her with an odd kind of companionship most of her life.

The pool had been her first exhilarating—and later, frightening—example of her power over the physical world.

She'd been six years old when she'd found the garden hidden on the hill behind her family's cottage. Michael had just left for the first time to take up the wandering life, and she'd run off, heartbroken that her only friend and playmate had abandoned her. She'd run and run and run. Aunt Brighid had told her she would make friends when she started school, but it hadn't happened. The other girls teased her and said cruel things, and she knew the teacher heard the girls and did nothing, encouraging them by keeping silent. So there were no friends, and without Michael to help her, school was hard. And Aunt Brighid hadn't wanted to admit that the same . . . something . . . that lived inside Michael and had driven him away from Raven's Hill lived inside her, too.

Her aunt would defend her against anyone—including the women who had been Brighid's Sisters on the White Isle—but privately, Brighid hadn't been able to hide the flinch, or the anger, whenever she saw evidence of Caitlin's and Michael's "gift."

So all Caitlin had known that day was that the difference that lived inside her and Michael was the reason Michael had gone away, and she ran, wishing with all her young heart that she could find someone, anyone, who would be her friend.

She'd tripped and ended up sprawled on the path. When she looked up, there was a stone wall in front of her and a rusted, broken gate.

She had found Darling's Garden.

Tangled and overgrown, desperately needing care, the garden tugged at her, and as she walked around it, her heartache eased. Here was something that needed her, wanted her, welcomed her.

Spotting something small that looked pretty but was almost buried under weeds, she pulled up a weed to get a better look. Then pulled up another. And another. When she finally cleaned out a circle of ground around the little plant, she still didn't know what it was, but it made her feel a little less lost and alone.

Years later, she learned the plant's name. Heart's hope.

She kept going back to the garden, escaping from school as soon she could to run up the hill to the secret place. Aunt Brighid's scolding and obvious worry about where a child that age was disappearing to for hours at a time couldn't eclipse the lure of a place where the light seemed to sparkle with happiness every time she slipped through the gate.

Then a girl at school invited all the other girls to see the expensive fountain her father had installed in the family's garden. All the girls except one.

Not you, the girl had said. I don't want you and your evil eye to look at our fountain.

Caitlin had stood outside the school, blinking back tears of shame as anger filled her.

"I wish your fountain looked as rotten as your heart," she whispered.

All the way up to the secret garden, she thought about a fountain and how lovely it would be to have one.

When she got to the garden, there it was—not the kind of fountain appropriate for a formal garden, but a tumble of stones forming a series of waterfalls into a knee-deep pool that was guarded by a young willow tree.

It was the most beautiful thing she'd ever seen—but it hadn't been there the day before. That was when she realized she could make things happen just because she wanted them to. She was excited, delighted, sure it was the best thing that had ever happened to her.

A week later, her aunt hauled her into their cottage, sat her down in a chair, and said, "Whatever it is you did, Caitlin Marie, I want you to undo it. There's enough talk about evil eyes without you causing trouble."

She didn't understand until Aunt Brighid told her about an expensive fountain that had turned foul. The water plants rotted overnight. The golden fish that had been bought from a merchant in Kendall and brought to Raven's Hill at great expense kept dying. And the water stank like a stagnant marsh no matter how often the groundskeeper cleaned the fountain and replaced the water. There was fear of sickness running through the village because of that foulness.

She'd cried and sworn she hadn't done anything bad, even though she suspected she *was* the one who had caused the change in the fountain, and she cried even more when Aunt Brighid yelled, "Where will we go if we're driven out of this cottage? This is all we have, and we have this much because it was your father's legacy, the only tangible asset he left his children. If we don't have this, we have nothing, Caitlin. Nothing."

Then Aunt Brighid started to cry.

She'd seen Aunt Brighid cry happy tears and the "little sadness" tears that came over the older woman from time to time, but not this heart-tearing sorrow.

So that night she wished as hard as she could that the fountain in her classmate's garden would be wonderful and clean and make everyone happy.

It didn't happen. Oh, the next time that fountain was cleaned, it didn't turn foul, but the plants and fish never flourished, and the water never quite smelled clean. Finally, it was drained for the last time and had stood empty ever since.

After that, she kept her wishes contained to the garden and never wished something bad on anyone. Which was hard for a young girl who had no friends, who the teachers looked at with distrust, who knew she was an outsider because of a difference in which she had no choice.

She had kept the garden her secret until Michael came home the first time. He, at least, was like her. He would understand that special place.

But he hadn't understood it. Oh, he'd admired it, had praised the work she had done all by herself to clean it up, but he hadn't felt anything for it.

And yet, he'd done the one thing Aunt Brighid couldn't do: He had accepted her strange communion with the world. It worried him, and it wasn't until years later that she realized he was worried for himself as well as for her. Magicians, the luck-bringers and ill-wishers who could change a person's life by doing nothing more than wishing for something to happen, had been driven out of towns when things turned sour. Some had been injured; some even killed. And in those places . . . Well, it wasn't safe for *anyone* to live in those places anymore.

When she was ten years old, her secret was discovered by two boys who followed her after school one day. She didn't know if they had intended to do more than follow her; she had heard nothing while she had worked in the garden. It wasn't until she had slipped out through the gate that she heard the screams for help and found the boys. One had a leg pinned under a fall of boulders. The other was sinking in a patch of bog.

Fortunately, it had happened during one of Michael's visits home, and he'd been walking up the hill to find her—or shout for her, since even he couldn't find Darling's Garden unless Caitlin was with him, but, oddly enough, his voice carried over the garden walls when nothing else did.

So while she had stood there, horrified that she might have done something that had caused the hill to create boulders and bog, Michael had come up the path.

A sudden crack, and a tree limb fell across the bog hole, just missing the boy and providing him with something to cling to—and providing Michael with a safe way to pull the boy out. That same branch became a lever for freeing the other boy from the boulders.

The boys recovered from their misadventure, but no one in Raven's Hill forgot the story that Caitlin had been seen entering Darling's Garden. Darling, who, it was said, had been a mostly benevolent sorceress who could command the world to do her bidding. There had been rumors that women in her father's family had found the garden a few times, but no one had known for sure that the garden still existed until Caitlin Marie had stumbled across it.

After the incident with the boys, Aunt Brighid began talking about the White Isle and Lighthaven, a place of peace, of Light. Maybe a place for a second chance, a new beginning—and, for Brighid, a return to the life for which she was best suited. For Caitlin, the stories about the White Isle were the seed that began a dream of friends and acceptance, of being part of a community.

Until the Sisters of Light, at Aunt Brighid's request, came to test her to see if she could be one of them.

She was not. Could never be. Wasn't welcome on their little piece of the world.

That she had failed the Light's test had been noticed by the villagers and had sealed her fate, branding her a sorceress.

And now . . .

Setting the tin cup back in its place among the stones, Caitlin moved to the bed in the garden that usually gave her the most comfort. Sinking to her knees, she studied the heart's hope.

The plant hadn't bloomed for the past three years—not since she had failed the Light's test. Oh, it continued to survive even though it didn't thrive, and it produced buds each year. But nothing came of those buds, of those small promises of hope. Even now, when it was well into the harvest season and most other plants had spent themselves, it was full of buds, as if it were waiting for some signal to bloom that never came.

Like me, Caitlin thought. *I can have my choice of professions in Raven's Hill—village sorceress or village whore. Take me out for a moonlight walk, tell me how lovely I am now that I'm all grown up, tell me my hair is so lush—like a courtesan in a story. Courtesan! Just because I didn't spend much time in school doesn't mean I haven't read the books Michael brought home from his travels, doesn't mean I wouldn't know a fancy word for whore.*

The pain of a lifetime of small hurts and snubs swelled up inside her until there was nothing left. There were plenty of people who were willing to use her in one way or another, but nobody really wanted her.

Swallowing down a sob as she remembered that young man standing in the moonlight, looking so romantic and saying things that ripped her heart open, she took the little folding knife out of her skirt pocket, opened it, and lifted it up to eye level. As she studied the blade, the breeze in the garden died, and it was as if the earth held its breath and waited to see what she would do.

"A whore needs to be lovely," Caitlin said. "A sorceress does not." Lifting the knife, she held the blade just above her cheek.

Imagining Aunt Brighid's horror and sorrowful acceptance upon seeing Caitlin's maimed face gave the girl a feeling of jagged pleasure. Imagining Michael's grief—and worse, the guilt that would live in his eyes ever after because he'd had to leave them in order to provide for them—made her lower the hand that held the knife.

"I can't stand this anymore," she said, staring at the heart's hope. "I can't stand being here, living here. If I wasn't around, Aunt Brighid could go back to the White Isle where she belongs. Then Michael wouldn't have to support anyone but himself and could have a better life than the one he has now. He *deserves* a better life." Tears filled her eyes. Her breath hitched. "And so do I. Why can't I go someplace where I can have friends, where I'm accepted for what I am? Why can't there be a place like that? I'm so alone. It hurts to be so alone. Isn't there anyone out there in the world who would be my friend?"

As she curled her body over her legs, her waist-length hair swung over one shoulder. Grief flashed back to anger, which deepened to a cold, dark feeling.

Sitting up, she grabbed the hair just below the blue ribbon that kept it tidy. Then she laid the knife's blade just above the ribbon and sawed through the hair. Tossing the length of ribbon-bound hair in front of the heart's hope, she continued to grab chunks of the shortened hair and cut it even shorter, feeling a terrible satisfaction at this act of self-violation.

Then she sliced her thumb, and the pain broke the cold, dark mood.

Folding the blade into the handle, she tucked the knife in her pocket, then went to the waterfall to wash the wound. Not so deep it would need stitching, but it was painful and—she sighed as she wrapped her handkerchief around her thumb—it signaled an end to working in the garden that day.

She looked at the tufts of hair that littered the ground around where she had been sitting. She looked at the tail of beautiful hair that used to make her feel pretty and no longer gave her pleasure.

Then she ran out of the garden, ran all the way home.

"Caitlin Marie!"

She found no satisfaction in her aunt's dismay at her appearance, but she lifted her chin in defiance. "That hair was only suitable for a whore. I won't be anyone's whore."

Aunt Brighid started to speak, then changed her mind about whatever she was going to say. Instead, she pulled out a chair at the kitchen table. "Sit down. I'll get my shears and see if I can tidy up what is left of your hair."

While Aunt Brighid trimmed the hair, Caitlin kept her eyes closed. There was a freedom to having hair so outrageously short. It would be seen as unfeminine, undesirable. Tomorrow she would look through the trunks stored in the attic. There might be a few things left that Michael had outgrown. With masculine hair and masculine clothes . . .

Maybe she would learn to smoke a pipe. And she would make it known that any man who showed interest in her did so because he had no *real* interest in women. No man in Raven's Hill would want to be accused of taking a moonlight walk with another man. Maybe, if she were mistaken for a young, somewhat effeminate man, she could even go traveling with Michael, get away from Raven's Hill altogether and see a bit of the world. Maybe even find people who could accept this strange gift inside her and would want to be her friends.

No longer feeling quite so bleak, she helped Aunt Brighid sweep up the hair trimmings, then prepare the evening meal. Later, as they both worked on the mending, she thought about the hairs she had wound around the heart's hope and belladonna plants she had given to Merrill.

When she'd gone up to get the plants, she hadn't paid attention to anything *but* the plants. Now, picturing that corner bed in the garden, she realized the stone that had come from the White Isle had been tucked behind the plants.

After Aunt Brighid began talking about Lighthaven, she had given Caitlin the stone that had come from the White Isle as a sort of talisman, and Caitlin had brought it up to the garden to be part of the flower bed she had made to honor the Place of Light. The bed never flourished. Some lovely little flowers bloomed in the spring, but the rest of the year that ground remained stubbornly bare, no matter what she tried to plant there—or tried to coax Ephemera to produce there. After she failed the test of Light, she stopped tending that flower bed, and even the little spring flowers died out.

She didn't remember doing it, but she must have moved the stone to that corner. And now that she thought about it without anger clouding the feel of the garden, it seemed a little . . . odd . . . that the plants had been with that stone. Remembering the feel of a hand clasping hers when she touched the plants, she realized something else. The plants hadn't felt quite in tune with the rest of the garden—as if she were singing one song while someone else sang another, and the melodies tangled and blended at the same time, working toward harmony but not there yet.

Not there yet.

Caitlin winced. No. Surely not. It had been a childish gesture, a bit of pretend. The two hairs she had wrapped around the plants' stems *couldn't* change whatever was going to happen when Merrill and the other Ladies performed their ceremony. Could they?

Glorianna fastened the gold bar pin to the plain white blouse, then stepped back to get a full view of herself in the mirror. The dark green skirt and the matching jacket that had flowers embroidered around the neckline and cuffs were probably too formal for this meeting. With her hair pinned up, she looked like she was attending some afternoon society function instead of meeting colleagues to discuss the danger to their world.

But we aren't colleagues, Glorianna thought as she dabbed a little scent on her pulse points. *I was never one of them.*

But she had to see the Landscapers who had found their way to Sanctuary, had to talk to them and hope they would be willing to work with her to protect Ephemera from the Eater of the World.

Guardians of the Light, please help them accept me, listen to me. If they can't, if they won't, Ephemera will end up more shattered than it is now.

The woman who looked back at her from the mirror had eyes filled with nerves instead of much-needed confidence. The woman in the mirror was tired of being an outsider who couldn't count on her own kind to stand with her in the battle that was coming. Even though she still believed in her heart that she would have to face the Eater alone, it would be a relief to know her family didn't have to shoulder the weight of being the only ones supporting her.

Which was why she had chosen these clothes for this meeting—as a reminder that her family *did* support her. Her mother had given her the blouse as a gift for her thirty-first birthday. Lee had purchased the fine green material, and Lynnea had made the skirt and jacket. Jeb, still a little uncertain of his place in the family beyond being Nadia's new husband, had given her the bar pin, which had belonged to his mother. Yes, the outfit was lovely, but it was the love and acceptance it represented that she had donned with each piece of clothing, like a shield that would protect her heart from whatever was to come.

As she turned away from the mirror, she was drawn to the watercolor that hung on the wall next to her bed. Titled *Moonlight Lover,* the view was of the break in the trees near Sebastian's cottage, where a person could stand and see the moon shining over the lake. The dark-haired woman in the painting wore a gown that was as romantic as it was impractical, and looked as substantial as moonbeams. Standing behind her, with his arms wrapped protectively around her, was the lover. His face was shadowed, teasing the imagination to provide the details, but the body suggested a virile man in his prime.

There was something about the way he stood, with the woman leaning against his chest as they watched the moon and water, that made her think he was a man who had journeyed far and now held the treasure he had been searching for.

Sebastian, the romantic among them, had painted it for her. He had captured the yearning for romance that she thought she kept well hidden. But in the same way that the secrets of the heart couldn't be hidden from a Landscaper, could romantic yearnings be hidden from an incubus?

It worried her sometimes when, in the dark of a lonely night, she conjured the image of a fantasy lover. When that shadowy lover began to feel almost real enough to touch, was she still alone in her fantasy or had an incubus joined her by reaching through the twilight of waking dreams? Or was something else trying to reach her through that yearning? Sometimes it almost felt as if she could extend her hand across countless landscapes, and touch—

Bang, bang, bang. "Glorianna?"

Muffling a shriek that would announce her abrupt return to the present—and give Lee the satisfaction of knowing he'd startled her—Glorianna pressed her hand against her chest to push her jumping heart back into place. There was nothing quite like a brother when it came to shattering a sensual fantasy. She hoped to return the favor someday.

Annoyed with herself for procrastinating and annoyed with him, since he wouldn't have been banging on her bedroom door if they weren't already late and that meant he *knew* she was procrastinating, she hurried across the room and opened the door.

All her annoyance disappeared, because all she could do was stare.

He was wearing his best black trousers and jacket, with a white shirt, a patterned green silk vest, and a black necktie. He'd worn those clothes for the weddings—Sebastian and Lynnea, and then, a week later, their mother and Jeb. Except for those two occasions, she couldn't remember the last time he had dressed so well.

"My handsome brother," she said, intending a light compliment. But seeing him standing there, polished up because he was as nervous about this meeting as she, was a sharp reminder that his life would have been so much easier if she hadn't been his sister.

Or if he had refused to acknowledge her after she had been declared rogue.

So she couldn't keep her voice light, couldn't wave aside how much his loyalty had meant to her over the past sixteen years.

"Don't get maudlin," Lee said, grabbing her arm and pulling her out of the room.

"I am *not* getting maudlin," she said, insulted because she was so close to feeling that way. "I was just trying to be pleasant."

"Uh-huh." He kept pulling her along, slowing down when they

reached the stairs to give her a chance to lift her skirt so she wouldn't trip and send both of them tumbling.

"Will you stop pulling at me?" Glorianna snapped when they reached the bottom of the stairs.

"No." He pulled her out of the house and around to the side. "We'll use my island to reach the rest of Sanctuary. It will take too long to use a boat. You spent so much time primping, we're late as it is." He gave her a calculating look. "Or did you get distracted by some-thing else?"

Heat flooded her face, and Lee, being an odious sibling, laughed.

"Sebastian will be pleased that you like his gift," he said.

"I wasn't mooning over a painting," she replied, clenching her teeth.

"Did I say mooning? I *never* said mooning." He stopped at the edge of where his island rested over hers, visible since there was no reason to hide it.

Lee's little island was anchored in Sanctuary. She had originally cre-ated it as a private place for herself, but it had resonated with Lee from the moment he'd set foot on it, and the connection was so strong that he could impose the island over any other landscape. Unseen unless he chose otherwise, the island provided safe ground if he found himself in a dangerous landscape.

"So," he continued, "do you want to sit around with the other Landscapers indulging in sterile, suffocatingly polite talk or just ask Ephemera to conjure up a big mud wallow?"

"*What?*" She stared at him. "Did you knot that necktie too tight? I don't think there's any blood getting to your brain."

"There's a custom in one of the landscapes—not one of yours but one I visited with another Bridge a couple of years ago. When two people—usually women since men tend to deal with things in other ways—start hurling insults at each other, and the disturbance starts dragging other people in to take sides, the village leaders have the two women—people—escorted to a wallow at the edge of town that was created just for that purpose. The two . . . contestants, let's call them . . . are assisted into the wallow—"

"Shoved, you mean."

Lee shrugged. "And they go at it. Every insult is accompanied by a handful of mud that is slung at the other contestant."

"Mudslinging in the literal sense."

He nodded. "So they scream and rant and rave and sling mud at each other until they're too tired to continue."

"Must be humiliating, to say things meant to be kept private."

"But they don't keep it private. They've been saying the same things to people behind the other person's back. This gets it all out in the open, and beyond showing everyone else how petty the argument truly is, it's also highly entertaining."

"Does it do any good?"

"Sometimes I think it really does clear things up between people who care about each other but stumbled somewhere along the way."

Glorianna cocked her head. "Like siblings?"

Lee grinned. "From what I gathered, some of them start a ruckus just to go play in the mud."

She laughed. "Too bad you didn't know about this custom when we were younger."

He laughed with her, then he turned serious. "You're not like other Landscapers, Glorianna Belladonna. You never were. You're a heart-walker as well as a Landscaper. Never forget that."

Tears stung her eyes, and she didn't resist when he put his arms around her in a comforting hug.

"Do you ever wish that I had been like them?" she asked, resting her head on his shoulder.

"Sometimes," he replied quietly. "But only because of what it cost you to be different." He hesitated, then added, "I wouldn't change anything, Belladonna. I've worked with other Landscapers. Had to. And I'll tell you this, not as your brother but as a Bridge. There is no one else I would want leading this fight against the Eater of the World. There is no one else I would trust enough to follow."

She lifted her head and looked into his eyes. Not that she needed to see the truth; she could feel his heart.

"Let's go meet with the others."

With their hands linked, they stepped onto the island. Within moments, Lee had shifted them back to the part of Sanctuary where the island physically existed. A few minutes later, they entered the guesthouse and found the room Yoshani had reserved for this meeting.

The Landscapers and Bridges in the room didn't look bedraggled, exactly, but there was a dazed expression in all their eyes. They had seen the end of their world as they knew it, and none of them were sure how to take the next step toward healing what had been savaged by the Eater of the World's attack on the Landscapers' and Bridges' schools.

Had the Guides of the Heart looked the same way? Glorianna wondered. *When the battle was over and they looked around at their shattered world, had they, too, felt lost and uncertain?*

Yoshani smiled when he saw them, but she felt the sadness resonating from his heart, felt the Dark currents of power that flowed through the room, fed by the five Landscapers and three Bridges who sat waiting. She didn't know any of the Bridges, and she didn't know the Third Level Landscaper or the three who wore First Level badges. But the oldest Landscaper had been an Instructor at the school during her brief time there.

"Hey-a," Yoshani said softly.

One of the Bridges looked over and saw them. For a moment, his eyes remained blank. Then anger filled him as he leaped to his feet and pointed. "What are *they* doing here?"

"They are the ones you have come to see," Yoshani said.

"Not them," the oldest Landscaper said. "Not *her*."

"There are things you need to know," Glorianna said, moving farther into the room. "Things you can do to protect your Landscapes if you just—"

"You did this!" the Third Level Landscaper screamed. "The wizards should have destroyed you when they had the chance!"

"Glorianna didn't release the Eater of the World, and she didn't destroy the school!" Lee shouted. "She's never done anything to any of you! The Dark Guides poisoned your minds and hearts against her, but she's the only one who can help you now."

"We don't need *her* help," the oldest Landscaper said, her whole body shaking with anger as she got to her feet. "She was declared rogue for a reason, and we've finally seen Belladonna's true face."

"Do you really see it?" Glorianna asked. "Can you calm your own hearts for just a moment to really see me for who and what I am?" She held out a hand and focused on the oldest Landscaper. "You don't need the garden at the school to connect with your landscapes. They resonate within you. You *can* reach them. If the landscapes you came from are secure, you can build another garden to help you protect the places in your keeping. And the Bridges can connect the landscapes the five of you hold. I need your help in fighting the Eater of the World."

"Our help?" the oldest Landscaper said. She laughed bitterly. "If anyone unleashed these horrors on the landscapes, it is *you*. You dare to come here to Sanctuary? This is sacred ground, a Place of Light. You sully it with the mere presence of your filthy heart!"

"Enough!" Yoshani shouted.

No, Glorianna thought. *It is not enough.*

The Dark currents inside her swelled with an anger that was black and undiluted. She stepped away from Lee. But before she said the words that were straining to break free, she sent out a command.

Ephemera, hear me. The anger in this room is nothing more than wind, a storm that cleanses and is gone. This anger manifests nothing, changes nothing.

But it would change everything.

"I am not like you," Glorianna said, the fierce anger that flowed through her making her voice rough. "I have *never* been like you, because I am a direct descendant of the Guides of the Heart who walked this world long ago. I am like *them*, and I am connected to the world in ways you cannot imagine. But I also have the bloodlines of the Dark Guides flowing through my veins, so I command the Light *and* the Dark. I am not human. Not like you. I am Belladonna. You have never wanted any part of me. Now I want no part of you." She raised a hand and pointed at the Landscapers and Bridges. "Ephemera, hear me! Know these hearts. Any place that resonates with me is closed to them for all time. They may leave this landscape of their own choosing, but if they do not leave, send them to the landscape that resonates with their hearts. This I command."

She turned and walked to the door. Then she paused and looked back at them. "The Eater of the World is free among the landscapes. If you don't hold on to your pieces of the world with all the Light in your hearts, It will destroy you and everything in your care."

She walked out of the room, walked out of the guesthouse. Then she ran from the pain that threatened to cripple her.

But even as she ran, she knew no one, not even Glorianna Belladonna, could run fast enough or far enough to escape the pain that lived in her own heart.

Yoshani stepped in front of Lee. "It is done," he said, keeping his voice low so that only Lee would hear. "There is no need to say more. Go away for a few hours. Go see your cousin."

Lee's green eyes were filled with icy anger. "My sister needs me."

"There is too much anger in your heart, my friend. You cannot help her. Let your feelings spill on someone who can drink them in and not be hurt by them. Sometimes anger needs an echo before it can be washed away. Go. I will look after Glorianna."

Lee glared at the Landscapers and Bridges, but he left the room.

Yoshani closed his eyes and tried to calm the turmoil in his own heart.

Opportunities and choices. It was a saying Glorianna often used to explain how the world worked to fulfill true heart wishes. He had seen the Light side of that saying, but until today, he had never seen the tragic side of it when the choices might cost so much.

He turned to face the eight people in the room.

"I am sorry," he said, "but you can no longer stay in Sanctuary."

He gave them a few moments to deny and protest his words, then he raised a hand to command silence. "You cannot stay."

"But we came here looking for help, looking for answers to what was happening in the landscapes—and what happened at the school," one of Bridges protested. "You said we might find the answer here."

"The answer stood before you, and you would not see. You chose to turn away from her, and now she has chosen to turn away from you."

The oldest Landscaper stared at him in disbelief. "Belladonna? *She* was the answer? She's a rogue!"

"And that is all you see," Yoshani said sadly. "For you, she is nothing more than a word that evil used to shroud your hearts. So now you do not resonate with the currents of power that flow through Sanctuary, and you cannot stay here."

"But *she* can?" one of the Bridges shouted.

"Sanctuary is one of Belladonna's landscapes," Yoshani replied quietly. "She altered Ephemera in order to bring the Places of Light together so that we might learn from each other, draw strength from each other."

They just looked at him, too stunned to speak.

The youngest Landscaper wrapped her arms around herself. "The school is gone. We can't go back to our gardens. How are we supposed to take care of Ephemera if we're all alone?"

"You are not alone," Yoshani said, looking at each of them in turn. "You have each other. So you find a place where you can build again, begin again." *And hope the Eater of the World does not find you again.* "Come. I will escort you to the bridge that, I believe, will still be able to take you back to your landscapes."

Glorianna kept her eyes fixed on the koi pond. She wanted to go back to the Island in the Mist and wrap herself in the comfort of solitude. But she sat on the bench and watched the koi while waiting for Lee to find her.

Except it was Yoshani who sat down on the bench and watched the golden fish.

"Where is Lee?" Glorianna asked, her voice husky from the storm of tears that had broken inside her after she'd run from the guesthouse.

"He has gone to spend a little time with Sebastian," Yoshani replied.

"But . . ." She pushed down the feeling of disappointment. Lee had to be upset about that meeting. He was entitled to venting in whatever way he chose.

"I suggested he leave for a little while," Yoshani said. "As close as you are to your brother, I think there are some things that you cannot say to him."

Glorianna didn't answer, so they sat together and watched the koi.

"Heart wishes are the most powerful magic that exists in our world," she finally said. "They can reshape the world, cause a cascade of events."

"Is it not true that any heart wish, no matter how powerful, can be thwarted by another heart wish that alters or disrupts that cascade of events?" Yoshani asked. When she didn't respond, he added, "What is it you fear, Glorianna Dark and Wise?"

Fear. Yes, there were things she couldn't discuss with a brother—or a mother. But here, now . . .

"I've known for sixteen years that I was different," she said softly.

"I've known I wasn't like the other Landscapers, even before I was declared rogue. But I've wanted to be one of them. I've wanted to belong and have friends and people who would understand the challenges and frustrations of being a caretaker of the world." She hesitated, then pushed on to the thing that had to be said. "Did I cause this, Yoshani? Did my own yearning to belong ripple through the currents of the world and set all this in motion, freeing the Eater and destroying the school so that the survivors would need to see me as one of them?" Tears welled up, stinging her eyes before they flowed down her cheeks. "Did I do this?"

"Glorianna, I say this with honesty and with the love of a friend." Yoshani took her hand in both of his and leaned toward her. "You are being a conceited ass."

She blinked at him, trying to see him clearly through the tears.

"Did you free the Eater of the World?" he asked.

"Maybe I——"

"Did you go to the school and set that evil free?"

"No, but——"

"Did you deliberately, and with malice, use your influence over Ephemera to cause whatever was done to set the Eater free?"

"No." Using her free hand, she wiped the tears off her face.

"Let me tell you a story about the world."

"I don't think there's time for a story," Glorianna said, feeling surly. He had called her a conceited ass. What kind of help was that?

"There is time for this one." Yoshani released her hand, braced a foot on the bench, and wrapped his arms around the upraised knee. "I wasn't a bad man, more of a youth whose wildness could have led him down a dark road. If there had been a place like the Den of Iniquity in those days, I might have chosen a very different life."

Glorianna studied him. "Teaser still gets hysterical when your name is mentioned."

Teaser was an incubus who lived in the Den and was Sebastian's closest friend. When she had gone to Wizard City to trap the Dark Guides, Yoshani had returned to the Den with Teaser to help that landscape remain balanced. The incubus was still having trouble accepting the fact that a man who lived in a Place of Light had been comfortable—had *enjoyed*—visiting the Den of Iniquity.

Yoshani smiled. "As I told him many times during my visit, I was not always a holy man."

"So why did you become a holy man?"

"Because of you."

Glorianna didn't know what to say, didn't know what to think, what to feel.

"My wildness was making things difficult for my family. At the core of that wildness was anger. Within my extended family there were several professions I could have chosen, several trades I could have apprenticed in. But none of them touched my heart, and in my own way I fought against being yoked into a life I wasn't meant to live.

"Finally my grandfather took me aside and told me I had a choice: I could go up the mountain and live in the community that served the Light and remain a member of the family, or I could continue my wild ways alone, shunned by all who had loved me. If at the end of three years I had not found my place or my purpose with the Light, I could come home and take up my old ways with no familial penalty.

"So for three years I worked in the community and studied with the elders and tried to find my purpose in the Light. And every day I prayed that something or someone would show me what, in my heart, I knew I was missing.

"And then you appeared one day, a girl from a strange part of the world, trying to make herself understood. The elders decided that you suffered from a sickness of the heart, a . . . poisoning. I was twice your age, and most unwilling, but the elders assigned me the task of staying with you as you wandered the land that made up our holy place. So I followed you through our gardens, through the fields and woods. Then you stopped suddenly, lifted your face to the sky, closed your eyes . . . and drank peace. I watched the Light fill you, felt it rejoice in the vessel, saw you bloom like a plant responds to rain after a dry spell.

"I watched, and I felt something shift in my heart. I understood the kind of work I could do in the world—helping others find that pool of calm, that moment of peace when they can truly hear the wishes of their own hearts and see the paths that are open to them for their life's journey. Because I was asked to watch over you, I found my place in the Light."

"If I hadn't gone to your community that day, the Dark Guides would have succeeded in sealing me in my garden at the school," Glorianna said. After a silence that seemed to fill the world, she asked, "Why didn't you tell me this story before?"

"Until we became friends and trusted each other enough to talk about delicate matters, I didn't know how you, as a Landscaper, saw the world around you. After I began to understand how you saw the world, it never felt like the right time to tell you this story. Until today. So now I will ask you, Glorianna Dark and Wise. Were my prayers, my heart wish, the reason Ephemera created a way for you to reach my part of the world? If they were, am I to blame for the sorrows in your life?"

"No, of course not," Glorianna said. "We make a hundred choices every day, and each of those choices, no matter how trivial, changes the landscapes we live in just a tiny bit. Enough tiny changes can change a person's resonance and open up another landscape as the next part of their life's journey."

"Or close a landscape?" Yoshani asked gently.

She nodded. "Sometimes people cross a bridge and never find the way back to a landscape they had known because they have outgrown that place. They have nothing to offer that landscape, and it has nothing to offer them."

"And sometimes when they reach that point, they know it is time to leave." Yoshani took her hand again. "You reached that point today. I think, in your heart, you never truly left the school. I think that by holding on to a landscape that was not yours, you denied your own heart's attempts to manifest a heart wish." He gave her hand a little squeeze. "You spoke the truth, Belladonna. You are not like them. You never were. Let them go. They have their own journey. It's time for you to look for the people who are like you."

It washed through her, a wave of power, as if a dam had finally broken to free what had been trapped for so long.

A heart wish.

Hers.

"Guardians and Guides," she gasped.

"What is it? What is wrong?" Yoshani grabbed her shoulders to support her.

"I think it's called an epiphany—or a heart wish released from its cage." She felt faint resonances. "Something is already in motion. I couldn't feel it before."

But she *had* felt it—in a stone Ephemera had brought into her garden.

"I need to go back to the Island in the Mist," she said as she sprang to her feet.

"May I come with you?" Yoshani asked, rising to stand beside her.

She hesitated, almost refused his company, then allowed the ripples still flowing through the currents of power to decide for her.

"Thank you. Your company would be welcome."

"And since you are so gracious, I will even cook a meal for you," Yoshani said as they walked away from the koi pond. "Do you have rice?"

"Yes. No. Maybe." She *did* cook when she was alone on the island for a few days and wanted to putter in the kitchen, but that wasn't the same thing as knowing what she had in the pantry at the moment. "Lee eats things."

Yoshani made a sound that might have been a snicker. "In that case, I suggest we fill a basket from the guesthouse larder. Simpler that way, don't you think?"

She had no opinions about the simplicity of using the guesthouse larder, but she knew with absolute certainty that her life was about to change—and nothing was going to be simple.

In the hidden part of the world known as Darling's Garden, air ruffled the water in the pool and murmured among the leaves. Fluttered the blue ribbon that tied a long tail of brown hair.

The garden resonated with New Darling's heart wish, sending ripples through Ephemera's currents of power, both Light and Dark: *"Isn't there anyone out there in the world who would be my friend?"*

An answering resonance rippled back from many places of Ephemera, but there was one place that had a stronger resonance, a better resonance. Because one heart wish could answer another. In response, Ephemera altered a little piece of the garden to provide an access point to a part of itself that resonated with that other heart wish. But New Darling did not cross over. So it took what New Darling had left for it to play with and brought it to the place that resonated with the other heart wish.

As the long tail of brown hair disappeared from the garden, one bud on the heart's hope bloomed into a beautiful, delicate flower.

Chapter Eight

*H*urry, *hurry, hurry,* Merrill thought as the ship closed the distance to Atwater's harbor. But not fast enough, despite having full sails. Something followed them. She could feel Its presence, feel the lure of It every time she looked at the water.

Would they have time to get back to Lighthaven and do . . . What? Shaela kept asking that very question, but Merrill had no answer. If that *was* the Destroyer—the Well of All Evil from the ancient tales— moving through the water in pursuit of their ship, how could two plants or a prayer circle stop It?

"It still follows," Shaela said when she joined Merrill at the bow. "It makes no attempt to catch up to us, but It follows."

"It doesn't need to catch us," Merrill replied. "All It needs to do is surround the White Isle, and we'll be trapped. Then It will consume the people living in the island's villages, just as It did in the old stories, until Lighthaven and our Sisters are all that is left—tiny candles in the dark. Candles that, in their turn, will be snuffed out one by one."

"Don't talk that way," Shaela said, her voice sharp. "You are the leader at Lighthaven. If *you* believe the White Isle is lost, our Sisters will believe it too. And then it *will* be lost. Our belief in the Light is the ship that brings the Light to all the people who live on the White Isle as well as our countrymen in Elandar. That's why we live apart—to maintain the innocence needed to nurture that belief."

"Your life wasn't sheltered," Merrill said.

"No, it wasn't. Which is why I cling to my belief in the Light. It is my raft, made from the planks of a broken life." Shaela rubbed her fingers against her forehead. "What will we do when we reach home, Merrill? There will be no time to sit and debate. We need to decide before we reach Atwater, since whatever we do must be done swiftly."

"I know, I know." But what could they do?

Merrill curled her hands around the railing, then closed her eyes and tried to picture a ceremony they could perform that would save the White Isle—and more importantly, Lighthaven—from the Destroyer.

And could picture nothing.

"We're heading into harbor," the captain called.

"This is what we'll do," Shaela said, shifting closer to Merrill. "We'll form a prayer circle made up of seven Sisters. We'll place the plants in the center of the circle. Four Sisters will chant the words that were heard in the dream. The other three will chant an affirmation as a refrain."

Merrill stared at her friend. "But that's— That's *sorcery*. You're talking about casting a spell, not participating in a prayer circle."

"It's all about belief, isn't it?" Shaela demanded. "Sorcery or prayer. What difference does it make what we call it? If we stand in front of our Sisters and say seven is a number of the Light, not a tool of magic, who will doubt us? Who will doubt you, our leader? If you say it is so, it will be so."

Suspicion too primitive to be shaped into words suddenly filled Merrill. She felt her body draw itself up, flinch away from the other woman. A broken life, Shaela had called the past that had brought her to the White Isle. A broken life—and not an innocent one.

"What were you before you came to the White Isle?" Merrill whispered.

"After all the years we've worked together and lived together . . . and now you ask me." Shaela smiled bitterly. "What do you believe I was?"

A sorceress. She looked at the scarred face, the blind eye and wondered, for the first time, if the wounds might have been deserved.

Why am I thinking this? she wondered, feeling off balance and a little desperate. *Why am I wondering about a friend when I need her emotional strength and purpose of will. Why . . . ?*

Then she knew. She didn't need to look at the stern or the water beyond the ship. It was so easy to picture a black stain on the sea, moving with the tide, coming closer and closer to shore.

Somehow, the Destroyer had reached into her mind and heart and was planting doubts, dividing her from her Sisters.

"I think your plan will work," Merrill said.

"And why would you think that?"

"Because the evil pursuing us doesn't want me to believe in the plan—or in you."

"Merrill?" Shaela's voice was sharp with worry. "Have you been tainted by the evil out there?"

"Touched but not tainted," Merrill replied, trying to smile. "I'll be all right. And we'll reach Lighthaven and perform the ceremony in time to stop the Destroyer from consuming the White Isle. I'll leave the preparation to you. I think you understand best what we need to do. I will gather the other five Sisters."

Shaela lightly touched Merrill's arm. "Heart's hope lies within belladonna. We don't have to understand what it means. We just have to believe it will save us."

Merrill nodded. Almost to the wharves now. Almost home.

But it's foolish to be hasty, whispered a solicitous voice. *Foolish to hurry through something so important.*

Yes, it would be foolish to hurry. Especially when they weren't even sure of *how* to do what needed to be done.

Best to think carefully. For the good of all. So important. And you . . . So responsible for whatever happens.

Leader. But not as good a leader as Brighid had been. Never as good.

No, not as good, the voice whispered sadly. *There is too much darkness in you, too many . . . unnatural . . . desires.*

Merrill sucked in a breath. Not true! *Not true!*

But something outside of herself wanted her to doubt her decisions enough to hesitate. And that meant any delay—even the time it would take to reach Lighthaven—would be enough to destroy all chance of them succeeding.

"We can't wait," Merrill said as the ship docked and the gangplank was moved into place. "We're going to have to take whomever we can find to make up our circle. Sailors, shopgirls, anyone."

"And what are we going to tell those people?" Shaela asked.

"We'll tell them we found the magic that can save them from what is coming, but it won't work without their help."

Which was, Merrill thought as she walked down the gangplank, nothing less than the truth.

She maintained a calm facade as minutes ticked away while she and Shaela selected the spot for the circle and considered who among the people present at the wharves and warehouses would be suitable participants. But underneath was the now-incessant drumbeat of *hurry, hurry, hurry.*

The Eater of the World drifted through the water, letting the sea carry It toward the land ahead that blazed with currents of Light. There was no hurry. The Dark currents on the island were swelling rapidly and now tasted of fear—and the certainty that It could destroy the humans who lived on the island. Even the ones who guarded the Light.

So easy to slip into that one female mind and plant a seed of suspicion in her heart where trust originally had been sown. But that trust, carelessly given and just as carelessly tended, had shallow roots and was not strong enough to survive when attacked. That female wanted to save the Place of Light, wanted to believe the magic she had acquired from the . . . sorceress . . . would be able to defeat It.

But the female had become a battleground. Her heart cried out with the need to save the Light. Her mind didn't truly believe the magic would save anything—or anyone. And because what her mind believed was just as strong as what her heart wanted, Ephemera would not answer.

It amused Itself for a little while, moving toward a ship or fishing boat, then savoring the fear when the humans realized the shadow in the water was no longer following the sea's currents but moving toward them with purpose. Cries of warning filled the air as ships and fishing boats maneuvered to escape. Some fled toward the safety of the harbor; others turned away from the island.

Heart by heart, the humans fed the Dark currents, changing the feel of the island. And whatever heart was supposed to supply the bedrock . . . Murky bedrock. The heart who held the island in its keeping did not care about the people here enough to tend the landscape, so there would be little resistance when It began changing the island's resonance to match Itself. Wasn't that delightful? But . . .

The heart that held the island also held the village where It had first noticed the guardians of the Light—another place equally neglected that It would change into a hunting ground. But there was something else on the island, tangled up in the Dark and Light currents. Something more. Something that It couldn't sense clearly, which made It uneasy.

No longer content to drift in the water, anticipating the feast, It moved toward the island with purpose.

"I'm flattered that you invited me to view your garden," Yoshani said.

Satisfied that there was no dissonance in the part of the garden that represented her mother's landscapes, Glorianna gave her companion a sly smile. "Would you still be flattered if I invited you to help me with the weeding?" She laughed at Yoshani's startled expression. But when he said, "This would be permitted?" she felt a flutter of sadness, so she linked arms with him and moved on to the next part of the garden.

"I have brought you sorrow," Yoshani said, seeing more than she wanted him to. "I am sorry."

"It wasn't you."

"Something in my words made you sad."

She stopped at the next bed but didn't focus on it. Not yet. "This garden represents my landscapes and is my connection to them. Oh, they're always connected to me here"—she tapped her chest to indicate her heart—"but this is a tangible . . ." She frowned as she tried to figure out how to explain. "Every landscape should have the Landscaper's actual presence on a regular basis to remain balanced—and because standing on that ground is the best way to sense if a particular part of a landscape needs special attention. The gardens are an easy way for a Landscaper to step between here and there to reach the pieces of the world in her care. It's an established path, an anchor that takes me to the same place in the landscape every time. Also, by working the soil, by planting and weeding, I can feel each landscape, so I know if any of them need immediate attention."

"But you invited me to work in your garden," Yoshani said. "Would that not interfere with your landscapes?"

Glorianna shook her head. "Your heart would not interfere with this garden." Then her voice was barely a whisper as the sadness washed over her again. "That's how the training begins. You work with an experienced Landscaper, weeding the beds in her garden, learning the names of the plants and what they symbolize and what they need to grow well. You learn how to combine things that are pleasing to the eye but also represent different aspects of a landscape. You learn the resonance of Ephemera's currents of power—the Dark as well as the Light. You learn all these things on safe ground because someone else's resonance maintains the balance." She forced herself to smile. "But that could all be a ploy made up by the older Landscapers to get out of doing all the weeding by themselves."

Yoshani looked around, then looked into her eyes. "Perhaps you need an apprentice."

Something rippled through her when he said the words.

Something is changing, she thought, suddenly feeling a tug from the section of the garden she specifically wanted Yoshani to see—the beds that represented Sanctuary. *No. Something has already changed.*

"Glorianna?"

She didn't answer him, just slipped her arm out of his and ran toward that other part of her garden, leaving him to hurry after her.

Was it luck and the restlessness of young women, Merrill wondered, or the Lady of Light's guiding hand that had brought three of their Sisters into Atwater? The girls had come to town to run errands and do some shopping for the community and—giving in to an impulse—had come down to the wharves to ask for news about Merrill and Shaela just as their ship's lines were being secured.

Only five of them in total instead of the seven Shaela had wanted, but five experienced in focusing their thoughts in order to connect with the Light were better than seven who would need to be coached.

Foolish to set up on the wharf in front of all the warehouses, Merrill thought as she and Shaela set the pots of heart's hope and belladonna side by side. Surely they could get away from the waterfront and the smells of seawater and fish? Atwater had a lovely little park. That would be a much more pleasing setting for a prayer circle and would take hardly any time at all to get there. Was this sense of urgency something that came whispering from the Dark so that they would act prematurely and ruin the chance of this "magic" succeeding? If she chose wrong, their failure would be her fault. How—

Her mind ceased its frightened chatter when she looked into Shaela's eyes—the one clouded and blind, while the other saw the world a bit too sharply.

Believe.

It was as if the word had been breathed on the air between them.

Shifting the pot of heart's hope, Merrill said quietly, "You take up the chant from the dream. I will lead the refrain."

Shaela shook her head. "As leader . . ."

"I can't believe, Shaela. Not strongly enough. Now that it comes down to it, I can't do what you can. But I can take up the refrain." She hesitated, then added, "We won't get a second chance."

Shaela looked toward the sea. "I know."

A crowd formed around them as sailors, merchants, and dockworkers were drawn toward their little gathering and word began to spread that the Sisters of Light were going to do a special circle of protection right there at the wharves.

"Ladies?" The captain of their ship, as well as several of his crew, eased through the crowd. "Is there something we can do to help?"

Before Merrill could refuse, Shaela spoke up. "Take up any part of the chant your heart can believe in without question. The more voices that are raised for this ceremony, the better our chances of having our prayers heard."

They took their positions, Merrill and Shaela facing each other while the other three Sisters filled in the circle, the heart's hope and belladonna at its center. Around them, the people formed another circle.

If this doesn't work . . . Merrill closed her eyes for a moment, trying to banish doubt, then focused on Shaela.

"Heart's hope lies within belladonna," Shaela said, raising her voice enough to be heard by the first few people around the circle.

"Guardian of Light, hear our prayer," Merrill answered as the refrain.

"Heart's hope lies within belladonna." This time, two of their Sisters took up the chant with Shaela.

"Lady of Light, hear our prayer." The other Sister's voice joined Merrill's.

"Heart's hope lies within belladonna."

"Guardian of Light, hear our prayer."

"Heart's hope lies within belladonna." Male voices joined the chant, a little hesitant but there.

"Lady of Light, hear our prayer." More voices.

Merrill felt the Light fill the circle, felt it spill over the crowd, felt it grow stronger with each voice that took up the chant. And for the first time since they had sensed the stain of evil that had followed them from Raven's Hill, she truly believed they would succeed.

Looking at her friend, Merrill added her voice when Shaela said, "Heart's hope lies within belladonna."

It gathered speed as It moved toward the island.

Something had changed. The fear was fading, and It felt the world becoming fluid as Ephemera prepared to manifest the need that was now held in many hearts.

No! It had not found the other Places of Light, so it would *not* be deprived of this one.

It fed Its rage to the Dark currents in the sea. Then It became the sea—and rose up as a deadly wave that moved toward the island with the speed of a wild storm.

The calling was filled with a desperation that felt like a lash against her skin. The resonance of that landscape grated against her senses.

But she had to answer. *Had to.*

"Glorianna!"

A hand grabbing her arm, holding her back.

"Something calls to me, Yoshani," she said, trying to pull free. "I am an ill-fitting piece being wedged into a place I don't quite belong, but I'm all there is." She stared at the bowl-shaped stone and the silver cuff bracelet beneath the water, feeling the need that rang in the hearts connected to those objects. Feeling a rhythm in the air.

"This is not a place you know, isn't that true? If you go there, can you get back? Glorianna!"

Yoshani shook her, and that startled her enough to focus on him. And seeing the look in his eyes startled her enough to hesitate. When she had seen that expression in other men's eyes, she had called it "warrior's eyes." She had never thought to see Yoshani's dark eyes look that way.

"A summons that powerful may not come from the Light," Yoshani said.

"I have to answer," Glorianna said. "If I don't, something precious will be lost. I know this, Yoshani. I can feel it."

He nodded, but the wild look in his eyes didn't fade. "You will not go alone."

"But—"

"Both of us or neither. I will not compromise, Glorianna."

There wasn't time to argue. Snatching the bracelet out of the stone bowl, she tried to ignore the grating dissonance, that conflict of resonances.

Whatever wants me will also reject me.

She closed her hand around the bracelet, then said to Yoshani, "Don't let go of my arm." When she felt his grip tighten, she thought, *There will be bruises tomorrow.* But she didn't tell him to ease his hold on her. She would rather have bruises than lose a friend while taking that step between here and there. Besides, she suspected that more than her arm would be bruised by the time she completed this journey. "When I tell you, take a step forward."

She waited, waited, let the resonance build until the rhythm felt like a chant.

"Now," Glorianna said, and felt Yoshani move with her as they took the step between here and there.

"Heart's hope lies within belladonna."

"Guardian of Light, hear our prayer."

Most of the people ran, trying to escape the destruction that was coming, but some stayed. Maybe they realized they couldn't get far enough away to save themselves. Maybe they believed their voices would still be able to tip the scale and save the White Isle.

Merrill glanced over her shoulder and shuddered as she saw the wall of black water coming toward them. Shaela, facing the sea and watching the wave come closer with every heartbeat, didn't falter.

"Heart's hope lies within belladonna."

"Lady of Light, hear—"

The man and woman came out of nowhere, breaking into their circle. The woman stumbled against the pots, knocking over the belladonna before breaking through the other side of the circle. The sailors and dockworkers caught the two strangers and steadied them, but the damage was done. Whatever "magic" had been made by the chant and the circle had been destroyed.

"You!" Merrill said, giving in to the slash of anger that wanted to drive the dagger of failure into someone else's heart.

But the black-haired woman just stared at the wall of water coming toward the island, then turned her icy green eyes on Merrill.

"What is this place?" she demanded.

"Guardians and Guides," the man said as he looked at the black wave. "We can't stay here, Glorianna."

"We can't leave yet," the woman, Glorianna, replied. Those eyes fixed on Shaela. "What is this place?"

"The White Isle," Shaela replied.

"An island? This is an island?"

Shaela nodded.

"Glorianna," the man said.

The woman shook her head. As she held up her clenched hand, Merrill caught a glimpse of something silver.

"This is a Place of Light, Yoshani," Glorianna said.

"And that is a killer wave that will drown this island and everyone on it."

Glorianna shook her head again. "No, *that* is the Eater of the World. I recognize the resonance of It."

Merrill gasped. How did this woman know? How could she speak with such certainty? Like the man, her speech declared her a foreigner, someone who came from a country far beyond Elandar. But there was something familiar about her, something . . .

It's like being around Caitlin Marie. Only . . . more so.

A shiver went through Merrill as the woman stared at the sea, then turned and looked inland as if she could see beyond buildings and hills right to Lighthaven.

"This place is mine and not mine," Glorianna said quietly, turning back to look at the sea. "Resonances are tangled up in a way I don't understand, but that other resonance isn't strong enough to keep me from holding on to this landscape—at least for a little while. I can try to save or I can try to destroy. If I try to destroy and fail, I will save nothing." She stared at the black wall of water, then took a deep breath and let it out slowly. "Ephemera, hear me."

✶   ✶   ✶

She was there! The True Enemy was there, on the island! It would smash her, drown her, destroy her! In this form, It was part of the sea. She could not cage It, could not stop It.

The black wave swelled even higher, moved even faster.

Glorianna watched the unnatural wave bearing down on the island. If there had been time, she would have considered each of her landscapes in turn to see if there were any borders that could be made that would connect this landscape to other pieces of the world. But there wasn't time. Besides, something wasn't right here. Despite being a Place of Light, that tangle of resonances warned her that something wasn't right.

They're going to be alone, she thought. *For a while, they're going to be alone.*

Couldn't be helped.

"Ephemera, hear me."

She felt the world changing to manifest her heart and will. But the change wasn't smooth, wasn't complete. Even in the moment when Ephemera altered the landscapes and the black wave disappeared, she knew the change wasn't complete—because this newly made landscape didn't quite resonate with her. The place itself felt secure enough; the currents of power were flowing as they should, although the Dark currents felt too thin to properly balance the hearts on this island.

Nothing to do about that, either, until she found the other Landscaper who controlled this island. Besides, now she wanted to solve her own puzzle.

"You're safe," she said, approaching the two older women. "The Eater of the World can't reach you."

They said nothing, but the three younger women all made a sign with their fingers. Yoshani responded by saying something under his breath that she suspected was a very bad word learned in his youth. Which confirmed that the sign was meant as an insult.

She took a step closer. They all took a step back.

Whatever wants me will also reject me. She felt the truth of it as she looked at the women.

One of the older women straightened her shoulders and lifted her chin—the movements of a leader reminding lesser beings that she *was* a leader.

"Your kind are not welcome on the White Isle," the woman said.

An echo from the woman rippled through the Dark currents inside Glorianna. Pain. But not pain received; this was hurt inflicted. And when she thought about the hurt inflicted and listened to that heart, her eyes were drawn to the two pots—the heart's hope and the belladonna, which was knocked over, its dirt partially spilled out on the wharf.

"Where did you get those plants?" Glorianna asked.

"That is not your concern, sorceress," the woman said. "Go back to whatever shadow place you came from."

Ignoring the woman, Glorianna crouched beside the spilled pot that held belladonna. Something there. She righted the pot, then scooped up as much of the spilled soil as she could without filling her hands with splinters from the wharf. As she pressed the soil around the plant's stem, her fingers touched a spot at the base of the stem that tingled, resonated, was so full of a wanting it made her ache.

"Yoshani," she said as she brushed the soil away from the stem, "can you see anything?"

He crouched beside her. As she tilted the pot, she saw something glint in the sunlight.

"There," Yoshani said, pointing to the exact spot on the stem. "It looks like a hair was wrapped around the plant."

A need so great even a hair carries its resonance.

More than that, the resonance in the hair matched the resonance on the island that was tangled with her own.

Handing the pot to Yoshani, she stood and faced the two older women. This time she focused on the one with the cloudy eye. "Where did you get those plants?" No answer. "Tell me now, or I will give you back to the Eater, and the Light will vanish from your part of the world."

They looked at her in horror. Then the leader said, "You have such darkness in you that you would condemn the innocent?"

"You will never understand the currents of power that flow through me." She opened her hand, revealing the silver cuff bracelet—and saw shock and recognition in the leader's eyes. "And you are not innocent. But you got what you asked for." Before the woman could move, Glorianna grabbed her hand and slapped the silver bracelet into it.

The woman stared at the bracelet. "Where did you get this?"

"In the future, be more careful what you ask for." She paused. "Heart's hope carried the need to be protected, and you are. You are no longer connected to the world. You will not be found by the Eater of the World—or anyone else."

The cloudy-eyed woman frowned. "But the dream said heart's hope lies within belladonna."

"It does," Glorianna replied. "*I* am Belladonna."

Ripples, murmurs. Ignoring the leader, she focused on the cloudy-eyed woman. "For the last time, where did the plants come from?"

"From a girl who lives in Raven's Hill," the cloudy-eyed woman replied. "She gave us the plants."

"Where is Raven's Hill?"

"On the eastern coast of Elandar."

That told her nothing, but she would wait until she was back on her own island before trying to figure out where Elandar was in relation to any landscape she knew.

She picked up the pot of heart's hope and handed it to the cloudy-eyed woman. "Tend this carefully. It's the only anchor you have left to the world. If it's destroyed, I don't know if you'll be able to touch the world again."

"Touch the world?"

"This island is all you have now. What can be harvested from the land and the sea within this landscape's boundaries is all your people can reach—at least until I find the other . . . sorceress . . . whose heart resonates with this place."

Glorianna stepped back and took the pot of belladonna from Yoshani. "Hold on to my arm. We need to leave now."

"Agreed," he said, looking around at the men who had remained at the wharves.

She focused her heart and will on her garden, on the beds that represented Sanctuary. The feeling of strength and peace and home filled her. "Now," she whispered.

Together they took the step between here and there—and stood in her garden, looking down at a bowl-shaped stone filled with water.

Glorianna set the pot of belladonna next to the stone. She wasn't sure the island was really one of her landscapes, but she would keep it safe for a little while.

"What now, Glorianna Dark and Wise?" Yoshani asked, striding to keep up with her as she headed for the part of the garden that would take her to Aurora.

"I need to talk to my mother and Lee—maybe Sebastian, too—and see if any of them have heard of Elandar or know how to reach Raven's Hill. If the Eater followed the ship, It may know how to find the girl. We have to find her first."

"Forgive me if the question sounds cold, but why is this girl so important?"

Glorianna stopped in front of the statue of a sitting woman that she'd taken from her mother's garden to act as an anchor for Nadia's landscapes. She kept her eyes on the statue as she felt the question flow through her.

Something is changing. Has already changed.

"Because, Honorable Yoshani, I think this girl is like me. There may be someone else out there who is like me."

It smashed water on water out of frustration at being cheated of Its prey. It raged at the True Enemy's cunning.

It could see the Place of Light, but as It got closer to the island, the land began to fade, becoming less substantial until It reached some invisible marker in the sea. At that point, the island vanished altogether.

Something had drawn the True Enemy to this place. Something . . . or someone.

Turning, It followed the ships fleeing south. If It couldn't have the Place of Light, It could—and would—have the sorceress who had helped deprive It of Its prey.

We're safe, Merrill thought as she stared at the calm sea. *The Destroyer is gone; the dark-hearted sorceress is gone.*

"Merrill."

The world can't touch us anymore. Isn't that what she said? We won't be tainted by the world anymore. But the Dark feelings are still here. The Dark still smears the Light. I am the leader. I will cast out the Dark. I can. I will. Somehow, I will.

"Merrill."

She looked at Shaela and smiled. "We're safe. From everything." She looked at the pot. "We should throw that into the sea. We can't take it with us. It would contaminate Lighthaven."

Shaela shook her head. "Hope is the Light's seed. We must keep it with us and tend it. We will need it in the days ahead."

Merrill looked at the pot of heart's hope that had come from Caitlin Marie and shuddered.

I will cast out the Dark. I can. I will. Somehow, I will.

Chapter Nine

"I'm not drunk," Lee said as he bumped into Sebastian.

"Of course you're not," Sebastian agreed, steering them both along the path that led from Sebastian's cottage to Lee's.

"Because *you* kicked me out of the Den."

"That's what family is for—to help you stop being stupid."

"That is not what family is for."

"You'll have to explain that to my wife. In point of fact, cousin, Lynnea was the one who decided you needed to go home and kicked you out of the Den. I'm just the messenger."

Before Lee could say anything about women not minding their own business—which would have gotten him into trouble—his feet got adventurous and decided to make flat ground dip and roll.

Damn the daylight, weren't all the chirpy-chattery critters supposed to get quiet when people walked through the woods? It seemed like they were all gathered just overhead and expressing their opinions at volumes little critters shouldn't be able to reach. And he'd drunk just enough that all that noise was threatening to fill up his head and change into a mountain-sized headache. As if that wasn't bad enough, he kept feeling like something was tugging him off balance—and it wasn't the whiskey he'd tossed back while he'd raged about Landscapers and Bridges who were determined to believe the worst about Glorianna because considering anything else might require them to use their brains.

But Yoshani had been right. Sebastian's anger when Lee had spewed out the things that had been said at that meeting in Sanctuary had been a cleansing fire reflecting his own feelings, and they had burned each other's tempers down to a smoldering opinion that the surviving Landscapers and Bridges had as much understanding of the danger they were all facing as what came out of a horse's ass, and—

He stumbled against Sebastian again and, this time, got a semi-friendly curse and shove.

Something pulled at the Bridge's power in him, wanting him to answer, wanting him to . . . what?

He grabbed Sebastian's shoulder for balance.

"Daylight, Lee! You didn't drink *that* much."

"No, I didn't." And he hadn't felt more than a little sloppy and tired until they'd crossed the border between the Den and Aurora. The closer they got to the spot where the path that started behind Sebastian's cottage branched and headed for his cottage or Nadia's house, the more he felt like he was being bounced and rolled and couldn't get a solid sense of where he was.

Then Sebastian was holding his shoulders in a bruising grip.

"Are you sick?" Sebastian asked, giving him a shake that wasn't the least bit helpful. "Lee, what's wrong?"

Good question. It was like everything was just a little out of focus, a little off balance. But still familiar, except . . .

"It's not me; it's Ephemera." Lee turned and headed up the path, stumbling because this connection to Ephemera was producing a fever-dream sense of the world around him, as if he were almost seeing some other place while his feet were hitting the solid reality of Aurora.

Sebastian walked beside him, swearing sincerely and creatively while keeping a supporting hand on his shoulder. Then they reached the boulder that marked the branch in the path. Lee stopped, throwing an arm to the side to block Sebastian.

"Guardians and Guides," Sebastian said. "Is that hair?"

A long tail of light brown hair tied with a blue ribbon lay next to the boulder.

They approached cautiously. Lee crouched to get a closer look, then held his hand above the hair.

"Careful," Sebastian said, his voice sharp.

"Don't be a collie," Lee replied absently, waving off Sebastian's caution while he focused on the hair. Finally he stood up and shook his head. "This is strange."

"These days, strange is *not* good."

"I don't think there is any harm in this," Lee said, rubbing the back of his neck. Damn it, he was getting the kind of headache that was going to climb up his neck and threaten to crack his skull. And he needed to *think.* "Besides, the magic in the hair is fading."

"How can you tell?"

"The ground is firming up. Or my sense of it is coming back into focus."

Sebastian pointed at the hair. "*That's* what was making you act so drunk?"

Lee nodded.

"We should burn it."

Lee shook his head. "Not yet. I'd like Mother and Glorianna to see it first. Maybe I reacted so oddly to it because my 'translation' of the magic wasn't correct. Sometimes a Bridge touches a place with opposing needs. The two landscapes will not resonate with each other enough for a bridge to be created that will connect them. But someone in those landscapes is sending out a heart wish that is so strong that I'm picking it up as a need to create a connection, but I can't pick up a sense of place."

"What do you usually do when that happens?"

"Create a resonating bridge." Lee picked up the tail of hair. Nothing but a little tingle now. Enough that he would probably recognize the resonance of the person's heart. He looked at the paths, then at the hair. "Three choices," Lee said. "Three chances?"

Sebastian studied the paths and swore softly. "For good or ill, this was aimed at someone in the family."

"Yes. So let's see what Mother can tell us about it."

Having decided that much, Lee headed down the path that would lead to his mother's house. Sebastian fell into step beside him.

"Does Ephemera usually bring you tokens like that?" Sebastian asked.

"No. So there's no point in the incubi asking me to send lovelocks to whomever they're currently entertaining as dream lovers." Lee glanced at his cousin and decided that whatever Sebastian was chewing over probably didn't concern the incubi. "Anything else you want to know?"

"Yeah," Sebastian said after a moment. "What does 'don't be a collie' mean?"

Lee just grinned.

Glorianna opened the kitchen door of Nadia's house enough to poke her head inside. "Anyone flying around in here?"

"No," Nadia replied. "The birds are all in their room."

Glorianna pushed the door open and entered the kitchen. "Yoshani came with me. Something happened that . . ."

Nerves. Tension. Eyes full of questions as her entire family turned away from whatever was on the kitchen table and looked at her. And something else in the room—a resonance that made her breath catch.

As Yoshani came in behind her, his greeting silenced before it began, she looked at Lee. He hesitated, then shifted to one side, giving her a look at the table.

Guardians and Guides. She could feel the air around her as she took the few steps that brought her to the kitchen table, could feel the currents of power that made Ephemera an ever-changing world. For a few heartbeats, the entire world consisted of a tail of light brown hair lying on a towel spread over the table. "Where did you get that?"

"Found it near the boulder where the path branches," Lee replied.

Glorianna set her hands on the towel, her fingers not quite touching the hair. The same resonance as the hair that had been wrapped around the two plants. This came from the sorceress who lived in Raven's Hill. But . . . how?

She heard voices murmuring around her, asking questions or, in Sebastian's case, demanding answers. Heard Yoshani answering. But it was all sound, like the rustle of leaves or rock hitting rock. Right now, the only messages she could hear came from a distant heart.

So much pain in that heart, so much longing, so much need. And anger in the hands that had sawed through the hair. But there was also strength in that heart.

How did this get here? Those women on the island didn't come from this part of Ephemera. So what does this girl want so badly that her need caused Ephemera to bring shorn hair from wherever it had been dropped to a place where it would be found by someone in my family?

"Do any of you know where Elandar is, or where to find a village called Raven's Hill?" she asked, finally looking up at the people around her.

Head shakes from everyone.

"I can ask around the Den," Sebastian said.

"One of Mother's landscapes is a village on the coast," Lee said. "I could go there, ask around."

As he spoke, Glorianna could have sworn a shadow fell across the table even though no one had moved.

"No," she said, taking a step back from the table. "We need to stay close right now—and we need to find this Raven's Hill."

"When I return to my part of Sanctuary, I will ask the scholars if they have any knowledge of Elandar or the White Isle," Yoshani said. "They may even have a map that would show its location."

Glorianna nodded, although she wasn't sure what use a map would be—unless she discovered that she or Nadia already had a landscape in that part of the world. Even then, it wasn't as if they would have to travel to get there. Any place that resonated with their hearts was no farther away than the step between here and there.

Lynnea touched the edge of the towel. "Do we really need to find the place?" She squirmed when they all looked at her, but her blue eyes met Glorianna's green ones. "It just seems this is really about finding the person."

"Agreed," Glorianna said. *And about finding her before the Eater of the World does.*

"So this is about a heart wish, isn't it?" Lynnea glanced at Nadia, who tipped her head in a way that indicated she wasn't ready to comment yet. "I read a story last week about a girl who doesn't know who she really is, and the people in the village where she lives don't like her because she's different. Her journey is full of hardships, but in the end, s-she finds her own people. She f-finds the place where she belongs."

Glorianna's heart felt a tender tug and ache as she watched Sebastian wrap his arms around Lynnea, loving and protective.

"You shouldn't read stories that upset you," he said, kissing Lynnea's forehead.

"No, it was a lovely story." Sheltered in Sebastian's arms, Lynnea looked at Glorianna. "I think this girl doesn't know who she is. They called her a sor—" She looked at Yoshani.

"Sorceress," he said.

Lynnea nodded. "Sorceress. So the people in her landscape have already decided that she's a bad person instead of seeing who she really is."

Like me, Glorianna thought, remembering the way the Landscapers and Bridges who had reached Sanctuary had looked at her.

"If she's a Landscaper and her heart wish is to find her own kind . . . ," Lee said.

"Ephemera opened an access point, but she didn't recognize it as a way to cross over to another landscape," Glorianna said, finishing the thought.

"So this time, Ephemera took what the girl had discarded and brought it to us," Nadia said softly.

"She can't find you in order to fulfill her heart wish," Lynnea said, "but you can find her."

Can we? Glorianna wondered. Another Landscaper. Someone who didn't know that she, Glorianna, had been considered a rogue all these years. Someone who had access to another part of the world.

A part now under attack by the Eater of the World.

A different understanding of the world. A different base of knowledge. Maybe even a clue about how to fit the shattered pieces of their world back together. Assuming it would be safe someday to put those shattered pieces back together.

"Mother, I'll need your kitchen shears," Glorianna said.

While Nadia fetched the shears, Glorianna untied the blue ribbon and divided the tail of hair into two pieces. "Since Lee and I are the ones who would recognize this resonance, I think we should both have a piece of hair."

"I don't feel anything now," Lee said. "Bringing it to the house seems to have fulfilled the need."

She wasn't feeling anything from the hair either now, but Ephemera had brought it here, as the world had brought her the bowl-shaped stone and silver cuff bracelet.

Nadia brought the shears. Glorianna cut the blue ribbon into four pieces.

When the two tails of hair were secured at the top, Lynnea said, "We should braid it. It will stay neater that way if you or Lee have to carry it."

Glorianna held up the tails and looked at Lynnea and Nadia, then rolled her eyes to indicate the four men who were doing the awkward-male foot shuffle.

"Why don't the four of you go out and get some air," Nadia said. "I've got a stew simmering that will be ready soon. Lynnea and Glorianna can help me finish the meal, and then we'll all enjoy some pleasant company."

There was a noticeable lack of movement. Finally Lee said, "You want us to leave the kitchen?"

"Yes, dear," Nadia replied. "I want *all* of you to leave the kitchen."

Sebastian hovered near Lynnea, whose teary moment had long passed.

"You'll be all right?" he asked, brushing his lips against Lynnea's temple.

"Don't be such a collie, Sebastian," Lee said as he walked out of the kitchen.

Glorianna snickered. She couldn't help it. And it wasn't helping any that Lynnea was turning red with the effort not to laugh and Nadia, who was displaying an admirable amount of control, just stared at the hair instead of braiding it.

"That's the second time he's said that to me," Sebastian said, giving the three women a sour look as he followed Jeb and Yoshani out of the kitchen.

Glorianna glanced over her shoulder. "You don't think Lee will actually tell Sebastian what that means, do you?"

"Of course not," Nadia said, swiftly braiding the two hanks of hair and tying them off with the other two pieces of ribbon. "Jeb will."

She laughed. "He's fitting in just fine, isn't he?

Nadia looked out the window and smiled. "Yes, he is."

"So what does that mean?" Sebastian demanded as soon as the four men were standing around outside.

Lee winced. He should have known better than to say it twice. "It's just a saying."

"A saying usually has a meaning," Yoshani said.

I guess being a holy man isn't the same as being helpful, Lee thought.

Sebastian gave Lee a narrow-eyed glare, then swung around and looked at Jeb.

Jeb scratched his head and shrugged. "Haven't heard the saying before, myself, but a collie is a herding dog. Protects a flock of sheep and keeps them from straying."

Sebastian swung back around to face Lee. "You're comparing me to a dog?"

"Protective," Lee said. "I just meant you're being a little too protective."

"Don't go ragging on the boy, Lee," Jeb said, giving Sebastian's shoulder a friendly pat. "He's just practicing to be a good daddy is all."

Lee watched all the color drain out of Sebastian's face.

"Daddy?" Sebastian said, his voice coming close to a squeak. "*Daddy?* Is she . . . ? Did we . . . ? *How?*"

"I thought he was an incubus," Yoshani said.

"He says he is," Jeb replied.

"Shouldn't he know how babies are made?"

"You would think so."

It's the drink, Lee thought. *It's the whiskey I had in the Den that's making me feel like I'm nine years old again and Mother has tossed us both outside because we were being a pain in the ass.* But knowing that didn't stop him from looking at Sebastian and saying in the same tone he'd used when he was nine, "Daddy. Daddy, daddy, daddy."

Sebastian didn't come up swinging. He just got paler.

Then Jeb said, "You know, the day Sebastian becomes a daddy, you become an uncle."

And Lee felt the blood drain right out of his head.

Jeb bobbed his head once, indicating approval. "Thought that would do it." He looked at Yoshani. "Have you seen Nadia's personal gardens? I just finished making a bench for her."

"I would be delighted to see other examples of your handiwork," Yoshani said, smiling.

"What do you think is going on out there?" Glorianna said, taking a quick peek out the kitchen window before setting the dishes on the table, which Lynnea had just cleaned off. "Jeb and Yoshani look amused, and Sebastian and Lee look like they've been sucker punched."

"Lee shouldn't tease Sebastian," Lynnea said. "He's still getting used to being a Justice Maker."

"Instead of being a troublemaker?" Glorianna asked too innocently.

Nadia turned away from the counter where she was rolling out the biscuits. "One of you girls might want to mention that if everyone behaves for the rest of this visit, I won't ask why Lee had been in the Den drinking enough that Sebastian had to bring him home. And let's have a little more help getting the meal on the table and a little less mirth."

As soon as Nadia had turned back to her biscuits, Glorianna grinned at Lynnea. It didn't matter that they were all committed to saving Ephemera from the Eater of the World. When it came to home and family, some things didn't change.

Chapter Ten

The closer he got to Kendall's docks, the more uneasy Michael felt. It was as if he were walking through ankle-deep tar, and every footstep was an effort. But the streets were as clean as they ever were in this part of the seaport, and that feeling had nothing to do with the physical world around him. This was something else, something different, something . . . evil.

And worse, the music that represented Kendall's docks sounded *wrong*.

He shuddered. The rattle of the pans on the outside of his pack sounded too loud, drew too much attention. He stopped walking and looked around, as if he needed to get his bearings.

He'd had this same feeling when he walked through the fog that had smothered Foggy Downs.

Michael tipped his head, even though the music he was listening to wasn't a physical sound. Yes, he recognized it now—the sly riffs of temptation, the trills of fear, the harsh rumble of despair. Whatever had touched this part of Kendall had been the same thing that had poisoned Foggy Downs. And Dunberry. He'd managed to turn Foggy Downs back to the rhythm and beat of his own tune. Maybe he could do the same here. He couldn't afford to lose the Kendall docks as a safe place where he could blend in. And, damn it, he couldn't afford to lose this particular port since he depended on the generosity of the ships' captains to make the traveling easier.

Hurrying now, he moved through the streets until he reached the Port of Call, a tavern that was cleaner than most, didn't water the drinks as much, and had a proprietor, Big Davey, who usually was willing to trade an evening of music for a bit of supper and a cot for the night.

But conversations sputtered into silence when he walked through the door. Hard-eyed men, toughened by a life spent at sea, studied him with a wariness and distrust that made him wonder if he would be able to back out the door without getting into a fight. He wasn't a stranger to fights—and had a few scars from broken bottles and shivs to prove it—so he knew when to hold his ground and when to back away.

He'd taken that first step back when a voice called from one of the tables. "There's the man! Barkeep, bring my friend a whiskey and ale."

The sailors, recognizing the voice, relaxed and went back to their conversations. Michael made his way to the table and shrugged out of his pack before sitting across from the man who had hailed him.

"Captain Kenneday," Michael said. He glanced up at the barkeep—a new man who hadn't been working at the Port of Call the last time he'd visited Kendall—and began digging in his pockets for the coins needed to pay for his drink.

Kenneday waved a hand. "On me." Then he raised his glass of ale. "To your good health, Michael."

"And yours," Michael replied, raising his own glass to return the salute. He looked around the room. "Doesn't seem to be a night to drink for the fun of it and get pissed enough to tell a bald-faced lie to your mates and believe it's the truth."

"No, no one is drinking for the fun of it." Kenneday drained half his glass, then wiped his mouth on the back of his hand. "Did you hear about the murders?"

Michael's hand stuttered, almost spilling the ale. "Murders?"

"Four streetwalkers and a young gentleman who had picked the wrong night to go slumming around the docks."

"Someone killed four women?" The young gentleman wasn't that surprising. Anyone who came around the docks at night dressed like he had money was a man begging to be robbed at the very least.

"Three women." Kenneday shrugged to indicate he didn't pass judgment on who was earning a living in the alleyways. "All viciously killed. Caused quite a stir."

"They didn't find the man who did it?"

"The constables didn't find *anything*. It's like whatever killed those people just melted away."

"Which is impossible."

"Is it?" Kenneday whispered. "Is it really, Michael?" He scrubbed his salt-and-pepper hair with the fingers of one hand, then smiled, clearly trying to change the mood. "So where are you off to now? Heading for your southern ports of call?"

How many other people realized his wandering wasn't as aimless as it seemed? It had started that way, but by the end of his second year he found himself making a circuit, returning to the same villages several times a year.

Just like his father had done. Odd that it had never occurred to him before, but the last year the family had traveled together, he'd been old enough to anticipate revisiting places but too young to appreciate what the pattern of traveling meant.

"Actually, I'm heading north," Michael replied, suddenly feeling cautious. Kenneday was ten years his senior and an open-minded man who usually wasn't inquisitive about another man's personal life, except for a bit of bawdy teasing. The question sounded friendly, but he couldn't shake the notion there was something behind it. "Going up to Raven's Hill to spend some time with my aunt and sister."

"I'm heading that way myself. Got cargo to take up to the White

Isle, so we'll be sailing past Raven's Hill. I can drop anchor there long enough to see you ashore."

"That's kind of you to offer," Michael said, feeling more wary by the moment.

Kenneday shrugged to indicate it wasn't worth mentioning. But he kept his eyes fixed on the table as he moved his glass in slow circles. "We'll be sailing with the morning tide, so I can settle you into a bunk for the night. Have you had dinner yet?"

"No." Michael glanced around the room, then leaned across the table. "I'm not saying you're not a generous man, Captain Kenneday, or that you haven't offered me passage at other times to make the traveling easier, but before I agree to anything this time, I'd like to know what's behind the offer."

For a moment, Kenneday looked up, and Michael caught a glimpse of a haunted soul. Then the other man fixed his attention back on the glass and the circles he was making on the table.

"Safety," Kenneday finally said. "Safety for my ship and my crew. That's what's behind the offer." He hesitated, then leaned forward so his forehead was almost touching Michael's. "I've been a sailor most of my life. Took to the sea as a boy, as soon as I was old enough to be hired on. So I've seen my share of the world, and I can tell you there's something strange about Ephemera and the way it responds to some people."

Magician. That was the word that now hung between them. First Shaney, now Kenneday. Maybe he'd never been as unremarked as he'd believed.

"There's stories coming down from the north," Kenneday said, "and the captains who sailed past the spot are swearing they'll sink their own ships before they sail that stretch of water again."

A twitch in the belly, a tightening in his shoulders. "What kind of stories?"

"Something evil has risen from the depths of the sea. A great, tentacled monster. It destroyed five fishing boats, killed everyone on board. Now fog covers that stretch of water—a fog you can't see until you sail into it. And while you're trapped there, you can hear men calling for help, calling for mercy, calling . . ." Kenneday swallowed hard. "Just calling. The voices of doomed men, already dead."

"There are stories about all kinds of monsters," Michael murmured. "They give a reason for tragedies that have no reason."

"Can you look me in the eyes and tell me there are no monsters in the world, Michael? Can you tell me there's no truth behind those stories?"

He couldn't. Not when he knew demons walked in the world. After all, Elandar had the waterhorses, who would give a man a fatal ride, and the Merry Makers, who would lure their prey into the bogs with their lights and music.

"I've seen the mood in a room change just because you started twiddling on that whistle of yours," Kenneday continued. "That's all I'm asking. We have to pass that stretch of water in order to go on to the White Isle, and I'll be sailing with half my crew if I try to haul anchor without some kind of talisman to protect us when we reach that foggy water. But if there's a luck-bringer on board, twiddling a bit of music to calm the sea and whatever stirs within it, my men will be easier for it."

"I don't know . . ." Michael jerked back as two meaty hands set two more glasses of ale on the table. "Big Davey."

Big Davey tipped his head toward Kenneday. "His won't be the last offer, just so you know. I reckon right now you can get passage on any ship for the price of a few tunes." He pulled a folded and wax-sealed paper from the pocket of the stained apron tied around his waist. "This came for you. The sailor who left it said a Lady of Light had asked him to leave it here for you since it was known that you stop here when you come to Kendall."

Michael's heart jumped into his throat, but his hand was steady when he took the paper.

"I'm thinking another whiskey might be in order," Kenneday said quietly, looking at Big Davey.

Big Davey nodded and went away. Kenneday picked up his glass of ale, then leaned back and half turned in his chair to look at the other men in the tavern, giving Michael the illusion of privacy.

Michael,

Come home as soon as you can. Things are happening. Dreams, portents. It is possible that the Destroyer has risen from whatever shadow place it has used as its lair.

I had a dream, Michael, and in the dream a voice said "heart's hope lies within belladonna." I do not know the answer to this riddle, but I feel certain the answer is the key to protecting Elandar from a great evil.

I hope you receive this message, and I hope you can come home. But if your heart calls you elsewhere, you must follow. Find the answer to the riddle. For all our sakes, find the answer to the riddle.

Your aunt,
Brighid

P.S. Do you remember the story about the Warrior of Light?

Cold hands closed over his heart . . . and squeezed.

The Destroyer? The Warrior of Light? What did two plants have to do with stories and dreams and a riddle? Did Aunt Brighid really expect him to protect their country by finding the answer to a *riddle*?

And what if finding the answer *was* the only way to protect Elandar?

Lady of Light, have mercy on me.

Michael folded the paper and tucked it into his pocket. Then he closed his eyes in order to close out the room and the other men.

Heart's hope lies within belladonna.

A warmth, a tug that suddenly turned into a longing so fierce it was almost painful. He could feel her, smell her, hear the music in her heart. The dark-haired woman who had been filling his dreams lately.

Dreams, Aunt Brighid had said. Portents.

Could his dream lover be the key to the riddle? Could she lead him to the Warrior of Light?

"Michael?"

He opened his eyes and noticed the glass of whiskey. He drank it down, wanting the heat of it to warm a cold that suddenly filled his bones.

"Trouble at home?" Kenneday asked.

"I'm not sure," Michael replied. "But I'll take your offer."

Kenneday started to push back his chair. "Then let's get you settled. We sail with the morning tide."

Michael shook his head, then leaned over and rummaged in his pack. When he straightened up, he held his whistle. "Give me an hour here."

Heart's hope lies within belladonna.

He let the rhythm of the words fill his heart, his body, and then let the words shape the music that flowed from him as he played no particular tune. He could sense something quivering in response to the music, had the strange sensation of the ground turning under the building to align itself with . . . What?

He had no answer, so he concentrated on the music—and hoped he would dream of his dark-haired lover. He wanted that last memory of her as a talisman when he sailed through water where Evil dwelled.

Chapter Eleven

It flowed from the sea to the land, a shadow under stone, a feeling of menace that made horses bolt and run wild through the village streets, made penned animals fling themselves at their enclosures until they broke free—or ruined themselves in the attempt—made women, for no reason they could explain, snatch up their children and bring them inside, ignoring the wails and protests that toys had been left behind.

As It flowed beneath the earth, It sent the force of Its own rage through the Dark currents that ran through the land around the village of Raven's Hill. It could sense the presence of the Landscaper who had helped the True Enemy hide the Place of Light, but It couldn't find her. Somewhere on that hillside. There and yet gone. Somewhere.

Frustrated and furious, It paused on the edge of a well-tended lawn, a darker shadow among the shadows cast by stones and trees. Paused and stretched Its mental tentacles to touch the minds of the villagers.

And, oh, wasn't this delicious? These foolish humans looked on the Landscaper with distrust, not realizing she was their protector, that her presence spared them from the stains within their own hearts.

Sorceress? Yes, It whispered. *Yes, she is a servant of evil. She covets what you have, wants to destroy what you hold dear. Nothing good has come from that family. Nothing ever will.*

Hearts wavered. Were seduced. Fed the Dark currents. One heart blazed with the Light and one heart was too anchored in the currents of Light to be completely swayed, but even in those hearts It found shadows of doubt.

It flowed along the base of the hillside until It reached the path that led upward. Like other animals, humans had game trails they followed. The Landscaper traveled this one often. It could feel her resonance in the earth.

It could feel something else too—a tangle of currents so bloated with the Dark and resonating so strongly with It that Ephemera gave up that piece of itself with no resistance.

And part of the meadow behind the cottage near the hill changed to rust-colored sand.

Satisfied, the Eater of the World rested—and waited.

Michael tucked the tin whistle inside his pack, secured the pack's flap, then set it aside where it would be out of the men's way but within easy reach when they finally dropped anchor at Raven's Hill.

He was glad his presence and his music had eased the hearts of Captain Kenneday's crew, but he hoped by all that was holy that he wouldn't be ready to leave when Kenneday sailed back this way, hoped he could find a reason—or an excuse—for taking the roads to head back to the villages that made up his circuit. Because he didn't want to sail through that stretch of water again, even knowing that it would be hard for Kenneday and his men to make that part of the journey without him.

What was out there was no story told by the surviving fishermen in order to explain a tragedy. Kenneday's ship had had a clear sky, a good wind, and no hint of anything unnatural. Then they sailed into fog.

He'd heard the voices of the dead men. A chill had gone through him, as if he'd stepped out of the sun into deep shadow. So he'd picked up his whistle, and he'd played. At first the tunes were laced with sorrow and were a salute to the dead and the families who mourned the lost men. Then he eased into tunes that threaded hope into the melody. The fog thinned, the voices of the dead faded, a hazy sun shown overhead, and he imagined he could see a faint glow around each man as, one by one, they shed their despair and believed they would reach clean water again.

When they finally sailed clear of that terrible stretch of water, Kenneday looked at his pocket watch—and discovered they had been lost in the fog for three hours.

No, he didn't want to sail through that stretch of water again, but as he had played, a thought had danced with his tunes. Maybe his brain had gotten addled in the fog, but if not, the feeling people had of a journey being shorter or longer than usual might not be just a feeling after all.

Leaving his pack, Michael made his way to the stern, where Kenneday was manning the wheel.

Kenneday smiled as Michael came up to stand beside him. "We'll have you home in time for tea, Michael. That we will." Then he looked away. "I'm grateful for your help. If you hadn't been on board . . . Well, we might still be sailing in that fog, becoming more of the lost men, if it hadn't been for you."

Michael gave the captain a sharp, assessing look and decided Kenneday believed what he said.

And it is true, Michael thought. *If this isn't more than fevered imaginings, a ship might never leave that stretch of water if the men on board start believing they'll never get free of that haunted place.*

"I think there's a way to avoid the fog," Michael said.

"What? Sailing clear around Elandar every time I have a supply run between ports in the north and south? That would put days on every trip."

"You don't have to avoid this part of Elandar, just that stretch of water." When Kenneday made a dismissive sound, Michael clamped one hand on the captain's forearm. "Listen to me. The bad water is where those five fishing boats were destroyed. Talk to the men who were in the other boats. You can be sure they know how far out they were when that monster rose from the sea. Damn the darkness, man, you and the other captains can figure out the position of a safe channel that will keep ships from sailing into that water. You mark other dangers; why not this one?"

"Because this one is different."

Kenneday might be arguing, but Michael heard the underlying hope in the man's voice.

"This one has boundaries, same as any other piece of dangerous water," Michael said. "I don't know how I know that, but I *know* it. And I'm thinking the area inside those boundaries is never any smaller than the area where those fishing boats were destroyed, but it can expand to be as big as a person believes it to be."

"That's crazy talk."

"Is it? Then how do you explain us being in that fog for three hours?"

Kenneday hesitated, then shook his head. "I can't."

"You said yourself there's something strange about this world. I'm thinking it's gotten stranger. So maybe there's someone out there who knows what is happening and what to do about it."

His dream lover's face filled his mind. Would she understand Ephemera's strangeness? Did she know the answer to the riddle his aunt had sent him?

Maybe you've been alone too long.

Where had *that* thought come from?

"Michael?"

The sharpness in Kenneday's voice brought him back—and he realized he was now holding the man's arm in a painful grip.

"Sorry. My mind wandered." He took a step back and tucked both hands in his pockets.

"I'll talk to the other captains about marking a channel." Kenneday tried to smile, but worry filled his eyes. "After all, we can't always have a luck-bringer on board with us."

The truth of it, and the unasked question under it, caused an awkward silence between them.

"I'd best pull my gear together," Michael said. Since Kenneday would have seen him checking his pack, it was a poor lie, but it served its purpose.

Michael paused near his pack, then didn't even pretend to check his gear. He went to the rail and looked toward the shore. He wanted to go home, *needed* to go home.

But as he looked at the shore, he suddenly had the feeling "home" was a place he hadn't seen yet.

"What are you playing at now?" Caitlin muttered. "If I don't get back in time to help Aunt Brighid put tea on the table, there will be nothing but cold silence this evening."

When there was no response to her words, she rubbed the back of her hand across her forehead as if that might scrub away the day's frustrations. How many times over the years had she used the old hoe to work the soil in that part of the garden? There shouldn't have been any stones there, let alone a big stone buried under the soil just deep enough and just at the wrong angle.

Giving the broken hoe handle a sour look, she used the jagged end to poke at what should have been the path leading down the hill to the cottage.

It should have been a simple day of weeding and tending the garden, but everything had been harder to do. The ground held on to weeds with a perverse tenacity. For the first time since it appeared in her garden, the knee-deep pool of water at the base of the little waterfall held no more than a finger length of silty water at the bottom, so she'd had to let the bucket fill by leaving it under the falls—and yet the surrounding beds weren't saturated.

"Maybe I've found where the water drained," Caitlin said, lifting the now-muddy end of the hoe. The path, which had been dry when she walked up it that morning, was now ankle-deep mud for several man-lengths. And now that part of the path was bordered by thorny, impenetrable bushes that had sprung up in the few hours she'd spent in her garden.

"I need to go home," Caitlin said. "I'm tired, I'm hungry, and I need to go home."

She waited and watched. The path didn't change. The bushes didn't sink into the ground to give her an easy way to skirt around the mud and pick up the path farther down the hill.

Giving the thorny bushes a hard whack with her hoe handle, she retreated up the path. Then she set off through the trees. If the hillside behaved, she should come down close to where the path crossed the meadow behind the cottage.

But as she picked her way through the trees, watching for ankle-twisting roots and dips in the ground, she couldn't shake the feeling that Ephemera really was trying to stop her from going back to the cottage.

The Eater of the World flowed through Raven's Hill, nurturing the bogs of doubt and fear that lived in human hearts.

Yes, it whispered to three boys whose hearts already embraced the Dark. *The woman in the cottage. Nothing but a hag, a whore, an old liar rejected by the Ladies of Light. She sullies the village with her presence.*

As the boys headed for the cottage that held the heart full of Light, the Eater of the World drifted back toward the harbor. Something on the water was producing a faint resonance with this place. Something strong enough to *leave* a resonance, despite the murky bedrock of the Landscaper's heart.

Whatever was coming would never leave again. The Eater—and the sea—would make sure of that.

Uneasiness became an itch under Michael's skin. He knew Kenneday and the crew were becoming infected by his uneasiness, but he couldn't stop prowling from one end of the ship to the other, watching the sea, the shore, the sky. Something out there. But what was it? And *where* was it?

Out of the corner of his eye, he saw Kenneday hand over the wheel to the first mate, so he stayed by the rail and waited for the captain to approach.

"Is there something you need to be telling me, Michael?" Kenneday asked.

Michael shook his head. "I need to get home." The moment he spoke the words, the certainty of it was like a fist pounding against his heart. "I just need to get home."

"We should have you ashore in another hour or so. Not in time for tea, I'm afraid, but maybe in time for supper if the wind doesn't die on us again." Kenneday hesitated, then added, "If you'd come north by land, it would have taken you longer, even with the delay we had in that fog."

Hearing a defensive apology in the words, Michael offered an understanding smile. "I know that. I've just been anxious since I read my aunt's letter. I'll feel easier when I find out the fuss turned out to be a trifling matter." *I'll feel easier when I know for certain that an hour from now isn't an hour too late.*

But that wasn't something he wanted to think about because he had the strangest feeling that if he thought about it, and truly believed it, he would make it true.

"Old hag! Old hag!"

"Come get what you deserve, old hag!"

Doing a trip and stumble—and just managing not to land on her face—Caitlin rushed down the last few man-lengths of the hill. She knew those voices. Coyle, Roy, and Owen were the village troublemakers, but they had always kept clear of the cottage.

"Old hag! Old hag!" That was Coyle.

"Owen! Stop diddling with yourself and bring us more rocks!" That was Roy.

Using the curse words she'd heard Michael say once—words that had earned him a slap upside the head because Aunt Brighid had also heard him—Caitlin paused at the bottom of the hill to decide what to do.

Coyle threw another rock, shattering the glass in an upstairs window, while Roy jumped up and down, yelling at Aunt Brighid, yelling for Owen. And Brighid was doing some yelling of her own but was sensible enough to stay inside.

Since her aunt's yelling was filled with anger rather than being the sound of someone crying out in pain, Caitlin decided to wait until the boys had thrown their last rocks. Then she could wade in. Maybe a hoe handle applied to their backsides would teach those hooligans a few manners.

But as she waited, she noticed the ground changing between her and the boys. Fear shivered up her spine.

There had been no sand when she'd gone up the hill that morning, but there was a large patch of it now, beginning at the base of the path she usually used to reach her garden and stretching out toward the cottage. It looked like someone had poured barrows of sand over the meadow to create a long-fingered, bony hand.

But there were no grasses or wildflowers poking up beneath the sand, which didn't look deep enough to have covered the plants. And she'd never seen rust-colored sand before and *knew* it hadn't come from any of the beaches around Raven's Hill.

As Coyle and Roy threw more rocks at the cottage windows, Caitlin watched meadow grass disappear as two of the sand fingers stretched a little farther toward the cottage.

There's something out there that can change the land, she thought. *Something . . . evil.*

The cottage was too isolated. She and Aunt Brighid would be nothing but hens waiting for the fox if they stayed. Which meant getting Brighid out of the cottage and escaping to the village proper. Which meant getting past those black-hearted boys.

Holding the hoe handle in a two-handed grip that would make it a useful weapon, Caitlin scanned the trees at the base of the hill, looking for some movement. Where was the third boy, Owen? It was rare to see just two of the boys when they were causing trouble, so the third had to be around.

Deal with the here and now, Brighid always told her. Well, the here and now was the two boys she could see.

This is my place, Caitlin thought as she stared at Coyle and Roy, who had their backs to her. *This is my land. You're not wanted here. You're not welcome here. Leave this place!*

She wasn't able to influence people, and she didn't expect anything to happen. The words were merely a way to bolster her own courage before she made a dash for the cottage that would bring her to the boys' attention.

You're not wanted here. You're not welc—

Her focus shattered as she saw three of the sandy fingers shrink, the sand changing back to packed earth. It was bare earth—the grass and flowers didn't magically reappear—but it was earth, not sand.

I can change the meadow back to the way it was. I can fight this evil, make it go away.

Then her attention came back to the boys. They were waiting for her, staring at her. Each boy held a filled whiskey bottle with rags stuffed into the necks of the bottles like a wick in an oil lamp.

The rags were already burning.

"No!" Caitlin yelled.

The Eater of the World flowed toward the hillside as fast as It could. The Landscaper was trying to destroy the access It had created into the bonelovers' landscape. She was sending her resonance into the world and Ephemera was responding.

It would stop her. Yes, It would. She was stronger than many of the Landscapers It had destroyed at the school, but not as skilled or powerful—or dangerous—as the True Enemy. It could pull her into Its landscape, just as It had done with the others. The bonelovers would do the rest.

Coyle and Roy flung the burning whiskey bottles through the broken windows. Then they grinned at her and ran, no doubt intending to be far enough away that they could claim ignorance when she accused them of setting the cottage on fire.

Because it *was* burning. Too much. Too fast.

"Aunt Brighid!"

The fingers of sand were stretching out again, reaching for the cottage, blocking her way to the back door.

Why hadn't Brighid come out the front door? They couldn't save the cottage. Not by themselves. Was Owen guarding the front door, holding some kind of club or other weapon so Brighid was afraid to leave despite the fire?

Caitlin turned, intending to run to the front of the cottage and rescue her aunt. But with her first step, the ground felt soft, fluid . . . strange. She staggered. Stabbed the hoe handle into the ground to maintain her balance.

"Earth isn't fluid," Caitlin said, putting all the conviction she could into her voice. "This earth isn't soft. It's solid, and it's *real.*"

She felt the ground firm up, but when she looked around, she let out a cry of disbelief and despair.

She stood in the center of a perfect circle surrounded by sand. She felt a pulse of evil at the edge of the circle. In front of her, bits of meadow still poked up like hummocks in a marsh.

It was as if something were daring her to jump from one hummock to the next in order to reach safe ground. As if something dared her to pit her influence with Ephemera against its power to control the world.

If I stay here, I'm safe, Caitlin thought. Except . . .

"Auntie!" Her heart swelled with relief when she saw Brighid staggering away from the cottage, coughing horribly, and bleeding from cuts probably made by broken glass.

Her heart shrank to a cold, hard lump in her chest as she saw a shadow thicken in the ground behind her aunt, saw a darkness rise up and take the shape of a man holding a knife. He looked at Brighid, then looked at her and smiled—and she understood the message.

He—it—can't touch me where I stand, but if I stay, he'll kill Aunt Brighid. One of us lives, one of us dies. My choice.

For a moment, she hesitated. Brighid hadn't been an easy woman to live with and she didn't think of her aunt with any warmth or joy, but Brighid had set aside her own life to help them when she and Michael were children, so she owed the woman for that.

My choice. My life. Doesn't mean I won't try to survive.

Watching the man-shaped darkness, Caitlin backed up to the very edge of the circle. She still had a chance. A running leap to land on the largest "hummock" and push off from there to solid ground.

Lady of Light, help me. Please, help me.

She held the hoe handle in one hand, its length evenly balanced. Probably better to leave it, but she didn't want to face the knife empty-handed.

She took off across the circle, driving with her legs, putting everything she had into the leap.

"Caitlin!" Brighid screamed.

She didn't need to look. She could feel the change in the earth beneath her as her aunt and the world she knew faded away, disappearing altogether the moment the "hummock" vanished and her foot landed on the rust-colored sand.

She stumbled, flailed, drove one end of the hoe handle into the sand. It caught on something, acting like a lever as it lifted an object up from the sand. The momentary resistance was enough to help Caitlin stay on her feet.

She paused, gasping for air as she looked around. Rust-colored sand beneath a sky the color of ripe bruises. Nothing else—except that shifting black mound not too far from where she stood.

Caitlin watched the mound, then shook her head. Couldn't be ants. Much too big to be ants.

The mound shifted. She caught a glimpse of . . . something. Thought she heard a wet-sounding cry.

She turned to free the hoe handle—and froze at the sight of the rib cage that had been pulled out of the sand. She stared at the clean bones, then at the black mound.

For one heartbeat—maybe two—something made a last, desperate effort to escape, knocking a few of the creatures away. In that heartbeat, she saw what was left of a boy's face.

"Owen," she whispered.

She couldn't help the boy. Even if she could pull him free of those creatures, she couldn't save the boy. So she freed the hoe handle from the old bones and backed away carefully and quietly to avoid attracting attention.

When one of those unnatural ants noticed her and moved toward her, she did the only thing she could do.

She ran.

"Friend of yours?" Kenneday asked as their dinghy approached the stairs that led up to the south side of the Raven's Hill harbor.

"He is," Michael replied, settling his pack as he watched the man waiting for them at the top of the stairs. Nathan had been a friend since boyhood and had remained one even after it became evident that Michael was a Magician. He came back to Raven's Hill out of love and duty; however, it was the time he spent with Nathan that made those visits tolerable.

But having Nathan waiting around the harbor instead of working in his shop boded no good.

Kenneday looked back at the crewman who had rowed them to the stairs. "Stay here and keep on eye on things in case we need to leave in a hurry," he said quietly.

"Aye, Captain."

Pretending he hadn't heard that exchange, Michael climbed the stairs. A cold fist squeezed his belly when he got close enough to see the worry—and regret—in Nathan's eyes.

"Ah, Michael," Nathan said. "It's bad. I'm sorry to be the one to tell you, but it's bad."

"What happened?" Michael asked. A nudge from behind had him shifting to make room for Kenneday.

"Well, a couple of boys got into some mischief and—" Nathan stopped, swore softly, then shook his head. "No. I won't whitewash it like others want to do. The fact is we have conflicting stories and some things just plain aren't right, but the nub of it is Coyle and Roy—and we suspect Owen was with them but he hasn't been found yet—started their mischief by throwing rocks at the windows of your aunt's cottage and ended it by burning the place down. We tried, Michael. The men rallied when the smoke was spotted, and they got the water wagons and pumps out there as fast as they could, but the fire had taken hold and . . . It was like that fire didn't want to be put out. And after Jamie disappeared right in front of us . . ." He raised his hands palm up to indicate helplessness. "I'd just come down to the harbor to see if there might be a ship that could take a message when sails coming up from the south were spotted. Your aunt said you would be coming, so I hoped . . ."

Kenneday's hand on his shoulder was a warm comfort, but it didn't ease the cold fist that still squeezed his belly. "Aunt Brighid? Caitlin?"

Nathan looked away. "Don't know why your auntie stayed inside so long. Fear, I'm guessing."

A shudder went through him, jangling the pots attached to his pack. "How bad?"

"She has some cuts on her back and arms. Most likely got them from the glass when the windows were broken. And her lungs sound a bit charry from the heat and the smoke, but the doctor figures she'll mend just fine with some care."

He couldn't breathe. He could feel his lungs fill and empty, but he still couldn't breathe. "Caitlin?"

Nathan rubbed the back of his hand across his mouth. "She disappeared. We thought your aunt meant she had run away—Caitlin was acting touched in the head, Michael; she'd gone and cut off her hair just because some boy had asked to go out walking in the moonlight. So at first, when Brighid said the sand had taken Caitlin, we thought she was just babbling because of the pain. But when Jamie disappeared right in front of our eyes . . ."

"What sand?"

"Something . . . evil," Nathan whispered. "A rusty color, like dried blood. Stretching out from the base of the hill right up to one side of the cottage. Brighid said Caitlin tried to jump it in order to reach her, but the ground just changed under the girl—and she disappeared."

Something thrummed under Michael's feet.

"Where's the aunt now?" Kenneday asked.

"At the doctor's house," Nathan replied. "She'll be looked after until she mends."

Thrumming. A harsh buzzing that vibrated up from the soles of his feet. Clashing chords. Grating notes that sliced at harmony.

He had brushed against this sound before in Foggy Downs and Kendall—and in a terrible stretch of water where the voices of dead men drifted on the fog.

He'd entertained the notion that it was another Magician trying to drive him out of the villages where he felt easy. But it wasn't another Magician that had touched those places and changed their songs. It was something more. Something out of myth.

"Listen," Michael said. "Do you feel it?"

Kenneday looked puzzled, but everything about Nathan sharpened.

"Can you still hear the feel of a place?" Nathan asked.

Michael nodded. It was all clashes and grating noise—but it was in tune with pieces of Raven's Hill, and that scared him more than anything.

Almost more than anything. Because when he looked at the land just beyond the harbor's southern spur, he saw a shadow flow over the earth and stone before it disappeared into the sea. And *its* song chilled him to the bone.

"Lady of Light, have mercy," Michael whispered. "It's here. The Destroyer is *here*." He spun around, looked at the crewman waiting in the dinghy, and shouted, "Get off the water! Up here, man! Up here!"

"Michael!" Kenneday said. "What's got into you?"

"The thing that destroyed the fishing boats. It's out there in the harbor. Right now. I can feel it." He looked at Nathan. "Give me your word that you'll give my aunt what help she needs once she's on the mend. And you, Captain, promise you'll give her passage to wherever she wants to go if she chooses to leave Raven's Hill."

"You have my word on it," Kenneday said. "But, Michael, where are you going?"

Dread shivered through him, but he pushed it aside. "Somehow, that thing took my sister. I'm going to get her back."

Michael pulled on the shoulder straps of his pack to resettle the weight. Probably smarter to leave it, since a part of him believed he wasn't going anywhere except the bottom of the harbor, but all that was left of what he could call his own was in that pack, including his whistle, and he wasn't leaving it behind.

"Michael," Kenneday said sharply. "Where are you going?"

Certainty flowed through him, swift and strong, replacing the cold feeling with a lovely heat as he filled his mind with the image of his dream lover.

He looked at the two men he considered friends and felt as if he'd finally removed a mask he'd hidden behind all his life. "I'm going to see what happens to evil when a Magician does some ill-wishing." Turning away from Nathan and Kenneday, he walked to the edge of the spur.

Light surrounded by a net of Dark currents. It knew the resonance of this heart, had felt the bedrock of it in the foggy village and the seaport. This was the resonance that was connected to the Landscaper in this village.

Smash it! Destroy it! Once this heart was gone, there would be no bedrock. There would be nothing to protect the people who lived in this place. It would snuff out the Light in each heart, and this place would change, would fester, and the people would curse and wail at a world turned harsh and bitter and dark, never admitting that their own hearts had shaped the world they had to live in.

But first, It would drag this male down into one of Its watery landscapes. And there It would feast.

As It rose toward the surface, It changed into the monster men of the sea most feared.

Michael felt his heart stop beating for a moment as tentacles rose out of the sea. This was the nightmare that destroyed ships and left dead men to haunt the sea.

He could feel the song of its darkness, could almost find the rhythm that matched the seductive lure of it.

No! He didn't want to find the rhythm of it. This *thing* had taken his sister, had used bad-hearted boys to hurt his aunt. This *thing* was going to dance to *his* tune.

And what tune do you know that is dark enough? a mocking voice whispered to his heart.

He didn't have an answer, and he faltered.

The tentacles, which were flailing around him like whips lashing the air, came closer.

No, Michael thought. *No!* But he suddenly realized the question hadn't been idle. The Destroyer knew something he didn't know, and his survival depended on that something. Which was why the *thing* was certain it would win.

The ground beneath his feet became soft, fluid. A wind that didn't touch his skin blew through him. The harbor faded, the sounds of men shouting or crying out in fear faded.

And what tune do you know that is dark enough?

The question echoed in his mind.

If I am condemned to a dark place, it will be a place of my own choosing, Michael thought with all the conviction he could summon.

What place? the mocking voice whispered. *I am the Eater of the World. I am the Destroyer of Light. There is no place you can go where I cannot follow.*

Despair filled him. He felt himself being lifted. Knew that his fate was about to be sealed.

The world was in motion. He felt things that had no language but music. And then, as he felt himself plunging toward water, he heard another song—and had an answer.

Once more, he filled his mind with the image of the black-haired woman of his dreams.

Her darkness is my fate. Her heart is my world. There is nothing else, nothing else, nothing. And when I stand within her heart, she and I will destroy you.

The *thing* screamed in rage and fear. The world tore apart, pulling Michael and the Destroyer in separate directions.

Michael fell—deaf, blind, helpless to do anything but cling to the image of a face . . . and a riddle.

Her darkness is my fate. Heart's hope lies within belladonna.

Falling. Falling.

Suddenly the world returned. Sound. Sight. He had one moment to see the land around him before he hit the water.

And when the water closed over his head, there was only darkness.

Chapter Twelve

Glorianna dashed from one section of her garden to the next. Looking. Searching. Listening with her heart and not understanding the messages coming through Ephemera's currents of power.

This felt like Heart's Justice, and yet it didn't quite feel like someone had been swept away in the currents of the world to end up in the landscape that most reflected that person's heart. This felt like someone crossing over a bridge from one landscape to another, but normally she wouldn't have felt the resonance of a crossing because someone who truly didn't belong in her landscapes shouldn't be able to reach them. That was disturbing enough, but . . .

"Glorianna!" Lee caught up to her. "Glorianna?"

"Someone—or something—tried to bring the Eater of the World into my landscapes," Glorianna said, staring at the part of the garden that held the access points to her dark landscapes.

"*What?*" Lee skipped back a step, as if he expected the Eater to burst out of the ground at any moment.

You touched a boy! You've got the ickies!

Lee's skip-step made her think of that taunt, which she'd heard, in one form or another, in so many villages—a taunt that seemed part of the rituals that transformed a girl into a young woman. Somewhere during those years, "icky" changed into "interesting," and after that, a girl's life was never quite the same. Of course, the boy's life was never quite the same either.

The moment's amusement settled her enough to think rather than react.

"Someone crossed over," Glorianna said, "but not in a customary way. And the Eater almost crossed over with that person."

"Almost." Lee wasn't asking a question so much as demanding the answer he wanted to hear.

Glorianna nodded. "Almost. The dissonance would be clanging through the currents of power if the Eater had come into one of my landscapes."

"It had slipped in before. Made an anchor point small enough to escape your detection until you were almost on top of that piece of ground."

"I know, but this is different. I don't think It was trying to enter my landscapes. I think . . ." Glorianna frowned. "A battle of wills. Maybe the person wasn't trying to bring the Eater in. Maybe the person was trying to get away, but that wouldn't explain the feeling of Heart's Justice."

"There is such a thing as spontaneous Heart's Justice," Lee said reluctantly.

Glorianna just looked at him.

"Bridges don't talk about it, but we know it happens. If two incompatible people cross a resonating bridge at the same time—especially if one person is trying to force the other to cross over to an . . . unsuitable . . . landscape—Ephemera sometimes responds with Heart's Justice, sending each person to a different landscape. In those cases, it seems that where the will is focused is equally important as what landscapes resonate with the person's heart."

"You have a mother and a sister who are Landscapers, and you've never mentioned this."

Lee shrugged, looking wary. "It's not talked about. It just seemed better if everyone believed Heart's Justice didn't happen unless a Landscaper initiated it." Then he gave her a look that wasn't brother to sister but Bridge to Landscaper. "Besides, doesn't a kind of Heart's Justice happen every time a person crosses a resonating bridge? When you cross one of those bridges, the landscape where you end up may be a place you've never seen before even if it does resonate with your heart."

He had a point. And maybe it was one of those bits of knowledge that seemed so obvious it was assumed everyone knew about it. At least, all the Landscapers and Bridges who kept Ephemera balanced and connected as best they could.

Lee stepped up beside her and studied the access points to the dark landscapes. "What are you sensing now?"

"Nothing. I'm fairly sure whoever crossed over ended up in one of the dark landscapes, but that heart has vanished in the overall resonances."

"A person who has died wouldn't leave a resonance, and if there was a fight with the Eater . . ." Lee lifted his hands in a helpless gesture.

"Even so, I'd better get a message to Sebastian in case any . . . unusual strangers . . . show up in the Den."

"I can do that," Lee said. "You're not going to feel easy about leaving the garden for a while."

She wrinkled her nose and smiled to acknowledge the truth of that.

Lee gave her a one-armed hug. "Just remember to go back to the house and get something to eat. And bring a shawl or jacket back out with you. It's getting too cool at night to be outdoors without one."

"Yes, Mother."

"That's brother."

"Sorry, I could have sworn the tone said *mother* even if the timbre of the voice was too deep."

"If you tell me I'll make a great uncle, I will wrestle you to the ground and push your face in the mud."

Glorianna blinked. Clearly this wasn't the time to offer an opinion about such things, even if she'd thought to say anything.

She couldn't recall what she said to him in response, but it must have been satisfactory since he left, intending to stop by their mother's house on the way to the Den.

"Well," she said to the garden as she deadheaded flowers on a few of the autumn plants. "Well, I'm sure he'd be a fine uncle as long as he doesn't depend on *me* to make him one." Which made her wonder why he'd even be chewing on the question.

Which made her think of one reason why he would.

Glorianna grinned. Sebastian a daddy?

Then the grin shifted into a pout. Lynnea should have told her. Even if it was too early to be sure, Lynnea should have said something to her or Nadia. Because, obviously, Lee had been given a hint.

Would giving Lynnea a present of baby blanket and booties be too unsubtle a request for information?

A tremor went through the currents of power—there and gone. But it was enough to remind her that something strange had happened and it was best to be cautious until she discovered who had entered her landscape in an unexpected way—and why.

The Eater of the World huddled in a cave within the water landscape It had shaped long ago. Its coloring matched the stones in the cave; Its only movement was the two tentacles extending beyond the cave, undulating in a way that made fish think they had found a meal when, in truth, they were about to become one.

Simple minds. Simple creatures. It had nothing to fear from these things. It had no enemies in this landscape.

The male who had escaped It was dangerous. The male had powers that made It uneasy because those powers stirred old memories too vague to be useful and too strong to be dismissed.

Not quite like the True Enemy, whose resonance had filled the male's heart, allowing him to pull away from the Eater's landscapes. No, not like the True Enemy . . . but like the *Old* Enemy. The ones who had locked It inside Its landscapes.

But It was safe here. The male could not swim so deep to find It here. And the True Enemy did not know how to find It within Its own landscapes.

It was safe here. It would eat and rest. Then It would go back to the landscapes filled with busy human minds. It would listen to the fears revealed in the twilight of waking dreams—and It would take more things from the natural world and shape them into nightmares. Fear would have a name and become stronger for the naming.

Fear already had a name: The Eater of the World.

Pleased that It had remembered this, It left the cave. The Landscaper It had ensnared in the bonelovers' landscape was probably nothing more than bones by now, but bringing those bones back to the cottage beside the hill would create more shadows in the people living in that village.

Especially in the hearts that would be pleased to see the bones.

Caitlin ran across sand that never ended toward a horizon that never changed. Light filtered through the bruise-colored sky, but she couldn't find the sun, so she had no way to tell which direction she was heading, and the only assurance she had that she wasn't walking in circles was the fact that she hadn't crossed her own footsteps or the lines and squiggles she occasionally made in the sand with the hoe handle for the sole purpose of showing herself where she had been just in case she *was* walking in circles.

Feeling the stitch in her side flare up again, she slowed to a walk, breathing hard, craving water. But when she looked back, she saw the dark shapes heading toward her. Closing the distance.

Can't, Caitlin thought as she stabbed the hoe handle into the sand and leaned on it. *Can't run anymore. Need water, need rest, need a way out of this place, need . . . help. Lady of Light, I need help.*

She looked toward the horizon and let out a sobbing laugh. More dark shapes. More of those creatures coming for a feast. Coming for her.

Caitlin closed her eyes.

Even if she could continue to outrun them, what would be the point? Survival? For what? There was no food, no water. She was going to die here, one way or the other. And even if she could get back to Raven's Hill with a snap of her fingers, living there wasn't much better than being lost in this place. Yes, she had Aunt Brighid and the garden, but her life was as barren as the sand.

I don't want to go back to Raven's Hill. And I don't want to die here. I need help.

The ground beneath her vibrated like she was standing on a giant tuning fork.

Her eyes popped open and she twisted her torso to look around, not daring to move her feet.

A long step away from her was a heart's hope plant, so tiny it could barely support the single bloom.

Her breath caught. Her heart rapped against her chest. And she remembered what she had done in the meadow, what she had said.

Maybe, she thought. *Maybe.*

She glanced around. The dark shapes were getting closer. Couldn't think about that. Couldn't think about anything but what Ephemera could do.

Shifting until she stood a shoulder-width from the heart's hope, Caitlin bent at the waist and held out the hoe handle with both hands. She rested the broken end on the sand; then, using herself as the center point, she drew a circle in the sand.

"This is my place," Caitlin said as she drew the circle. "Within the bounds of this circle is a place of Light and hope. My heart dwells within the bounds of this circle, and creatures of the Dark are not welcome here. You cannot touch this ground. You cannot touch me."

As she closed the circle and began tracing it again on the sand, she felt the world beneath her feet become soft, fluid.

Come on, Caitlin Marie, think about what you need here while you have the chance to get it.

Water. Food. A place that wasn't *this* place.

As she finished the second tracing of the circle and began the third, she saw the creatures running toward her, and her focus almost snapped. But she held to the thought that she was safe inside the circle. She had to believe that. *Had to.*

The world beneath her feet was no longer soft. Whatever Ephemera could do had been done.

Caitlin bit her lower lip to hold back a cry of despair. No food, no water. Nothing but the tiny heart's hope within a circle sketched in the sand.

She widened her stance. Shifted her hands on the hoe handle for a better grip.

Then she watched as the ant creatures reached the circle and disappeared, reappearing on the other side of the circle moments later. They didn't go far before they began milling around, searching for something.

Caitlin slowly lowered her arms, letting one end of the hoe rest on the sand.

The creatures couldn't see her, couldn't sense her. Couldn't find her. She was close enough to that awful place to see it—and them—but she was no longer *there.*

She sank to her knees and watched the ant creatures.

Slowly, she noticed the difference in the sand—and the difference in the air, which smelled of fish and seawater. Within her circle, the sand was no longer rust-colored. Scooping up a handful, she let it sift through her fingers until all that was left was a small shell like the ones she used to bring home when Michael took her for a walk on the beach.

She had done this much. Maybe after she rested a bit, she could try to shift herself from this little patch of Raven's Hill beach to her garden.

She waited until they were gone, having accepted that their prey had somehow escaped. Then she stretched out beside the heart's hope and gently brushed a fingertip over the bloom.

She didn't have food or water, and she would be in desperate need of both very soon. But she was safe from the creatures, and even though she didn't know how to take the next step, she had gotten back to the part of the world she knew. For now, that was enough.

It found the remains of the young male—one of the three boys whose hearts had embraced Its whispers to harm the Light that lived in the cottage. But It couldn't find the Landscaper. She was here but not here. It could feel the resonance of the current of Light that had formed in the bonelovers' landscape because of her presence, but It couldn't find *her*.

A spot in the sand. Nothing there—and yet something there. This had the same there/not there feel as the garden hidden on the hill behind the cottage.

She was strong, but she had seemed unskilled, like the young ones at the Landscapers' School, who had been so easy to kill. But she had known how to escape from one of Its landscapes. No one had escaped from Its landscapes before.

At least, not until that incubus had managed to elude Its attempt to bring him into the bonelovers' landscape. The incubus lived in the Den, one of the True Enemy's landscapes.

Then the male who had fought It at the village where the Landscaper lived. He had broken free by resonating with the True Enemy's heart.

And this young female was somehow connected with the True Enemy because of the Place of Light they had taken away from It.

These human creatures were all connected to *her*, to Belladonna . . . the True Enemy. It couldn't reach her landscapes. Even when It felt the male crossing over and tried to hold on to him, It had been pulled away to one of Its own landscapes. If the Landscaper found a way into one of Belladonna's landscapes, It wouldn't be able to reach *her*, either.

But there were Dark hearts in every landscape, and It could always reach *them*.

And one of *them* would be able to find Belladonna's companions— and destroy them.

"What, exactly, am I looking for?" Sebastian asked for the third time.

Lee was ready to pound his cousin's head against a wall. "I told you. I don't know *exactly*. Someone who doesn't belong. Someone . . . different."

Sebastian looked down the Den's main street, where two men and a succubus were staggering toward a brothel that provided slightly more privacy than having sex in the alley. He looked in the other direction, where three bull demons stomped out of a tavern, bellowing.

"Guess someone had a good night playing cards," Lee said.

"Omelets all around," Sebastian muttered, watching as three horned, shaggy heads turned in the direction of Philo's place, where Lynnea waited tables and cooked a few "special" dishes.

"I hear Lynnea's got the bull demons clearing out some of the brush around your place and cutting another path so folks aren't walking through your back yard when they want to get from the Den to Aurora."

"Yeah," Sebastian said, stepping aside to let the bull demons stomp over to their favorite table and then wait politely for Lynnea to notice them. "She made a cake—with a buttercream frosting, mind you—and brought it to Philo's during one of her work shifts. Gave each of the bull demons a piece of cake and offered to make each one a cake of his very own in exchange for clearing brush and cutting the new path. The negotiations got . . . noisy."

Lee grinned. "I heard you almost had to lock up your own wife."

"You hear too much. Anyway, they each get a cake for clearing the brush, and another cake for cutting the new path through the woods so we can maintain some privacy at home."

"Did you get a taste of the sample cake when all this bartering was going on?"

Sebastian just sighed.

Lee laughed.

"So," Sebastian said, watching Lynnea and the bull demons. "Tell me again about noticing someone in the Den who's different?" When Lee didn't answer, he turned and looked at his cousin. "Lee? *Lee!*"

"I have to go. Someone needs . . ." So strong. The need was so strong. "I have to go."

He started to step back, to step away. Before he'd completed that first step, Sebastian grabbed his jacket and hauled him back so close that the only things separating them were Sebastian's fists.

"Where are you going?" Sebastian demanded.

"I don't know. It's not a place. I don't get a sense of place."

"You're the only Bridge Nadia and Glorianna can count on. Maybe the only one living in their landscapes. If something happens to you . . ."

"I know." Lee tried to free himself, but even if he decked Sebastian, Lynnea was heading toward them—and the bull demons were on their feet, waiting to see what the humans were going to do—and out of the corner of his eye, he saw Teaser hustling toward them. He wasn't going anywhere until Sebastian let him go. Unless he took Sebastian with him. All it would take was a stumble and a step back, but . . .

"I know," he said again. "But I have to go. I'll use my island to cross over to the place where I feel the need. I'll be careful. As long as I stay on the island, I'm connected to Sanctuary. I can get back. I'm not going to take a risk that will put us in danger, Sebastian, but I can't leave a heart out there when the need is so strong."

Sebastian uncurled his fists but didn't quite let go of Lee's jacket. "You're exhausted now, practically asleep on your feet. How long will this take?"

"You can't pin a time on something like—"

The hands tightened into fists again. *"How long?"*

This isn't about me being the only Bridge in Nadia's and Glorianna's landscapes. This is about family. "Give me four hours. If you don't hear from me by then, figure I've run into bad trouble." *Not that knowing that would do you any good. If I'm in the kind of trouble that makes it impossible to reach my island, there's nothing you can do to help me.*

Sebastian let go of Lee's jacket and stepped back. "Four hours."

Using his unusual gift of being able to impose his small island over another landscape, Lee brought the island to the Den's main street. He extended one hand back and felt the bark of a tree. One step back and he was standing on the island, vanished from the sight of the Den's citizens even though he could still see them.

Slipping one hand into his jacket pocket, he fingered the coiled braid he carried everywhere. Resonance and need rang through him, confirming what he'd already suspected. He was about to let Ephemera's currents of power take him to an unknown landscape in order to find the woman who belonged to a discarded braid of hair.

And he hoped she was worth the risks.

Chapter Thirteen

"Iz dead."

"Iz sleeping."

"Iz *dead.*"

"Iz *sleeping.*"

"How you know iz sleeping?"

"Cause I poked it? See?" *poke poke poke.*

Michael jerked awake, coughed up more bog water, then groaned. "I'm not sleeping now, you brainless twits, and I'm not dead, either."

Silence. Then the first one said, "We could kill it. Iz enough flesh on it to feed the clan."

Clan. Bog. *Lady of Light, have mercy on me.*

Michael pushed himself up to a sitting position and carefully rubbed his eyes, which felt hot and gritty. Then he looked at the two youngsters standing in front of him—and the adults silently moving closer.

The Merry Makers were human-shaped, and a full-grown one came up as high as a human man's chest. But they looked like they were formed from the bogs they claimed as their own: thin brown bodies with limbs that looked like animated branches; hands that had long, twiggy fingers; faces that could have been carved from gnarls of wood; hair like the moss that hung from the trees that grew on the bog's islands.

There was a vicious strength in those thin limbs that could easily overpower a grown man, and humans lured into the bog by the lights and the music seldom found their way home.

Unless they could bargain.

"I am not familiar with this clan," Michael said, feeling the need to step as carefully with his words as he would with his feet in order to get out of this dark place. "But I have been among your people before." Early in his wandering, when he'd been young and foolish and lost one night—and had learned firsthand that the stories about the demons who lived in their world weren't just stories. "We shared a night of music."

They didn't speak. Their large yellow eyes just stared at him.

There was no place for him to go. The Merry Makers were in front of him. A quick roll would have him back in the water, but the water offered no real escape from them—and trying to escape would be enough to condemn him.

Then one clear note sounded through the air.

Michael looked toward the sound and noticed his pack sitting close by, open.

He didn't remember taking off the pack, but his memories of what happened after he hit the water were jumbled bits of images. At least now he understood why he'd thought trees had reached down and saved him from drowning.

The Merry Maker who stepped forward held Michael's tin whistle in its long fingers. "Magician." The voice was deep and harsh and yet fluid—and sounded like it belonged to the bog itself. "We have heard of you, Magician."

There was something more primal about this one, something more dangerous. Which made Michael wonder if he was looking at this clan's Heart of the Bog. He'd heard the name the last time he'd been among the Merry Makers. They wouldn't explain what it meant, but he figured the name itself pretty much said it all—especially in terms of who made the decision of whether or not a human lived or died.

"Luck-bringer," the Heart of the Bog said, watching Michael. "Ill-wisher."

"I have never wished ill on your people," Michael replied.

"No, you have not." A pause. "You appear without warning, deep in our piece of the world, at a time when nothing should be able to cross over into the protected dark places."

Protected? Michael wondered. *By who?*

A lovely face once again filled his mind, and he was very much afraid he knew the answer.

"Why are you here, Magician?"

His life hinged on what he said next. He knew it; they knew it. So he listened to his heart and gave the Merry Maker the same answer he had given the Destroyer. "Her darkness is my fate."

Bodies shifted. Murmurs rose and fell until the Heart of the Bog raised one hand, commanding silence.

When the Heart of the Bog just watched him, Michael added, "Heart's hope lies within belladonna."

The Heart of the Bog tipped its head to one side and smiled a sweetly chilling smile. "You seek Belladonna?"

Something about the look in the Merry Maker's eyes told him he had misunderstood the riddle. It wasn't about the plant, it was about a *person*. It was the name of his dream lover, who must be a dark-hearted woman if she protected *this* part of the world. But he sensed she was also the key to getting away from the Merry Makers.

"Yes," Michael said. "I seek Belladonna."

The Heart of the Bog walked over to the pack and tucked the whistle inside before fastening the pack's straps. "We will take you to the Justice Maker. He has powerful magics." That chilling smile again.

"Deadly magics. See-bastian will decide if you are a friend . . . or a meal."

A gesture of its hand, more frightening because of the gracefulness of the movement, indicated that Michael should pick up his pack.

When he had his pack settled on his shoulders, they closed in around him. He saw no weapon in any hand, but he knew all the Merry Makers carried a knife and a slingshot—and were lethal with both. So he followed the Heart of the Bog and hoped this Justice Maker with the deadly magics was someone he could reason with.

A hand pushed her shoulder into the sand, holding her down. Another hand clamped over her mouth. And a stranger's voice said, "Stay quiet. I'm not going to hurt you. The boundaries are so thin the bone-lovers can sense prey even though they can't reach this landscape. But this place is so small, I already broke the boundaries in order to reach you, so I don't think your access point is going to last much longer."

The words made no sense to Caitlin, but she understood enough. Someone had come to help her, and those ant creatures—bonelovers?— were nearby. She relaxed her muscles, which was the only thing she could think to do to let him know she wasn't going to fight him.

The hand lifted from her mouth. The other still rested on her shoulder, but now lightly enough to feel like offered comfort rather than a restraint.

She didn't move except to turn her head enough to look at the man kneeling beside her. About her brother Michael's age, give or take a year. A good face. Handsome even, with the black hair and those green eyes framed by lashes that were unfairly lush. And the beginnings of those crinkle lines at the corners of the eyes that gave a man's face character and made women just look old.

When she shifted to push herself up, his hand moved from her shoulder to her arm, pulling her up to a sitting position.

She looked beyond her circle and clamped her hand over her mouth to stifle the scream. The sand all around them swarmed with bone-lovers, and not too far beyond her circle . . .

"They found something," the man said. "Might not be human. If there's only a border between two landscapes, animals can cross over easily enough. Most instinctively avoid landscapes that are dangerous, but if they're scared and running, they could end up in a landscape like this and then not be able to get back out." He stood, then offered her a hand to help her up. "Let's go while they're occupied."

Go where? Caitlin wondered, since she didn't see horses or a buggy or any other way to outrun the bonelovers. Then again, he *had* gotten here. Somehow.

As she raised her hand to clasp his, she remembered the heart's hope. She twisted around on her knees and began scooping a channel in the sand around the tiny plant. Couldn't have many roots. Not a plant this size. And certainly not deep.

"What are you doing?" the man demanded. "That's probably the only thing holding this access point intact."

She looked over her shoulder and glared at him. "I'm not leaving it in this place." She didn't know how much time had passed between when she'd created the circle of sand and when the stranger found her, and she wasn't sure she could explain to this man how often she'd awakened during those hours and felt like the presence of the heart's hope was a sip of courage. "I'm not leaving it."

He held up a hand to stop her. "Wait. Don't pull it out of the ground. Don't move. Just wait."

He moved to the edge of the circle, studied the bonelovers mounded over the unknown prey. Then he took a step and disappeared.

"No." The word came out as a whimper. Caitlin just stared. He'd left her. She hadn't been willing to leave the plant behind, so he left her.

Then he was back, reappearing inside her circle as suddenly as he had disappeared.

"Here," he said, handing her a sturdy bowl. "It's been cleansed, so it doesn't resonate with any earth that's been put it in before."

She understood the individual words, but the way he was stringing them together, the meaning escaped her. And his accent said plain as plain that he wasn't from a part of the world she knew. But she wasn't about to start asking questions that might have him thinking he'd be better off leaving her behind.

She worked her fingers under the tiny heart's hope. Yes, just as she thought. Not much root. She scooped up the plant and the sand, but there was too little of it for the size of the bowl.

"Just hold it at the right depth," the man said. He scooped up sand and poured it into the bowl while she held the plant in place. When he scooped up a shell, he looked at it, then at her. "Beach?"

Caitlin nodded. "I'm thinking it's the one near the village's harbor, but I can't be sure."

He set the shell aside and scooped up more sand. "And where would that be?"

"Are you asking the name of my village or my country?"

Now *he* looked puzzled. "Both."

"I live in Raven's Hill, and my country is called Elandar."

There was less warmth and more wariness in his green eyes.

"That should do it," she said, trying to sound cheerful as she pressed the sand down around the plant. On impulse, she set the shell next to the heart's hope.

He brushed off his hands, then reached into his jacket pocket. "Is this yours?"

She looked at the coil of braided hair tied with blue ribbon that he pulled out of his pocket—and shivered. "Where did you find that? I left it . . ." She wasn't about to tell him where she left it.

"It appeared near my mother's house," he said, looking and sounding more wary. Then he looked beyond the circle and stuffed the braid back into his pocket. "Let's finish this discussion in a safer place."

A bonelover was right at the edge of the circle, staring at them.

"It can see us!" Caitlin said.

"No, it can't," the man said with an oddly heavy emphasis. "But I think the boundaries have thinned to the point that it can hear us and it knows there's prey close by, so we need to leave here now." He helped her to her feet, then took a step closer to the bonelover and picked up her broken hoe handle. Stepping back, he wrapped a hand around her upper arm and led her to the spot where he had disappeared.

"This will be easier for you if you close your eyes," he said.

What would be easier? But she closed her eyes. He moved away from her, but not so far that he released his hold on her arm.

"Imagine stepping over a log," he said. "Lift one foot up and over."

"We're too close to the edge," Caitlin protested. "If I take a step, I'll be out of the circle."

"You'll be all right," he said. "Take the step."

Wasn't much choice, so she took the step.

Her breath caught. Not sand beneath that foot. Firmer ground. Where . . . ?

"Now the other foot," the man said. "Now is not the time to day-dream or dally."

"Where did you hear *that* saying?" Caitlin muttered as she obeyed him. For a younger man, he suddenly sounded like a querulous uncle. Or how she'd imagined a querulous uncle would sound.

"From my mother. I heard it often at one point in my life."

She smiled—and had the strange feeling that she'd almost fallen but had recovered her balance.

"Open your eyes. Give me the bowl."

She opened her eyes, but she hugged the bowl to her chest as she looked around. Trees and dappled sunlight. The cool air of autumn.

But to her left was the circle of sand from the Raven's Hill beach and beyond that the rust-colored sand that belonged to a nightmare. "How . . . ?"

"We'll discuss it later. Right now . . ." He pulled the bowl out of her hands, then gave her the hoe handle. "Undo this access point to the beach before the bonelovers find a way to cross over. If they manage to get through to your beach, they'll have access to everything it connects to, including your village."

"How do I do this? I don't know how to do this!"

He stared at her. "You really don't know what you've done, do you? You don't know what you are."

Sorceress.

"Ask Ephemera to take your beach back where it came from. Tell Ephemera to leave nothing connected to the Eater's landscape—not so much as a shell or grain of sand."

She hesitated.

The man lifted the bowl. "The sand and shell are enough to create an anchor point. You can get back home."

If I knew how this worked. "I can't be talking to the world while you're watching."

"I'll go up the path a ways. But we need to get away from this land-scape as soon as you're done." He touched her arm lightly. "Don't step off the island."

As if she needed the warning.

The moment he was out of sight, she wished she could still see him. Pretending to be brave was easier when she wasn't alone.

Just get it done, she thought as she knelt at the edge of the island. *He sounds like he sees this sort of thing all the time. Why would he see this sort of thing all the time?*

She shook her head and put her mind to the task. He was right; there was no time for anything except getting away from this place.

By the time there was no trace of the circle she had made, she was sweating and panting—and fighting panic as she watched a bonelover move toward the island.

"I wasn't sure you could do it," the man said, coming up behind her.

"You certainly *sounded* like you expected me to do it," Caitlin replied testily.

"That doesn't mean I was sure you could. Better close your eyes again."

The bonelover was moving toward them, heading right for the path she knelt on.

She squeezed her eyes closed . . .

. . . and heard a roaring. And beneath it, closer, the lap of water.

She opened her eyes and threw her body back from the edge, knocking into the man and almost sending him tumbling.

"Easy," he said, grabbing her to steady them both.

"Lady of Light, have mercy." A wall of water, curved like a horseshoe, coming down from the land high above to meet the river.

"Haven't you ever seen a waterfall?" the man asked.

"Not like that." Even though their little bit of land was a safe distance away, the sheer sound of it made her tremble. Closer to them was another falls, its water breaking halfway down on a tumble of boulders as big as houses.

"They're called the Guardian Falls," the man said, crouching beside her. "The river has several names, depending on which landscape you're in. Some call it the Wish River; others call it the River of Prayers." He paused and looked at her. "What do people call you?"

"Caitlin Marie. And you?"

"Lee." He rose and moved to the edge of the island, and raised a hand in greeting as a boat sailed past.

Seeing the men on the boat return the greeting, Caitlin scrambled to her feet. "They can see us! Why can they see us?"

"Because I want them to see us. The island resonates too closely with the river. Even if the people couldn't see it, the boats on the river would still run into it. So the people here can see it until I shift it back to the place where it actually exists."

"You don't seem to be drunk, so you must be daft because most of what you say makes no sense."

"It makes sense," Lee said. "In this part of the world, it makes sense." He leaned against the trunk of a tree and studied her. "Caitlin Marie, I don't know the customs of your people, so I hope you won't take this in a way it isn't meant."

"Take what?" she asked, suddenly too aware that she was alone with a man she didn't know on a small bit of land she couldn't leave.

He smiled. "I think it's best if I take you home to meet my mother."

Chapter Fourteen

"Sentinel Stones," the Heart of the Bog said, pointing to the two massive stones that rose out of the bog on either side of the "trail."

"I never thought I'd see the likes of them out here," Michael said quietly, awed and uneasy. He'd seen Sentinel Stones before. They were always placed outside a village in a field beside a main road. Easy enough to reach, but set back far enough that going to them would be intentional.

There was power in the Sentinel Stones, and some strange magic in the air between them. People disappeared when they walked between the stones. Sometimes they came back with wild tales of seeing different countries or of suddenly finding themselves walking the streets of a town on the other side of Elandar; more often they were never seen again.

"No," Michael said, stopping when he realized the Heart of the Bog intended to walk between the stones. "We can't go there."

"That is the border," the Heart of the Bog replied, turning back to face him. "There is no other way to reach the other landscape from here." Its yellow eyes studied him. "You afraid, Magician?"

"Yes." No point blunting the truth.

The Heart of the Bog was silent for a moment. Then, "You must pass between the Sentinel Stones to find the Justice Maker. He is the next step in your journey. If you do not find him, you will not find her."

Damn the darkness. "People disappear when they walk between Sentinel Stones."

"That is the purpose of the Stones. But these mark a border and only go to one place."

That is the purpose of the Stones. Lady of Light, did anyone besides the Merry Makers know this?

Michael swallowed hard, trying to push his heart back down his throat. *You don't have many choices, lad. You can't stay here, and it seems a walk between the Stones is your only way out. The world has turned strange, and a great evil is out there, somewhere. And Caitlin Marie is out there, somewhere.*

"What do I have to do?" Michael asked.

"Hum a note that sounds like what you seek," the Heart of the Bog replied.

He thought about the woman who stirred him in dreams in ways other women had never done and who was somehow connected to this dark piece of the world. He took a deep breath and hummed the note.

A moment later, another note filled the air, creating a simple harmony.

The Heart of the Bog nodded, then wrapped its long fingers around his wrist. Humming the two notes, they walked between the Sentinel Stones.

Michael felt the lightest tingle of power. Then he was through the space between the Stones and . . .

The bog was gone. From what he could tell in the moonlight, there was open country in front of him and some lights in the distance that might be a village. The air felt different—and it didn't smell like home.

He looked back and saw a handful of Merry Makers appear between the Stones, but there was no sign of the bog now. The Stones were just standing in the middle of a field.

"Not much farther," the Heart of the Bog said, releasing Michael's wrist and heading toward the lights. "Humans will find us soon and take you to the Justice Maker."

Nothing to do now but follow. The pots on the outside of his pack clacked and clattered to the rhythm of his walk. After a minute or so, two of the Merry Makers pulled out their reed whistles and began playing a tune that turned the rattle of pots into percussion.

Well, Michael thought, *if the lanterns and the musical clatter don't attract someone's attention, nothing will.*

They were halfway between the Sentinel Stones and the lights when the Heart of the Bog stepped onto a cart path that began in the middle of a field for no reason Michael could discern. But a few minutes after that, two men came riding up to block their path.

"Halt!" the older man said. "State your business."

"This human came to us without warning, appearing deep within our piece of the world," the Heart of the Bog said. "He seeks the Justice Maker."

Not by choice, Michael thought. Who were these men? Law enforcers? Thugs? He couldn't tell by the look of them.

"Do you want us to take him the rest of the way, or are you bringing him to the Den?" the man asked.

The Heart of the Bog considered for a moment, then shook its head slowly. "Take him. If the Justice Maker is pleased with the Magician, we will trade him for another kind of meat."

Michael stared at the Heart of the Bog. "What kind of meat?"

The Merry Maker shrugged.

"What kind?" Michael demanded. Lady's mercy, would they drag some poor fool to those Sentinel Stones and hand him over to the Merry Makers? Or . . . different meat. Did the Merry Maker mean a woman . . . or a child? "I'll go no farther until I know what kind of meat." And if he didn't like the answer, he would do the most harmful ill-wishing he could think of before he was dragged away.

The Heart of the Bog studied him. Then it smiled. "Cow. Sheep. Maybe goat."

Michael's huffed out a breath as relief shivered through him.

The Heart of the Bog stepped closer. "You are worthy of what you seek, Magician. Remember that." It tapped Michael's chest above his heart. "In here."

Then the Merry Makers turned away and headed back toward the Sentinel Stones.

Michael looked at the two men. "My name is Michael. Who would you be?"

"Addison," the older man replied. "This here is Henley." He hesitated, then added, "From the sound of you, you come from a landscape that's a fair distance from here."

"I come from a country called Elandar."

"Country? Huh," Addison said, nodding as if Michael had just confirmed something. "Didn't take you for a city dweller, since most of them wouldn't know what to do with a pack like that, let alone be able to carry it. Come on, then. It's not too far a walk for someone who's used to using his feet."

Michael walked in front of the horses, torn between wanting to lengthen his stride to walk off his annoyance and wanting to slow down to delay getting to their destination—whatever it was.

Obviously they thought a wanderer was an uneducated man and couldn't tell the difference between being *from* the country and living *in* a country. So let them underestimate him and judge him by his clothes and the pack on his back. All the better for him to get away from this place and figure out how to find Caitlin.

It didn't take long enough before they passed stables, paddocks, and a line of hitching rails as well as . . . Yes, those wooden slats *were* bicycle racks. Looked like everyone left their conveyance here and went the rest of the way by foot.

The street was cobblestone, which was common enough. The colored lights that lit up the street . . .

There was a feel of a harvest fair about the place, and he almost expected to see the booths that offered games of chance. Of course, it felt like the seedy side of the harvest fair, where the games of chance weren't as innocent as a ring toss to win a stuffed animal for your sweetheart.

There had been times, when his belly had been as empty as his pockets, when he'd accepted a coin or two in exchange for bringing someone a little more luck at those games of chance—or a little bad luck if the coins had come from a man's rival.

"Is there some kind of festival going on?" Michael asked.

"Nah," Addison said. He dismounted and handed the reins to Henley. "The Den of Iniquity always looks like this. You can leave the pack here. No point in jangling down the street, is there?"

Lady's mercy. The last time someone suggested he leave his pack, they hadn't wanted anything worth selling to be ruined if things got messy when they killed him. Music had gotten him out of that bad patch, and he'd made a point of avoiding that particular fork in the road ever since.

He looked at the two men—and noticed that each of them had a hand resting on a weapon. The Heart of the Bog had cleaned his tin whistle, valuing the instrument far more than the man, but he hadn't had time to assure himself it was in any condition to be played. So it was best not to offer entertainment he wasn't sure he could deliver—especially to men already suspicious of him because he was a stranger.

He slid the straps off his shoulders and set the pack on the ground.

"This way," Addison said. "If Sebastian isn't at Philo's, the folks there will know where to find him."

"And he rules this place?"

Addison pondered for a moment, then nodded. "That's a way of saying it."

Wondering what kind of justice would be found in a place called the Den of Iniquity, Michael followed Addison, who headed for a courtyard full of tables and statues.

Then he shoved Addison aside and ran to the woman standing next to a table with her back to the street.

He spun her around and grabbed her arms in a bruising grip. "Damn the darkness, Caitlin Marie, you scared me out of a decade of my life pulling a stunt like this! If you weren't a grown woman, or close enough, I'd take a strap—"

He was dimly aware of the sound of chairs crashing as men shoved away from the tables, dimly aware of men and . . . something shaggy . . . moving toward him with deadly purpose. But what he saw with painful clarity was the fear in the woman's blue eyes. He gentled his grip but still held on to her, ready to catch her if she swooned.

"I am sorry," he said, working to make his voice soothing. "When I saw you standing there, I thought you were Caitlin Marie."

"Who deserves a strapping?" Her voice trembled with fear, but there was an undercurrent of anger now—the kind that came from a woman who knew the feel of a leather belt against tender flesh.

The men and the shaggy things were closing in, and he was pretty sure he was holding the one ally he might have in this place—if she chose to be.

"She's my sister," he said quickly, too aware of how little time he had to explain. "My little sister. She disappeared. Just vanished from the village where she and my aunt live. I have to find her. There's something evil out there, and I have to find her. And I thought, when I saw you—the right height, the right color hair—I thought I'd found her."

"Take your hands off my wife."

Hearing the "or else" under the command, Michael released the woman, took a step back, and took stock of how much trouble he was in.

The blond-haired man on his left was holding a sharp table knife, but not in a way that said he was used to street fighting. On another day, the two shaggy, horned creatures that looked like bulls walking on their hind legs would have scared him out of half his wits—especially since one of them was carrying a club and the other had a large knife, and they *did* look like they knew a lot about street fighting. But it was the dark-haired man coming up on his right that held Michael's attention. He was dressed in black leather and had cold green eyes, and there was something about the way he rubbed his thumb against the fingertips of his right hand that produced a ball of fear in Michael's gut.

The woman hesitated a moment, then shifted enough to half block the man's approach. "Sebastian," she said, taking hold of his arm with both hands.

So this was Sebastian, the Justice Maker who was going to decide his fate. *I'm a dead man.*

"He wasn't trying to hurt me," she said. "His sister is missing, lost in the landscapes."

"And this is how he responds to finding his sister?"

The woman's mouth primmed as she looked at Michael and made a lightning-flash decision. "I've been told that men who are scared tend to yell at a loved one as a way of showing relief. Which is totally unfair since the person being yelled at has already had a difficult time because otherwise she wouldn't have been late. But unfair or not, I've been told that this is a male thing to do and men have to be forgiven, eventually, when they do it."

Irritation tightened Sebastian's mouth when the blond-haired man choked back a laugh, but it was enough to break the coldness in his eyes.

"I thought we agreed that discussion was finished," Sebastian said.

"It is finished," she agreed. "I was just reminding you of it."

He would have found the domestic byplay more amusing if his life didn't depend on Sebastian's temper.

The woman looked at Michael. "You came here to find your sister."

"I came here by mistake," he replied.

"No one comes to the Den by mistake," Sebastian said. "By accident, yes, but not by mistake."

Michael nodded to indicate he understood the distinction. "By accident then."

"The Merry Makers brought him across the border in order to see you," Addison said from behind Michael.

"Why?" Sebastian asked.

"I'm looking for the answer to a riddle," Michael replied. It wasn't really a riddle anymore since he'd already figured out "belladonna" was a woman and not the plant, but if he kept these people intrigued about why he was among them, he might be able to talk his way out of this place.

"You said you were looking for your sister," the woman said, shifting so she no longer blocked Sebastian's right hand.

Damn the darkness, these people were too suspicious of strangers to be intrigued by anything. And if the woman stopped believing his reason for grabbing her . . . He had a feeling Sebastian could kill him in cold blood right here on the street and no one would say a thing about it.

"I *am* looking for my sister," he said, putting all the conviction he could into his voice, "and the answer to this riddle. I'm thinking finding one is the only way of finding the other."

Sebastian stared at him. "What's the riddle?"

"Heart's hope lies within belladonna."

He didn't expect a reaction, so he wasn't sure what it meant when Sebastian rocked back on his heels as if he'd just felt a fist jab him in the ribs.

"Who are you?" Sebastian asked.

"Michael. The Magician."

No response to the word. Might have given him some leverage if they'd been a bit fearful of him. Then again, he wasn't sure being an ill-wisher measured up to whatever "deadly magics" Sebastian wielded.

"I'm Sebastian Justicemaker," Sebastian said. "This is my wife, Lynnea," He tipped his head to indicate the blond-haired man. "That's Teaser."

Michael nodded to Lynnea, then to the blond-haired man, who just gave him a measuring look before returning to his table.

Sebastian lightly touched Lynnea's shoulder. "Why don't you clear that far table and ask Philo to bring some food."

"Best make it downwind," Michael muttered, pinching his shirt. Since everything he owned had gone into the bog, everything smelled like the bog. "I'd be grateful for some food and something warm to drink. And some water."

The customers at the chosen table were shifted to another, and Michael noticed no one grumbled about the change in seating. At least, not out loud. He washed his hands in the bowl of warm water that was offered, glad to have that much clean. The beverage Lynnea called koffee was hot and strong, which made him realize how cold and tired he was.

"I suppose you want the whole story," Michael said after Lynnea delivered the food—thick stew, slices of fresh bread generously buttered, a white cheese, and some round black objects in their own small bowl.

"Be careful biting into the olives," Sebastian said, pointing at the small bowl. "They have pits. Eat while it's hot. Then I'll listen."

He didn't need to be told twice. He dug into the meal, but he studied the street and the people while he ate. Strange place. There was a mean edge that reminded him of the streets around the docks in Kendall, and certainly enough taverns . . .

A beautiful woman strolled toward the table, gave him an assessing look, then smiled in blatant invitation. Michael felt the heat of a blush as he looked down at his meal and pretended not to see the invitation.

. . . and there were brazen streetwalkers.

"What do you think of the carnal carnival?" Sebastian asked, sounding amused.

That was the perfect way to describe the Den of Iniquity, Michael thought. "It's interesting."

"You've never seen a succubus before?"

"A what?"

"The female who made you blush." There was something about Sebastian's smile that was sharp and just a little mean.

"Is that what you call streetwalkers here?" Michael asked, looking up to meet Sebastian's eyes.

"No, that's what we call female sex demons."

Michael's jaw dropped. He'd *heard* of such females from a few sailors who had docked at Kendall, but he'd figured the men were just telling tales.

Sebastian's smile got a little sharper. "A male sex demon is called an incubus." He raised his koffee cup in a mocking salute.

"Lady's mercy," Michael whispered.

"More koffee?" Lynnea asked, coming up to the table. She looked at Michael and frowned. "Is something wrong?"

"He's just wondering why a sensible woman would want an incubus for a husband," Sebastian said.

"That's because he's not female," Lynnea replied as she refilled their cups. "If he was, he'd know why a sensible woman would want you for a husband."

Michael took his time stirring a lump of sugar into the koffee, trying to decide if prudence or curiosity would win the battle of whether or not he kept his questions to himself.

Prudence had no chance of winning.

"Those men," he said. "They're going into a brothel?"

Sebastian nodded.

"Do they know the woman . . . the female . . . is a . . ."

"That's why they come to the Den."

Teaser set a bottle of whiskey and two glasses on the table. "Philo figured it was time for this."

"Philo was right," Sebastian said, his eyes never leaving Michael's face. "Teaser is an incubus. As far as the women who cross over to visit are concerned, he's one of the Den's assets."

Michael glanced up at Teaser. "Are you a Justice Maker, too?"

Teaser laughed. "Having one wizard in the Den who can call the lightning and sizzle people is enough. I'll stick to making women very happy and leave the other part to Sebastian."

Well, Michael thought when Teaser strolled away, that told him what sort of "deadly magics" Sebastian could wield.

Sebastian poured whiskey into both glasses, then set the bottle aside and rested his forearms on the table. "Now. Tell me your story, Michael the Magician, and make it a good one. Your life depends on it."

I've no doubt of that.

Michael took a sip of whiskey to give himself time to think. Where to begin? And how much would Sebastian believe when none of the things that had happened recently seemed believable?

So he started with meeting Captain Kenneday and hearing about the lost fishing boats. He told Sebastian about the letter that had come from his aunt that contained the riddle she had heard in a dream. The hand holding the whiskey glass trembled as he talked about that haunted piece of the sea, and his voice broke when he got to the part about his aunt being injured in a fire and his learning that Caitlin Marie had disappeared. But his voice held steel and fear when he recounted seeing the monster, and of his battle of wills with that evil in order to choose the darkness that would claim him.

Throughout the telling, Sebastian never moved. Just watched him with unnerving intensity.

"So that's how I ended up with the Merry Makers, and they decided to let you decide," Michael said. He tossed back the glass of whiskey and poured himself another to fight the chill that was back in his bones.

Sebastian picked up his glass of whiskey and sat back. "You don't know the incubi and succubi, but you're familiar with the Merry Makers?"

Michael nodded. "Ran into them once before, in the early days of my wandering. They liked my music, so they let me go."

"Are there any other demons in your landscapes?"

"In my country, you mean?"

Sebastian tipped his head, as if considering. "A person's landscapes can hold many places, so I have a feeling we aren't talking about the same things. But we'll go with your way of looking at the world—for now."

Michael frowned. "What country is this?"

"This landscape is the Den of Iniquity."

He huffed in frustration. "But it has to connect to something!"

"It has borders with the Merry Makers' landscape, as well as the waterhorses' and the bull demons'. There are stationary bridges to several daylight landscapes."

Michael braced his head in his hands. "One of us has a brain fever."

"No, one of us has spent his life in the part of Ephemera that was shattered the most during the battle between the Guides of the Heart and the Eater of the World. And the other has probably moved through landscapes all his life without realizing it."

He stared at the table. At some point the dishes had been cleared away, but he couldn't remember who had done it or when. His mind went blank, and in that moment of restful emptiness the things he'd seen recently, the things he'd said, and the things he'd been told drifted through that emptiness and came together to form a new pattern.

"This vanishing from one place and appearing in another," he said slowly, as if feeling his way. "You don't see anything strange about it, do you?"

"In this part of Ephemera, you gamble with your life every time you cross a bridge," Sebastian replied. "So, no, I don't see anything strange about your crossing over from one place to another. At least now we know where the Eater of the World was last seen, and that's more than we knew before." He pushed his chair back. "Come on. You look ready to fold."

Michael nodded. "I could do with a bit of a wash and some sleep."

"You can use our room at the bordello, since Lynnea and I will be staying at the cottage. I'll come fetch you in the morning and take you to Sanctuary."

"Sanctuary?"

"The next step in your journey to answer the riddle."

Michael stood up, but didn't follow Sebastian when the other man started to walk away from the courtyard. "Sebastian Justicemaker?"

Sebastian stopped and turned to face him.

"Do you know the answer to the riddle?" Michael asked.

"I should," Sebastian replied. "I'm the one who sent it out through the twilight of waking dreams."

His heart started beating harder, faster. "Then you know how to find Belladonna."

"I know how to find her. But whether or not *you* can find her . . ." Sebastian shrugged. "That's what you're going to find out."

Chapter Fifteen

Michael looked at the creatures waiting in the street, then pulled Sebastian back inside the bordello and firmly closed the door. The pushed-in faces and tufted ears made the things look like mangy but somewhat loveable critters—if a person overlooked the razor teeth, the powerful arms and upper bodies, and the curved talons that could gut a man with one swipe. And that was just the front half. The back half looked like a draft horse version of a bicycle, complete with saddlelike seat, but lacking wheels. Of course, since the things were floating above the ground, the lack of wheels wouldn't trouble them. But it was that last detail that was a little too much for *him*.

"That's the transportation you arranged?" he asked.

"Demon cycles," Sebastian replied too agreeably.

"You expect me to straddle one of those things and put the family jewels within reach of its teeth and claws?"

Sebastian's lips twitched as he glanced down at Michael's groin. "Is that what you're packing under your belt?"

"You know what I mean. Don't you?" He wasn't going to make assumptions about what these people did or didn't know. Not after having breakfast with Teaser and hearing the incubus's ideas of how the world worked.

"If they were interested in any organs, it would be your heart and liver, not your penis," Sebastian said, opening the door. "Come on. You've got a ways to go today."

"Well, isn't that just grand," Michael muttered as he followed Sebastian.

When he swung a leg over the demon cycle, he wished Lynnea and Sebastian had found him some broken-in hand-me-down clothes rather than these new ones that felt a little too stiff to be comfortable. Or maybe it was his feelings that were a little too stiff. He could count on one hand the times when he'd had a truly new garment in the past dozen years, and here they were giving him a whole new set of clothes. And he *hadn't* done any luck-bringing on his own behalf to bring it about!

Then he scolded himself for being ungrateful. He was a stranger from another land who had dropped in among them with a story of a lost sister and a battle with a terrible monster. Instead of running him out of town, they had given him clothes and a place to stay, had loaned him a travel pack and filled it with basic supplies, and were cleaning up his gear from its dunking in the bog so that it would be ready for him when he got back from this bit of the journey.

If he got back from this bit of the journey.

None of them said it, but it was there, unspoken, under everything they *did* say.

He might have enjoyed the new experience of riding a demon cycle if he really believed Sebastian and Teaser's assurance that the creatures didn't harm the people they'd agreed to transport.

He didn't consider "they usually don't eat their passengers" to be sufficient assurance. "Demon cycles are safer to ride than waterhorses" wasn't much comfort either since the whole reason the horse-shaped demons gave humans a ride was to drown their victims.

But if he survived this and found his way home again, he'd have a story that would buy him a meal and a bed in any inn he chose to stay at, and an always-full glass in any pub he walked into.

When they reached an odd spot in the dirt lane, Sebastian told the demon cycles to stop, then looked at Michael. "Which way do you want to go?"

Michael studied the land ahead as best he could in the available moonlight. The dirt lane ran straight ahead, but the odd spot was nothing more than a bump of road that formed a half loop, reconnecting to the straight lane. At the midpoint of the half loop were two boulders set far enough apart to allow a wagon to pass between them.

"What's the difference?" Michael asked.

Sebastian pointed to the straight lane. "If we go on that way for another mile or so, we'll reach the border that connects the Den to the waterhorses' landscape." He pointed to the half loop. "That's a stationary bridge that leads to Aurora, which is where we have to go in order to reach Sanctuary."

Michael stared at Sebastian. "I'm in a part of the world that's nowhere close to home. I know that. I can *feel* that. But you're saying that a mile down the road I can pass between a couple of stones and end up within walking distance of a village I've stopped at once each season for the past ten years?"

"That's what I'm saying."

He'd met some crazy people in his travels, but he'd swear by the Light that Sebastian wasn't one of them. Which meant he could be back in Elandar, no more than a long day's walk from Dunberry. Not that he'd go to Dunberry. Not anymore. But . . .

"If I make that choice, I won't find Caitlin Marie, will I?" Michael asked.

"Probably not."

And I'll never find Belladonna. An unshakable certainty rang through him. If he didn't make this journey, he would never find the woman who haunted his dreams.

"We'll go on to Sanctuary."

Sebastian nodded. "Best clear your mind of everything but the thought that you need to cross over to Aurora."

"Teaser said these stationary bridges only go to specific places, so you can be certain of where you end up when you cross one of them."

"Nothing is that certain in Ephemera," Sebastian replied. He tapped the demon cycle on its shoulder. "We're crossing over to Aurora."

"Do we need to hum a particular tune?" Michael asked.

The demon cycles jerked to a stop, and they and Sebastian looked at him with the same quizzical expression.

"I had to hum a note when passing between the Sentinel Stones in order to get from the Merry Makers' bog to the Den," Michael mumbled, feeling his face heat as Sebastian continued to stare at him. "So I just wondered."

"That spot between the Merry Makers' landscapes and the Den is a border, not a boundary," Sebastian said.

Michael's only response was a lift of his shoulders to indicate the explanation lacked any useful information.

"A boundary requires a bridge," Sebastian continued blandly. "A border is a place where two landscapes connect without need of a bridge. They're usually marked with stones just to make it easier to find the spot."

"So what was the humming all about?"

Sebastian shrugged. "They might have had a reason for you to do it, but it had nothing to do with reaching the Den."

"That ripe—" Michael caught himself and considered the wisdom of roundly cursing one demon in the presence of another, larger demon. That he was riding. Not to mention that the man escorting him was at least part demon. "As you say, there was probably a reason."

"Indeed."

He could hear the laughter in Sebastian's voice. Fine. Grand. Let the ripe bastard laugh at him. Wouldn't be the first time someone had laughed at him.

"Aurora," Sebastian said to the demon cycles.

Aurora, Michael chanted silently. *Aurora. We need to reach—*

Sebastian and the demon cycle passed between the stones and vanished right before his eyes.

"Lady of Light!"

Even though he'd done this twice now himself, seeing someone else disappear was more frightening somehow. If he'd had time, he would have jumped off the demon cycle, but they were passing between the stones before his brain could tell his body what to do.

Then . . .

"Arrgh!"

Michael ducked his head and closed his eyes against the sudden daylight. When he could see again, he looked around—and swallowed hard.

They weren't in the same place anymore. Close enough by the feel of the land that, if he'd been walking a circuit back home, he might have considered the distance between the two places as a reasonable bit of travel. But nothing was reasonable in this part of the world, and it finally started to sink into his heart and brain that he was a lot farther from home than could be measured by something as simple as distance.

"Does that still lead to the Den?" Michael asked, tipping his head to indicate the straight lane.

Sebastian shook his head. "Follow the lane from this side and it will take you to the road that goes to the neighboring village, which can be reached without using a bridge. When the Landscaper initially altered the landscapes a few weeks ago, there was a border between Aurora and the Den. A bit unusual since one is a daylight landscape and the other is dark. But it turned out a border was a little too easy to cross, so a bridge was put in to keep the mothers in Aurora from worrying overmuch that their sons—or, worse, their daughters—would be slipping over to the Den."

"But some still do."

"Some do."

"If that's a stationary bridge, why can't all of them go the Den?"

Sebastian smiled. "Even with a stationary bridge, you have to resonate with the landscape in order to cross over."

He heard the message. "You're saying I resonate with the Den."

Sebastian tipped his head in acknowledgment. "Like I told you last night, no one comes to the Den by mistake. Shall we go?"

Michael didn't see the signal Sebastian gave the demon cycles, but as they neared a tidy cottage, the creatures swung to one side, keeping to the edge of the cleared property before heading into the woods. The cycles followed a footpath, the kind of shortcut that was made by friends and neighbors in order to reach each other's houses instead of taking the long way around. At a fork, they followed the part that curved to the right. When the path ended, Sebastian hesitated, then swung away from the house and grounds that must have been the usual destination in order to reach another path that ran through another patch of woods.

The demon cycles finally stopped on the edge of a clearing with a pair of stones Michael was starting to recognize as a bridge.

"Whose house was that?" he asked.

Sebastian dismounted and walked toward the stones, leaving Michael little choice but to follow.

"My aunt's," Sebastian replied. "My cousin Lee has a cottage nearby."

Probably reached from the left-hand fork in the path. "And your cottage is the one near the bridge between Aurora and the Den." When Sebastian nodded, Michael felt a pang in his heart. Family living in the same village, their homes connected by well-used paths in the woods. Distant enough for privacy, close enough for comfort. And not together out of need or duty, but because they enjoyed each other's company. What would it be like to live that way instead of following a pattern of rootless wandering?

"That's a resonating bridge," Sebastian said, pointing to the space between the stones. "Keep your mind focused on why you want to reach Sanctuary, and you should get there."

Michael stopped adjusting the straps of the travel pack Sebastian had loaned him. "Should?"

"A resonating bridge can take you to any landscape that resonates with your heart."

"I suppose that's a comfort," Michael said, eyeing the stones.

"Is it? Do you know every facet of your heart, Magician?"

Michael shivered, suddenly comprehending the magnitude of what he was about to do and how many things could go wrong.

The Heart of the Bog stepped closer. "You are worthy of what you seek, Magician. Remember that." It tapped Michael's chest above his heart. "In here."

The memory steadied him, even though he wasn't sure why it should. "All right. I'm ready."

"On you go, then."

Michael waited a beat. "You're not coming?"

Sebastian shook his head. "You have to find Sanctuary on your own. When you cross over, you'll see a large building nearby. That's a guesthouse. Someone there will be able to help you take the next step."

Michael held out his hand. "Thank you for all you've done. And for the loan of the pack. I'll get it back to you." *Somehow.*

"It's a kindness," Sebastian replied as he shook Michael's hand. Then he stepped back. "Travel lightly."

"How do you know the Traveler's Blessing?" Michael asked, startled.

"It's called Heart's Blessing in this part of the world," Sebastian replied. Then he smiled. "There's hope for you yet, Magician."

Hope. *Heart's hope lies within Belladonna. I need to find Belladonna.*

Taking a deep breath and blowing it out slowly, Michael walked between the stones.

✶   ✶   ✶

Sebastian stared at the empty space between the stones. "Guardians of the Light and Guides of the Heart, if he is who I think he is, keep him safe on this journey."

Turning away from the stones, he walked back to the demon cycles. "I'm going to visit my auntie, so you two should go back to the Den."

He could almost feel the friction caused by bits of demon cycle brain rubbing together to spark a thought.

"Cottage?" one of them finally said.

"Lynnea's still at the cottage."

They left him without a second thought, zooming through the woods at reckless speed in order to get to the cottage.

Sebastian set off at a leisurely pace, enjoying the quiet of a crisp autumn morning as he followed the almost-hidden path that would take him back to his aunt Nadia's house.

He just hoped Lynnea wouldn't be annoyed at him for the unexpected company. And he hoped Dalton, who had been a guard captain in Wizard City and was now working as a law enforcer in Aurora, wouldn't have a reason to cross over to the Den and inquire about the whereabouts of missing livestock, since they both knew that if the demon cycles were responsible, missing livestock translated to thoroughly eaten livestock—although the farmer did find a hoof and the end bit of a tail the last time Dalton had felt the need to come calling. And the three demon cycles that had given him, Lynnea, and Teaser a ride to Nadia's house on that particular occasion had rattled for days, sounding too much like bones and hooves being shaken in a metal barrel.

Not that he'd mentioned that detail to Dalton. When a man was the Den's Justice Maker, as well as being an incubus and wizard, he had a more flexible definition of law enforcement than the men who performed similar duties in the daylight landscapes.

Reaching Nadia's house, he gave the back door a perfunctory knock before he opened the door and stuck his head in the kitchen. "Anyone flying around in here?"

No one flying, but the stranger standing near the kitchen table spun around and dropped the cup and saucer she'd been holding.

"Who are you?" the young woman said in a shrill voice. She darted around the table to put it between them. "What do you want here?"

Sebastian was in the kitchen with his right hand halfway raised to call the wizards' lightning when Nadia rushed into the room.

"Caitlin, darling, what's the— Oh." Nadia stopped, then brushed her hair back with one hand. "Sebastian. I didn't hear you come in. Caitlin, it's all right. Sebastian is my nephew."

Caitlin.

Sebastian lowered his hand and took in the young woman's details. A little younger than Lynnea, but the same height and general size. Same color hair but straight instead of wavy—and very short. No one would mistake one face for the other, but seen from the back, he could understand Michael's error.

Oh, Guardians and Guides.

He walked out of the kitchen and ended up in front of a flower bed that still had some late-blooming plants. He just stared at them, even when Nadia caught up to him.

"Sebastian." She sounded harried and a little breathless, and he wondered what sort of emotional mess he'd left behind in the kitchen. "What is going on?"

"That's Caitlin Marie, isn't it?" he said, keeping his eyes fixed on the plants rather than looking at his aunt. "Her hair is so short because she cut it off. That was the tail of long hair we found a few days ago."

"Yes. Lee found her in the bonelovers' landscape. She had altered the landscape enough to create a protective circle that kept the bone-lovers from reaching her, but that's all she knew how to do. And even that was instinctive rather than a true understanding of what she was doing. She held on and held up until Lee brought her here. Once she truly believed she was safe, she . . . fell apart. Just as well that she did it here where my will dominates, so she's not manifesting."

"I didn't talk to Jeb directly when he came to deliver Lee's message," Sebastian said. "He met up with Teaser near the edge of the Den and said Lee had gotten back safe and sound. I don't think Jeb mentioned the girl, Caitlin."

Nadia drew in a deep breath, then blew it out in a huff as she frowned at Sebastian. "Then how did you know who she was?"

"I just saw her brother Michael off on the next stage of his journey. He's heading for Sanctuary, so he crossed over the resonating bridge near here. He's searching for his sister—and Belladonna." He finally looked at his aunt. "I almost brought him here. I figured you would be up by now, so I almost brought him to the house so you could see him, talk to him. If I had, he would have found his sister, and maybe he would have chosen not to go on to Sanctuary."

"He wouldn't have needed to. Lee intends to drop in on Glorianna to tell her about Caitlin and ask her to come here to meet the girl as soon as she can." Nadia paused. "Why didn't you go up with him? If a stranger shows up asking to see Belladonna, no one at Sanctuary will tell him anything or ask her to leave her island. He'll have made the journey for nothing."

"He'll be able to see her," Sebastian said, turning back to stare at the flowers since that was easier than facing his aunt. "If he's worthy."

She gasped. "Oh, Sebastian. You sent him there to be tested by the river?" When he nodded, she put a hand on his arm, a silent command to look at her. "Why?"

"I painted him, Aunt Nadia," Sebastian said, obeying the command. "With her."

Nadia remained silent and frozen for a moment. Then she blinked with slow deliberation. *"Moonlight Lover."* She pondered for a moment. "You saw him in a dream?"

"A waking dream, yes, and never clearly enough for the details, which is why his face is in shadow. But I recognized the feel of him. Gave me quite a start when he came to the Den—especially after I learned he'd ended up here after fighting the Eater of the World."

Nadia's hand clenched on his arm before she regained control and released him. "Well. I'll still have Lee take a message to the island, but we'll wait until midday."

"Aunt Nadia." He'd made the decision, and he would stand by it. "I liked him well enough, but I'm not sure I trust him. I—" He felt his face heat a little. "Sometimes I become aware of . . . things . . . without actively trying to link with someone through dreams. Romantic daydreams, I guess you could call them, that slip in under my guard."

She blushed as she realized the implications of what he was saying. "Do you still . . . ? You're *married*, Sebastian."

"I *know* that." He closed his eyes, trying to recapture the feeling that had washed through him, giving him the inspiration for the painting. "She's lonely, Aunt Nadia, and the romantic side of Glorianna's heart . . ."

"I know," Nadia said softly.

"After I met him, I started wondering if the inspiration for painting *him* as the fantasy lover had come from a yearning flowing in the currents of Light . . . or if it had come from something in the Dark."

Nadia's breath caught.

"There are things he didn't say last night, reasons he's looking for Glorianna that he didn't share. So I'm not sure I trust him. But a person can't lie to the river. If it lets him reach the Island in the Mist, we'll know he's worthy of what he seeks."

Nadia pressed her fingers against her eyes. Then she lowered her hands and sighed. "Should we tell Caitlin her brother was close by?"

He considered that for a moment, then shook his head. "There's no reason to tell her anything about Michael until we know if he survived."

*   *   *

"I'm sorry," Caitlin said as Lee gently pushed her hands aside and began picking up the broken pieces of cup and saucer. "I'm so sorry."

"It's just a bit of crockery, Caitlin Marie," he said.

"But it's your *mother's* bit of crockery."

He gave her a look that was friendly and exasperated. Not like a brother. Not quite. But not like the boys in Raven's Hill had looked at her either. He liked her, but he didn't want her, didn't expect anything from her. He was a friend. Just a friend.

The relief of that made her eyes fill with tears.

"Ah, don't go getting weepy over a broken dish," Lee said. "Especially when you did us a favor by breaking it."

Caitlin sniffled and blinked back tears.

"Do you think these are pretty?" Lee asked, holding up half the cup. "No."

"Neither do we. And we're pretty sure Mother doesn't like them either, but she's developed a stubborn streak about using them as the everyday dishes. And since we're not company, we get stuck with them. We've been fairly subtle about it, but we've accidentally broken almost enough of these things for her to pack up what's left and start using the set of dishes we bought her as a wedding present when she and Jeb got married." He paused. "She was getting suspicious about the sudden clumsiness when someone besides herself washed the dishes, so you did us a favor since she can't accuse *you* of doing it on purpose."

"Still, they're your mother's dishes."

"We could pack them up and send them home with you."

"I don't want them." The words came out so fast and so emphatic that she startled them both. And it wasn't practical. There was no telling if anything had been saved from the fire. She should welcome being given a few dishes to help her and Aunt Brighid set up housekeeping again.

But she didn't want these dishes. Really, really didn't want them.

Lee grinned, as if he knew what she was thinking—and was maybe planning on how to give them to her at a time when she wouldn't be able to refuse.

Caitlin sniffed again. "Do you think breaking a dinner dish or two would be enough to get the rest sent up to the attic?"

"That might just be enough," Lee agreed. He dumped the pieces into the trash container, then fetched the broom and dustpan to clean up the rest.

They were sitting at the table, sharing a plate of sweet rolls and a pot of koffee, when Nadia walked back into the kitchen.

Something happened out there, Caitlin thought, watching the older woman for a moment before glancing at Lee. Yes, he saw it, too, but he was understanding more.

"We pulled the sweet rolls out of the oven," Lee said. "They browned up a bit too much, but they're still good. Isn't Sebastian coming in?"

Nadia fetched a cup and poured koffee for herself. "He had to get back to the Den."

Lee took a sip of koffee and watched his mother. "I'll go to the island right after breakfast."

"I'm making soup for our midday meal," Nadia said. "Wait until later so you can take some to your sister."

Later. Ever since she'd arrived here yesterday, Nadia had been promising that they would send a message to Glorianna first thing in the morning because Glorianna would be able to explain things in a way Nadia could not. Now that promise was being bent, the message was being delayed. Why?

Because something happened out there. Caitlin looked out the window at the garden.

She had been so young when her mother died; she didn't remember the death itself, but she remembered the feel of the people around her—the hushed voices, the things that were said with nothing more than a look or within a silence.

That same feeling filled the kitchen now. Nadia and Lee knew something, but they weren't going to tell her. Not yet.

And they wouldn't tell her as long as she acted like a weepy child instead of a grown woman strong enough to face the world.

"Would you like some help making the soup?" Caitlin asked.

Nadia studied her for a moment, then smiled. "Yes, I would."

Chapter Sixteen

Sanctuary. The song of it flowed through him, sweet and gentle, but with just enough spice to give the heart delight as well as peace. He wanted to walk the grounds and the gardens, wanted to sit on one of those little islands he'd spotted and twiddle on his whistle, letting the notes become part of whatever message was passed along by the water.

You're almost home.

The thought seemed to float on the air, seemed to slip into his body with every breath. *You're almost home.*

He wasn't anywhere near the land of his birth. Which made him wonder what sort of answers he might get from the man now escorting him to the next stage of his journey.

He still wasn't sure Sebastian and Teaser weren't playing games with him. Oh, he couldn't deny that this part of the world was much stranger than anything he might have imagined, but how could people live as a people if they didn't know *where* they lived?

"Yoshani," he said hesitantly. "I was wondering if you know what a country is?"

"I know what a country is," Yoshani replied with a smile. "And I understand what a landscape is. There can be many landscapes in a single country—and there can be many countries in a single landscape."

Michael frowned. "That makes no sense."

"Which part? Both are true, depending on how one sees the world."

"They can't both be true. The world—"

"—is fluid. Ever-changing. A reflection of ourselves."

That thought wasn't comfortable—or comforting. Not after the things he'd seen lately.

"Which is why I am grateful daily that I can walk here," Yoshani added quietly. "That this place reflects a piece of my heart."

And mine? Michael wondered, almost staggered by the power of wanting that to be true.

Yoshani raised a hand and pointed. "There is the path. It is not much farther now."

For a few steps, the only sound was their shoes on the path.

"Do most people know about the world's . . . odd behavior?" Michael asked. "I've never met anyone in Elandar who knew about this." No one who had admitted it, he amended. But they all knew about people who had walked between the Sentinel Stones and disappeared forever. Crossed over to another landscape. That's how Sebastian and Teaser had explained walking across an ordinary-looking bridge and ending up in another part of the world. Did all the Sentinel Stones work the same way? How could these bridges have existed in Elandar for centuries without anyone but the Merry Makers remembering how they worked?

Maybe people didn't want to remember. Maybe it's time for people to remember once again.

"It is not odd behavior, Michael," Yoshani said. "It is the nature of Ephemera." He stopped walking and stared at the land in front of them. "And no, most people do not understand our world. They are protected from its nature—and their own—by the bedrock of the Landscapers' hearts. But because they have lived in the part of the world that was most shattered by the war between the Dark and the Light, there are many people here who understand the truth."

"And what is the truth?"

Yoshani turned and placed a hand on Michael's chest. "That no matter how much you know about the world and its vastness, the only landscapes you can truly see are the ones that resonate with your own heart." He stepped back. "Come. The border is at the end of that path."

A shiver went down Michael's spine. He'd met Yoshani a few minutes after he crossed the bridge into Sanctuary, and had trusted the man on sight. But when he'd explained his purpose, something had flickered in Yoshani's dark eyes. That flicker hadn't altered his trust in the man, but it did worry him—especially after Yoshani explained that he'd have to cross over to another part of Sanctuary in order to continue his journey.

Now the border—and another piece of the world—was at the end of the path. At least there was comfort in knowing he wouldn't be leaving Sanctuary just yet.

"What's that?" Michael asked when they reached a statue of an otterlike being standing upright and wearing an open, full-length coat or robe. The top of the statue reached his chest, which reminded him of the Merry Makers because they stood at about that same height. And even though the creature looked benign, seeing something else that looked humanlike but wasn't human made him very uneasy.

"That is a River Guardian. They built their homes in the face of the gorge and have tended the River of Prayers for as far back as their race has memories. Their magic is very powerful and has become part of the currents of the river, even beyond the landscape they call home. Just stay on the path and walk past the statue. That will take you to their part of Sanctuary."

Michael hesitated. "Can you come with me?"

Yoshani studied him. "I can accompany you a little farther on the journey if you like."

"I would like. Very much."

Yoshani smiled. "Come then." He walked past the statue and vanished.

Michael hurried after Yoshani, not wanting to get lost or left behind. But when he passed the statue and found himself in another part of Sanctuary, he forgot about his companion and the reason for this journey. Forgot about everything because the river pulled at him, the clash and harmony of its songs commanding all his attention.

Yoshani grabbed Michael's arm to keep him from moving closer to the rushing water. "This river runs through many landscapes and, even here in Sanctuary, the banks are not always safe."

Power, Michael thought as he stared at the river. He'd never felt such a powerful flow of water. Some parts of it looked tame and no deeper than an easily waded stream, and the dainty waterfalls that spilled from small slate islands were restful to the eye and heart. But the rest of it . . .

"It's a battle," he whispered, his eyes drawn to the places where the current seemed to fight itself, and the speed of the river mesmerized him until the lure of becoming part of it was almost irresistible.

"Michael."

He still couldn't take his eyes off the river, was almost deaf to everything except its sound, but he allowed Yoshani to pull him back a few steps.

"What is this place?" he asked.

"I think it has other names in other landscapes, but here it is called Wish River," Yoshani replied. "The River Guardians say it reveals the conflicts that arise when one heart's wants and needs are directly opposed to another heart's wants and needs."

Michael forced himself to look away from the furious energy in the rapids and focused on the serene islands of stone with their dainty waterfalls and calm pools.

Yoshani followed his gaze and smiled. "Not all heart wishes are in conflict with another." He tugged on Michael's arm. "Come. Your journey has not ended, and if you delay too long, you may not find what you seek."

Troubled by the words, Michael turned away from the river—and became aware of an odd sound, like a low, steady thunder. A mist was rising up from the river, softening the air and forming rainbows. Where the mist rose, the river disappeared, and Michael began to suspect he knew what that sound of steady thunder meant.

But he wasn't prepared when Yoshani stopped and looked at him.

Michael's heart pounded in his throat. The river poured over the edge of the world, smashing on tumbles of huge boulders before the water found its way back to the river in the gorge.

"The path down to the river is over there," Yoshani said.

"And why would I want to be going down *there?*"

"Because the River Guardians live down there, and they are the only ones who can help you on the next stage of your journey."

Michael studied the other man. "You're leaving now."

"Yes. But I hope we will meet again, Michael." Yoshani paused, then added, "Remember the river's lesson: A heart wish that is not in conflict with another—or with itself—more easily finds its way." He raised a hand in farewell. "Travel lightly."

Michael watched Yoshani until the man was no longer in sight. Then he turned to the path that led down into the gorge.

More like a staircase carved out of the stone than a path, Michael decided by the time he was halfway down. And the wooden railing not only provided the comfort of a handhold, it distinguished the stairway from the rest of the stone. The River Guardians probably didn't need that distinction, but he figured visitors appreciated being given that much guidance.

By the time he reached the river and a flat area that was a dock, a dozen of the otterlike creatures Yoshani called River Guardians were waiting for him.

"Greetings," Michael said, wishing he'd thought to ask Yoshani if there was a particular greeting that was required or expected.

The River Guardians all bowed slightly, the pads of their paw-hands pressed together chest high. They looked at him out of bright black eyes, and none of them so much as twitched a whisker.

"I seek Belladonna," he said.

Whiskers twitched in response to *those* words. Then one of them—maybe the leader—took a step forward. "Dangerous journey to reach Island in the Mist."

"Where is this island?"

They all turned and pointed.

He looked at the falls and the spume of mist that rose up to the top of the river. Then he looked at the spume rising farther up the river—a spume that reached for the sky and obscured whatever lay behind it.

He took a deep breath and let it out slowly. *I do this to find Caitlin Marie. I do this to find Belladonna. I do this to understand a riddle.* "If that is where I must go, then I will go."

The leader bobbed its head. "This way."

They crowded around him, herding him to a boat that was secured to a post-shaped piece of rock by a leather collar connected to a rope.

Not much of a boat. Fine for rowing around a pond or small lake, but the thing didn't look big enough or sturdy enough to test the strength of that river. Then he realized what else was missing besides size and sturdiness.

"Where are the oars?"

"No oars," the leader said. "Magic boat. Won't work with oars." It pointed at the boat, then at Michael. "The heart is the sails, the will is the tiller."

"You expect me to steer that thing by *wishing* it where I want to go."

"The heart is the sails, the will is the tiller. When the river tests you, it does not hear mind wishes, only the heart." The River Guardian stared at him. "If you are worthy of what you seek, you will find Island in the Mist. If you are not meant to find it, the boat will bring you back here. If your heart needs another place, you will find another landscape. But if your heart tries to deceive the river about why you seek, the river will take you."

I could die doing this, Michael thought as he stared at the boat. "Nothing is ever simple around here, is it?"

"Ephemera is as simple as the heart," the River Guardian replied. "Go or leave?"

He was about to tell the River Guardian the words meant the same thing. Then he realized they didn't, not the way the creature meant them. He could go to the island or leave this part of Sanctuary. What was unspoken between the two words was that if he left he would never find what he sought.

"I'll go."

Only one seat in the stern. *Guess these things aren't meant to hold more than one person,* Michael thought as he gingerly stepped into the boat and settled himself in the center of the seat. He gave a moment's thought to slipping off the travel pack and placing it in the bow of the boat, then decided against it. Except for his whistle, now wrapped in a clean square of cloth, the pack and everything in it was a loan from Sebastian or Teaser, and he didn't need it bouncing out of the boat when he hit rough water. And he had no doubt there *would* be rough water.

One of the River Guardians removed its robe and handed the garment to a companion before it slipped into the water next to the boat. Another River Guardian lifted the leather collar from the stone post and tossed it to the one in the water, who slipped the collar over its head.

It swam against the current, pulling the boat to the center of the river. When they got to that point, the distant spume seemed to pull into itself, giving Michael a good view of what waited to test him.

The river above him split, divided by a large spar of land. The falls he'd seen had been awesome enough, but these . . .

Walls of water. A huge half circle of white thunder falling to the river with nothing to break its long descent. Churning water and wild currents filled the bowl formed by those falls. And the spume of mist that rose from the center of that wild water marked the spot that held the prize—if he could survive the river long enough to reach it.

Suddenly the collar and rope were tossed into the boat and he was adrift, alone, with the currents tugging at the boat, pushing him back down the river, away from the place he needed to go.

The heart is the sails, the will is the tiller, Michael thought. *I seek the Island in the Mist.*

Against all logic and reason, the small boat began moving against the current. On either side of the river, he caught glimpses of buildings shaped from the native stone, blending in so well it was hard to tell where the intentionally created began and the naturally created ended. He wished someone else could steer the boat so he'd be free to just look at the world around him. But every time his attention strayed for more than a few seconds, the boat floundered.

Well, he'd just keep his mind on his business. When he reached the island, he'd be able to stand on the shore and look his fill at the falls and the river.

Except he couldn't see an island, and he was now close enough to the walls of water that the currents were vicious.

What do you seek? It might have been a thousand voices whispering the question—or only one.

"I seek the Island in the Mist." It seemed right to say the words aloud, to give them the weight of his voice.

Why do you seek?

"Heart's hope lies within Belladonna. I seek Belladonna. I seek her help in fighting the Destroy—"

Insanity or rage. It didn't matter. The river turned against him. It flung the boat out of the water, sending it smashing back down into savage currents that were intent on killing him.

What do you seek?

"I seek—" Why was this happening? He was being honest about what he sought!

A wave crashed against the boat, almost knocking him into the river. He flung himself to his knees, grabbing the side of the boat with one hand while the other fumbled to slip the leather collar over his arm to give him that much connection to the boat.

What did he seek? Caitlin Marie. The answer to a riddle. Help defeating the Destroyer of Light before it consumed the parts of the world he knew.

The currents changed, knocking him this way and that.

What do you seek?

Like a series of pictures, the world changed around him. For a moment, he was surrounded by fog, and he could hear the voices of doomed men forever lost. A moment later, he was gliding over a mist-filled lake toward an island he could barely see—and didn't want. A moment after that, he saw a rib cage partially buried under rust-colored sand. Then the currents, the river, and walls of water.

"I seek Belladonna!" he screamed.

Why do you seek?

Going under. Going under. No chance of surviving.

And in that moment, as he surrendered to fate, he felt the warmth of her as she leaned against him, as he wrapped his arms around her in dreams. Almost home. Almost . . .

My heart's hope lies with Belladonna.

Yes, the river whispered. *Yes.*

Glorianna leaned against the wall next to her garden's gate, catching her breath and her balance.

A heart wish that was full of joy and yet bittersweet. Separation and homecoming.

Right here. On her island.

She recognized the resonance of that heart. It had struggled to free itself from the Eater of the World, had almost pulled the Eater into her landscapes.

Now that heart was here on *her* island—and Ephemera was responding like a pet whose best friend had returned home after a long journey. Responding like that to another heart here, on *her* island. The world didn't respond that way to Lee or Nadia when they came to visit. Didn't respond to anyone that way. Not *here*.

Until now, something inside her whispered.

Then she saw him coming up the path from the little harbor. He looked scruffy, despite clothes that appeared to be fairly new. And clearly the river had given him a hard ride, which meant he had tried to hide his true purpose in coming to the island. That was reason enough to be wary of him, even if he hadn't come into her landscapes in such an unusual way.

He stopped and looked around, his smile as warm as spring sunbeams after a long winter as he took in the grounds that were carefully balanced between created flower beds and the natural flow of the land. As he turned toward her two-story house, she stepped away from the garden. She didn't want him in her house until she'd taken a better measure of the man.

Catching the movement, he turned toward her. Moved toward her.

Another jolt of recognition when he got close enough for her to get a good look at his face. Here was the moonlight lover from the painting Sebastian had made for her. But that man had been a fantasy that was . . .

. . . *as real as a dream, a wish, a desire.*

A yearning washed through her. It flowed into Ephemera's currents before she could stop it or deny its importance.

But it didn't go beyond the island. Didn't have to in order to find fulfillment.

More than wariness jangled inside her now. She wasn't sure she could—or should—trust the man coming toward her. But she knew with absolute certainty that, where he was concerned, she couldn't trust herself.

He smiled at her and raised his hands as if to prove he held no weapons.

No weapons? Ha! She'd wager he had toppled a good many women's defenses by wielding that oh-so-charming smile. And did he think she didn't notice his eyes doing that quick, assessing sweep men always did when they saw a woman whose body appealed to them and got them wondering if . . .

Guardians and Guides. Heat flooded her face when she remembered she was dressed in her grubbiest gardening clothes—and had been working in her garden all morning, so she certainly wasn't looking her best.

Which meant the look of appreciation in his eyes was nothing but a deceit.

You said once that the only man worthy of being loved was one who saw you in your gardening clothes and still thought you looked beautiful, her romantic side murmured.

Shut up, she told her romantic side. "What are you looking at?" she growled at him.

His smiled warmed. That son of a succubus was *amused* by her!

"More than an image that haunts my dreams," he replied, his voice flowing over her like warm, silky water. "A woman. A beautiful, real woman."

And because her stupid heart actually went pitty-pat in response to the words, she whipped her temper awake.

"Wasn't sure that bit of a boat would make it," he said, still giving her that charming smile.

"You'll have to be tested," she said, putting an edge in her voice to warn him she wasn't the least bit charmed.

"Already was."

When she didn't respond, his smile faltered. Good.

"What is your name?" he asked.

"Glorianna."

He looked puzzled. And a trifle disappointed? But he rallied fast enough and polished up the smile.

"It's obvious you passed the river's test since you're here," she said. "But there is another test."

Now the charming smile gave way completely to frustration and a hint of ripening anger. Which only stoked her own temper since being mad at him seemed the safest thing to do until she could get him off her island. Not the fairest thing, true, but the safest. Besides, she *needed* to see the results of *this* test.

He slapped his hands against his legs. "*Another* test? Don't you people do anything for fun?"

"Yes," she snapped. "We give strangers tests and then laugh at them while they make fools of themselves."

The frustration vanished as quickly as it had come. He grinned at her as if he'd figured out the answer to a puzzle. "You're just snappy because you got caught out wearing your old clothes."

A mortifying assessment of her temper. Especially because it was partially true.

"Since this is my island, what I wear is no one's business but my own. And I am *not* snappy!"

He rocked back on his heels. "Oh, but you are. Which is a fine thing because the temper brightens your eyes and puts color in your cheeks. Makes you even more beautiful."

He was taller than her and heavier than her, but at that moment, riding on temper and embarrassment, she was pretty sure she could pick him up, haul him down to the shore, and toss him into the river. "Take the test or go back to the river. With or without the boat."

He gave her his most woeful wounded-male look.

She just stared at him.

"Got a brother, don't you?" he asked after a long moment of silence.

"I do." And Lee had perfected that woeful look by practicing on her until *she* had perfected the Stare.

"Thought so." He sighed. "All right, then. Let's get this test done before you have time to think up another."

He followed her to the spot she called the playground. Then he scratched his head and pursed his lips as he looked at a calf-high wooden box that was about the size of a marriage bed and was filled with sand. Another box, about half that length, was attached to it and held a wooden bench and gravel.

"It's a sandbox," he finally said. "Darling, if you're wanting me to build you sand castles, I'm going to need some water along with the sand."

"You won't need anything that's not already with you," Glorianna said. "Leave the pack on the ground out here. You'll want no distractions."

He shrugged off the pack and set it on the ground, then looked at her, clearly waiting for more explanation.

She pointed to the gravel. "You can sit on the bench or stand on the gravel. But don't step into the part with the sand, or you might never find your way back."

She saw a flash of alarm in his eyes and watched his face pale. And wondered what kind of landscapes he'd already seen.

"Heart's hope lies within Belladonna," he said. No charm now. Not even any confidence. Just a vulnerable truth that she could feel resonating inside her like a pure note when he added, "My heart's hope lies with Belladonna."

"Maybe," she replied, her voice rough from trying to control her own tangle of emotions as she silently acknowledged the difference in those two phrases. "It depends on the test."

He hesitated a moment longer, then stepped into the wooden box holding the gravel.

"Don't leave this space until I return for you," she said. *Ephemera, hear me. Show me the landscapes of this heart.*

She walked away, ignoring his "Now just a minute here!" protest. She kept moving away until he turned his attention to the sand. Then she doubled back to quietly come up behind him.

"Fine," he grumbled, lightly kicking at the gravel. "Play tricks on a stranger just because he doesn't know much about . . . *Lady's mercy!*"

Fist-sized stones—many with jagged edges—filled the box that had held sand. A moment later, half the stones sank beneath a foul-smelling bog.

"Just a trick," he whispered. "Can't be real. I can't be doing this. Land doesn't change this fast. Not this fast."

Yes, it can, Glorianna thought. *Under the right—or wrong—circumstances, it can.*

The far corner of the sandbox disappeared under a heavy fog.

Dark landscapes, she thought, feeling a chill go through her. Was there nothing inside him but dark landscapes?

"Lady of Light, have mercy on me," he said, sinking to his knees. Then he cocked his head, as if hearing something. His eyes widened in shock, swiftly replaced by wonder. "The wild child."

The words resonated through the currents of power, leaving Glorianna breathless. It wasn't the way she would have described Ephemera, but it felt exactly right.

"Come on, now. Come on," he said, his voice cajoling. "You know me. You listen to me when I play tunes in the pubs, when I've given people a reason to sing and laugh and put aside their troubles for a while. And I've played tunes for you, when I'm on the road and it's just the two of us. I'm a long ways from home, and maybe you don't know me because of it, but . . ."

Stone rose out of the bog in front of him. Not fist-sized rocks, but a hefty piece of granite that had veins of quartz glinting in the sunlight.

"Well," he said after a brief hesitation, "that's a good stone."

A patch of grass covered the area in front of the stone, and the bog under it turned to earth that smelled like fertile ground after a soft rain.

He laughed, sounding relieved. "Yes! That's the way of it."

A small heart's hope plant grew in front of the quartz-veined rock.

Hold, Glorianna commanded as she moved around the box to where he could see her.

He stood slowly. She kept her eyes on the box that now reflected some of the landscapes of his heart. She didn't need to see his eyes to know they held vulnerability and wariness.

A good heart shadowed by doubts. A hard life when he deserved something better. A balance of Dark and Light.

But the test didn't answer one question: What *was* he?

"Anger makes stone," she said quietly, pointing to the fist-sized, jagged-edged stones. Then she pointed to the granite. "And strength makes stone. Doubt and fear are bogs in the heart. Fog can come from many things, but despair makes the deserts—and hope the oases." Now she looked into his blue-gray eyes. "You don't understand the meaning of what you see, but you know the world listens to you, that you can make things happen. Don't you?"

He looked reluctant to admit to anything, but he nodded.

"What do they call you?" she asked.

"My name is Michael."

She shook her head slowly. "What do they call you?"

A stronger reluctance. She watched his throat muscles work as he swallowed. "Luck-bringer. Ill-wisher." He paused, then added, "Magician."

He said the word as if it had been the bane of his life.

And it has been, she realized. *Just as being declared rogue has been the bane of my life.*

She studied him a little longer. Then she smiled. "Welcome to the Island in the Mist, Magician."

There was real warmth in her smile, honest welcome in her words. And the music of her heart . . . Bright notes entwined with dark tones, forming a song that held the promise of everything he had searched for, waited for, wanted with all his heart. Love and happiness and home all held within a body he hoped to be kissing by the end of the day—and to keep on kissing for the rest of his life.

He'd misunderstood, had gotten things tangled up in his own mind. But . . . No, that wasn't right. He'd gotten here because he'd told people he was seeking Belladonna.

He watched her smile fade and knew it was because he was staring at her, but the music inside her—and its possibilities—held him. Bright notes and dark tones. Could the answer be that simple?

"Glorianna . . . Belladonna?"

Her green eyes chilled as she nodded. "I am Belladonna."

Her darkness is my fate. He grinned at her, and got a narrow-eyed stare in return. That was all right. He was here; so was she. They would build a grand life together—once they figured out how to deal with the Well of All Evil.

"What landscape do you call home?" Glorianna asked.

"My coun—" He stopped. Why bang his head against the wall of stubbornness these people had for refusing to understand the word *country?* "My landscape is called Elandar. My family comes from a village called Raven's Hill."

"Do you know the White Isle?" she asked.

Not knowing why she had tensed in response to his answer, he nodded. "I know of it. My aunt was a Lady of Light there before she came to live with us when my sister and I were children."

"Come with me." She turned toward the enclosure.

Michael started to follow, then stopped so fast he had to pinwheel his arms to keep his balance. "Wait. What will happen if I step out of this box?"

"Nothing. Your heart doesn't dominate here." Now she looked thoughtful. "But it does resonate here."

"Is that going to stay like that?" he asked, waving a hand at the bog, fog, and sand—and that little bit that, in his own mind, represented home and hope.

"No, it's just a playground where Ephemera can safely express itself. It will go back to resting sand when you step out of the gravel box."

He stepped out of the box and silently counted. Before he reached "ten," almost everything had changed back to sand.

"Ephemera," Glorianna said in a warning voice.

"Can't it stay?" Michael asked, feeling a heaviness in his chest at the thought of the heart's hope going away.

"When you feel its resonance, what does it mean to you?" He gave her a puzzled look, so she pointed to the rock, grass, and heart's hope. "What does that represent for you?"

"My homeland," he said without hesitation.

She hesitated, then said, "An access point. All right. It can stay there for the time being. Come with me."

He picked up the travel pack.

She stared at the pack. He didn't see anything that would distinguish it, but when she looked troubled, he wondered if she recognized it as belonging to Sebastian. Should he say something? Reassure her that Sebastian had loaned it to him? Or should he reassure her that he barely knew the incubus–wizard–Justice Maker who ruled a place called the Den of Iniquity?

Not sure what to say, he offered no information—and she asked for none as she led him to the gate in the walled enclosure.

Then he walked into a garden that would change his understanding of the world forever.

*   *   *

Glorianna fiddled with the gate to give herself a moment to think.

He was carrying Sebastian's pack. She recognized it because of the luck piece Lee had given Sebastian—a small, flat stone with a natural hole. It was tied to the pack with a strip of leather and wasn't something that would draw anyone's attention. But that stone was one of the two one-shot bridges Lee had created to assure that Sebastian would be able to reach the Den, no matter what landscape he might find himself in.

Which meant this stranger, this Magician, had been to the Den— or to Aurora—and had met Sebastian.

"How did you get to the River Guardians?" she asked.

"A man named Yoshani showed me the way to their part of Sanctuary."

So Yoshani *and* Sebastian had met Michael—and they, having ways to send her a message, had made the choice to let the river test him. Why?

So I would know he is worthy of what he seeks—even if I'm not sure I trust my response to him or his to me.

"There's something I'd like you to do while I show you the garden," she said, turning to face him.

"Another test?"

The weariness in his voice tugged at her. "Yes, in a way it's another test, but not a difficult one. I'd like to know which parts of the garden resonate for you."

"You mean which ones I feel in tune with?"

"Yes."

He immediately moved to the first bed on the left side of the garden and crouched in front of the statue of a seated woman. "A bittersweet tune for this one. A mother's tune."

"Why do you say that?" Glorianna asked, intrigued by his choice and the way he described his resonance.

"I look at this"—Michael waved a hand to indicate the bed—"and I hear the warmth and strength of a woman who loves and knows how to laugh but has also felt the sorrows that come in a life. So . . . a mother's tune."

Glorianna studied the statue she'd taken from her mother's garden in order to protect Nadia from the Eater of the World. So. This Magician from Raven's Hill resonated with Aurora, which was Nadia's home village.

"Any others?" she asked.

With many of the access points to her landscapes, he held out a hand and tilted it back and forth to indicate a so-so response. He wasn't repelled by those particular places, but they also weren't landscapes that resonated with his heart.

Then they reached the part of her garden that held the dark landscapes. Michael immediately pointed to two of the access points. Then, after a moment's hesitation, he pointed to a third.

"You know the waterhorses," Glorianna said.

Michael nodded but gave her a puzzled look. "How did you know?"

"You pointed to their landscape."

That slight blankness in his eyes. He wasn't a Landscaper in the way she would normally use the term, but he clearly had a strong connection to and power over Ephemera. It scared her to think that he'd been going about his part of the world, influencing Ephemera when he had so little idea of what he was doing.

"And you know the Merry Makers," she said, and added silently, *And the Den of Iniquity.*

He nodded again.

"What about these?" Now she moved quickly through the garden, not giving him a chance to tell her about other connections he might have to her landscapes. She stopped in front of the section that held the Places of Light.

"Oh." He swayed to a stop, then closed his eyes and smiled. "Oh, this is a grand part of the garden."

She could see the truth of it in his face, could feel the air pulse between them as he resonated with those Places of Light. While it hadn't affected him in the same way, he had resonated just as strongly with the three dark landscapes he had pointed out.

"Does any one of them appeal to you in particular?" she asked softly.

He said he was from Elandar, came from the village of Raven's Hill. She wasn't sure what to think when he passed over the access point for the White Isle and pointed to the access point that led to the part of Sanctuary that was connected to Aurora.

Michael turned in a slow circle, but the way she had designed the beds that represented her landscapes made it impossible to see all of the garden from any one place.

"I wouldn't want her to face the dangers of the journey," he said, "but I wish my sister could see this garden. She found an old walled garden on the hill near the family home, and she's struggled for years to make something of it."

She could still hear him talking, but Glorianna was no longer listening to the words. "Your *sister* has a garden like this?"

"Oh, nothing so grand, but this place reminds me of her bit of garden."

Guardians and Guides, she thought. *There are Landscapers out there who don't know who they are or what they can do when they play with a bit of land. Especially if they come from the old bloodlines and are like me.*

Raven's Hill. A garden. A resonance that tangled with her own on the White Isle. And a man who had dared the river in order to find her. A dream lover who wasn't just a dream.

"Glorianna?" Michael reached for her. She took a step back. "What's wrong?"

"You came seeking Belladonna. Why?"

A blush stained his cheeks. "I've seen you in my dreams. Loved you in my dreams."

She could feel the warmth of his hands—a memory held within a dream.

"I came to find the answer to a riddle—and I found you. 'Heart's hope lies within belladonna.'" He looked around the garden. "I'm thinking the answer to defeating the Well of All Evil is right here in this garden. Because this garden is your heart, isn't it, Glorianna Belladonna?"

She felt breathless. Felt light enough to float with the clouds—and heavy enough to break the earth as she sank into it.

A test of the river to prove he was worthy of what he sought. *A different kind of Landscaper,* who might be able to show her an answer she couldn't see by herself. And maybe—*maybe*—someone with whom she could share her home and the island. Someone who could accept Belladonna as well as Glorianna.

"I think I need to hear the whole story of how you ended up here, but I would rather you tell it to the whole family at the same time," she said. "So we'll have to go to my mother's house."

"She lives on the island?"

His hopefulness was so transparent that she had to smile. "No, she lives in Aurora. We'll have to cross over to that landscape."

He paled. "Cross over. Then it's a ways from here."

"Yes, in some ways it is a ways from here," she replied. "And in others it's no farther than a heartbeat away."

He took the step that brought him close enough to brush a finger along her cheek. "Well, that's true of a good many things, isn't it?"

Who are you, Magician? "Yes," she said. "It is."

Chapter Seventeen

"Damn the darkness," Michael said, bracing his feet as if that would help him regain his mental balance. Glorianna had told him that reaching Aurora and her mother's house required nothing more than taking a step between here and there, but he'd expected a little more ceremony. He'd expected a little more warning than "hold my hand and take a step forward." Although why he should keep expecting something more was a puzzlement.

Face it, my lad. You just don't want to look this straight in the eyes and admit you've never known half of what must have been going on around you.

"I don't hear the falls anymore," he said, turning in a circle to look around. Nice house, but not too grand. Well cared for grounds and . . .

He felt his heart skip a beat when he saw the stone walls on the other side of a narrow brook.

"My mother's walled garden," Glorianna said. "Come to the house. By now you'd probably like a bite to eat."

"I would, thank you." He'd been grateful when she'd taken him up to her house on the island to freshen up and put on a clean shirt before making this visit to her mother. And he'd wondered if it had been her own manners or a customary lack of hospitality that had left out an offer of food or drink—until he realized her embarrassed mutter about reaching her mother's house in time for the midday meal meant she'd checked her larder while he'd been washing up and had found it a bit too bare.

Which made him wonder if that was due to a lack of attention on her part or a lack of means to keep food on the table. Maybe he could offer to till some ground for a kitchen garden. Of course, after they were married, he could—

Whoa! Slow down, lad. Just because your heart has settled on the matter doesn't mean she's thinking of sharing home and hearth with the likes of you.

"I don't think my mother is serving meals out in the garden today," Glorianna said, sounding amused. "If you want food, we have to go into the kitchen."

"What? Oh." How long had he been staring at that garden while he'd been dreaming up a future that . . .

You won't grow old together, some part of him whispered. *Except in your dreams.*

Why not? he asked that shadow self, feeling defiant. *No one else has put a ring on her hand. She might settle for the likes of me.*

"Michael?"

Pulling himself out of the argument going on in his head and heart, he smiled at her without answering the "what's wrong?" question he'd heard in her voice. They hadn't gone more than a few steps when he stopped again and studied the trees and the shape of the land. "I think I was near here early this morning."

"If Sebastian was your escort to the bridge that led to Sanctuary, you were"—Glorianna turned slightly and pointed—"less than a mile from here in that direction."

"That ripe bastard," Michael muttered.

Her green eyes chilled, warning him off.

"You have feelings for him." Seeing the truth of that scraped at him enough to ignore the warning chill. "When he was whispering to you in the moonlight, did he mention he has a wife?"

"Well, he was whispering," she replied with insincere sweetness. "I may not have caught everything he said."

Michael clamped his teeth together to keep from saying something that might have her showing him the door before he ever got the chance to know her—or for her to know him. Because he wanted to know her, both for himself and for . . .

Ah, Caitlin Marie. Now that you're lost in a world gone mad, I finally found someone who might understand your heart.

When they reached the house, Glorianna opened the door just enough to poke her head inside and ask, "Anyone flying about?" He didn't hear an answer, but she swung the door open, stepped inside the kitchen, and said, "Sebastian, darling, when you were whispering sweet nothings to me in the moonlight, why didn't you tell me you had a wife?"

As Michael stepped into the kitchen, he registered the presence of other people in the room, but his focus was on the ripe bastard sitting at the table looking much too much at home. It gave him a mean pleasure to see Sebastian turn red and choke in response to Glorianna's words.

"Daylight!" Sebastian said when he was able to breathe again. "Who would have said a thing like . . . Oh. *You.*"

"Yes, it's me," Michael said, approaching the table as Sebastian rose to face him. "Despite your little trick this morning, you haven't seen the last of me yet."

"That's obvious since you're here," Sebastian replied.

"And it's obvious to me that your kind have no respect for the marriage vows."

"My kind? *My kind?* I wouldn't be slinging mud if I were you, Magician. *Your* kind takes off his wedding ring when he comes to the Den and pretends he doesn't have a wife, but we figure it's better to have the succubi play with the randy human goats than have those men making promises to girls in their own landscapes. The girls would get their hearts broken—or worse; the succubi just give those men what they came for and lighten their pockets in the bargain."

"And you think that's honorable?"

"It's honest."

"That's enough." A black-haired, green-eyed man wedged himself between them and shoved hard enough to push Michael and Sebastian back a step.

Two against one, Michael thought bitterly. Brothers or first cousins, if the family resemblance was anything to go by. But if he was going to get a beating, he was going to take one last jab at earning it. Looking at Sebastian, he said, "You shame your house and your family."

Cold fury leaped into Sebastian's eyes. Michael braced for whatever a pissed-off wizard would do to him. And then . . .

"Why is everyone shouting?" Lynnea asked, stepping into the kitchen.

Michael took a step back, distancing himself from the interrupted fight. How long had she been standing there? Did she know about Sebastian and Glorianna? Or had his own ill-considered words revealed her husband's betrayal? He'd be delighted to see the ripe bastard shut out of the marriage bed, but Lynnea didn't deserve having her heart trampled. And it didn't speak well of Glorianna's heart that she would act the friend while helping herself to another woman's husband. Which might be Sebastian's fault entirely, him being the incubus and all.

Fool. You should have held your tongue and just done a little ill-wishing so Sebastian would get what he deserved.

"Michael?"

At first glance, he thought the person coming into the kitchen behind Lynnea was a feminine-faced boy, but the voice . . .

"Caitlin?" He stepped around Sebastian and the other man. His little sister was *here*, alive and well. "Caitlin Marie?"

He knew that particular smile, had looked for it each time he'd come home from his wandering. Her smile of welcome.

He snatched her off her feet and hugged her hard, feeling laughter bubbling up while tears stung his eyes. He set her down, and leaned back to get a good look at her and assure himself that she was, indeed, well. Which is when the little detail that had caused him to mistake her gender really registered.

"By the Light, girl! What did you do to your hair? You've cut it so short people will be mistaking you for a boy."

"No, they won't," Teaser said, suddenly appearing in the doorway beside Lynnea. "Not with a nice pair of tits like she's got."

Michael spun around, pushing Caitlin behind him. "And what business do you have to be noticing her titties?"

Teaser shrugged. "I'm just saying."

Caitlin gave him a shove, which made him turn and stare at her. Raising her chin, she said defiantly, "I don't want to look like a girl— and I'm not going to be any man's whore."

Before Michael could roar about that, someone grabbed his ear and tugged him to a place at the kitchen table.

"Sit," an older, dark-haired woman said, ignoring his yelp when she gave his ear another tug. "All this shouting over foolishness. And now you've got the birds upset."

That's when he focused again on the room in general and realized the noise filling the kitchen wasn't coming from anything human.

He sat long enough for her to release his ear. Then he popped up from his chair, intending to give Caitlin Marie—and Teaser—a piece of his mind.

The dark-haired woman whacked him on the head with a wooden spoon. "Sit!" she said. "You too, Sebastian. Lee. Teaser." Each name was accompanied by her pointing to a chair. "Glorianna, you and Caitlin Marie need to talk, so you girls go into the parlor. Lynnea, you go with them. And the rest of you *be quiet!*"

In the hush that followed, Michael looked at Glorianna and recognized a woman who was working up to being well and truly mad. He figured her anger was going to be generously heaped on *his* head for making everyone aware of Sebastian's infidelity, but he intended to do his best to see that the ripe bastard got a fair share of it.

"I think the Magician and I need to discuss a few things and clear the air," Glorianna said.

"Mud wallow?" Lee asked.

"Lee!"

He hunched his shoulders when the older woman smacked the table with her spoon. Then she looked at Glorianna. "And I think you need to speak to Caitlin Marie. You may be a powerful Landscaper and a Guide of the Heart, but in this house you are my daughter, and you will do as you're told."

The air snapped and crackled between the two women.

Lynnea put an arm around Caitlin's shoulders. "Let's go into the parlor like Nadia asked." She and Caitlin disappeared into another room.

Glorianna hesitated for one more crackling moment, then followed them.

"You should be ashamed of yourselves," Nadia said, glaring at the men around her kitchen table. "You're grown men and you're acting like . . . like . . ."

"Hooligans?" Michael suggested, giving Nadia his charming smile.

She whacked him on the shoulder. Apparently charm didn't work with the women in this family.

"Hooligans," Nadia said. "I don't know what that means, but it sounds like the way you're behaving. Yes. Hooligans."

"Thanks very much," Lee said dryly. "Now you've taught her another name to call us when she's annoyed about something."

Nadia gave Lee a whack.

"He started it," Sebastian said, pointing at Michael. "Coming in here and acting all pissy. Accusing me of being unfaithful—and with my cousin no less."

Cousin? Glorianna hadn't said anything about being Sebastian's cousin. In fact, she . . . No, a prick of jealousy had spurred his assumption that she was defending a lover. But after making what he considered to be an honest mistake, she had helped him down the wrong path by not correcting that assumption. "She's got some brass to be blaming *me*," he muttered.

"That's enough," Nadia snapped. She gave each one of them the Stare. "You're not little boys who can call each other names and waggle your privates at each other."

"Trust me, Auntie," Sebastian said, "there's no one sitting at this table who is interested in waggling his privates at another man."

"Sebastian Justicemaker."

Sebastian winced.

Michael felt a foolish urge to stick out his tongue and say "Nyah, nyah," but Nadia was standing next to him and beat his Aunt Brighid by a long arm when it came to retaliating against male foolishness. He hadn't had anyone whack him with a spoon since he was fifteen, and he'd figured he'd outgrown that stage of his life.

Apparently not.

"As I said"—Nadia gave each of them another dose of the Stare— "you're not little boys who can indulge in name-calling and taking pokes at one another. You're powerful men who have a powerful influence on this world. And starting trouble just to make trouble is unacceptable behavior from every one of you. And that goes for you too, Teaser."

"I didn't do anything," Teaser muttered, slouching in his chair. "Just said the girl had a nice pair of tits."

"Where I come from, if a man says something like that to a girl's brother, the next thing he'd better be saying is the date of the wedding," Michael said darkly.

"Well, we're not in your part of the world, are we?" Teaser replied in a prissy tone of voice. "If you're going to get all scrappy about the way we live, go back where you came from."

I don't know how.

Powerful men . . . who had a powerful influence on the world.

Remembering the sandbox—and how the world had changed to reflect his feelings—he leaned back in his chair and looked out the kitchen window. Nothing appeared different, but how could he know how much influence he had on the world? Was a nearby village filling up with heavy fog at this very moment? Was some farmer's field suddenly full of stones that might lame a horse or break a plow? How was he to know?

"Did I break the world?" He almost expected to hear Aunt Brighid's voice saying, *You're puffing up your consequence, boy.* But no one in that kitchen dismissed his question—and a true, pure fear began to shiver through him as he looked up at Nadia. "You said we were powerful men. I'm a Magician. A luck-bringer. An ill-wisher. The world listens to me. I can make things happen." Memories stirred, and he added in a horrified whisper, "Even when I don't mean to."

Nadia tossed the wooden spoon onto the table, then hurried to the back door, pausing long enough to yell "Glorianna!" before she was out the door and running toward her walled garden. A moment later, when Glorianna rushed into the kitchen, Lee pointed to the door and said, "Go."

She hesitated a moment, and Michael saw the flash of understanding as their eyes met. Then she was gone, following her mother into the gardens.

Michael's stomach started rolling. It was getting hard to breathe. "Rory Calhoun." The memory sank its teeth into his heart.

He'd been sixteen years old and already planning to leave Raven's Hill the day young Rory Calhoun and two friends met their fate in the old quarry.

He'd gone for a walk, wearing the new coat Aunt Brighid had bought him as a fare-thee-well gift. Inside, he was a swirl of fear and excitement at the prospect of leaving home for the first time since his father had settled him, his mother, and baby Caitlin into the cottage that, along with the land that came with it, had been the sole inheritance the man could offer his wife and children. Then his father had resumed the wandering life and, two years later, his mother had walked into the sea.

But that day, Michael wasn't thinking beyond the dimly remembered romance of the wandering life, had seen it as a way to escape the looks people gave him and Caitlin Marie. He had seen a way to earn some coins with the music he'd taught himself to play on the tin whistle he'd found in a trunk of his father's belongings.

That day, his mind and heart had been filled with the sense of adventure and the pleasure of wearing a new coat instead of a patched, secondhand one. Then Rory and two friends began following him, taunting him, throwing clods of dirt that just missed hitting him and dirtying his new coat.

Until Rory had thrown a clod that hit him square in the back. Stung that the people in this village wouldn't let him have one nice thing, he turned and looked at Rory. "May you get everything you deserve."

"Ooooo," Rory said, waving his hands. "He's ill-wishing me. Ooooo."

They continued to follow him until they reached the old quarry. Then they abandoned him to play "dare you"—a game all the boys in the village had played at one time or another to prove manliness or bravery or some other foolish thing. Usually the game was played on the other side of the quarry, where there were slabs and ledges of stone that weren't too far below the top. A fall on that side of the quarry might end with a broken leg or arm. On this side was a steep slope that changed to a sheer drop to the quarry floor. Any boy who fell on this side of the quarry would end up at the bottom, broken and dying.

He'd sometimes wondered what would have happened if he'd kept going, kept walking. But the air around him had trembled with a discordant song, and something about those young voices pulled at him. So he'd turned and saw them standing much too close to the edge. But that was the whole point of playing "dare you." The quarry's edge wasn't stable. Walk too close and a section of stone might break away. The winner of the game was whichever boy stood closest to the edge and stamped a foot, daring the stone to break.

"They're not bad boys," he'd whispered as he'd watched the three shuffle up to the quarry's edge. "Well, two of them aren't. Without Rory, the other two would settle down and grow up."

In that moment before things changed forever, he heard notes so harshly abrasive they made him wince. One harsh note, actually, and two others that weren't quite in tune. Two that might fit back into the song that was Raven's Hill if given a chance.

In that moment before things changed forever, he saw all three boys jump up and land on the edge with a two-footed stomp.

Before he could move, the boys disappeared, replaced by the roar of stone and air filled with dust.

Michael ran to the quarry, stopping a man-length from the new edge, then testing the ground, step by step, until he could look into the quarry.

Rory Calhoun hung on the edge of a new, sheer drop, impaled on a broken spire of stone. His eyes stared unblinking at the sky, but the fingers twitched, the hands tried to clench. Alive then . . . for a few moments longer.

As he stared at the boy, Michael realized he was hearing terrified mewling. Realized Rory's legs hung over the drop.

"Boys?" he called.

"Help! *Help!*"

Two of them, alive. Clinging to their friend's legs. Which had probably contributed to that spire of stone punching through Rory's body.

As he stripped off his coat and dropped it, he studied the side of the quarry. There were now juts of stone he could stand on and knobs of stone for handholds. Best to belly over the side and lower himself down to the first ledge, which would get him close enough to reach the boys. He hoped.

The moment before he eased his legs over the edge, two things occurred to him: that the ledge might be a little too far down for him to get himself back out of the quarry, and that he couldn't let the boys see what had happened to Rory.

He grabbed his coat. With a wrist flick to spread the cloth, he dropped the coat over Rory. Then he lowered himself over the edge.

Stretched to his full length, his fingers clinging to the edge, his toes barely brushed the ledge beneath him. Would it hold him? Would it hold him and the weight of a boy? It had to hold. *Had to.*

Saying a quick prayer to the Lady of Light, he let go of the edge, landing solidly on the stone beneath him. He pressed himself against the quarry wall, hardly daring to breathe while he waited a few moments to see if the ledge would hold. Then he pulled off his belt, made a loop at one end, and wrapped the leather around his fist a couple of times before he shifted his weight to bring himself closer to the other boys.

As clear as the memory was up to that point, the rest was fragmented images: a boy's terrified face looking up at him; the weight as a boy slipped a hand through the loop in the belt and let go of Rory's leg; the arrival of his friend Nathan, who had come looking for him; the look in the eyes of the men who had helped pull the boys out of the quarry—a look that said they weren't sure if they should praise Michael for helping rescue the boys or blame him for the fall; the sound of men half swearing, half crying as they brought Rory out of the quarry and saw the damage that had been hidden under the coat.

He stayed in Raven's Hill long enough to see Rory buried and stand with his aunt and the rest of the villagers to offer his condolences to the family. The next day, he set off on his wanderings. His new coat had been ruined, of course, and there wasn't enough money to spare for another extravagance. So he'd started off on his new life wearing a patched, secondhand coat—and wondered if it was all he deserved.

"It wasn't your fault," Lee said.

Michael braced his head in his hands. He hadn't realized he'd been talking out loud while reliving that memory. "There were some in Raven's Hill who thought otherwise."

"It wasn't your fault," Lee said again. "If you hadn't been there that day, most likely all three of those boys would have died."

He remembered Glorianna as she stood beside the sandbox, studying the landscapes of his heart. *Anger makes stone. And strength makes stone.*

"So I willed a piece of stone to punch through a boy's body? Is that what you're saying?" Knowing now that he might have done exactly that made him ill.

"Don't argue with him, Lee," Sebastian said, sitting back. "He's not ready to listen."

A cold spot on his back. It took Michael a moment to realize it was the loss of the weight and warmth of a hand resting on his shoulder blade that he was feeling now. That warmth had been there all through his memory of Rory. That comfort of a human touch telling him silently he wasn't alone.

Until Sebastian sat back.

Who were these people? Michael wondered at the same time something inside him asked, *How can I be one of them?*

Before the silence around the table could become awkward, Glorianna and Nadia walked into the kitchen at the same time Lynnea and Caitlin eased into the kitchen from the doorway leading to the rest of the house.

"Is everyone done shouting?" Lynnea asked.

"For the moment," Nadia replied. She looked at the people in her kitchen and nodded. "We'll have to use the dining room. The kitchen table is too small for so many. Girls, you'll set the table and help me fix the soup and sandwiches. That will be a simple-enough meal."

"After we eat, I think we'll"—Sebastian gestured to indicate Lee and Teaser—"take Michael to the Den for a few hours."

"We'll see," Nadia said, going over to the counter to start another pot of koffee. "You're not ten years old anymore, but the rules still apply. If your behavior creates stones and weeds in my personal garden, you will clear the stones and weeds out of my personal garden."

"But—" Sebastian studied his aunt for a moment, then huffed. "Yes, Auntie. The four of us will be happy to clear the stones and weeds out of the garden."

"Teaser and I weren't involved in this," Lee protested.

"Now you are," Sebastian replied, which earned him a scowl from his cousin.

"And after the meal," Glorianna said, looking at Caitlin, "you're going to tell me everything you know about your garden. And you"—those green eyes locked onto Michael—"are going to tell me exactly how you got to this part of Ephemera."

Glorianna stood by the kitchen window, watching four men spend an unfathomable amount of time sorting out a few gardening tools. "Do you think they'll actually get anything done?"

"Two of them might dither and not take me as seriously as they should," Nadia said, bringing two mugs of koffee to the table, "but Sebastian and Lee aren't likely to forget what will happen if I go out to inspect the beds and find a stone or weed."

She turned away from the window and grinned. "It was more devastating because you were so polite about it, smiling at them as you handed them lanterns and informed them you would keep their dinners warm, no matter how long it took them to finish cleaning up the garden."

"They were at an age when food was a fine motivator," Nadia said, smiling. Then the smile faded. "So what do you think of this Magician?"

"He doesn't see the way we do, doesn't feel the resonance the way we do," Glorianna said, sitting down at the table. "He talks about luck-bringing and ill-wishing and the music of a place. I'm not sure if he's a Guide of the Heart or a Landscaper or some combination of both. Then there's Caitlin, who definitely *is* a Landscaper, but more like me than the Landscapers who were at the school. She's been tending a garden with no knowledge or understanding about her connection to the places held within those walls. And Michael looks after his landscapes by wandering from place to place, making a circuit in order to tend to each of them before going back home for a few days to rest in a place that resonates with another's heart. Which is not so different from the Landscapers who traveled through their landscapes and then returned to the school to rest." She sipped her koffee. "They may have borders in this Elandar, but they have no boundaries, no bridges. Their piece of the world didn't shatter. Maybe if I can understand how the landscapes work in their part of the world, I can find a way to make this part of the world whole again."

"Do you really want to do that?" Nadia asked.

Glorianna stared out the window rather than look at her mother.

"The Eater of the World is out there, Glorianna. It has touched Elandar three times that we know of. Four if you include that haunted stretch of sea that Michael passed through. Instead of putting the world back together, maybe you should be thinking of breaking more of it."

She rubbed her forehead, trying to deny the headache starting to brew behind her eyes. "Lee is the only Bridge working with us. He can't take on the burden of doing more."

"Then what are you going to do?"

Glorianna glanced out the window. It looked like the men were getting something done now. "I think Sebastian is right. Caitlin and Michael need some time together, and the rest of us need a few hours to set aside the weight of the world. Tonight we'll go to the Den and eat at Philo's, listen to music, and . . ." *Remember what romance feels like?*

When she had first seen *Moonlight Lover,* she'd wondered if the fantasy lover was an incubus—someone Sebastian knew and had used as a model for the painting. Then Michael had showed up on her island—someone who was, and wasn't, like her.

Considering the assessing way he had looked at her and that slip of jealousy he'd shown when he'd thought Sebastian was a lover, the odds were good that he would be interested in a night's romp in bed. But did she really want that from him, with him?

In some ways, she wanted that very much. But her heart needed more. With Ephemera so dependent right now on the choices she made, she had to be careful.

"We're going to eat at Philo's, listen to music, and . . .?" Nadia asked.

"And tomorrow Caitlin and I will pay a visit to the White Isle," Glorianna said, tucking the idea of romance away, along with her heart.

Long ago, beyond my memory and yours, spirits who were the voice of the world walked among us. And they knew things no ordinary human could know. Like the secret to using the Door of Locks.

Now the Door of Locks was hidden in a garden that lived in the heart of a magic hill, and that hill was the country home of the spirits who resided in this part of the land. When a person had a powerful need for something that was just beyond his grasp, he would set his feet on the road and follow his heart—and if the spirits decided he was worthy, he would find that garden.

And when he reached the garden, which was protected by high walls and a barred gate, a spirit would appear and ask, "What do you seek?"

Now, a foolish man might say he was seeking gold or jewels or some other kind of treasure. He might be allowed to enter the garden after giving such an answer—but he might not. Because the correct answer to the question—and this is most important to remember—the correct answer is "I seek the hope that lives within my heart." Give the spirit *that* answer, and the garden's gate will always open.

And then, once you're inside . . . It's a lovely place, as beautiful as a dream, and you're allowed to wander and look and sit for as long as you please. When you're ready, the spirit takes you to the Door of Locks.

There are one hundred identical locks on the door, and while you're standing there, trying to fathom it all, the spirit reaches into your heart and takes out a key, and says, "Every lock leads to a different place that lives within you. Some are dark places, some are light places, some are full of struggle and sorrow while others will shower your days with joy. Choose a lock. The key will fit any one of them. Choose where your heart needs to go. Choose."

And that is what you must do—choose. Now, some people are hasty, ignoring the spirit's warning about the nature of the locks and thinking that since the locks all look the same they'll all be the same. And some people don't ask for the lock they truly want because it's high up in a corner of the door or too low to the ground and they don't want to be inconveniencing the spirit and they figure a lock that's easy to reach will do just as well.

But it won't do as well. I'll tell you that now. It won't do, and if you settle for what is easy instead of what you truly want, you may never discover the hope that lives in your heart.

So you choose wisely, and you choose well, and you pick the lock that matters the most to you at that moment. Then the spirit takes the key that was plucked from your heart and slips it into that lock.

It changes you. It doesn't matter if you end up in a place you didn't know existed or in the village where you've lived your whole life. It changes you—and you will never again see the world in quite the same way.

Except we've lost the way of it, you see.

A dark and terrible Evil swept through the land in that long-ago time, and the spirits disappeared. Some say they were all destroyed in a great battle against that Evil. Others say that those who survived went into hiding and still tend the magic garden. No one knows the answer, just as no one knows how to find the magic hill or a spirit who can pluck a key out of a person's heart and open the Door of Locks.

But I can tell you this. That magical place still exists. And someday someone will remember how to find it—and how to open the door that leads to all the hope that lives in the heart.

—*Elandar story*

Chapter Eighteen

Boredom gave birth to bravery.

The True Enemy had not found It. The male Enemy had not pursued It. The voices of the haunting dead entertained It, but no living humans had sailed into Its watery landscape recently, so there had been no minds to play with, no fear to savor. As It explored the borders of this landscape, trying to sense the presence of either Enemy, It remembered the delight of being among so many minds that did not know the Eater of the World, that were unaware of the source of the whispers that floated through the twilight of waking dreams, urging humans to make choices that would dim the Light a little more. Most of the humans It had encountered in the seaport called Kendall enjoyed the shiver produced by scary stories but no longer truly believed in the things that moved in the dark, ready to hunt them.

It would go back to Kendall and help them remember, give them a reason to believe.

And then It would feast.

The carnal carnival. The Den of Iniquity certainly was that—and more than a girl who had spent her life in Raven's Hill could imagine.

The colored lights that gave everything a festive, make-believe quality. The people strolling down the streets—or performing in the streets. And the music! Oh, Michael played his tunes, and she liked the music of her own country well enough, but this! Hot and edgy, pumping through the blood and making the heart pound with the need to move with the rhythm.

And Teaser, all cocky and full of fun, teaching her how to dance while Michael got all stony-faced. Until Glorianna started dancing, too. That had changed the man's tune fast enough. And did her prissy-prig—how she loved that word!—brother think no one had seen him kissing Glorianna after the dancing? Ha! So when Teaser . . .

"You've never been kissed?" Teaser had asked.

Caitlin shook her head.

Glancing around, he nudged her into the alley next to Philo's place.

"It's just a bit of fun, you know that?" he asked. "I don't want to get into trouble for a little kiss."

"In trouble with my brother?"

"No, with Sebastian's auntie."

The fact that Nadia could worry him tickled something inside her—and also made her feel safe. "Just a bit of fun," she agreed.

Oh, it was more than a bit of fun, that first kiss. It started out sweet and gentle—and ended as hot and edgy as the music. Might not have ended at all if Michael hadn't walked into that alley with Glorianna in tow.

Probably just as well that they had all spent the rest of the visit within sight of Sebastian's auntie.

Caitlin stood at the end of Nadia's personal gardens and breathed in the crisp morning air. Across a little stone bridge—which Lee had assured her was nothing more than an ordinary bridge—was the walled garden that protected Nadia's landscapes.

Landscapes! According to Nadia, the world was made up of lots of broken pieces fitted together but not necessarily in a tidy way of one village fitting with the next if you kept following a road. Oh, no. Nothing as simple as that. And them—Nadia and Glorianna—sitting at a table with her last night and asking, as calmly as you please, what landscapes, what parts of her country, were held in her garden. How was she to know? And why was Glorianna so sure they would be able to reach the White Isle? *How* was she planning to reach it? Was she figuring to have Lee cart them around on his little bit of an island?

"Like a magic carpet with trees," she muttered.

"Talking to yourself, Caitlin Marie?" Michael asked as he came up the garden path to stand beside her.

She stiffened. She'd missed him so much, had wanted to see him so much—and now he seemed like just another bully, the way he had yelled at her yesterday and acted like a surly dog when they all went to the Den last evening.

Thinking about the Den made her think about Teaser and *that* made her think about . . .

"You're blushing," Michael said.

"You had no right to be so mean to Teaser," she replied, giving him her coolest tone. Not cold, because he was her brother and she wouldn't be cold to him, but chilly enough to warn him off. "We weren't doing anything wrong." At least, not by the Den's standards. Even Nadia had said as much, hadn't she?

"Can we not talk about Teaser? I don't need a sour belly so early in the morning. Here. I brought a peace offering. Will you accept?" He held out a mug of rapidly cooling koffee.

She took the mug of koffee but wasn't sure if she was ready to warm to him. "Teaser was nice to me. The boys in the village were never nice to me."

"He's an incubus. There were things he was wanting from you that you wouldn't be knowing anything about."

"I'm not a child, Michael," Caitlin snapped. "What he wanted was no different from what the boys back home wanted, but at least Teaser was showing me a good time, and he *didn't* expect me to go down on my back!"

She saw pain slash across Michael's face before he looked away, focusing on that walled garden that led to other parts of the world.

"The world has disappeared right out from under me, Caitie, and I've lost my balance," he said quietly.

He hadn't called her "Caitie" since she was a little girl. She hadn't allowed him to call her "Caitie," not since he'd taken up the wandering life. That had been his punishment for leaving her. But she didn't have the heart to slap at him for it. Not when she was feeling lost too.

"I thought I knew my life," he continued. "I thought I was resigned to the bitterness of it and the hardship of it and the fear that I'd enter a village just as I'd done for years but this would be the time the people would turn against me because I was a Magician, and all their troubles would be laid on my shoulders. I thought I was resigned to the things I couldn't have because of what I was, and I had found a kind of contentment, even joy, when my being in a place made a difference to someone. But the world is so much more than I thought it was— and I'm not sure of who or what I am anymore. I'm scared for myself, and I'm scared for you. I've seen the monster, Caitlin Marie. I've seen the thing that wants to chew up the Light and leave us all in the Dark. And may the Lady of Light have mercy on us, because I don't know how we're going to stop that thing."

Caitlin looked back toward the house and saw Glorianna and Lee heading toward her and Michael. There was still enough distance between them not to be overheard, but she lowered her voice just the same. "Do you think they know how to fight the monster?"

"I'm thinking if they knew, they would already be standing on the battleground. It's clear from the things that were said—and not said—last night that they all think Glorianna is the key to fighting this battle."

Caitlin's breath rushed out of her, leaving her light-headed for a moment. As clearly as if she'd done it yesterday, she could feel herself as a girl sitting near the attic window, looking at an old storybook she'd found in a finely made wooden box, puzzling out the words with her newly acquired reading skills.

"The Warrior of Light," she whispered, staring at Glorianna.

No.

Michael denied the words with all his will, but the truth of it clanged through him like alarm bells shattering a peaceful morning.

No, he thought, struggling to breathe. *Glorianna is the key to finding the Warrior of Light, but she isn't the Warrior.*

"I remember now," Caitlin said loudly. "The Warrior of Light must drink from the Dark Cup."

Michael flinched, remembering the day he'd gone searching for Caitlin and found her sitting in the attic with the book open in her lap, crying for the woman in the story. Had she been old enough to understand the full tragedy of the tale?

My heart's hope lies with Belladonna. She can't be the Warrior of Light. Can't be. Lady of Light, please let it be someone else.

"What did you say?" Glorianna asked sharply, hurrying those last steps to reach them. She stared at Caitlin. "The Warrior of Light must drink from the Dark Cup. Isn't that what you said?"

Michael felt a wind blow through him. Felt Caitlin shudder in response to the force of it. Saw Lee tense and lean as if to bend with it. And saw Glorianna Belladonna standing before him—face cold, green eyes wild, a flame in the Dark.

A flame that would destroy everything in its path.

Then the moment passed, and he wondered if he'd just imagined that wind blowing through him—until he looked at Caitlin and saw the same conflict in her face.

He had imagined nothing. Something *had* happened. The world had changed, and nothing would be the same for any of them because he was standing in a garden in a part of the world he hadn't known existed, looking at a woman who was the living version of an ancient tale that was part of his family's legacy.

On his ninth birthday, his father, Devyn, had taken him up to the attic and showed him the box of books that held the old stories.

"I've little enough to give you, Michael," Devyn said, resting a hand on the box he'd taken out of a specially made cupboard. "There's this cottage, but it's usually passed on through the female side of our family line. Since it came to me, I guess there are no others anymore who can lay claim to it. But this is just a place, boy. Just wood and stone. And if you have to leave it, let it go without regrets. But this . . ." He stroked the wood. "What's in here is your real heritage."

Devyn opened the box and took out a book. He set it on Michael's lap, then opened it.

After turning a few pages to try to understand why this book was so important, Michael looked up at his father, puzzled. "They're just stories."

"Aye. To most of the world, they're just stories, and you've heard them told here and there, since they've been spread across the land over the years. But the stories in that book you're holding and the ones still in the box . . . Our family's history is hidden in those stories. The heart of it, anyway, if not the ordinary truth of it. Do you know the story about the Door of Locks? Well, it's like that, you see." Devyn tapped a finger on the book. "We've got all the locks, but somewhere along the way we lost the key that would show us how they work."

Michael took a long swallow of koffee to ease the sudden dryness in his throat. He had found a key of sorts, because he had the feeling that Glorianna would understand his family stories better than he did. But he wasn't sure he wanted her to know those stories. He wasn't sure he wanted her to be anything other than the woman he'd seen in the Den last night—vibrant, alive, and smoldering with sexual energy.

If he didn't give her the stories, he might be able to keep the woman who was Glorianna.

In order to survive, the world would need the warrior called Belladonna.

Michael looked at Glorianna and knew she would never forgive him if he withheld the answers that would help her fight the Destroyer of Light. Even so, he would hide one story for as long as he could. But the other . . .

He cleared his throat to catch the attention of the people around him. "Before we get on with this journey, I'd like to tell you a story that's been in my family for a good many years."

Glorianna stepped off Lee's island and took a half-dozen steps toward her garden before she spun around and headed for her house instead. They needed to be gone; there were things to do. But she couldn't guide them to the White Isle while she felt so unsettled.

"I'm sorry it upset you," Michael said as he caught up to her, "and I won't pretend to know why it did. It was just a story, Glorianna."

She stopped and faced him. Conflicts smashed inside her, like a stormy battle between sea and shore, revealing things she hadn't known she was feeling until Michael had told them that story.

"You don't know!" she shouted.

"Women have been saying that to men since the beginning of time, so is there something in particular that I should be knowing?"

She heard amusement in his voice, but it was the sadness in his eyes that made her bite her tongue to hold the words back, to hold the feelings back just long enough to shape a command. *Ephemera, hear me. These words, these feelings, are just storms passing through the hearts that are present. They change nothing.*

Having done that much to protect her island, she flung at Michael all the turmoil inside her. "You tell me a story that's been handed down in your family, but you have no sense of what it means."

"That's right. I don't know what it means. I don't have the answer."

"You *are* the answer! Luck-bringer. Ill-wisher. Magician. You dress it up as a story with spirits and magic hills—which, considering the lineage of the Guardians and Guides, isn't dressing things up so much. But you're the spirit in the story, Michael." She saw the shock in his eyes and knew she'd hit him with a big enough bit of truth, but she couldn't stop. "You're the one who helps people use the key inside themselves to open the Door of Locks—to take the next step in their life journey. To cross over to another landscape."

"How?" he demanded. "How can I help them cross over to something I didn't know existed?"

"I don't know! Your landscapes aren't broken!" She rammed her fingers into her hair, pushing and pushing as if she intended to shove her fingers through her skull and pull out the thoughts that plagued her now. Especially the one that made her hurt inside so much.

"Your landscapes aren't broken," she said again, feeling something squeezing her heart at the same time it was pushing at her ribs so hard she wouldn't be surprised to feel bone break. "When the Eater of the World attacked the Landscapers' school and killed all the Landscapers who were there, Mother and I were afraid we were the only ones left. And we could only tend the landscapes that resonated with us, so that left so much of the world unprotected. But we hoped there would be others like us in parts of the world that had been less shattered—and there are. You. Caitlin. There must be others as well, not just in Elandar but in other pieces of the world. But you don't remember what you are. You don't remember why you're needed. And—" A sob broke through her punishing effort to hold it back.

Michael moved closer. "Say it," he said quietly. "Get the rest of it out."

"Your world isn't broken." The tears fell now, hot and fierce. "The Guides of the Heart shattered the world—broke it and broke it and broke it again until they were able to isolate the Eater of the World in one of those broken pieces and build a cage that would contain It. But they couldn't leave that place unprotected, not with the Dark Guides hiding somewhere, and the power within them changed, got divided between the men and women somehow. They couldn't leave that place. They couldn't go home." Her voice changed to a harsh whisper. "I have lived on that battleground my whole life. Lee, my mother, all of us here have lived on the s-scars of a war, and we're reminded every day of what it cost to stop the Eater of the World."

"And the rest of us only know it as a story," Michael said.

She fisted her hands in his shirt, desperate to make him understand. "They broke the world, and they broke something in themselves by doing it. But your part of the world is whole and your gift is whole, and I don't know how your part of Ephemera works. The Eater of the World is out there, Michael. It's out there with no boundaries to stop It and no one who will recognize the signs of Its presence and It can go where I can't follow because *my* world is bound by my landscapes and if I can't stop It the Eater will change the world into a dark and terrible place and It can go *anywhere* now and I'm tired of living on a battleground and I'm tired of being alone and I—"

A storm of feelings broke inside her, and all the words were swept away.

There were some kinds of tears a man could accept easily enough, even be amused by in an affectionate way, but when a strong woman broke enough to reveal her pain, those tears were a fearsome thing to behold. And seeing the shock and confusion on Lee's face was enough confirmation that the woman weeping in his arms rarely broke enough to cry, even in private.

A look at Caitlin was all it took to have the girl linking arms with Lee to draw him away.

"Cry it out, darling," Michael said as he shifted slightly to settle Glorianna more firmly against him. "Just cry it out. You'll feel better for it."

I have lived on that battleground my whole life.

What must it be like to grow up in such a place, where you and everyone you loved was dependent on the caprice of the world? But it wasn't the world, was it? It was the heart that made things, changed things.

"I've got you, darling," he murmured as one hand moved over her back in comforting circles. "We'll learn from each other, Glorianna Belladonna, and we'll find a way to do right by the world." *And you don't have to be alone now.*

He felt her body tighten, felt her pushing against his chest in order to step away, get away, escape from the knowledge that she had shown a man she barely knew emotions she had kept hidden from her family.

"I have to wash my face," she said, sniffling. "I can't go to a landscape looking like this."

He let her go, watched her run to the house. Even with her brother here, she wouldn't leave without them. He didn't think she would leave anyone, even kin, alone on this island. Not when that walled garden held the lives of so many.

"I've never heard her cry like that," Lee said, coming up beside him. "I don't think she *has* cried like that."

"She's cried like that before," Michael said quietly. "But I'm thinking it's the first time she's let anyone witness the tears."

"Maybe." Lee stared at Michael, and the bewilderment of dealing with Glorianna's tears gave way to a steely resolve. "She's not like the other Landscapers. She's more, and she was declared rogue because of it. Even now, with the world crashing down around us, the other Land-scapers who survived won't acknowledge her."

"And you're saying that if Caitlin and I learn from Glorianna, we'll be tarred with the same brush?"

"That's what I'm saying."

Michael looked at Caitlin, who was hovering nearby, and thought about a young girl shunned by the other children, a young girl who had found something far more wondrous than she knew when she had discovered Darling's Garden. And he thought about himself and his desire to hear the music in one woman's heart rather than experience the bodies of many.

"Well, then," he said. "Since I've never enjoyed dealing with fools, it's lucky for me that I met up with you first." He hesitated, remembering what Nathan had told him just before that monster rose from the sea. "Lee, if it can be done, I'm thinking it would be better to go to Raven's Hill first. I'd like to check on my aunt, who was injured in a fire, and see the cottage to find out if anything remains." *Like a box of books that might provide some answers.*

"Does your village have a beach?"

"Aye. Nothing grand, mind you, but enough of one for those who want to wade in the sea or look for shells."

Lee nodded and looked at Caitlin. "Then I think we have a way to get to your village."

Chapter Nineteen

For the second time in an hour, Glorianna stepped off Lee's island. But this time she stood on a beach that wasn't hers in a place that wasn't anywhere she knew.

Not a comfortable place. Not a landscape that held a companionable resonance like she felt when she visited one of her mother's landscapes. She couldn't have reached this village by crossing a bridge. Her heart wouldn't have recognized this place.

Which made no sense since this was Caitlin's home landscape, and the girl's resonance fit in just fine with hers and Nadia's.

Caitlin doesn't belong here either, Glorianna thought as the currents of power lapped around her like the waves lapped the beach. *She's a dissonance and . . . someone else is the bedrock. Someone's heart anchors Raven's Hill* against *the influence of a Landscaper.*

She felt Caitlin come up beside her, heard Michael and Lee step off the island, but didn't turn her head to look at any of them. How did one explain the delicate and courageous act of relinquishing a landscape to someone who hadn't known there *were* landscapes until a few days ago? And it would have to be done with care since the Eater of the World already had some hold on this village.

Guardians of the Light and Guides of the Heart, show me the right path for what needs to be done.

The currents of power shifted around her, flowed through her, set things—

Wait!

—in motion.

Glorianna stood frozen, scarcely daring to breathe. She had been offering up that small prayer since she was a little girl. She had never been answered like this. Not like *this*. She had been thinking about Caitlin, but Ephemera had answered a different meaning to that prayer because here, in this place, it could.

Opportunities and choices. She would help Caitlin find her place in the world. In doing so, *she* would find the Guardians and Guides who could show her how to defeat the Eater of the World.

All she needed was the courage to follow the path.

"I'm grateful for the loan of the coat," Caitlin said.

"Should have brought gloves," Glorianna replied, shoving her hands in her pockets. She felt off balance, so she said nothing more, just turned to watch Lee light the two lanterns he kept on the island.

Caitlin rubbed her own hands briskly. "When the wind comes from the north, it does have a wicked bite."

"That's the breath of the ice beast," Michael said, smiling. "He blows on the sea to create floes of ice so he can float down to the world of men and snatch a pretty maid to take back to his lair to be his wife."

"Or to be his dinner if the maid doesn't prove to be an interesting companion," Caitlin added.

Glorianna shivered. A year ago, their words would have done no harm. Now . . . "Don't tell that story to strangers."

Lee swore softly. He, at least, understood. But Michael shook his head and said, "It's just a story."

"A year ago, it *was* just a story. Now there is something out there that can pluck the image of the ice beast out of a person's mind and make it real. Change a story into truth. That's what the Eater of the World does. It takes your fears and makes them real—until all that's left in the world are the things you fear."

She watched Caitlin's and Michael's expressions change as the import of her words took root. Caitlin looked unnerved, but Michael . . . For some reason, being reminded that stories could be more than stories had been a blow to his heart.

"Shall we go?" she asked.

"Here," Lee said, handing a lantern to Michael. "Is it usually dark?"

"We got here ahead of the dawn," Michael replied, looking at the sky. "Sun's not up yet."

"Ah."

Lee had asked one question; Michael had answered another. This village was teetering on the edge of becoming a dark landscape, slipping over at times but always being pulled back toward the Light.

"But the sun was up when we left Aurora," Caitlin protested.

"We're in a different part of the world now," Glorianna said. She touched Caitlin's sleeve to get the girl's attention. "Currents of Light and Dark flow through this place, although the Dark currents are a little stronger. Maybe because of things that have happened here recently."

"Like boys setting fire to a cottage?" Caitlin muttered.

"Yes." Glorianna studied Caitlin. What had she been doing by the time she was eighteen? What had she known by that age that this girl didn't even begin to realize? "Can you feel their resonance? Can you feel the currents of Dark and Light?"

"I don't know," Caitlin whispered. "I'm standing next to you, and I feel . . . something . . . but I don't know. I don't think I'm allowed to do this."

The girl has been stumbling through her life because there wasn't anyone who could help her identify the sensations flowing all around her. She could have done so much harm if someone else's heart hadn't struggled to keep the village as balanced as it is.

"Take my hand." She offered her hand to Caitlin. "I'll show you the way my mother showed me."

When you were learning to walk, Glorianna, you held my hand to keep your balance. Hold my hand again to learn another way of walking.

Caitlin gasped and tried to pull away.

"Don't be afraid of it," Glorianna said quietly, tightening her grip on Caitlin's hand. "That's the world you're feeling. Ephemera flows through the heart, manifests the heart. Your heart. A Landscaper is the bedrock, the sieve through which all other hearts flow. Who she is becomes the resonance of a place." *Usually,* she amended silently.

"But I can't be good all the time. I can't!"

"No, you can't. There are shadows in every garden, Caitlin Marie. There is darkness in every heart. Even the Places of Light have slim currents of Dark flowing through them. No heart is purely one thing or another." She felt a tremor of relief go through the girl at the same time that she thought, *There is an answer in those words.*

Places of Light needed some Dark, and dark landscapes still needed a thread of Light. Why did the dark landscapes need the Light? That question had teased her when she had stood before the walls of Wizard City and unleashed Heart's Justice on the Dark Guides. It teased her now.

The Warrior of Light must drink from the Dark Cup.

And wasn't it inconvenient that, having warned Michael against telling stories, she would have to persuade him to tell her the story about the Warrior of Light?

Be patient, a gentle, ageless voice whispered. *When the time is right, he will tell you.*

"Lee," Michael said, "since you've got one lantern and I've got the other, why don't you give Caitlin Marie a hand up the beach? The path leading up to the village is just a bit of a ways over there."

Before Glorianna could tell him they could see well enough, Caitlin looked back at her brother. Grinning, she pulled away from Glorianna, linked an arm with Lee, and said, "Come on, then. I'll show you the path and we'll let the lollygaggers catch up when they can."

"Lollywhat?" Glorianna said. Then a hand closed over hers. Bigger. Warm. A little work-roughened.

"Something I've wondered about Lee," Michael said, smiling at her. "Is he your older brother?"

"Younger."

"Younger?" He sounded surprised. "But we're of an age."

"Which makes you twenty-eight or -nine. I'm thirty-one." A couple of years shouldn't make any difference at this stage of their lives, especially since it wouldn't have mattered if *he'd* been the one who was older. But she could still remember when those couple of years between her and Lee made a *big* difference.

"Ah. An older woman."

The laughter in his voice, as if he knew exactly what she was thinking, made her feel foolish—and that made her defensive.

"Yes," she snapped. "Older. I'll be gray-haired and wrinkly in a few years."

"But now you're a woman ripe with the juice of life."

Her breath caught, her heart stumbled, and those juices warmed, ready to flow.

"Are you going to be showing me that trick of feeling the currents?" Michael held up their linked hands.

"It's not your landscape." Wasn't Caitlin's either in the purest sense, but she wasn't going to tell him that.

"Ah. Well, you could still say you were trying to show me. Or you could tell your brother we're holding hands because you like the looks of me and you were wondering when I'm going to kiss you again."

Looking into her eyes, he lifted her hand and kissed her fingers— and an odd little thrill tickled her belly and stirred those juices.

"I have *not* been wondering about that," she sputtered, glad the lantern light would hide the blush caused by the lie.

"I have."

His smile changed. The humor in it faded, replaced by some quality she couldn't name—or wasn't sure she *wanted* to name. Because it was more than lust or desire.

A sharp whistle made them both look up the beach to where Caitlin was ineffectually tugging on Lee's sleeve and Lee, may the Guardians bless him, was just standing there, staring back at them, not having lost the timing required to be a perfectly annoying younger brother.

"So what are you going to tell him, Glorianna Belladonna?" Michael asked as Lee began walking back toward them. "Are you going to tell your little brother that you were helping me learn about the currents— or that you were thinking of trying me on as a lover?"

Her body hummed. Her brain went blank.

And his words resonated through her like a promise—and yet felt oddly hollow.

He gave her hand a friendly squeeze and walked up the beach, passing Lee.

"Glorianna?" Lee said as soon as he reached her, his voice sharp with concern. "What's wrong?"

She looked at her brother and blurted out the answer. "He wants to kiss me again."

She could hear her heartbeats in the silence that hung between them. Then Lee said, "You just figured that out? When we were in the Den last night, the man was wrapped around you snug enough to have Sebastian muttering, so it's not surprising he wants to kiss you again. At least, it's not surprising to the rest of us."

How was she supposed to figure that out? Sure, they'd had fun in the Den last night, but since then she'd been a bit preoccupied thinking about other things—although knowing her behavior had caused her cousin the incubus to mutter was rather gratifying. But Michael being younger than her was reason enough to put thoughts of kisses—

and lovers—aside. Even if he wasn't so much younger that it should make any difference.

But there had been something bittersweet in the resonance of his flirting just now, something that hadn't been there last night in the Den. As if his feelings had changed in some way, but he didn't want anyone to know they had changed. Didn't even want to admit to himself that they had changed.

She closed her eyes and focused on her breathing.

"Glorianna?"

She held up a hand to signal Lee to wait.

Distractions. Lures that tugged a person away from the path she needed to follow. Or signposts that confirmed the way. Were these thoughts about kisses and age a signpost warning her to turn away from a man who could easily distract her, or a lure nudging her away from a person who could help her fight the Eater? She didn't fit into this landscape, and the Dark currents were working on her in ways they couldn't in her pieces of the world.

She opened her eyes and looked at Lee. "Do you trust the Magician?"

"If you're asking if I think he'll act responsibly with regard to the world, then, yes, I trust him. Do I trust him with my sister?" Lee patted her cheek. "Not a chance."

Should have known better than to ask a brother.

But the answer felt right and steadied her.

She tugged the lantern out of Lee's hand. "I'll go with Caitlin to take a look at her garden. You're going with the Magician."

"I don't think that's what he had in mind."

Michael watched Caitlin and Glorianna head in the direction of the hill that would take them to Darling's Garden, then turned to look at his remaining companion. "Tell me again how I ended up with you?"

"You make my sister nervous," Lee replied.

He snorted. "That one has more brass than an orchestra and more nerve than a sore tooth. So I sincerely doubt I make her nervous. Her *brother*, on the other hand . . ."

Lee just grinned, and that made him like the man even more, despite the feeling that neither Lee nor Sebastian was pleased by his interest in Glorianna. But she was a grown woman, and what she did with a man behind closed doors was none of their business, was it? Not that he'd say that to Lee. Or Sebastian.

So he sighed for show and said, "Come along, then. We'll go to the harbor and see what news is to be had, then find out where my aunt Brighid has been staying."

He struck out for the harbor, settling into the easy stride that covered ground but let him keep the pace for miles. A couple of minutes later, his conscience pricked him. He'd wanted to discomfort Lee, but he didn't want the man pulling a muscle in the effort to keep up.

But when he started to suggest they slow down, Lee just looked at him and smiled. That's when Michael realized the other man had settled into the same rhythm.

"Travel on your feet a lot, do you?" Michael asked.

Lee nodded. "A fair amount. Depends on how far I'm traveling and where." He stopped suddenly and pressed the palm of one hand against his forehead.

"Is your head troubling you?" He hadn't noticed Lee indulging to excess last night, but drink took men differently.

"Something is," Lee muttered.

Now Michael focused on the man—and on the music inside the man. A good tune, solid and steady. Reminded him of his friend Nathan. But there were sharp riffs now that hadn't been there last night. As if the song that was Raven's Hill was working on Lee.

"Maybe you should go back to your little island."

Lee lowered his hand and shook his head. "I'm all right."

No, you're not. If something about Raven's Hill was so troubling to Lee, what might it be doing to Glorianna?

"It's not much farther." With luck, he'd catch Nathan before the workday started. Whenever he felt ragged during a visit home, a few hours with Nathan settled him again. Maybe the same would be true for Lee.

They both lengthened their strides, moving with purpose until the harbor was in sight. Then Michael stopped sharply enough that Lee took several more steps before realizing something was wrong.

"That's Kenneday's ship," Michael said, pointing. "I came up with him before things . . . happened. He should have set sail by now." Unless the ship no longer had a captain. Kenneday had been standing near him when that monster rose out of the water. "Come on."

They ran the rest of the way, travel packs bouncing against their shoulders. When they neared the water, Michael veered toward a tavern that was favored by captains and merchants who wanted a drink and a meal while conducting business. Even now, with the sun barely lifted above the horizon, the tavern was open for business and filled with customers.

And there he found Kenneday, sitting alone at a table, looking ashen and years older.

Michael strode up to the table. Upon seeing him, Kenneday cried out and stood up so fast the chair toppled.

"Ah, Michael, have you come back to haunt me? I swear by all I hold dear, there was nothing I could have done to save you. When that . . . *thing* . . . disappeared, I took out a boat to look for you. I did look. But I'll understand if your soul feels a need to plague me."

Michael looked at Garvey, who was working behind the bar—and was staring at him out of a face wrung clean of color. "Can we have a pot of strong tea over here?" He waited for the nod before turning back to Kenneday and putting some sting in his voice. "You've told me more than once that a captain who loses himself in drink risks losing his ship. And I know you're a man with a fair share of courage, so I know you aren't holding your ship, crew, and cargo in the harbor because some beasty rose out of the deep."

Kenneday's hand curled into a fist. "If you weren't a dead man, I'd blacken your eye for using that tone of voice with me."

"Does he always think people are ghosts, or does this happen only when he's drunk?" Lee asked.

"Drunk, is it?" Kenneday shouted. "I'm not so far down into the bottle as to be called a drunk!"

"Then listen," Lee said. "If you throw a punch and hit Michael in the eye, he'll throw a punch and lay you out on the floor, and then I'll get dragged into it because these kinds of fights never end with two punches, and we'll end up trying to explain to his sister and mine how we landed in the guardhouse for a fight that wasn't our doing."

"Are you another spirit, then?" Kenneday asked.

"I'm a Bridge, and I'm sober, and I'm very much among the living."

And you're getting more pissy by the minute, Michael thought—and wondered whether he should be more worried about Kenneday or Lee.

"So why don't we all sit down and you can tell Michael why your ship is still in the harbor and why you think he's dead," Lee said.

"I saw him go down into that terrible darkness, didn't I?" Kenneday collapsed into another chair at the table while Lee righted the toppled chair and Michael pulled out a third. "Saw that thing rise up out of the sea and him standing there, facing it. And then the air turned black and the sea turned the color of blood, and when we could see again, Michael and the creature were gone."

The pot of tea and the cups rattled as Garvey put them on the table. "Your auntie will be pleased you've come back to the living."

"I wasn't—" Michael shook his head. They were going to believe what they chose to believe. "Nathan said Aunt Brighid had been taken to the doctor's house after the fire. Is she still there?"

"She's at the boardinghouse now on Trace Street," Garvey replied.

"Doctor looks in on her every day, even though she's well enough not to be needing him. Grieving for you and Caitlin Marie, of course, so I'm guessing she'll be pleased to see you."

If the shock of seeing us doesn't kill her. But another thought occurred to him, and he wondered if, in fact, Brighid *would* be glad to see them.

"As for why I'm still in the harbor," Kenneday said, "I had cargo for the White Isle, so I went once I felt sure there was nothing to be done for you. But it's gone, Michael. You can see it. Sure as I'm sitting here, you can see it. When you're coming up on it, the island looks as solid and real as your own hand. But then it starts to fade away. The closer you get, the more it fades until you sail over water where land should be—and when you get far enough away, you can see it again, behind you. Can't be reached, though. No ship can dock there. So I came back, with my holds still full, and I didn't have the heart to go farther. Not just yet."

"Is the cargo in your hold staples that will last or supplies that will rot?" Lee asked.

"Mostly staples," Kenneday replied. "There are things that will go bad, but not just yet."

"Before you shed your cargo at a loss, give it another day," Lee said.

"You know what became of the White Isle?" Michael asked.

Lee sipped his tea and grimaced. Since Michael found nothing wrong with the tea, he assumed the beverage wasn't to Lee's taste.

"Belladonna altered the landscapes to keep the White Isle away from the Eater of the World," Lee said. "But her resonance is tangled with another Landscaper's. Maybe that's why the island is visible at all. It shouldn't be."

Kenneday looked from one to the other in disbelief. "Are you saying a *sorceress* made the White Isle disappear?"

Silence suddenly filled the tables around them, then carried like a wave throughout the tavern. Everyone turned in their direction. Everyone waited for an answer.

And the song that was Raven's Hill turned dark and jagged.

Without some help, we're not going to get out of here alive, Michael thought as he studied the faces of the men around him—some he had known for most of his life.

Lee sat back in his chair, reached into his pocket, and pulled out a small, smooth stone. "What does a sorceress do that a Magician doesn't?"

Bad question. Beads of sweat popped out on Michael's forehead.

"Are you a Magician then?" A man at the next table stood up and cracked his knuckles while he gave Lee a nasty grin.

"No, I'm not," Lee said calmly, rubbing his thumb over the stone. "But I can tell you this. If the Magicians and sorceresses in your . . . country . . . walk away from you, you won't survive a month. Because they not only protect you from Ephemera, they protect you from your own hearts. That thing you saw in the harbor killed most of the Landscapers and Bridges in my part of the world—and the world is going mad because of it. Before you blame someone else for your ill luck, consider this: Nothing comes to you that doesn't live within your own heart. That is the way of the world."

"You're begging for a lesson," the man snarled. As he took a step toward them, Lee threw the stone at him. The man caught it, an instinctive action . . .

. . . and disappeared.

Another wave of silence filled the tavern.

So fast, Michael thought. *It happens so fast.* "Where did he go?"

Lee pushed away from the table. Everyone in the tavern tensed—but no one dared move.

"I don't know," Lee said. "He crossed over to whatever landscape most reflected who he was at that moment."

"So he'll be able to come back?"

A sick, nasty expression flickered across Lee's face, like a note that was out of tune and out of tempo. "Depends on whether or not he can survive what lives within his own heart."

Michael rose to his feet. "How can you be so callous with a man's life?"

"Callous?" Lee let out a harsh bark of laughter. The nastiness gave way to something darker and more honest—and more painful. "He comes at us, wanting to shed blood, with everything in him resonating a pleasure for inflicting pain, and you think *I'm* callous? Don't stand there and tell me you couldn't feel it. Not when you were that close to him. And the truth is, if he really belonged here, nothing would have happened when he caught that stone. *Nothing*, Michael. That's how the world works. And if he didn't belong here but wanted to stay, something would pull him away from this place, no matter how hard he tried to hold on. That, too, is the way of the world."

"All right, fine," Michael said, just wanting to get them out of there before the other men began to consider the odds.

"No, it is not all right!" Lee shouted. "My sister is going to die trying to save Ephemera from the Eater of the World. So is yours. So are you. You're Ephemera's defense against It, so you are going to die, Michael. And then they are going to die." He swept his hand out to indicate the men in the tavern. "There is nothing they can do to fight something that was formed out of the darkness that lives in human hearts. They can gather armies to fight this thing, but without the sorceresses and Magicians that they hold in such contempt, their own fear will kill them. Their own despair will consume them. Their own doubts will devour their families. Do you know what is out there, Magician? Do you want to know what the Eater's landscapes hold?"

No, he didn't.

"The bonelovers look like ants, but they're as long as your forearm. They're called bonelovers because that's all that's left of anyone who stumbles into their wasteland. The trap spiders are big enough to pull a full-grown man into their lairs. The wind runners are as big as dogs and have jaws powerful enough to crush bone. The death rollers—"

"Stop it," Michael said. "Stop it now. That's enough."

"—are like the crocodileans, which are native creatures that live in the rivers of warmer landscapes. But the death rollers are bigger, meaner—they are crocodileans swelled by human fear. That's what is out there, Michael. That's what is going to sink its teeth into your villages and your people. You think these are stories. I've lived with the truth of it all my life. I trained in the school where the Eater had been caged. I felt Its presence under all the currents of Light that flowed through the school. But all those currents of Light, all those hearts . . ." Lee's eyes suddenly filled with tears. "I knew a lot of the people who were slaughtered when the Eater destroyed the school. And in the days to come, most of you will stand at a memorial stone and grieve for lost comrades or loved ones."

"We have graveyards here," Michael said softly.

Lee wiped his eyes and gave Michael a smile that was painfully sad. "Magician, most times there won't be anything left to bury."

He saw Kenneday shudder, and he thought about the fishermen who now haunted a stretch of sea. And he thought about what it would be like for men to take out the boats in order to feed their families if most of the sea was haunted with the dead, and there were only pockets of safe water left.

"Are you saying there's a war coming?" a voice asked.

Michael looked toward the door. Nathan stood there—and the dark, jagged notes that had filled the tavern faded away, replaced by a rhythm that was as strong and steady as a heartbeat.

"It's already started," Lee replied wearily. "And it's already reached your shores."

Kenneday stared at the table for a long moment, then looked at Michael and Lee before nodding sharply. "I've got a duty to my ship and my crew, so I can't be putting aside all my cargo runs. But she's a good ship, and they're good men. I'll put them all at your disposal whenever I can to haul cargo or passengers. Whatever you need." He stood up and looked around the room. "I sailed through the haunted water, and I was glad to have Michael on board."

"Ill-wisher," someone muttered.

"That's enough," Nathan said sharply, coming into the room. He tipped his head toward Lee. "I don't know this man, but I heard what he said. And I'm wondering if we haven't misunderstood some things about sorceresses and Magicians—and the world—for a long time now. So I for one am willing to offer a hand in friendship." He held out a hand to Lee, who clasped it.

There was no actual sound in the room, but Michael could hear a dissonance shifting into the harmony of a different tune.

Something has changed.

He looked at Lee, who sank into a chair at the table, and he thought about the woman climbing the hill with his little sister.

Neither Glorianna nor Lee understood the world as he knew it— but they understood it in ways he'd never even dreamed.

Who was this woman? Caitlin wondered as she watched Glorianna study the outer walls of Darling's Garden. What kind of person talked about resonances, dissonances, and currents of power flowing through the world?

And what kind of power flowed through Glorianna Belladonna that she could change the physical world simply by asking it to change?

"Ephemera, hear me," Glorianna had said.

Caitlin stood beside her, trying not to look at the burned husk of the cottage that had been her family's home. In front of them, the rust-colored sand had swallowed even more of the meadow.

"This sand does not belong here," Glorianna said. *"This landscape is not welcome here."*

Listen to her, Caitlin thought as fiercely as she could. Please, listen to her.

A quiver along her skin, as if the air had asked a question. Glorianna watched her, waiting.

Feeling self-conscious and foolish, Caitlin stared at the sand and said, "This is my place. The sand that comes from that dark . . . landscape . . . does not belong here. It is not welcome here. I do not want that sand to touch what is mine."

Something rippled through the land, then flowed through her, making her feel as if she were being lifted up to ride a wave in the sea. And then she watched the land change right before her eyes, and within moments, bare earth replaced the sand.

Filled with a blend of delight and disbelief, along with a helping of fear, Caitlin laughed nervously. "Isn't Ephemera going to fill in the bare spots?"

"Yes," Glorianna said. "The meadow will reseed itself, as it does every year."

"That wasn't what I meant."

"I know. But there is a difference between being playful and being careless with what you ask of the world."

"This garden is loved," Glorianna said, brushing her fingers over the stones.

"I tend it as best I can," Caitlin said, pleased that she sounded modest—and puzzled that Glorianna could tell what she'd done to the garden when they hadn't gotten inside yet.

"You repaired the mortar?" Glorianna asked.

"What?" Now that it was pointed out, she could see signs of recent work.

"Maybe Lee's ability to impose one landscape over another isn't unique after all," Glorianna said. Then she smiled at Caitlin. "The garden doesn't actually exist on this hill. It's here because you need it to be. But it is grounded somewhere else—and it is loved there, Caitlin."

"Then . . . it's not mine?" It hurt to consider it. The garden had been her friend most of her life.

"Of course it's yours. It wouldn't be here if it didn't resonate with you."

"Then what are you saying?"

Something in the air between them. Something in Glorianna's eyes. Compassion? Knowledge? Caitlin couldn't put a name to it, but she understood with unshakable certainty that whatever happened in the next minute would change her life—and would change the world.

"I think you should find out where this garden is rooted. Where you're rooted. It isn't here, Caitlin Marie. I'm not even sure this is one of your landscapes. This village and the surrounding land should be one of the pieces of the world that is in your keeping, but something isn't right here. And I don't think this is really home."

"No," Caitlin whispered. "It's not. We never quite fit in Raven's Hill." A different place where the other girls wouldn't see her as a sorceress and the boys wouldn't think of her as the new village whore? "How do I find this place?"

"Let's take a look inside the garden."

Michael was the only person who had seen her garden—and Michael hadn't understood. This was different, exciting, strange, terrifying.

"At this time of year, it's not at its best," Caitlin said, twisting her fingers as Glorianna studied each bed.

"No, it's not," Glorianna said absently. "You'll have to work on that. You want balance reflected through the seasons, just as you want a balance between the currents of Light and Dark. This." She stopped in front of a stone. "This came from the White Isle."

Caitlin gaped for a moment. "How can you tell?"

"I can feel the island's resonance in the stone." Glorianna studied the stone a moment longer, then looked at Caitlin. "Why did you put it here in the garden?"

Flustered, Caitlin felt her face burn. "My aunt Brighid used to tell me about the White Isle and about Lighthaven, which is the heart of the island. For a while she thought I might be accepted into training there, but . . ."

"You don't belong to Lighthaven," Glorianna said with such careless certainty it took a long moment before Caitlin felt the pain of that statement. Then Glorianna looked at her and she had the same light-headed feeling that the world was changing right under her feet. "Lighthaven may hold the Light, and it may provide you with a place to rest and renew the spirit, but I think you'll find the heart of the White Isle in a different place."

My place. The yearning that swept through her was so fierce, she felt as if she could ride that sensation to another place. Another life.

"No no no," Glorianna snapped, grabbing her and giving her a hard shake. "You haven't been trained yet to take the step between here and there. And since none of us knows where this garden actually stands, we'd have no way to find you."

Grounded. Jammed back into her skin. Shoved back into this village that deadened her heart.

"You should have let me go," Caitlin whispered.

"Not yet," Glorianna whispered back. Then she stepped away and said briskly, "Let's take a look at the rest."

"Not much left of it, is there?" Lee said, shielding his eyes as he studied the remains of the cottage.

"No, not much left," Michael said. The winter clothes he'd be needing soon. The books he'd carefully selected and scrimped to buy so that he could share them with Aunt Brighid and Caitlin. The little treasures he'd accumulated over the years and couldn't carry with him. All gone. His life, his boyhood, all burned away.

Nothing left of me here, he thought. *Nothing left for me here. Except, hopefully, my father's legacy.*

Stepping around broken, burned timbers, Michael looked up at the one corner that still appeared to be fairly intact. But even if they hadn't been touched by the fire itself, would the books have survived?

Only one way to find out.

"If we can steady a ladder up to that spot, I think I can get what I'm looking for," Michael said.

"We can set a ladder up there right enough," Nathan said, "but it won't take much to have the rest of this place coming down on us."

"It will hold long enough," Michael said softly, pouring every drop of his luck-bringing into those words. A dark tune playing here. The same tune he'd heard during the years he'd lived in the cottage, with only a sprinkle of bright notes coming from Nathan. Just like always.

Lee met his eyes for a moment, then helped Nathan and Kenneday find the most solid spot for the ladder.

Oh, the wood was weak and trembled under his feet when he eased his way across what was left of the attic. A board cracked ominously as he pulled the box out of its special cupboard. Carrying the whole box would add too much weight to his own—and the image of Rory Calhoun impaled on stone suddenly filled his mind. Two boys were saved by the death of another. He didn't want to repeat that particular tune by saving the books but dying in the process.

"Lee," he called. "Come up the ladder so I can hand these over to you." He opened the box and took the books out one at a time, stretching as far as he could and moving as little as possible to pass the books to Lee who, in turn, handed them down to Nathan and Kenneday.

"Careful," Lee said as Michael finally eased his way back to the ladder.

Wood creaked and groaned as Michael started down. The wood supporting the top of the ladder suddenly broke, and he might have fallen among all the broken timbers if Lee and Nathan hadn't been holding the ladder steady.

"Go," Lee said, looking at Nathan. Kenneday was already outside, his arms full of books.

Nathan shook his head. "He said it would hold until we were safely away, so it will hold."

As soon as Michael had both feet on the floor, Nathan took one end of the ladder and Lee took the other. He followed them out, and as he cleared what had been the threshold of the front door, the cottage gave out a sound of creaking, wailing, agonized groaning.

Lady's mercy, Michael thought as the rest of the roof and attic flooring that had supported the box of books came crashing down.

"I told you it would hold long enough," Nathan said to Lee. Then he looked at Michael. "What comes next?"

Michael shook his head and watched the two women walking toward them. Glorianna looked upset. Caitlin looked dazed, like she'd tumbled into a tree while running flat out. "I think what comes next is up to them."

"Aunt Brighid," Caitlin said, lightly brushing her fingers over her aunt's hand. "Auntie, it's me. Caitlin Marie."

Not so bad, the doctor had said. The cuts and burns had not been significant, and Brighid was a strong woman.

It looked bad enough to her.

Then Brighid stirred, opened her eyes. "Caitlin?" Her hand shook as she raised it to touch Caitlin's face. "Caitlin Marie? I saw you disappear. I saw . . ."

"I know," Caitlin said hurriedly. "I know. But I found a way back. Michael, too. He's here. See?" She half turned in the chair by the bed and looked up at her brother.

"Aunt Brighid," Michael said.

"You came," Brighid said. "You got my message?"

"Yes," he replied.

Currents of power suddenly flowed through the room as the third person moved to a position at the end of the bed where she would be clearly visible.

Caitlin watched, helpless to understand what was happening while Brighid and Glorianna stared at each other.

"I am Belladonna."

Brighid sucked in a breath and coughed it out, a rasping sound. "You're a sorceress like Caitlin, aren't you?"

"I'm a Landscaper, like Caitlin," Glorianna replied. "We are the bedrock that protects Ephemera from the human heart."

"Lady of Light," Brighid whispered. "You . . . could show her who she's meant to be?"

"I can show her."

"There's nothing for her here."

Grief filled Glorianna's eyes, and Caitlin wondered again what the woman had seen in her garden that had caused such distress.

"No," Glorianna said, "there's nothing for her here."

"I'm sitting in the room," Caitlin said, guilt that she had done something wrong making her testy. "And I'm old enough to do some deciding for myself."

Glorianna's eyes never left Brighid's, but she smiled. "Then we'll let your auntie get some rest while we discuss those decisions."

That didn't sound like she was going to be the one doing much deciding, but at least she'd have her say.

"I'll be back a little later," Caitlin said, smiling at her aunt. As she rose, she saw the undiluted sadness in Michael's eyes before he made an effort to hide his feelings.

She held on until they were in the hallway outside her aunt's room before the feelings spewed out. "I don't want her here. There's a syrupy meanness in that room. They're taking care of her right enough, but they're *glad* she's hurt. It's her punishment for taking care of me and Michael all these years." She glared at her brother. "You know that's what they're thinking."

"Caitlin," Michael said.

She wanted to shout, wanted to scream out the anger, but she kept her voice low. "You've been gone, Michael. These past twelve years, you've been gone. And you only stayed four years after Mother died. Then you were off having your adventures."

"I was off trying to earn enough money to take care of the three of us," Michael said heatedly, but he, too, kept his voice down.

"Let's go to one of the rooms we've taken before continuing this discussion," Glorianna said.

"There's nothing more to discuss," Caitlin snapped.

"Caitlin."

She didn't respond to Glorianna. She was too stunned by the way Michael suddenly paled.

"What did we do to the world?" he whispered.

"Somewhere around this village, a fine crop of rocks has sprung up," Glorianna replied after a moment.

"What?" Caitlin asked, wondering why Michael looked ready to faint while Glorianna looked sympathetic but amused.

"Anger makes stone," Glorianna said. "Something you can't afford to forget. Now, would you like the rest of this to be discussed in private or would you rather go down to the parlor and put on a show so the people downstairs who are trying to eavesdrop won't have to strain their ears?"

"What does sass make?" Caitlin muttered.

"Tart fruit."

She wasn't sure if Glorianna was teasing or not. Based on his expression, Michael wasn't sure either, but the answer had brought some color back to his face. So she let herself be herded into one of the rooms they had rented while Michael knocked on the door of the other to fetch Lee.

Once the four of them were seated, Caitlin plucked up her courage to have her say. "Aunt Brighid doesn't belong here. Michael has been on his own for a time now, and I'm old enough to make my own way. Besides, we're going to have to start over in one place or another, and I don't want it to be here."

"Ah, Caitie," Michael groaned. "Why did you never say things were so hard here?"

"It was all we had."

He closed his eyes as if her words had hurt him.

"A piece at a time," Glorianna said. "What do you want for your aunt?"

"She's a Lady of Light," Caitlin replied. "She should go back to the White Isle. I don't think she'll ever really heal if she stays here."

"And you?" Glorianna asked.

"I want to find where my garden truly belongs. And I want to learn who I am. I want to learn to be Landscaper."

"Aren't you going to ask what I want?" Michael asked.

"No," Glorianna replied quietly. "I feel your heart well enough."

"So we go to the White Isle?" Lee asked.

"If you have a way of reaching it once we get there, I have a ship that can take us," Michael said.

Glorianna nodded. "Then it's settled."

"Captain Kenneday and Nathan are having a meal downstairs," Lee said. "I don't know about the rest of you, but my stomach says it's mealtime."

Since there was nothing more to be done, Caitlin followed the rest of them down to the dining room.

Michael stripped down to his drawers, then slipped into bed and stared at the ceiling. "Tell me again why I'm sharing a room—and a bed—with you?"

Lee tucked his hands under his head and grinned. "Because we could only afford two rooms, and the beds being what they are, you cut up stiff about sharing one with your sister. And as much as I like her, I didn't want to share a bed with Caitlin Marie either."

"You're damn right you wouldn't be sharing a bed with her. No matter how grown-up she thinks she is, the girl is just eighteen and an innocent."

Lee rolled over on his side and propped himself up on one elbow. "My sister is thirty-one and, in some ways, just as innocent."

"Nooo," Michael said, shaking his head in denial. "You aren't telling me a woman as lovely as Glorianna has never been pleasured by a man."

"I won't tell you she's never had sex, and I hope it gave her pleasure. . . ."

"But?" Michael prodded when Lee seemed to sink into his own thoughts.

"None of them would have had enough heart to reach her island."

Lee's words filled him with hope and scared him right down to the bone. He wasn't sure if he wanted to be Glorianna's first love, but he kept thinking he wanted to be her lifetime's love. Because he was certain she was *his* lifetime's love.

If you do what you must, you won't have a lifetime with her.

Lee rolled onto his back. After a long moment of silence, he said, "So how old were you?"

"What?"

"If you're thinking Caitlin is too young at eighteen, how old were you when you were initiated into the pleasures of sex?"

Recognizing Lee's effort to lighten the mood, Michael said, "Are we talking brag or lie?"

Lee closed his eyes and smiled. "Whichever provides the best story."

Chapter Twenty

"I've never seen a landscape do that," Glorianna said. As Kenneday's ship sailed closer to the White Isle, she watched the island fade like a mirage in the early-morning light.

"It's not a comfort to hear you say that, Glorianna," Michael scolded. "Couldn't you tweak the truth a bit and say it doesn't happen often?"

She pulled her scarf up to cover the bottom half of her face, both to hide her smile and to warm up skin that was chilled by the brisk sea air. Then she pushed the scarf back down long enough to say, "It doesn't happen often."

Michael looked at the now-empty sea beyond the bow of the ship, then looked back at her. "I'm thinking there's not much sincerity in that answer."

This time she laughed out loud. "Half the time I'm not sure if you're teasing or really mean what you say. You're a hard man to please, Magician."

"Not so. I don't ask for much, I'm grateful for what I'm given, and I'm willing to give a great deal in return."

Glorianna looked away, glad for the cold air that soothed her suddenly burning cheeks. The man wasn't talking about enjoying each other for a few nights of sex. And yet, there was always that bittersweet resonance in his words. "You barely know me."

And she barely knew him.

The heart has no secrets, Glorianna Belladonna. Not even yours. That's why he scares you. If you let him, he'll slip into your life—and you'll slip into his—as if you had always been there for each other. As if there had always been love's shining light welcoming you home.

"I can hear the music in you," Michael said quietly. "It's a glorious song, as heartbreaking as it is beautiful, so full of sorrow and joy. A man could listen to that tune for a lifetime and not grow tired of it."

"I don't know what you're saying."

He took a step closer, his body now sheltering hers from the wind. "You know exactly what I'm saying, and it scares you. If it's any comfort, it scares me too. Maybe it should. Love is not a small thing. It can change a life."

"It can change the world," she whispered.

"Maybe it can." For a moment, he looked troubled by her words. Then he stepped back and smiled. "Well. I'd best let you gather your thoughts. Kenneday said he'd hold this course so you could see the White Isle vanish and reappear, but he's fidgeting like an old maid with the effort not to ask you when you're going to do your magic, and your brother is giving me a look that makes me want to punch him in the face or buy him a drink, I'm not sure which."

"What have you got against Lee?" Glorianna demanded, feeling her temper ruffle in automatic defense of her brother.

"I've got nothing against the man," Michael replied. "In fact, I like him. But being your brother, he feels honor bound to be a pebble in my shoe."

Before she could decide where the tease ended and truth began, Michael walked away and Lee came toward her, carrying the White Isle stone she and Caitlin had removed from the Garden before they set sail out of Raven's Hill yesterday morning.

"I don't want this place," Caitlin had said when they paused at the bottom of the hill behind the cottage. "If, as you say, this place is tied to me in some way, I want to be shed of it."

"Caitlin," Glorianna said in quiet warning, feeling Ephemera gathering itself to manifest the girl's will. "You lived here."

"And wanted to leave the way Michael did. We survived here. Had to, because it was all we had. That's not the same as belonging to a place."

No, Glorianna thought, it isn't the same.

"I don't care if I'm supposed to be the guardian or Landscaper or sorceress or whatever you choose to call it," Caitlin said defiantly. "I don't want the dead feeling that fills my heart when I think of Raven's Hill. I don't want this place. Let someone else be its caretaker."

The words had no sooner left Caitlin's mouth when Glorianna felt Ephemera change the resonance of the world around them. Caitlin gasped and stared at her in fearful wonder.

"You did this," Glorianna said. "Not me."

A heartfelt choice. Even though it had not been done with care and had been spurred by dark feelings, Caitlin's rejection would not leave the village floundering. Which was as clear a message as any that the girl had not been the right person to hold this landscape.

Now that Caitlin's heart was no longer interfering, Glorianna could feel the heart that acted as the anchor for Raven's Hill. Solid. Steady. It would need the help of a Landscaper to strengthen the bedrock that would protect Ephemera from the chaos that lived in the human heart, but . . .

Not me, Glorianna thought as she and Caitlin made their way to the harbor. There was an appeal to the solid steadiness of that anchoring heart that made her uneasy. There was temptation in its resonance. Not because there was a dark intent toward her, but because it was comfortable and could turn her away from the path she needed to follow— and the man who was part of that journey.

"I've never seen a landscape do that," Lee said, staring at the open, empty sea.

"We're not supposed to be that truthful," Glorianna replied.

"Any ideas about why it did that?"

Glorianna looked toward the stern. How far would they need to go before the island began to reappear? Would they have to sail for hours to cross the same amount of water as the length of the island? "A couple. One is that, since my resonance and Caitlin's are tangled on the White Isle, it didn't shift completely when I altered the landscapes to protect the Place of Light from the Eater."

"What is the other idea?"

Glorianna kept her attention focused on the island. "A conflict of wills and heart wishes." She thought that over and frowned. "Actually, it's not so different from your island and mine."

"More like yours," Lee said, nodding. "A place that can't be reached unless you truly need to reach it and your heart resonates with it. But your island doesn't hold a town's worth of people hostage. They need to be connected with some part of the world, Glorianna."

"I know. But the first task is to find a way to reach the island and get Brighid to Lighthaven." Half turning, she called, "Caitlin. We need you up here."

"Do we?" Lee asked quietly as Caitlin hurried to join them.

"She's connected with this island. She should be part of anything that's done here. And we're going to need a bridge. I can cross over without one, but the ship can't."

"All right, I'll—"

A malevolence in the water up ahead. A knot of Dark currents that felt unnatural in a way she understood intuitively but couldn't explain.

Spinning around and almost knocking Caitlin to the deck, she screamed, "Turn around! Turn away! Now!"

For one frozen moment, Kenneday stared at her. Then orders were shouted and men scrambled. Sails luffed before catching the wind again. Then the ship was turning away from the Dark water.

Glorianna sank to the deck and closed her eyes to block out the visible world and focus on the feel of that part of Ephemera, but something powerful washed over her as the ship brushed the edge of that undiluted darkness, and the world, like the island, faded away.

Moments later, she floated on a cushion of warmth and solid strength. Protected. Cherished. And she could hear music, lovely music, with a beat that was steady as a heart. But it was faint, so she moved toward the sound, trying to hear it better.

"That's right, darling," a voice said close to her ear. "That's right. Come back to us now. Your brother doesn't want to be turning grayhaired with worry at so young an age—and neither do I."

"I like your voice," she said, not interested in his confusing talk about men turning gray. She didn't really care what he said; she just wanted to hear that lovely music in his voice.

"Open your eyes for me, darling, and I'll talk all you want."

She obediently opened her eyes and discovered she was braced between Michael's thighs and held firmly against his chest. Turning her head a little gave her a clear view of Lee's white face.

"You promised you wouldn't faint again," Lee said accusingly.

"I didn't faint," she grumbled.

"Did a good imitation of it," Michael muttered.

"Then what did you do?" Lee asked, grabbing her hand in a bone-pinching grip.

"I—" What *did* happen? "Did we get clear of those Dark currents?" she asked, trying to free her hand from Lee's grip so she could grab his hand in turn.

She didn't think he could get paler, but Lee paled.

"Yes, we turned away before we caught more than the edge," he said. "Although I think you scared Kenneday and the crew out of half their wits when you started screaming."

"I wasn't screaming."

"Trust me, darling," Michael said. "Before you didn't faint, you were definitely screaming."

"Just caught me by surprise is all."

"Then remind me not to give you any surprises."

That didn't seem fair, but now that she was regaining her emotional balance, the puzzle of why she had reacted that way to those Dark currents commanded her attention.

She needed help getting to her feet, which embarrassed her enough to snap at Michael and Lee. Then she caught sight of Caitlin, clinging to the railing, with a sailor hovering nearby looking as though he dearly hoped he wouldn't need to be helpful.

"What's wrong with Caitlin?"

"Suddenly couldn't hold her breakfast," Michael said. "Have to confess, I was feeling a bit queasy myself for a bit, but I figured it was from you giving me such a scare."

Lee looked from one to the other. "Three Landscapers, to one degree or another. Three reactions to a knot of Dark currents. You feel them all the time. Why was this different?"

Formal training. Glorianna looked into Lee's eyes and felt relief that there was someone else here who understood the world as she did—and who knew enough to ask the question.

"Can we approach that spot more slowly?" she asked.

"Why would you want to be doing that?" Michael said.

"Because that spot is not natural. I think that's why we all reacted to it. So if the Eater of the World didn't create it, I'd like to figure out what did."

Michael sighed. "I'll talk to Kenneday. Although, with the excitement you've given him, I don't know if his offer of a ship is going to hold beyond this voyage."

As soon as they were the only ones at the bow, Lee said, "What are you expecting to find, Glorianna?"

"Maybe nothing," she replied. "Maybe more than one answer." She shivered. She'd felt warm enough before, but now, without the comfort of Michael's sheltering presence, she couldn't seem to hold off the cold as well.

Caitlin made her way over to them, looking green and shaky. Before she could say anything, Michael returned. Kenneday was clearly unhappy about returning to water that had produced such a reaction, but he turned the ship back toward that spot, running with fewer sails to cut their speed.

"Tell the captain to stay to the right of those Dark currents," Glorianna said.

"How is he supposed to tell?" Michael asked. "It's not like the water is a different color."

Ephemera, hear me.

"Lady of Light," Michael whispered a minute later at the same time some of the sailors began shouting and pointing.

Some kind of seaweed now filled a large patch of the sea, defining the knot of Dark currents. Glorianna held on to the rail and opened herself to those currents. Prepared this time for the strength of it, she recognized it for what it was. It sickened her and saddened her. And excited her.

There was something awful and seductive about that patch of water with its undulating seaweed, something compelling in its malevolence. And the lure to join that water, to feel the embrace of those seaweed limbs as desire became an anchor that would pull her under was almost overwhelming.

She gripped the railing until her hands hurt, and forced herself to focus on the clear, clean sky until the ship was once again turning away from that spot.

"It's an anchor," Glorianna said, still keeping her eyes fixed on the sky. "That's why the White Isle is visible as ships approach it. But who could have done this?" *And why would anyone who cherished the Light create something so deadly?*

"Glorianna, darling, I'm hearing the words but they're not making sense," Michael said.

His voice steadied her enough that she let go of the rail with one hand so that she could turn and face him.

"There is Dark and Light in all things, Magician. In all people, in all places. Somehow the dark feelings have been cast out, but the connection can't be severed completely. By trying to create a place that stands only in the Light, the people on the White Isle have created a dark landscape."

Hours later, Michael sat in the stern, his whistle held loosely in his hands while he stared at the water and wondered if he would ever trust the look of anything again.

"This is sweet water," Kenneday said happily, his hands steady on the wheel. Gone was the man who had grimly followed Glorianna's request to head south again in order to find a current of Light that would help them approach the White Isle. "Not the direction I'd usually take to reach Atwater's harbor, but I've made note of it in my log, and I'll be looking for this channel from now on." He glanced over his shoulder at Michael. "Why don't you play us a tune?"

"Don't feel like it," Michael replied, not meeting Kenneday's eyes.

Kenneday jerked as if hit. "I've never known you to refuse to play a bit of music. What's troubling you? That your lady friend recognized that dark water and you didn't?"

"I don't feel like playing," Michael snapped—and then flinched. What damage had he done in that moment?

"More to the point, you don't want to feel at all," Glorianna said, joining them.

"Leave me be," Michael warned. Those green eyes of hers saw too much. That heart of hers understood too much—and not enough.

"To do what?" she asked. "Close yourself off? Refuse to be what you are? You can't hide from your feelings, Magician. You can't hide from your own heart."

He surged to his feet, aware that the sailors near them had stopped their work, and that Kenneday was watching and listening. But the feelings bubbled over. "This morning we brushed the edge of a place dark enough to make you faint. A place made by ordinary people, if I understood what you were saying." He waved a hand to indicate the men on the ship. "For days now, you've been telling me I can do more to the world than the people around me. So how can I dare feel *anything* when so many people's lives hang in the balance of a mood? Happiness is safe enough, I suppose, but no one stays happy all the time. People call me an ill-wisher, but I've no desire to be the unintentional cause of misery." And how would he ever know how much misery he *had* caused— or if he had unknowingly created dark places in the world?

"You are the balance, the bedrock, the sieve that protects Ephemera from all the wind wishes and surface feelings that flow through the hearts of all the people who live in your landscapes."

"What about my heart, my feelings?" Michael asked, raising his voice close to a shout. "What happens when I want to piss and moan about something?"

Glorianna put her hands on her hips and glared at him. "You tell the world you have emotional gas and it should ignore you when you fart!"

There was no sound except the wind in the sails and the ship slicing through the water.

Then someone farted, a little *poot* that broke the silence.

One sailor choked on a snort of laughter, which made another man sputter, which made another laugh out loud, and suddenly all the men around them were guffawing while Michael faced a woman who looked ready to tie him to an anchor and throw him overboard.

He opened his mouth, not sure what he was going to say but sure he had better say something. Before he had the chance, Glorianna turned on her heel and walked away.

Scowling, Michael went to the rail, wanting no comments, no discussion, no company.

"I've heard there's an art to groveling," Lee said.

Figures that one would ignore the emotional "no trespassing" signs, Michael thought sourly. "I'm not groveling."

Lee, the ripe bastard, laughed.

Michael tucked his whistle inside his coat. "Maybe I'm groveling."

"There's no maybe about it," Lee said cheerfully. "You make her nervous, so she's going to find you more annoying than most people."

"I can't seem to keep my balance these days," Michael said softly. "I sound like a fool half the time and act like a fool the other half."

"Not as bad as that," Lee replied, smiling. "Nothing has changed, Michael."

"Everything has changed."

"Yes. Exactly." Lee braced his hands on the rail. "You're beginning to understand the world, Magician."

"Maybe." Michael waited a beat, then added, "I'm not groveling."

Lee's smiled widened. "Suit yourself."

The man could be more helpful, Michael grumbled to himself as he made his way to the bow, where Glorianna was doing a fine imitation of a merciless figurehead. *After all, it's not like I can pick a few flowers and try to charm her out of her mood.*

He stopped suddenly, remembering another man trying to charm an unhappy woman by giving her a bouquet of wildflowers. He'd loved the man. Still did when the images came back to him so painfully clear. And he'd loved the woman, despite her pain and rages.

"Nothing has changed, Michael."

"Everything has changed."

Feeling breathless, with his heart pounding, he joined Glorianna at the bow of the ship.

"I'd like to tell you a story," he said quietly. "Will you listen?"

Did she know how vulnerable he was at this moment? Could she understand what it meant that he was about to hand over the whole of his life to her judgment?

"I'll listen," she replied just as quietly.

Knowing he couldn't say the words if he was looking at her, he fixed his eyes on the sea. "My father was a wanderer who, it was said, could charm the birds into changing their songs into gold so he could have a few coins for his pocket. I never saw such a thing happen with the birds, but I'm thinking that, before my mother came along, more than one lady slipped a few coins in his pocket as a farewell present. And to be fair, he was a hard worker who could turn his hand to just about any kind of labor and was usually cheerful about it."

"He was a Magician?"

"He was. But he had an easy way about him, so people weren't eager to tar him with that particular brush. Anyway, he had two older brothers who took to the road to make their fortunes. They came back to visit their parents and kin a couple of times in the beginning, then were never heard from again."

He glanced at her to see how she was reacting to his story so far, but, like him, she kept her eyes on the sea and just nodded to indicate she understood.

"So my father, Devyn, went out on the road like his older brothers, needing more than he could find in the village where he'd been born. Sometimes things were good, sometimes they weren't, but he settled into a route that kept his feet moving and his heart happy, and for a few years he wandered from place to place with no ties because, as much as he traveled, he never seemed able to get back to the village where most of his kin lived."

"Maybe he couldn't," Glorianna said. "Often when a person crosses over to another landscape it's because they need to take the next step of their life journey. Sometimes that means adding something more to the life they've known—and sometimes it means not going back to the places and people they had known."

"Maybe," Michael said softly, thinking of how he would have felt if he'd never managed to get back to Raven's Hill to spend time with Aunt Brighid and Caitlin Marie. "Maybe." Would that have been a comfort to the family Devyn had left behind, to know that his not coming back might have been a decision made by the world and not the man himself? *And which family are you thinking of, my lad?* "So one year he ended up in a village that he'd never visited before and saw a pretty girl who captured his heart. Maureen had fire in her eyes and a voice, when she sang, that could make you weep with gratitude just for hearing it. She had an older sister who had gone to the White Isle to become a Sister of Light, but unlike Brighid, the White Isle didn't call to Maureen. She wasn't a wicked girl, just restless and a little wild because of it. Then she met Devyn, who offered her a wedding ring and a way to get out of the village that was smothering her.

"For a while, things went well between them. There was Maureen's pleasure in seeing new places, even ones that made her feel as restless and edgy as her home village. There was Devyn's pleasure in showing his pretty wife those places that lifted his heart. And there was the pleasure they shared in the marriage bed.

"There were places where things went well for them. Money came easy enough, and when it didn't come easy, there was still enough to get by. And there were places where things began to sour after a day or two. And people would look at my mother and mutter about an ill-wisher being among them. So Maureen and Devyn would pack up and move on."

"She created dissonance without intending to, and then, when blamed, probably fed the Dark currents with her own unhappiness. And Devyn, being unhappy about the troubles, wasn't able to balance things out." Glorianna shook her head. There was pity in her eyes. "She was a Landscaper who was unaware of her heritage. Mother and I speculated that there had to be other Landscapers beyond the landscapes that were held within the gardens at the Landscapers' School. The world would be too unstable without them. But we never considered what it would be like for those people to be so connected to Ephemera and not understand why some places would feel right and some wouldn't." She hesitated, and Michael heard her whisper, "Just heart's rain. It will pass, changing nothing."

As she said the words, clouds formed in what had been a clear sky.

"Your mother never found her landscapes, did she?" Glorianna asked, her eyes swimming with tears.

"No, I don't think she did." He stopped, needing a moment to regain control before going on with the story. "They first went to Raven's Hill when she was heavy with me. Devyn's mother's cousin lived there. That branch of the family had once lived in a grand house and were among the landed gentry. But bit by bit they lost the knack of it, and by the time Maureen and Devyn came to Raven's Hill, all that was left was a cottage and some land. Including a hill where the ravens gathered, which was considered an omen of a dark heart.

"Devyn put his hand to whatever work he could find, and Maureen did some fancy stitching that she'd learned as a girl, which earned a few coins and helped put food on the table. And if Maureen sometimes had dark moods and Devyn sometimes had long silences whenever he worked around the harbor and had to watch the ships leaving . . . Well, such things aren't unusual for a couple waiting for the birth of their first child, because nothing would be the same for them.

"They stayed in Raven's Hill for the birthing and a few weeks after until Maureen felt strong enough to take to the road again. But it was different now. A woman carrying a baby can't be hauling a pack as well, and one man can't carry what three people need. So when they left Raven's Hill, they had a horse and a traveling wagon that held all their gear and provided Maureen with privacy when she needed to tend the baby.

"Once they adjusted to being a bit . . . harnessed . . . instead of feeling free and easy, luck rode with them. Devyn found work that paid well enough to put by a few coins for the traveling days, and Maureen, shining with a new mother's pride, made friends with some of the women in the villages.

"I remember those years," Michael said, his voice rough with the feelings, good and bad, that came with the memories. "For a young boy, it was an adventure, and sometimes I felt so daring that I was traveling about Elandar when most of the boys I played with hadn't gone beyond the boundaries of their own villages."

"And your parents?" Glorianna asked. "What about them?"

He said nothing for a minute. "I can remember them dancing together in the moonlight. I can remember the way they looked at each other, with heart and heat. And I can remember the bleakness in his eyes when she would start raging about seeing the same places and why couldn't they find a different road?

"When I was nine, her belly swelled with another child, but it was harder for her and she was more sickly, so they went back to Raven's Hill. Devyn's mother's cousin was dying, and they were there to look after her and be with her in the end. Before she died, the cousin wrote up the papers giving the cottage and land to Devyn to hold in trust for a girl child because the cottage always went to female issue.

"There was no work for him. They got by, especially after Devyn dug up a small money chest filled with gold and silver coins when he was turning the soil for a kitchen garden. But after Caitlin was born, it was like the village had closed up its heart and its pockets where he was concerned. So he took up his pack and went back to traveling. The first few times he came back, he came with pockets bulging with coins and a song in his heart. Things would be good for a few days, and then she would tumble into one of her rages and the bleakness would fill his eyes. He'd wait until the storm passed and she was calm again—until she was close to being the girl who had captured his heart all those years before. Then he would head back to the road.

"When Caitlin had a first birthday, he sent a present and a packet of money by way of a ship heading north. A few weeks later, he sent another packet of money and a letter by way of another ship. A few weeks after that, there was just a packet of money. We never heard from him again. But the cottage belonged to Caitlin Marie, since she was a daughter of his lineage, so we still had a place to live.

"During that time, after Devyn went back to the road without her, Maureen began sending letters to her sister Brighid, who lived on the White Isle. I don't know how many letters she sent. She got a few in return, but whatever was said never eased her heart."

His throat closed with the pain of remembering.

"Finish it," Glorianna said gently.

"When Caitlin turned two, Maureen tried to bake a cake as a special treat. Didn't turn out right. Don't know why it didn't, but it wasn't edible—and it was all she had to give. She wept and raged and smashed things." His eyes filled with tears as he thought about that day, with him holding on to Caitlin to protect her from the shards of dishes and glass while his mother screamed out the pain of a broken life. "She walked out of the cottage—just left us there in the debris. And that night, she walked into the sea."

"Guardians of the Light and Guides of the Heart," Glorianna whispered.

Michael wiped the tears away. "You understand my mother, don't you, Glorianna Belladonna? You know why she hurt, and what she should have done to ease the pain. Don't you?"

"It wasn't your fault, Michael. It wasn't Caitlin's fault—or Devyn's. She was a Landscaper who needed to connect with the places that resonated with her heart. The world was always calling, and she was always searching for something she couldn't name but knew she needed.

There were places that resonated for your father where she was comfortable, but they were his places, not hers. And there were some places where she became a dissonance because she didn't fit at all. She never found the place her heart recognized as 'home,' and the pain of it eventually broke her."

"Will that happen to Caitlin Marie?" Michael asked.

"I think the White Isle holds some of the answers Caitlin has been looking for," Glorianna replied. Then she turned away. "I'd better see how Lee is coming with that bridge."

He held out a hand to stop her. "I'm not sure what I'm asking, so if I'm out of line I need you to tell me so."

She looked at him and waited.

"I need to know what I do when I'm in one of my . . . landscapes. After things are settled with Caitlin, could you come with me to visit one of them?"

For a moment, while they looked into each other's eyes, he could have sworn the world itself held its breath waiting for her answer.

"Yes," she said. "I'll come with you."

He stepped away to let her pass just as the ship sailed under that one bit of cloudy sky.

Kenneday raised a hand, hailing him. He hesitated, wondering what excuse he could give. And then there was no reason to hesitate, no need for an excuse—because no one would be able to distinguish the clouds' tears from his own.

Chapter Twenty-one

Merrill didn't know what to think, didn't know what to feel as she watched those . . . *people* . . . escort Brighid to the wrought-iron gate that served as the visitors' entrance to Lighthaven. *Brighid,* who had been the heart of this sanctuary of Light and never should have left the White Isle to tend those demon-spawn children. Brighid, who was coming back to them maimed in body and spirit by her time in the outside world.

When Shaela had told her someone was coming up the road in a hired carriage, she had rushed outside and locked the gate, unable— and unwilling—to hear Shaela's objections over the pounding of her own heart. She had known on some level who was coming, and locking the gate was the only way to protect what she loved best. Not the people, despite her affection for the Sisters who nurtured the Light. No, it was the place itself she truly loved. Because it was the only *safe* thing to love.

Anger clogged her throat, clogged her lungs, thickened the blood trying to pump through her heart. The carriage had stopped some distance away, but she could tell who crawled out of it as though it were some pus-filled womb. Not just the demon-spawn children of Brighid's sister coming to foul a Place of Light, but the sorceress called Belladonna was with them, along with a dark-haired man.

Belladonna. How had that *creature* managed to reach Lighthaven?

Hadn't she done everything in her power to cast the Dark out of Lighthaven? Since the day Belladonna appeared on the White Isle, hadn't she stood in the gardens for hours, focusing her heart and will on the effort of casting out the Dark? Hadn't she spent hours in the prayer room cleansing her own heart of any feelings that didn't belong to the Light? Hadn't she spent just as much time praying that the hearts of all her Sisters would be equally purified?

It had worked. Almost. She had not been strong enough to cast out the shadows lodged in Shaela's heart, and she had not been strong enough to cast out a friend who had served the Light for so many years. But those shadows must have provided the crack through which sorcery could reach the Light.

She couldn't let the crack widen, couldn't let the contamination spread.

She watched Brighid approach the visitors' gate, leaning on the brown-haired man she assumed was Caitlin's brother Michael, while Caitlin Marie kept pace with them. Belladonna and her companion were trailing far behind the others. Good. She had no desire to shame Brighid, but she was Lighthaven's leader and had a duty to this place, so the words had to be said.

She took a deep breath and let her authority and conviction ring in her voice. "It is with joy that we look upon our lost Sister and welcome her back to the place where her heart truly dwells. But the rest of you are not welcome here. I will not allow the darkness that crawls within your hearts to poison the Light. Brighid may come back to us—if she turns away from you, who are unclean."

A few man-lengths away from the carriage, Glorianna tripped, caught herself, then looked back to see what had snagged her foot.

"What's wrong?" Lee asked softly, stopping with her.

"Nothing," she said just as softly as she studied the ground. "Everything."

It wasn't visible to the eye, but if she let her mind and heart drift in the currents of Light and Dark that flowed through the White Isle, she could almost see it as a physical reality: the border that separated two landscapes.

"Brighid said she could tell the moment she took the first step on ground that belonged to Lighthaven," Lee said. "And she's right. Between one step and the next, everything *does* feel a little different. We must have crossed a border."

Glorianna kept studying the ground as the currents of power flowed around her, and through her.

From the moment her feet had touched the White Isle, she had felt that same odd dissonance she'd felt when she'd taken the island out of reach of the Eater of the World. Since Michael tended to describe things in terms of music, she guessed he would say the island was playing two different songs and, because the notes were tangled together, both sounded slightly out of tune.

But they were untangling now, becoming clearer, more distinct. And . . .

"It was a border," she said, not quite believing what she was sensing, "but it's becoming a boundary."

"Boundaries require bridges," Lee said sharply. "And these people don't know about boundaries and borders and bridges, so this doesn't usually occur."

That's right. It didn't. Maybe Elandar and this island weren't as seamless as people thought, but it was still a whole, unbroken piece of the world.

But that didn't answer the question of why Ephemera was altering a border to become a boundary that would make the separation of places apparent. Was it because she and Caitlin were on the island together? Or was something else spurring this change in the world?

The currents swelled suddenly, washing through her. She spun around and looked at the people standing on opposite sides of a gate.

Three women—Brighid, Merrill, and Caitlin Marie. Three heart wishes in conflict with each other. And yet . . . the *same* heart wish.

"Guardians and Guides." She staggered as the ground suddenly dipped and swayed beneath her, as the world itself cried out for help.

"Hey!" Lee grabbed her. "Don't you faint on me again. Don't you do that, Glorianna."

She gave him a shove that had him stumbling back a step and uttering a shocked curse. "We have to stop them before . . ." No time to explain. The bedrock of a Landscaper's heart wasn't established well enough here, so Ephemera was gathering itself to manifest those heart wishes without guidance.

She ran for the gate, aware that an argument was taking place, aware that the Dark currents in this place had been extinguished to the point where they couldn't absorb the bad feelings now swelling in a Place of Light, aware that the ground had become soft and the air heavy, that every heartbeat was a distant clap of thunder, a warning peal of the storm about to break.

She couldn't move fast enough. She would never reach them in time to tell them to stop, to wait, to think. So she did the only thing she could since she had a connection to the White Isle and Ephemera trusted her to guide it through the most ever-changing landscape of all—the human heart.

Ephemera, hear me. Give those hearts what they desire. But manifest those heart wishes through me. Through ME.

As she felt the world gather itself to obey her command, she heard two voices, raised in anger, say at the same moment, *"I don't want you."*

Thunder. Avalanches. The crash of the sea. The scream of the wind when it was filled with wild insanity.

The roar of a world tearing itself apart.

Everything snapped back into focus. Her last step had her knocking into Caitlin before she put her hands out to catch herself as she fetched up against the stone wall beside the gate. She leaned against it, rested her cheek against it as she closed her eyes.

Good stone. Solid stone. Not the stone of anger, but the stone of strength.

All the tangled currents were no longer tangled. Her resonance formed the bedrock for Lighthaven, but what lay beyond the boundaries of this landscape . . .

"I thought shattering the world had been difficult, but it wasn't," she said as strong hands settled on her shoulders. "The difficult part is keeping the pieces in harmony enough to stay together."

For a moment, she thought it was Lee standing behind her. Then she realized the shape of the hands wasn't quite right. And the warmth of those hands, the way they touched her . . . No, those weren't her brother's hands.

"Darling, I'm hearing the words, but they have no meaning," Michael said as he drew her away from the wall and back against him. "And if you're going to be scaring me on a regular basis, I'm telling you now I want kisses. The kind that make a man's head swim and will kick his heart back out of his stomach."

"Isn't there a saying about the connection between men's hearts and stomachs?" Foolish to be flirting, but she felt oddly light and happy, as if she'd taken in that first breath of spring after a hard winter.

"I haven't the foggiest idea what you're talking about," Michael said, laughter in his voice.

Then Lee said in a strained voice, "Fog is a good way to describe it," and the breath of spring vanished as she eased away from Michael and looked back toward the place where she had tripped.

Dark currents flowed through Lighthaven again, but they were slender threads that resonated with her. That fog, however . . .

She brushed her fingers over Michael's arm. "Go with Lee. See if you can find out the source of that fog."

He gave her a questioning look, then nodded. Good. Since they both knew he didn't have the training to figure out the reason for the fog, he was assuming she just didn't want her brother going alone to investigate. Which was true.

The other part of the truth was she wanted the men out of hearing before she let her anger flow.

She waited until Lee and Michael were halfway between the gate and the fog before she turned to look at the women. Shock and fear on Merrill's face. Fear and confusion on Caitlin's. Confusion . . . and an awakening . . . in Brighid's eyes. And a recognition: *I know you.*

Merrill first.

"Open the gate," Glorianna said coldly. "You got what you wanted. More than you wanted. Now you have to live in the landscape your heart helped shape."

"I don't . . . ," Merrill stammered.

"Open the gate."

Pebbles popped out of the ground all around the gate.

"Sorceress," Merrill whispered.

"Landscaper," Glorianna replied.

This time, the stones that popped out of the ground in response to her anger were fist-sized and had sharp edges.

Shaela stepped up to the gate and nudged Merrill to one side. Her hands shook as she unlocked the gate, but she pulled it all the way open.

Satisfied with that step, Glorianna glanced toward the spot where Lee and Michael were standing, thankfully still visible. Since the men didn't need her, she turned her attention—and her temper—on Caitlin Marie.

"Did you learn nothing in the past few days?" she asked, making her voice as sharp and hard as stone. "You have seen what happens to the world when you become careless. *You have seen,* Caitlin Marie. You no longer have the excuse of ignorance for what you do or the harm you cause."

The girl took a step back, shocked by the deliberately aimed emotional blow.

"I didn't do anything," Caitlin said, now looking sick and scared.

"You're a Landscaper," Glorianna snapped. "You can't lie with words when your heart knows the truth. *Feel* the difference. This place has changed." *For the better,* she added silently, but she still had one more of them to deal with before she acknowledged *that.*

"It wasn't just me," Caitlin cried. "It *wasn't.* Why aren't you yelling at her?" She flung out an arm to point dramatically at Merrill. "She started it by saying I don't belong here. She—"

"—is right."

Silence. Shock and pain. And in that silence, when the hearts of those women had no defenses, Glorianna, as Landscaper and Guide, heard all their secrets. Especially the ones they had kept hidden from themselves.

Now she could gentle her own heart. Because now she understood the tangles between herself and Caitlin.

"You don't belong here, Caitlin Marie," Glorianna said quietly. "You never did. If you had come when you had first learned of Lighthaven, if you had been welcomed when the dream of it was still a fluid dream, I think you could have walked here in harmony with this Place of Light. But always as a visitor. Now you resent the place and feel bitterness toward the people who live here. Now you are a dissonance. You are not the bedrock of Lighthaven." She turned to look at Merrill. "I am."

Merrill's eyes widened. She clamped a hand over her mouth to stifle a cry. Then her hand slowly lowered as she stared at Glorianna in wonder. "I know. I feel you in the Light in a way I couldn't before."

"I am the bedrock. And you are the anchor." She looked at Brighid.

"Just as you were once the anchor." She saw wariness in Brighid's eyes. It must have been hard for the woman to hide her true nature, even from the people she loved.

She took a step toward Brighid, then tipped her head toward Merrill and Shaela. But her eyes stayed locked with Brighid's. "They are Sisters of the Light, but you are a Guardian. A true Guardian, descended from the first ones who were shaped by Ephemera in response to a cry from the human heart. What we came from was not human, and even now, generations later, we are not completely human. But it's time to stop hiding, Brighid. The Eater of the World is loose in the world again, and people need to know they do not stand alone."

Brighid studied her, hope now battling wariness. "My family line has been a secret kept for generations. A secret entrusted only to the daughters destined for Lighthaven. Even Maureen didn't know because she wasn't . . . like me. You're not a Guardian. How do you know about these things? Why do you talk as if we're the same? We're not. I know we're not."

"Two branches from the same tree," Glorianna replied. "You came from a line of Guardians, the ones who remained apart from the world in order to nurture the Light. I came from the line who walked in the world in order to know the human heart. I'm a Guide."

Four women sucked in their breaths as they understood the significance of that word.

"You're a Heart Seer?" Brighid asked.

Glorianna nodded.

"But I'm not," Caitlin said, looking heart-bruised.

"No, you're not," Glorianna replied gently. "But you are a very strong Landscaper, Caitlin, and it's time for you to knowingly take care of your pieces of the world."

"I don't know how."

"My mother and I can teach you."

Caitlin looked at her with eyes drenched in unshed tears. "I don't know where I belong."

Glorianna stepped close enough to brush her fingers over the girl's short hair. "That's all right," she said, smiling. "I do."

Then she looked past Caitlin and saw the men coming back to the gate. Michael's face was pale as ice, and Lee's . . . She had never seen her brother look so grim—or so scared.

She looked at Brighid, then at Merrill. "I think the rest of this conversation should be more private."

"And *I* think this conversation would be best held in a well-stocked pub," Michael said. "But we're not likely to be finding one here, so . . ." He raked his fingers through his hair.

"We do have some brandy," Shaela said. "For medicinal purposes."

Lee brushed a foot from side to side to create a narrow path that was clear of the pebbles and fist-sized stones made from Glorianna's anger. He worked his way up to the gate and past the gate. Once he was inside the walls that surrounded Lighthaven, he turned and looked at all of them. "Then I suggest we all have a large glass of medicine before we talk about this. We're going to need it."

Michael cradled the glass of brandy and stared at the dark liquid, waiting for someone else to ask the question, voice a concern, do something. But Lee and Glorianna, who were the only ones in the room who might have the answers, seemed content to drink brandy, stare at nothing, and brood.

"All right," he said. "What happened out there?"

Glorianna and Lee looked at him. Then Lee said, "In response to some powerful heart wishes, the White Isle shattered into two landscapes, separating Lighthaven from the rest of the island. Right now, that's all we know." He turned to his sister. "Isn't it?"

Glorianna nodded. "And we know Lighthaven is one of my land-scapes, and I'm almost certain the rest of the White Isle is one land-scape that is in Caitlin Marie's keeping."

He waited, but they didn't say anything more. "What happened to the horse and driver when things . . . changed?"

"That mist-covered lake might not look so big from the other shore," Lee replied. "Not likely to be a puddle-jump, but—"

"Did a man die when this happened?" Michael's voice sharpened. "Is that what the two of you are trying not to say? That because people had an argument and some harsh words were said, the world changed and a man died because of it?"

Shocked gasps. One of the women—maybe Caitlin—whimpered.

"We don't know," Glorianna said, giving him the courtesy of look-ing him in the eyes. "I don't think a chunk of the road suddenly dis-appeared out from under the carriage, dropping man and horse to the bottom of the lake. I think it's more likely the landscapes altered, and Ephemera created a moat, of sorts, around Lighthaven."

Suddenly Michael realized what she wasn't quite saying: The lake was that unnatural dark patch in the sea, the place where Glorianna had fainted in his arms. Somehow, Ephemera had plopped Lighthaven in the middle of that dark patch, which Lee and Glorianna were now call-ing a lake. And since that made no sense to him, he focused on some-thing he hoped wasn't quite so slippery to grasp.

"So the driver might be standing in the same spot, wondering why the road is suddenly leading right into a lake?"

"He could be." Glorianna took a healthy swallow of brandy. "Or he could have stared at it for a minute or two and then driven back to At-water as fast as he could."

"To tell them what?" Brighid asked.

Michael studied his aunt. She looked pale, and she had to be hurt-ing still from the injuries caused in the fire. It would have eased his own nerves a bit if she'd gone off to rest. But he hadn't known, and she had never said, that she had been more than a Lady of Light, that she had been their leader.

She belonged here. He could see it. Even in pain, even in distress over the things that had happened, there was an ease in the way she held herself, as if the land itself nourished something inside her—something that had starved during the years she had lived in Raven's Hill.

He'd had no idea what she had given up in order to answer the plea of a young boy who had been desperate to avoid being put in the orphan's home and just as desperate not to lose his little sister, the only family he had left.

Brighid caught him looking—and returned the look.

Power in her eyes. The kind of power that had been kept hidden all the years she had lived outside these walls. Maybe—he glanced at Merrill, making a quick judgment of the way *she* was watching Brighid—had been kept hidden all the years she had lived here as well.

"We won't know that—or what's on the other side of the boundary—until one of us is standing in the other landscape and looking at the lake from that side," Glorianna said in response to Brighid's question. "The problem is, we don't know if the rest of the White Isle *is* the landscape on the other side of the lake. And Caitlin hasn't had the training to know how to take the step between here and there to reach one of her landscapes or her garden, so—"

"She's not going back to Raven's Hill," Michael said fiercely. "Especially not alone."

"Her garden isn't rooted in Raven's Hill," Glorianna said. "It never was. Our immediate problem is how to get across a lake of undetermined size with neither boat nor oars—and no idea of what now resides in that lake since it's still a dark landscape."

Michael shuddered. The weeds that floated just beneath the surface *had* looked similar to the seaweed that had marked that patch of dark water, but Lee had felt reasonably certain the water was fresh, not salt. Different . . . and yet the same.

So Michael took a long swallow of brandy and wished there wasn't a reason to wonder . . . and worry . . . about what might be waiting for any fool who tried to cross that lake.

Lee dug in his jacket pocket. "I've got a solution to that particular problem. Kenneday gave me this." He held out a compass and grinned at his sister.

Glorianna looked at the compass and started hooting with laughter while everyone else just looked puzzled.

"I asked him for something small that I could carry and use if I needed a way back to the ship. So he gave me this."

Glorianna almost got herself under control—and then got the hiccups.

"One shot—*hic*—bridge?" she asked.

Lee nodded. "It should put me on the deck of the ship. If I leave now, I shouldn't be too far behind the driver and whatever story he'll be telling. Might even get there ahead of him. I'll reassure Kenneday that we're all in one piece, then have him help me get a wagon and maybe a rowboat. We couldn't see the other shore because of the fog, but a person should be able to cross that distance."

"Depends on the heart, doesn't it?" Glorianna said cryptically. She set her glass aside and scrubbed her hands over her face. "All right. If you're feeling up to it, it would be better to get ahead of the wildest stories. We'll figure out what should be connected and how once we know what we're looking at."

"Done." Lee stood up and headed out of the room.

"If I'm not here when you get back, don't worry," Glorianna said as he opened the door.

He shut the door with a control that was worse than a slam. "And where will you be, Glorianna Belladonna?" Lee asked, turning back to face her.

She narrowed her eyes at him. He just stared back. Michael admired the backbone it took for a man to do that.

Glorianna looked at Merrill. "Do you have riding horses here?"

"Y-yes," Merrill stammered. "They're not fancy, but we have some."

She turned those eyes back on her brother. "The Magician and I are going to ride the perimeter of this landscape and find out what it has and what it lacks."

He was so surprised by her plans for him that he inhaled the fumes of the last swallow of brandy and coughed until he thought his eyeballs would bounce right out of his head. Of course, then he got a double whack on the back, which helped neither cough nor eyeballs.

"If you're done with killing me, then get me some water," he wheezed. He heard someone scrambling. Not either of the two who had been whacking him, but someone with a kinder heart.

Then Caitlin was kneeling in front of him holding a glass of water.

"Drink it down now. There's a lad," she said.

I'm not seven, he thought, feeling surly enough to think it but still having enough sense not to say it.

He took the water and drank it down—and got his breath back.

"It's settled then," Glorianna said.

"Now that you've settled things to your satisfaction, kindly satisfy the curiosity of the rest of us," Brighid said.

Michael, hearing her voice edge toward the cold side of discipline, winced. Glorianna, however, just watched his aunt, as if looking for something no one else could see.

"I won't know precisely until I ride the perimeter, which, I suspect, will take no more than a day," Glorianna said. "I'm guessing Lighthaven is now an island within an island. The connection between this Place of Light and the rest of the island was already fragile." She nodded at Merrill. "That, I think, was your doing. Your heart fears the world beyond these walls. You wanted Lighthaven to be unreachable, untouchable."

"And you wonder why?" Merrill asked. She waved a hand toward Brighid and Shaela. "Look what the outside world does."

"I didn't say you were wrong, Merrill," Glorianna replied. "I'm simply explaining." She waited, then she closed her eyes, as if she needed to shut them all out in order to make a decision. When she opened them, she looked at Brighid. Only Brighid. "The White Isle has been split into two separate landscapes. Maybe more. Until a Bridge comes in and establishes bridges that can connect those landscapes to other places, they stand apart from the rest of the world and each other. In Ephemera's attempt to balance the heart wishes that altered the White Isle, the Dark currents that had been cast out of Lighthaven have now formed a lake that keeps the Light from being touched by the outside world."

"That isn't right," Brighid said quietly. "The Light should not be hidden away."

"It should be protected!" Merrill protested.

"A beacon of hope must be seen, Merrill, or it cannot shine in the dark and warm the hearts that need it most." She focused her attention on Glorianna. "What must we do to touch the world again?"

"Glorianna?" Lee asked softly.

She waved a hand in his direction. "Go. Travel lightly."

She waited until Lee was gone before leaning back in her chair and looking up at the ceiling, as if she needed a moment to mentally step away from all of them.

Michael watched her. There were fine lines at the corners of her eyes. Had they been there before now, or had the strain of this journey cut those lines into her skin? Was he partly responsible for those lines? Was Caitlin, with her childish tantrums that created consequences not easily fixed—if they could be fixed at all?

"Is that how it is then?" he asked no one in particular. "People do foolish things, or say things in anger that they would regret in a clear-headed moment, and the world changes?"

"Opportunities and choices, Magician," Glorianna said, sitting forward. "Every day, every person makes a hundred small choices. Most of them are not so clear-cut as choosing between Light and Dark. There is so much room in the gray spaces of the world. But when weighed at the end of the day, that heart leans a little more toward the Light or the Dark—and then resonates a little closer with the Light or the Dark. Make enough choices, one way or the other, and the day comes when you have grown beyond who you were and it's time to take the next step in your life's journey."

"To cross over to another landscape, you mean?" Michael asked.

"The world doesn't care if you call it crossing over to another landscape or if you believe a spirit will remove a key from your heart and tell you to choose the lock that will open the door to the next stage of your life. What matters is that where you end up will match the resonance of your heart, good or bad, Light or Dark." She rested her forearms on her knees and clasped her hands loosely in front of her. Then she looked at each of them in turn. "Life journeys. On the way, you are influenced by others, helped by others, harmed by others. Some things happen because you have earned them. And some things happen because cruelty flickers through the Dark currents and rises up without warning, causing harm, causing pain, causing tragedies that can devastate one person or an entire village. What I feel in this room is a conflict of hopes and dreams and desires. No one who stood at that gate is innocent of shattering the White Isle. And no one is more to blame than the others. So many choices were made to bring you to this moment. Now that you know what your choices can do, make the next ones with care."

She pushed up and went to the door.

"What about you, Glorianna Belladonna?" Brighid asked. "Are you accepting responsibility for the choices you made?"

Oh, the look in Glorianna's eyes when she said, "I always accept responsibility for my choices." Then she slipped out of the room and quietly closed the door.

Chapter Twenty-two

Michael spread the blanket at the top of a gentle slope that led down to the lake. Maybe he should have offered to set things up where there was a bit of shade, despite the coolness of the day, but right now he needed to feel the sun's warmth seeping into him, and he didn't think Glorianna, despite being so fair-skinned, wanted to hide her face from the sun today either.

"You're more practical than my brother," Glorianna said as she walked up to him, her saddlebags over one shoulder.

"How so?" He smoothed the last corner, feeling more awkward than the first time he'd had a private picnic with a girl. Woman, really. She had been older than him and knew a few things he was more than willing to learn. Still, that first time with a new girl, when a boy wasn't sure if he'd get a hand cracked across his face or if the girl would smile and say "more," always made the heart beat a little harder.

"Lee would have put the blanket *on* the slope and then gotten stubborn about moving it until he'd spilled something on himself. You chose flat ground."

"I prefer eating food to wearing it." The image flashed into his mind, of him dipping his fingers into whipped cream and mounding it, ever so gently, over her bare breasts. No need to add a berry on top because the berry—

"Are you all right?" Glorianna asked. "You look flushed."

"I'm fine." He shifted on the blanket and sat in a way he hoped would hide just how fine he was feeling.

She waited for a beat, then set the saddlebags down on the blanket. "Why don't you set out what's there while I get the rest."

He winced at the tone but didn't offer to get up and help. Despite feeling troubled by what he had seen during their ride that morning, this was the first time they had been alone since he'd showed up on her island, and he was hoping for a little romance before they got back to Lighthaven's community. He didn't want to scare her off by having her notice just how ready he was for a little romance.

"This is a clever idea," he said with hearty enthusiasm as he lifted the container of cold chicken out of one saddlebag, followed by the water skin that had been nestled beneath it. Judging by the way her eyebrows rose, maybe he'd sounded a bit too hearty. "Well, it is," he muttered.

"No one has ever thought to fill up a water skin and put it in the ice house overnight, and then use it to keep food fresh when you're traveling?"

"If someone has, I haven't heard of it."

They divided the food, then settled down to eat.

As long as he kept his eyes away from the lake, he could enjoy having a picnic with the woman who heated his blood and warmed his heart, and could imagine them having more times like this, a lifetime of days like this. But the lake always intruded.

"It's not a natural fog, is it?" he asked, turning his head to look at the lake—and the fog that still shrouded its surface.

"Since that is the nature of this lake, you could call it natural," Glorianna replied.

He shook his head. "If it was just fog, it would have burned off by now."

Setting aside the bones of the chicken leg she'd devoured, she delicately licked her fingers clean. Watching her just about broke his restraint.

"Fog obscures," Glorianna said. "It hides things—dangerous pieces of ground . . . or dangerous facets of a person's nature. It's also a warning about the nature of a landscape, that the Dark currents are strong there."

"Lady of Light, have mercy," Michael murmured, dropping his head to his raised knees.

"Michael?"

Her hand on his shoulder, a comforting stroke. He turned his head to look at her. "The place I wanted you to see is called Foggy Downs. They're good people, Glorianna. I was hoping you would know how to help them."

"Wanted me to see?"

She was closing herself off from him, backing away emotionally. He could see it in her face. When she stretched out on her back and stared at the sky, he knew he'd slipped badly, but he wasn't sure what he'd done to upset her.

Then he thought about what he'd said and just sighed. No point chiding himself for words being taken in a way he hadn't meant. At least he knew how to fix this.

He packed up the remains of their meal and set it aside. Then he stretched out beside her, propped on one elbow so he could see her face.

"I still want you to see it," he said quietly. "I want that for myself and for those people. But I'm beginning to understand how much weight you already carried on your shoulders, and now you have more. I don't want to add to the burden more than I've already done."

She'd been staring straight up, ignoring his closeness even though his face must have blocked half her view of the sky. Now she frowned, and those green eyes shifted to look straight into his.

"Ever since I met you, you've been helping my family in one way or another—and putting aside your own tasks to do it. You haven't been on your island looking after your own because you've been looking after me and mine."

She gave him an odd look. "What makes you think one is different from the other?"

Am I yours? Something in him shimmered with joy, and for a moment he could have sworn the air tasted sweeter and the sun shone brighter. Suddenly, this delicate connection between them was more important than anything else in the world. Her feelings were more important than anything else.

He shifted until he halfway covered her, so that, when she looked up, he was all she would see.

"If I'm yours, how would you feel about a few kisses?" he asked, giving her a smile that was equal parts playfulness and charm in an effort to lighten the mood.

She looked more amused than charmed. "Why are you so interested in kisses?"

He did his best to shift his expression to confused sincerity. "I'm a man."

Laughter lit her eyes while she struggled to keep a straight face. "I suppose we could indulge in a few kisses."

"Maybe more than a few," he said, touching his lips to the corner of her mouth as he changed the tone of the song forming between them. "But not more than kisses. Not here. Not today." He raised his head and saw the confusion in her eyes. "Not for our first time. For that, I want a bed . . . and candlelight. I want to drift on the scent of your skin and float on the touch of your hand. And in all the years to follow, when we're laughing and quarreling and living, I want to see the memory of that first time shine in your eyes whenever I touch you, fill you, love you. I want that, Glorianna, for both of us. So, for today, I promise nothing but kisses."

"Do you keep your promises, Magician?" she asked, her voice husky with desire.

He brushed his lips against hers. "I do." And the truth of that was bittersweet. "I most certainly do."

Then his mouth closed over hers, and he spoke to her in a language that had no need of words.

Who was this man who could kiss her and make the world melt away and still had the self-control to roll to his side of the blanket and say, "Best to stop now, darling, while I still have a few brains left in my head"? How could he understand so much and still understand so little?

But he understood the land, understood what he was seeing—and not seeing. It had sobered both of them after they'd gathered up their things and continued the ride.

No word was spoken, but they both reined in as soon as they came within sight of Lighthaven's buildings.

"Well," Michael said. "It could have been worse. There's fresh water and fish in the streams. There's woodland, so there's game for food and wood for the fires. And there are meadows and pastureland and the acreage that's been farmed."

"The land is sound and can sustain itself," Glorianna agreed. "Can the people?" She noted his reluctance to look at her and had her answer. Unfortunately, it matched her own opinion of the people who tended this Place of Light. "They hobbled themselves, Michael. The Places of Light tend to be separated from the world around them because, long ago, the Guardians who took up the task of nurturing the Light decided that a simple life helped the heart and mind remain at peace. But the people who live in those places usually are not without resources . . . or knowledge. They may live simple lives, but there is nothing simple about their skills. If isolated, they could survive."

"Until they died out." Now he looked at her. "I don't know how it is in the other Places of Light, but I'm not blind to the look and feel of *this* place, Glorianna. Lighthaven belongs to the *Ladies* of Light. Men may come up from Atwater and the surrounding farms to do manual labor—of all sorts—" he added in a mutter, remembering the hungry, speculative looks he'd gotten from some of the younger Sisters while he was saddling the horses. "But they don't live here. And I'm thinking we're not going to find anyone outside this community on this land. Not a cottage, not a farm. No one."

"My concern is more immediate," she said. "How many of these women have ever nocked an arrow to a bow and gone out to hunt their dinner? How many have chopped down a tree or even chopped wood? How many have thrown a line in the water to catch fish? How many have tilled the land before they planted a kitchen garden? What about feed for the animals? Oats? Hay?"

He swore softly and scrubbed his fingers through his hair. "Well, can't you—no, I guess it would be Lee, wouldn't it—can't he put in one of those bridges?"

"To go where?" She waited to see if he understood the question, but there was only confusion.

Reminding herself that, until a few days ago, his view of the world had been fairly linear, and a straight road between two places actually would have taken him between one place and the other, she dismounted and gave the horse a long rein so it could graze while she gave the man her full attention.

He hesitated, as if trying to figure out the reason for her action, then did the same.

"Borders and boundaries." She fisted her hands and held them out, pressed together. "When two similar landscapes belong to the same

Landscaper, they can be fitted together as a border—a place where people can cross over without using a bridge."

"Like the Den butting up against the part of Elandar where the waterhorses dwell?" Michael asked.

"Yes, like that. The waterhorses are demons and live in a dark landscape. The Den is a dark landscape inhabited by humans and demons. Both are mine, and they resonate with each other."

He brushed a finger over her fists, pausing at the line made where they were pressed together. "It's a wonder, isn't it, that two places physically so far apart can be reached just by stepping over a line."

She separated her fists, leaving a fist-sized gap between them. "Boundaries are formed between the pieces of the world that belong to different Landscapers and also between places that belong to the same Landscaper but don't resonate with each other in a way that forms a border. Those require bridges in order for people to cross over from one to the other. Even then, a stationary bridge can be created only between two landscapes that *want* to be connected. The hearts in both of those places have to want something that forms a link. Do you understand, Michael?"

"I think so." He frowned at her fists, then tapped one. "Lighthaven." Tapped the other. "The rest of the White Isle. Two . . . landscapes . . . now. Two Landscapers."

"Yes," she said softly.

"So . . ." He tapped a finger on one fist, then formed an imaginary arch to the other fist. "Lee makes one of his bridges and connects—"

"No." This was going to hurt him. She knew him well enough now, could feel the depth of his heart and know this would hurt him. "Heart wishes are powerful magic, Magician. A true heart wish can change your life. It can change the world. In those moments when Ephemera was manifesting the heart wishes that were reshaping this part of itself, two women said in anger, 'I don't want you.' And they meant it, Michael. They meant it." She lowered her fists, watched him physically brace for the verbal blow. "These two landscapes will reject each other because the hearts that Ephemera used to define these land-scapes had rejected each other. So these landscapes can't meet. At least, not right now. Maybe never. Lee could build a thousand bridges to connect Lighthaven to the White Isle, and every one of them would fail."

"But . . ." He sank to his knees. "Does Caitlin know?"

She crouched in front of him. "No. And there's no reason to tell her. Not yet."

"She's not a child," Michael said, the snap of temper in his voice. "Don't you think she should know what she's done?"

"Not yet." She touched his cheek. He immediately reached up to press her palm against his face, holding on to the contact. "She's been told for so long where she doesn't belong. Let's find the place where she does belong. I said it yesterday, and I'll say it again. No one who stood by that gate was innocent, and no one is more to blame than the oth-ers for what has happened to the White Isle."

"I started this," he said, his voice rough with the clash of emotions. "I started this by writing a letter sixteen years ago."

Who would have guessed the man would even think of wallowing in blame, let alone actually do it? "Opportunities and choices, Magi-cian. You wrote a letter; Brighid chose to answer it. And she chose to have the three of you live in Raven's Hill. She could have brought you back here to the White Isle and found a family willing to foster the two of you if it wasn't possible for you to live with her at Lighthaven."

He let out a sharp, bitter laugh. "The demon-spawn children? Our new 'family' would have thrown us in the sea as soon as Brighid was out of sight."

That he believed the words was a weight on her heart. But she gave him a light kiss and stood up. "As a child, you believed that," she said briskly. "As a man, it's time to adjust some of those beliefs. Let's go."

She meant to ride on to the buildings enclosed within their stone wall. Like the Landscapers' walled gardens. Something to think about since no other Place of Light had shut itself away quite like this. But the lake pulled at her, and she reined in a man-length from the edge and studied the black water.

Brighid had been Lighthaven's anchor at one time. While the Guardian's heart had maintained the simple way of life that suited a Place of Light, Glorianna suspected the ebb and flow of feelings within the community of Sisters had been more natural. For one thing, there must have been children in order for the bloodlines to continue. Therefore, there must have been lovers, however temporary.

Now Merrill was the anchor. And Merrill, so fearful of the feelings that lived within the human heart, had managed to deny the Dark currents so strongly that Ephemera had created a dark landscape to provide an outlet and a balance.

A shimmer of thought, a butterfly of feeling fluttered through her. Something there. Something to remember.

Then the moment was gone, and it was time to face the next part of the journey—and all the troubled hearts now stirring up the currents in this landscape.

Merrill brought in a tray and set it on the table before studying the woman who stood at the window, staring out at the gardens they had both helped plant so many years ago.

"Does it look the way you remember it?" Merrill asked.

"Yes," Brighid answered quietly, sadly. "It hasn't changed."

"I kept it as it was. Shaela wanted to change some things, but I was the leader, and I kept it the same." *For you.*

"Why didn't you let it change?" Brighid asked, turning away from the window, the dried tracks of tears still visible on her face. "The songs that mark the waxing and waning of the day should remain the same because they are tradition. They ground the heart and give us the comfort of knowing that these same words have flowed through the air and seeped into the land going back to ancestors who are nothing more than myth. But living things should change, must change. Shaela loves you in ways I never did, never could. You should have let her change the gardens, Merrill. The two of you should have planted something new."

"But now that you're back . . ." Something in Brighid's face strangled the rest of the words.

"I'm not staying," Brighid said. "Something is missing. Has always been missing. I was destined for Lighthaven, and I did my duty and came here. As much as I loved this place, it was like a shoe that should have fit but always pinched a little. I don't know why." She paused, then sighed. "You blamed Michael for writing the letter asking me to come to Raven's Hill."

"I didn't blame you for leaving. You were obliged to stay with the children and—"

"I chose to stay."

The steel in Brighid's voice reminded Merrill of why Brighid had been chosen as their leader at so young an age.

Brighid shook her head. "Leaving here wasn't a completely selfless act. Yes, the children needed me, but I also needed to go, and that letter gave me a reason to leave."

"What was out there that you couldn't find here?" Merrill cried.

"I don't know!" Brighid's voice rang with frustration. "Life. Love. Maybe something as simple as lust. I don't know. I never found it." She pressed the heels of her hands against her temples. "I never found it. Just like Maureen never found whatever her heart needed. She loved Devyn. I know she did. But it wasn't enough. And Caitlin . . ."

"Doesn't belong here," Merrill snapped, feeling the sting of rejection all over again. They were back to where they were sixteen years ago. Despite what Brighid said about things changing, nothing had changed. Nothing. "Even the other sorceress said so."

"Guide of the Heart," Brighid murmured. "I never thought I would stand face-to-face with a true Guide of the Heart."

Everything should have been wonderful, but it was all breaking apart.

Merrill looked down at the cuff bracelet she had worn for so many years, thinking it had meant . . .

She pulled it off and held it out. "You gave me this. When you left. A family heirloom, isn't that what you said?"

"That's what it is," Brighid replied.

"You gave it to me as a reminder of what we had meant to each other, what we might have meant if you hadn't . . ." She trailed off.

"I gave it to you as a farewell gift," Brighid said softly. "I never intended to come back to the White Isle."

Merrill dropped the bracelet and turned, knocking into the table as she rushed to the door. Before the sound of the slamming door faded away, she heard the crash of cups and saucers hitting the floor.

Michael took a seat between Lee and Kenneday, more relieved than he wanted to admit that he was no longer the only man at Lighthaven.

"Never saw anything like it, in all my years at sea," Kenneday said. "One minute the deck is clear; the next, this one is standing behind me. And then, when we're standing on the shore of a lake that hadn't been there a couple of days ago, he's calmly transferring all the gear we had packed in the wagon onto this bit of an island only he can see."

"That's not quite true," Lee said, helping himself to some bread and cheese. "There are times when everyone can see the island."

Kenneday just snorted.

Michael helped himself to some of the food on the table and said nothing. Clearly everyone had had an exciting time over the past couple of days.

"It was the strangest thing," Brighid said, responding to Caitlin's question about the different table. "The leg just gave way. It must have been loose—may have been loose for years—and getting bumped with the weight of a tray on top of it was enough to break that leg."

Michael noticed the look exchanged by Glorianna and Lee, then did a quick survey of the room. Where was Merrill? Wouldn't Lighthaven's leader want to be here for this meeting? Besides his aunt Brighid, the only Sister in the room was Shaela.

"So," Lee said, accepting a cup of tea with a polite smile, "the lake does, in fact, circle Lighthaven. Dark, cold water. Weedy. Foggy. I spotted animal tracks going to and from the water, so I think we can assume the water is drinkable. Might be fish in there that are edible. And we confirmed that you can see Lighthaven from the White Isle shore."

"Like a dream it is," Kenneday said. "Like something that fades away as soon as you reach for it."

That got Glorianna's attention. "It's doing the same thing that the White Isle did?"

"We didn't get in a boat to find out, but my guess is it will do the same thing in that you can see it from a distance, but it will fade away completely before you get close to it," Lee said. "I'm wondering if that's the nature of this Place of Light. Maybe it was never meant to be found. Maybe it was meant to be like a dream—you take comfort in knowing it exists, but its allure is even more potent because so few people can reach it."

"Being hard to reach isn't the same as being impossible to reach," Glorianna said. "And some people will need to find it."

"Why?" Shaela asked. "We're supposed to remain apart from the turmoil of the world."

"How many of the Sisters were born here?" Glorianna asked.

Not many, if any, Michael thought, watching Shaela take in the significance of the question.

"A resonating bridge would work," Lee said. "Stationary bridge won't hold between the two landscapes—I did try to create one—but a resonating bridge isn't keyed for specific landscapes. Thing is, since people around here don't know about landscapes and bridges, we'd want something no one would mistake for something else."

"Too bad you can't put a pair of Sentinel Stones in the middle of the lake," Kenneday said, cutting another hunk of cheese off the wheel. "Be romantic like, taking a boat out with the dawn breaking and the mist on the water, and those great black stones rising up from the middle of the lake, and you watching that shore that looks as wispy as a wish and not knowing if it will fade away completely or become real." He glanced around at the people now staring at him and cleared his throat. "Just a passing thought."

"Tell us about these Sentinel Stones," Glorianna said.

When Kenneday just squirmed under her intent stare, Michael jumped in. "You've seen them. You've got a pair of them as the gate—bridge—between the Merry Makers' bog and the Den. Walked between them in order to cross over."

Now Glorianna *and* Lee were staring at *him*.

"Those are common in this land—in Elandar?" Lee asked.

"Common enough," Michael replied warily. "Every third or fourth village has a pair of them in the fields beyond the village proper."

"Tell them what the Stones do," Kenneday said, giving Michael an elbow in the ribs.

"It depends," Michael said, not sure if he needed to be more worried about Glorianna or Lee jumping on him. "Sometimes you walk through the Stones and nothing happens. Sometimes you don't go anywhere . . . but things change." Oh, this was starting to sound familiar in an unfamiliar sort of way. "And sometimes a person walks between the Stones and disappears. Sometimes for a few days—and sometimes forever."

Glorianna sat back and blew out a deep breath. Lee scrubbed his hands over his face.

"They've got resonating bridges all over this landsc—country, and they don't know what the things do," Lee said.

"In point of fact," Michael said testily, "we *do* know what they do. We just never knew *why* things happened to people when they walked between the Stones."

Lee looked at Glorianna. "A pair of those Stones would take care of the problem of people recognizing the bridge." His eyes shifted to look at Michael and Kenneday. "And if the storytellers were to spread a new 'legend' about Lighthaven and why it disappeared, then we'll have an explanation for everyone."

"And who are you expecting to come up with this story?" Michael asked, since he was beginning to feel like a mouse cornered by a pair of black-haired, green-eyed cats.

Lee cocked a thumb at Kenneday. "He's already come up with the part about how to find the mystical island of Lighthaven. The least you can do is come up with the reason it disappeared."

"So," Kenneday said, looking thoughtful, "you steer a bit of a boat between the Stones, and if you're worthy you'll reach Lighthaven's shore. And if you're not, you'll just keep going until you reach the other side of the lake and never find the island?"

"It will be a resonating bridge," Lee said. "So, yes, you might keep going until you reach the other shore. Or you might suddenly find yourself on another lake in another part of Elandar."

"Or on a river in some part of the world you've never seen before," Glorianna added.

"Or you could find yourself sitting in your bit of a boat in the middle of a farmer's potato field," Lee said.

A startled silence. Then Kenneday said, "Well, that would be a crap on the romance of it, now wouldn't it?"

Lee leaned forward a little farther to look at Kenneday. "Welcome to our part of the world."

Michael slapped his hands on his knees. "This is all well and good, and I'm willing to try my hand at spinning a story, but you're all forgetting one thing. How are we going to get two of those Stones and how do we plop them in the lake where they need to go?"

Another silence. Or maybe the room was full of sound that he couldn't hear. Because now he looked at Glorianna Belladonna, who said softly, "Ephemera, hear me."

She didn't leave the room to see what she had done. Neither did Lee. But he went out, along with Kenneday and Caitlin, and walked down the road that now ended at the shore.

The Sentinel Stones rose up midway between the shores. Huge, black stones Michael *knew* hadn't been there a few minutes ago. Stones that were both guard and doorway to a place that didn't want to be touched by the world.

"Lady of Light, have mercy," Kenneday whispered.

"I'm thinking when you stand in this place, the person you should be asking for mercy is called Glorianna Belladonna," Michael said. *Because she can remake the world.* He glanced at Caitlin Marie, who looked so young and scared as she stared at the Stones. He put his arm around her. "Come along. Let it go for tonight. I'm thinking tomorrow is going to be another long day."

She turned and pressed her face into his shoulder. "I'm scared, Michael."

He kissed the top of her head. "So am I, Caitie. So am I."

Hearts full of dissonance, unhappiness, yearnings. Glorianna drank the tea, wishing it were koffee, and let the hearts of the two women in the room flow through her. One needed to stay; the other needed to go. But there were other things that needed to be done first, so she gave Lee a pointed look.

"You're going to need a bridge," Lee said. Seeing their blank faces, he clarified, "A connection to another landscape. You'll need supplies, a way to purchase things you can't make or grow. And you're going to need strong backs to help with some of the labor. Even if we could have done it, which we can't, Atwater wouldn't have been the best choice. My sense of the place was that the people wouldn't be open-minded enough right now to being connected to another landscape in that way."

Glorianna waited for some response, but neither Brighid nor Shaela disagreed with Lee's assessment.

"So," Lee continued, "is there another village on the White Isle that might be a suitable host for a bridge?"

There were advantages to talking to people who weren't familiar with landscapes and bridges, Glorianna thought. Lee had already said he couldn't create a stationary bridge between Lighthaven and the White Isle, but they needed a starting point to begin searching for Caitlin's garden, and that meant finding another community of people on the island.

Brighid and Shaela exchanged a look.

"There is Darling's Harbor," Brighid said reluctantly, "but the people there have always been a bit strange."

"And they've gotten stranger," Shaela murmured.

"How so?" Glorianna asked, trying to remain calm. Darling's Garden. Darling's Harbor. Couldn't be a coincidence.

"For one thing, during my years here, their young people would show up before the summer or winter solstice and bring a gift, then say they were going to be journeying and would we hold them in the Light," Brighid said. "They always struck me as a simple people who were supremely confident that they were exactly where they were supposed to be."

Glorianna felt Ephemera's currents of power brush playfully against her own currents. She sat up straighter. There was one explanation for an entire village of people feeling confident that they were where they belonged, and it had nothing to do with them being simple.

"This village wouldn't have a pair of Sentinel Stones, would it?" she asked.

"It does," Brighid replied.

Glorianna knew that Lee was watching her, adding up the pieces as fast as she was.

There was a resonating bridge in the village of Darling's Harbor, and the people there used it to go journeying. Some of them must have crossed over into landscapes beyond Elandar. Maybe they weren't simple; maybe they didn't want to admit they knew more about the world than the people around them.

"Anything else you can tell us about Darling's Harbor?" Lee asked.

"They've gotten stranger," Shaela said, more loudly this time. "Two or three times a year, a pair of them comes to Lighthaven, cap in hand, and asks if we've had news about the Seer, did we know when the Seer was coming back. A few years ago, when a bad storm swept over the whole island, they came to say the Seer's house had been struck by lightning and burned clean to the ground, and should they be waiting to build another. Then this spring they came back to say they had built a new house and it was ready for the Heart Seer and did we have news of when she was coming."

Glorianna's heart beat fast and hard. "When did this start? How many years ago?"

Shaela shrugged. "A few."

"How many?" When both women stared at her uneasily, she set down her cup and struggled for patience. "This started twelve years ago, didn't it? They started asking about the Seer twelve years ago."

Shaela frowned, but it was thoughtful rather than annoyed. Finally she nodded. "Yes, I think it was a dozen years ago that this started."

Brighid gasped.

Glorianna nodded and said, "That's when Caitlin found Darling's Garden, wasn't it?"

"But Caitlin's not a Heart Seer," Brighid protested. "Besides, that garden was hidden somewhere on the hill behind our cottage. According to stories, the women in Devyn's family had found it a few times in the years since Darling first came to live at Raven's Hill."

"Caitlin isn't a Heart Seer," Glorianna agreed, "but she is a Landscaper who is a descendant of the Guide who had shaped that garden. That's why it appeared for some of the women in that family. It came to them because they were Landscapers who no longer remembered how to go to it."

"The garden acts as a separate landscape that can be imposed over another place, like my island?" Lee asked.

"Yes." Glorianna looked at Brighid. "That's why no one else living in Raven's Hill could find it. It only existed on that hill for Caitlin Marie. The rest of the time it was here, on the White Isle. Where it had been created."

"Looks like we're going to Darling's Harbor," Lee said. "I'll talk to Kenneday when he gets back from staring at the Sentinel Stones, and see if he's sailed to that village."

"We'll wait until morning." She wanted a few hours to go back to her own garden and make sure there was no sign that the Eater of the World had found Its way into one of her landscapes. And she needed to talk to Nadia.

Lee looked disapproving, since he knew her well enough to figure out the reason for the delay, but he didn't say anything. Not much he could say since she knew he wouldn't be turning in early either but, instead, would be making notes about the possible landscapes that might be connected to the White Isle or Lighthaven.

Lee pushed out of his chair, then proceeded to stack cups and dishes on the tray. He lifted the tray and smiled at Shaela. "Could I give you a hand with the clearing up?"

Not subtle, Glorianna thought as she watched Shaela stumble over the veiled order to leave the room, but not as blunt as he might have been.

"Your brother has a way about him," Brighid said when they were alone.

"That's one way of putting it," Glorianna replied, smiling.

Brighid didn't return the smile. "I don't know how to say this."

"You don't belong here."

Brighid closed her eyes. "I don't belong here. I should . . . but I don't."

When Brighid opened her eyes, Glorianna saw confusion, but there was no confusion in the yearnings that came from Brighid's heart. This heart needed the Light—and more than the Light.

"Do you need to live in this kind of secluded community?" Glorianna asked.

Brighid shook her head. "I've felt secluded in one way or another all my life. When I went to Raven's Hill to take care of the children, I had hoped . . ." Her voice trailed off as sadness filled her face.

No, Glorianna thought. For a descendent of the first Guardians of the Light, the toil of the world would have been too hard to bear—especially living in that cottage. But there was a way for Brighid to live in the Light and meet the world.

"Do you feel well enough to travel with us tomorrow?" Glorianna asked.

"Well enough."

"In that case, we'll go to Darling's Harbor to search for Caitlin's garden." Glorianna smiled. "And then I will show you Sanctuary."

Chapter Twenty-three

"Can you feel it, Caitlin?" Glorianna asked, stepping up beside the shivering girl. "Can you feel all the knots and tangles in the currents of power unraveling the closer we get to the harbor? Can you sense how those Light and Dark currents feel when they flow unobstructed?"

"Maybe," Caitlin said, her voice almost too low to hear. "I don't know." Her throat worked, as if she were trying to swallow something unpleasant—or hold something back. "I'm sorry I broke the world. I didn't know I could do that. Nothing like that has happened before."

That you're aware of, Glorianna thought—and couldn't quite hide the shiver that went through her. How had the world survived the combination of ignorance and power? How many landscapes had disappeared because an untrained Landscaper's heart had rung with a pure note of anger?

"Are you nervous too?" Caitlin asked.

"Yes." *But not for myself.* "I'm going aft to talk to Captain Kenneday. Do you want to come?" When Caitlin shook her head, Glorianna went back to the wheel, where Kenneday was guiding his ship to the docks and Michael and Lee were standing nearby.

"Looks like someone knew we were coming," Michael said, raising his chin to indicate the people they could see gathering at the docks.

"Nah," Kenneday replied. "Someone spots sails on the horizon and the word goes out. By the time a ship docks, the whole damn village is waiting to greet it. It's happened every time I've put into port here. It's like they're all waiting for something."

"Or someone," Glorianna said quietly. "If these people have known about Guides of the Heart and their connection to the world . . ."

"How many generations has it been since a Landscaper lived among them, tending her garden?" Lee asked, picking up the thought. "How many years have they been coming down to meet the ships, hoping that a descendant of their darling has come home?"

Home. Even though this wasn't her landscape, she felt the resonance of the word, the rightness of it. Heart wishes and yearnings were coming together for that moment of opportunity and choice.

She glanced at Michael—then thought of Brighid, who was belowdecks, resting—and recognized the two stumbling blocks that could end something before it began.

Grabbing Michael's arm, she pulled him away from the others. Judging by his smile, they had very different reasons for wanting a semiprivate moment.

"Listen, Magician," she said, giving her voice enough punch to wipe the smile off his face. "No matter what you or Brighid think about this, you must keep your thoughts and concerns to yourself. This is Caitlin's life, not yours. This has to be her choice, not what you want for her."

"What are you—"

"Your mother walked into the sea because she never had this moment to stand in the place where her heart was rooted. Sometimes we're given opportunities over and over again to make the choice that will lead to what the heart yearns for. And sometimes that opportunity, that moment when everything is right, only comes once."

Anger hardened his face, reminding her that he, too, had Dark currents flowing through him that connected with the world. That he was, in his own way, a Guide.

"Do you think so little of me that you believe I'd hurt my sister?" he asked.

"No, you wouldn't hurt her intentionally. But your doubts could influence her enough to have her making a choice that is not in her own best interest."

"She's eighteen," Michael snapped. "And not an old eighteen, if you take my meaning."

"Then it's time she grew up. She's not a child, remember?"

"Don't be turning this around on me, Glorianna. Don't be using my own words against me."

"Then remember that you left home at sixteen, that if the Landscapers in your . . . country . . . had received formal training the way they do in my part of the world, you both would have left home to attend school at the age of fifteen." She wasn't getting through to him. She could see that by the look in his eyes. But she was getting a good measure of the depth and breadth of his stubborn streak.

"Consider this, Michael," she said softly. "How would you feel if you never again heard music except for the sound that drifted through a locked door? When you pressed your ear against the wood, you could hear enough to crave the sound, to know something inside you needed it, but you could never open that door and hear the full richness or intricacy of the song." She watched him pale. "I'm asking you to think carefully before you speak. Don't become the locked door that stands between Caitlin and her heart."

He walked away from her—and for the first time in memory, she wasn't able to read someone's heart.

Michael curled his hands around the railing and squeezed until his bones hurt. He wanted to yell at her, rage at her, call her names, and say things that could never be taken back.

Not because she had the nerve to tell him not to be a stone around his little sister's neck, but because she had explained what was at stake in a way that scared him to the bone.

To lose the ability to hear the music in people's hearts? To lose the ability to play music that would help people find the harmony in themselves? Worse than that, to have that ability but to be denied the use of it until it became a thwarted, crippled thing festering inside you. What would that do to the person who had that ability?

He knew what that would do to a person. After all, hadn't his mother walked into the sea?

Door of Locks. Images. Stories.

Truths. Choices.

His family was splintering. It didn't matter that he'd spent the past dozen years on the road, only coming back to Raven's Hill for a few days at a time. It had been home because there had been family. Now the cottage was gone, and the sense of belonging somewhere was gone too.

Face it, lad, if there was a house that had a peg by the door that was for your coat and yours alone, and if there was a woman in that house who would laugh with you and quarrel with you and love you even when she wanted to knock your head against a wall . . . If you had those things, even if they were in a place far away from anything you had known, would you be resisting the idea of Caitlin settling so far from the places you know? You're afraid to let go because Glorianna hasn't offered you a place in her life, let alone a place in her house or in the piece of the world she calls home. And you're afraid because when you lose Glorianna, there won't be anyone left.

Lee stepped up to the railing. Said nothing.

Michael sighed. "How do you find the courage to let go?"

Lee shrugged. "Parents have been asking that question for generations. Most of them find the courage."

"It's just . . . If she stays here, Caitlin is going to be so far away."

Lee gave him an odd look. "You still don't understand, do you, Magician? All you need is one piece of common ground. If you have that landscape, she'll only be as far away as she wants to be."

Michael grimaced. "Sure, I know about you making bridges, but Caitlin's never been anywhere beyond Raven's Hill, and I can't see her wanting to go back there."

"She's been to Aurora," Lee countered. Then he gave Michael an evil grin. "And she's been to the Den of Iniquity."

He jumped as if a steel rod had been jammed up his backside. "Ah, no. Don't be doing that to me. You've got a sister too—"

"And a cousin who is the Justice Maker in the Den."

"Mentioning Sebastian is not a comfort." And thinking of Caitlin with her lips locked to Teaser's was a whole lot less than comfort. "She's just eighteen and innocent. And Teaser is neither, and a walking temptation in the bargain." Maybe if he kept saying it enough, it would make an impression on someone besides himself.

Lee's evil grin got wider. "So that story you told me about your first time. Which was it, brag or lie?"

"Damn you." But even as he said it, it occurred to him that he'd never had a friend who would poke at him like this. Even Nathan wouldn't have poked fun at him.

"Tell you what," Lee said, clapping a hand on Michael's shoulder. "You don't show too much interest in Caitlin's sex life—and I won't show too much interest in Glorianna's."

"That's different."

"So you say."

"It is."

"We're docking," Kenneday called out. "If either of you care."

"Could be worse," Lee said, taking a step back. "*Sebastian* could start taking an interest in Glorianna's sex life."

"Lady of Light, have mercy," Michael muttered, wincing at the reminder that the incubus had already showed a bit too much interest in his cousin's relationships. *And I haven't even talked her into bed yet.*

Lee walked away laughing, the ripe bastard. Then Brighid appeared from belowdecks, looking pale but determined.

Let them go, he thought as he moved to intercept Brighid and have a few words with her to convey Glorianna's message. *Have the courage to let them both go on with their own lives.*

Their eyes met, and he realized she had faced this moment twelve years ago—when she had let *him* go.

He offered her a smile and his arm. "Shall we go out and meet the world?"

She linked her arm in his. "Yes, I think we shall."

Can you feel it, Caitlin?

That's what Glorianna had asked. But she couldn't feel it. Wasn't sure of anything anymore. She hadn't meant to hurt the White Isle or Lighthaven, hadn't meant to break the world. It felt too much like the time she had indulged in a temper tantrum. She couldn't remember now what it was Aunt Brighid had denied her, but she could remember that moment of wanting to be spiteful beyond words. Could remember picking up the cobalt blue glass statue that represented the Lady of Light—one of the few possessions her aunt had brought to Raven's Hill and the one Brighid had truly prized. Could remember the terrible glee when she threw the statue on the floor to express her displeasure.

And she could remember the naked pain on Brighid's face when that statue broke—and the way Brighid had sounded broken when she said, "Do as you please, then." Brighid had gone into her bedroom and locked the door—and had spent the afternoon crying.

Such a frightening moment for a young girl, to wonder if anyone loved you anymore.

The statue had broken into a handful of pieces. She picked them up and put them on the kitchen table, then carefully swept the floor to pick up all the little shards. She got out her little glue pot and did her best to put the statue back together, but it still looked like something that had been broken and badly mended. When Brighid finally came out of her room, she stared at the statue for a long moment, then picked it up and threw it in the trash bin.

"Some things can't be mended, Caitlin Marie."

She hadn't done this breaking on her own this time, but the result was the same: The world couldn't be mended. Not even Glorianna could mend it. Why would these people want her to live among them?

Can you feel it, Caitlin?

Her fear that she was being dropped off in this village so that Michael and Brighid—and Glorianna—could wash their hands of her began bubbling up as resentment as she followed Glorianna down the gangplank. No, she *couldn't* feel it. People expected her to know things but couldn't be bothered to *explain* things. And then they blamed her for doing something wrong when she hadn't known she *could* do something wrong.

Then she stepped onto the dock and staggered into Glorianna, vaguely aware that Lee, coming down behind her, had grabbed her arm to steady her.

The light dazzled. The air felt heavy and so richly potent that just breathing made her feel a little drunk. And something flowed through her that was joy and sadness, anger and laughter, rich loam and hard rock, sweet water and brine.

"The currents of Light and Dark that flow through this landscape are aligning themselves to resonate more fully with the currents that flow through you," Glorianna said. "This is what it's like to be the bedrock of a landscape. Can you feel it, Caitlin?"

"Yes." *I'm home!* "Yes, I feel it."

Glorianna smiled. "Then let's see what we can do about getting you settled."

"For a place that's supposed to be a small, backward village, they have a good harbor," Lee said. "Could be they do a lot more trading than anyone else on the island is aware of. So it's likely they also have a rooming house or inn for travelers where Caitlin could stay until she finds a place that suits her."

"Let's find out," Glorianna said, smiling at Lee as if sharing a secret. Then she linked arms with Caitlin to lead her toward the welcoming committee.

Caitlin glanced back. Michael gave her an encouraging smile, although it wobbled a little around the edges. Aunt Brighid . . . Well, it was hard to tell what her aunt was thinking at the moment.

The people waiting for them were all smiling. When she and Glorianna were two man-lengths from the committee, the men swept off their caps in a move that was so smoothly in unison that it made her wonder if they rehearsed it on regular occasions.

Then the smiles faded. The people stared until an old woman stepped forward, smiling despite the tears that filled her eyes.

"It has finally happened," she said, looking at Glorianna. "All the years of waiting . . . done now. The Heart Seer has come back." Her eyes shifted to Caitlin, and her pleasure turned to puzzlement.

"I am the Guide, the Heart Seer, for Lighthaven," Glorianna said. "Caitlin Marie is the Landscaper for the rest of the White Isle. She is the one who has tended Darling's Garden these past twelve years."

"Aahhhh." The sound breathed through the crowd, as if something that had always seemed peculiar now suddenly made sense.

"I'm Peg," the old woman said. "This is my youngest granddaughter, Moira. I've been the village's cornerstone, so to speak. Been training up young Moira, since she has the feel of the place in her bones, if you take my meaning."

Before Caitlin could admit that the words made no sense, Glorianna said, "You're the anchor."

Hushed anticipation. A feeling like a light breath blowing over the hairs of her arm.

"You know," Peg said, her wrinkled face lighting with joy even though there was a hint of doubt in her voice.

"Anchors help Landscapers keep the world balanced and sane," Glorianna said. "But most don't realize what they do for a place and its people."

"*We* haven't forgotten our traditions," a gray-haired, middle-aged man said. "Not like some in the south."

"Hush, Colin," Peg said. "We'll not speak ill of our neighbors—even if they act like two-headed goats most of the time," she added in a barely audible mutter.

Caitlin tried to stifle a laugh, which came out in a snort.

"Do you need a handkerchief?" Glorianna asked with a politeness that would have cowed even Aunt Brighid.

"No," Caitlin said meekly.

Peg looked at Glorianna—and smiled. "You're a strong one, aren't you?"

"I understand how strong—and how fragile—the world can be," Glorianna replied.

"Didn't get your name."

"Glorianna Belladonna."

Another hush. Uneasy shuffling of feet.

"There's a pair of Sentinel Stones beyond the village," Peg said. "Some of our young go journeying. Some are meant for other places. Some return to Darling's Harbor. So we've heard of Belladonna."

Glorianna said nothing, but there was now a chill in her green eyes that made Caitlin wish Michael would step up and do something, say something.

Peg looked worried. "We've also heard stories that the Destroyer of Light has awakened."

"Where I come from, we call It the Eater of the World," Glorianna said. "And, yes, It is loose in the world—and has already touched Elandar."

Peg nodded. "Then it's glad I am to have seen the Warrior of Light with my own two eyes. And we're grateful that you were the one who brought the Seer back to us." She sniffed once, then squared her shoulders. "Now then . . ."

"Captain Kenneday!" Colin called out, raising a hand.

"You'll not be doing business now!" Peg scolded.

"And what better time to be doing it?" Colin demanded.

Peg opened her mouth—and finally huffed out a breath. "Very well, then. You talk to the captain. Kayne! You've got younger legs anyway. You show them a bit of the village on the way to the Seer's house."

"There's a house?" Caitlin asked. Something made her glance at Glorianna and Lee—and she realized they had already known about these accommodations.

"Sure there's a house," Peg said. "Old one burned a few years back. Just as well, I suppose. Meaning no disrespect, since she would have been kin to you, but the last one to tend the garden lived in the house from time to time. I was just a girl then, but I remember my mother talking to friends and saying how they had scrubbed that house from top to bottom and still couldn't get rid of the sour smell. It was like that woman's disposition had seeped into the wood and stone. The one that stands now has been tended but not lived in. We've been waiting, you see. We always knew one of Darling's girls would find her way home for good."

"That was her name?" Caitlin asked, startled.

"Sure it was her name," Peg said. "Darling by name, darling by nature. She was the Seer who first made the garden in order to tend her little bits of the world. Then she fell in love, but her man wasn't easy living here, so she went with him to live in his home village and added the place to the bits she tended. But she never quite came home again, even though we knew she still looked out for us. Her daughters and their line never quite came home either. Until now."

Kayne stepped up to be properly introduced, and Caitlin heard

Glorianna make the rest of the introductions. Heard Peg invite Brighid to ride with her in the pony cart. But those were just sounds rippling over the surface. There was a bell tolling in her head, and the sound rang out as "Raven's Hill, Raven's Hill, Raven's Hill."

As the others got sorted out, she tugged on Glorianna's arm, and a look from Glorianna Belladonna was all it took for everyone else to give them some private space.

"Raven's Hill is in the garden?" Caitlin asked, keeping her voice low.

Sadness filled Glorianna's eyes, and the weight of that sadness dragged on Caitlin's heart.

"It's there," Glorianna said reluctantly.

She waited, and then realized Glorianna wasn't going to say anything else unless asked. "Where?"

Glorianna hesitated. "Under the compost heap."

She thought about how Raven's Hill had felt these past few years—and blinked away the tears suddenly stinging her eyes. "Can I fix it?"

"No."

Some things can't be mended, Caitlin Marie.

"Why did you choose that spot to dump the debris from the rest of the garden?" Glorianna asked.

"It felt . . . bad," Caitlin said. "Trashy. Weedy. And . . . the other parts of the garden were weedy and overgrown, but I could still see some of what they had been. That spot . . ."

"Not your fault then, Caitlin," Glorianna said. "It's only a guess, but if too much of the nature of Landscapers had been forgotten by Darling's descendants, then one of them didn't resonate with Raven's Hill and should have let it go. Dumping garbage over the part of the garden that provided the access to the village was a cruel thing to do because it fed the Dark currents and never allowed Raven's Hill to be the place it was meant to be." She sighed and brushed her hair away from her face. "Maybe a need that had no other way of expressing itself acted through you. Whatever the reason, and even though it wasn't done prudently, you did what should have been done a long time ago; you severed your family's connection to Raven's Hill and the village's connection to your garden."

"But it won't have a Landscaper anymore," Caitlin said. "So won't more bad things happen?"

"It doesn't have a Landscaper at the moment," Glorianna said. Then she smiled and added softly, "But it does have an anchor. Another will has been pushing against yours all these years, resisting the village's slow change into a dark landscape."

A whistle made them look over to the spot where Michael, Lee, and Kayne waited. Lee cocked his head and raised a hand in an *are you coming?* gesture.

"Enough," Glorianna said, lifting a hand to acknowledge that they were coming. "For now, let's find out what is here. We'll deal with what was on another day."

Kayne wasn't much of a guide, Michael thought as they followed the lane that led to a house on a rise. For one thing, the man didn't know how to pace himself to a woman's walking speed. He'd push on ahead, leaving Caitlin and Glorianna trailing behind, and outside of tossing information any fool could figure out for himself by reading the shop signs, hadn't said anything useful about the village.

When Michael started lagging behind again to give the women time to catch up, Kayne looked back and sighed.

"So," Kayne said. "Should we dance around this or take the straight road?"

"Meaning what?" Michael asked. But Lee chuckled, indicating that *he* understood the question.

"Michael is Caitlin's brother," Lee said. "I'm Glorianna's brother. I'm not courting Caitlin."

"I'm noticing there's a step missing," Kayne said with a gleeful sparkle in his eyes.

"That's because Glorianna and the Magician here *are* dancing around the question," Lee replied.

"Ah," Kayne said, looking back at the women. But it was clear—to Michael, anyway—that Kayne wasn't looking at Glorianna.

"Caitlin Marie is only eighteen," Michael said darkly.

"A blooming age for a women," Kayne replied, smiling.

"Could be worse," Lee said in a singsong voice. "Could be Teaser."

Wondering why he had ever wanted friends, Michael stopped walking and stubbornly waited for Glorianna and Caitlin to catch up while Lee and Kayne went on ahead.

"Problem?" Glorianna asked.

"Men are a pain in the ass," he grumbled.

She smiled and patted his cheek. "Women have known that forever, but we love you anyway."

Caitlin sputtered and laughed. "Why don't I—" She shook her head and took off. She was laughing too much to run well, but she caught up to Lee and Kayne.

"He's practically licking his lips over her," Michael complained. "She can't be living here on her own when the first man who meets her gets that look in his eyes."

"And what look might that be?" Glorianna asked sweetly.

"You know the one. And if Aunt Brighid is going to be going her way and I'm going . . ." Deciding that was best left unsaid since he didn't know where he was going, he added, "You know what I'm saying."

Glorianna pursed her lips. A bad sign.

"You're saying Caitlin is going to have all this unsupervised time, and despite being a grown, albeit young, woman living in a community that not only understands her connection to the land but also values it, she will become a flirtatious, blithering idiot just because a man with a nice smile and muscles has shown a little interest in her. Is that what you're saying?"

"Maybe." He was pretty sure that *wasn't* what he was saying, but right now he wasn't going to make a definite statement about anything.

"And you're saying that my mother isn't an adequate chaperone, and that I'm not an adequate chaperone, since we'll both be coming here to give Caitlin lessons. And Caitlin will also need to come to Aurora for lessons."

Too close to the Den! Michael thought, hearing Lee's singsong, *Could be worse, could be Teaser.* "Ah . . ." Nadia as chaperone? That would be sufficiently intimidating. But Glorianna was too young to be strict enough when it came to a little sister's . . . flirtations. Which was something he couldn't say without digging a hole for himself that he'd need a ladder to climb out of.

So he focused on the house to buy himself a little time—and stopped in his tracks. It was stone and, for the most part, one story. A house built to weather the moods of the sea.

A house built to be a home that would hear the sounds of children playing, hear the laughter and tears of a life well lived. He could hear its music—and its music was good.

"Oh," Caitlin said. "What a darling!"

Wondering what Kayne had done to earn *that* tone of voice—and why Lee, the ripe bastard, hadn't stopped the man from doing it—Michael hurried forward to put a stop to whatever it was.

Except Caitlin wasn't paying any attention to Kayne. She was crouched down with a hand extended toward a small brown-and-white dog that probably would be a darling once he'd had a bath and a good brushing. The dog came forward, wary and ready to run, clearly wanting Caitlin and just as clearly *not* wanting the rest of them.

"First spotted him near the Sentinel Stones about a month ago," Kayne said as the dog finally got close enough to sniff Caitlin's fingers and then did his best to make friends. "A young animal. Spaniel of some kind, judging by the look of him, but no one here could name the breed. Anyways, we figured he'd come over from somewhere else, but short of catching him, chucking him back through the Stones, and hoping he would end up where he'd come from, there wasn't much to be done about him. It was Moira who pointed out that he seemed to think he belonged here at the house. He would come down to the village once a day to beg for scraps—and with those eyes staring at you, he didn't need to beg hard to get a good feeding—but most of the time he's been up here."

There was a radiance to his little sister that Michael had never seen before. *She's home*, he thought, feeling his heart break just a little because, in a way he couldn't quite explain but was beginning to understand, he knew he *wasn't* home, would never feel truly at home in this village, despite the music of the house. Because of that, and because he realized Glorianna was right and he could undermine Caitlin's confidence enough to have her turning away from the very thing her heart needed, he had to find a way to be an idiot she could defy.

"Up here all by yourself?" Caitlin crooned to the dog as she stroked the long, once-silky ears and was rewarded with lavish lick-kisses. "Poor baby. But you're not by yourself anymore, are you, Andrew?"

"Andrew?" Michael said, putting his hands on his hips. "What kind of name is that for a dog?"

Kayne frowned at him. Lee gave him an odd look and said, "What do you care? They both seem fine with it, and you don't have to answer to it."

"But . . . *Andrew?* He doesn't look like an Andrew. He looks like a Timothy."

Now everyone turned to stare at him. Including the dog.

"His name," Caitlin said, dropping each word like a stone, "is Andrew."

Michael raised his hands in surrender and took a step back when Andrew growled at him. "Fine. His name is Andrew. And you shouldn't be thinking of bringing him into the house until he's had a bath, Caitlin Marie."

"I know that," Caitlin snapped. "I'm not six, Michael."

Kayne, Michael noticed with satisfaction, winced. Good. Let the man realize the girl wasn't always sweet and cooey.

"Maybe we could start the mud-slinging tradition here," Lee said to no one in particular.

"Don't encourage them," Glorianna replied, looking back toward the village. "Here come Peg, Moira, and Brighid. Discussion of Andrew's bath can wait. For now, let's take a look at the house—and the garden."

The house was spare on furnishings, Michael thought as he walked through it, but the people weren't filling it with their cast-off furniture, so he understood the sense of not beggaring the village to furnish a house no one lived in. Still, there was enough to start with. A couple of times his eye caught Brighid's, and he was sure there was the same blend of worry and relief in his eyes as he saw in hers.

And he saw the undisguised relief on Peg's, Moira's, and Kayne's faces when Glorianna Belladonna gave her approval of the house.

Warrior of Light, Peg had called her.

Images. Stories. Truths. Choices.

This is the second time someone has called her the Warrior of Light, Michael thought. *She knows it's not a coincidence, so she won't dismiss it forever. The day will come when she'll ask you for the story. If you lie to protect what your own heart desires, what harm will you do to the world?*

"We've done some repairs on the walls," Kayne said, now sounding nervous as they walked to the walled garden behind the house. "On the outside. We would have fixed the gate—put on a new one—but we weren't sure if that would be intruding too much."

Michael watched Caitlin hesitate at the gate, then turn and look at Glorianna. And saw, in that moment, the transition from girl to woman, from child to adult.

"She'll be all right, won't she?" he said softly as Caitlin and Glorianna slipped into the garden.

"In all ways," Lee replied. "Come and help me pick out a couple of
locations for a stationary bridge."

"I thought you said you couldn't build one."

"I can't build one between the White Isle and Lighthaven. But between here and Aurora? Shouldn't be a problem. Caitlin's resonance is
in harmony with Nadia's and Glorianna's—and yours, by the way." Lee
gave him a long look. "Every bridge I build now adds to the risk of the
Eater of the World finding a way into Glorianna's landscapes and,
therefore, finding the Places of Light. Caitlin's landscapes aren't isolated from the rest of the world; neither are yours. But if it will help
you rest at night, I can build a bridge between one of your landscapes
and Darling's Harbor to make it easier to visit."

"That offer is being made from one brother to another, yes?"
Michael asked.

Lee tipped his head in agreement.

"What would the Bridge say?"

"He wouldn't be making a bridge between here and anywhere. But
Caitlin needs what Nadia, and especially Glorianna, can teach her. So
I will make a bridge."

"And pray to the Light that the Eater doesn't find this place?"

"Yes," Lee said. "That's exactly what I'll do."

Michael took a deep breath and let it out slowly as he studied the
walls of a garden he'd last seen on a hill in another part of his country. "All right then. I'll think on your offer. For now, let's see about this
bridge you've already decided to make."

Chapter Twenty-four

Michael sat on the bench and watched the fish flash gold among the water plants in the koi pond. His mind was carefully blank, but the absence of busy thought wasn't restful. Not like it should have been. Because he was busy not thinking about the woman who wasn't there.

"Are you stewing, brooding, pondering, or just letting a part of your brain float on the water?" Lee asked, settling on the other end of the bench.

"Anything tries to float on that water is going to get eaten," Michael replied. "Doesn't anyone ever feed those fish?"

"Sure. Doesn't mean they won't forage for themselves when the opportunity presents itself." Lee studied him. "Still worried about Caitlin?"

Michael rubbed his hands over his knees. "Kayne seemed a bit too interested in a girl her age."

"He's interested," Lee countered. "He's also smart enough to know the male who is currently holding Caitlin's attention is small, brown, and fuzzy."

He grunted. Not an eloquent response, but better than admitting

Lee was right about Andrew the dog being Caitlin's companion for the foreseeable future. Then he sighed. "My heart aches because someone else is happy. Does that make me a ripe bastard?"

Lee said nothing.

Michael kept his eyes focused on the pond. "I respected my aunt Brighid because she came to help me and Caitlin when we needed her, and I suppose I loved her, but it was a duty love, if you take my meaning." He glanced over long enough to see Lee nod. "I couldn't hear the music of her heart. Crashing chords and odd rhythms, but not the melody, not the tone that usually gives me a sense of who a person is."

"She wasn't where she belonged," Lee said quietly. He waited a beat. "What do you hear in her now?"

"A grand song. Something I never would have imagined was in her. Even before I listened for the song, I saw her face when we stepped off your island and she set foot in Sanctuary—and I realized I had never seen her truly happy or at peace with herself and the world around her. That's a hard thing to swallow since I'm one of the reasons she didn't have that peace."

Lee leaned forward, resting his forearms on his knees. "She wasn't happy at Lighthaven either, Magician. She knew she needed the Light, but that wasn't the place for her. And yet she never went up to Darling's Harbor to walk between the Sentinel Stones. I think that's one of the differences between your part of the world and mine. You can avoid a resonating bridge and stay where you don't belong. But it can't be an easy thing to deny your own heart day after day, year after year. And in the end, you can't deny it. Ephemera won't let you."

"She wouldn't have abandoned two children."

Lee nodded. "Having decided to help, she wouldn't have left you to fend for yourselves—especially while Caitlin was so young. But we're not talking just about your aunt. That's the thing about heart wishes. You might have to travel through several landscapes—and spend time in each one, living and learning and changing inside—before you're ready for the place you truly belong, the place your heart recognizes as 'home.' Brighid has found her place. So has Caitlin. What about you? Do you have the courage to cross over to the landscape where you belong?"

Michael turned enough to look at Lee straight on. "And you're thinking you know where I belong?"

Lee shook his head. "Your heart does."

He knew where he *wanted* to belong. Which wasn't the same thing.

"My father left when I was . . ." Lee paused. "Well, I was so young I don't have my own memories of him. My mother didn't know if he had crossed over a bridge and couldn't get back to us, or if he didn't *want* to come back to us and had crossed over to a landscape where she didn't belong. It was only a few months ago that we found information that makes us think he was killed because he had learned the wizards who were purebloods weren't human; that they were really the Dark Guides."

"It changed things, his leaving," Michael said, having a clear memory of his father walking down the road, alone, for that last time.

"Yes, it changed things."

"But your mother's heart didn't turn barren of everything but storms and rages."

"My mother was where she belonged, in a house that had been in her family for generations. And my mother has always known the nature of her gift and the way of the world. She wouldn't have stayed in a place where she didn't belong."

"Well, my mother didn't stay either," Michael said, hearing the bitterness in his voice. "Of course, where she thought she would end up by walking into the sea is anyone's guess. Where she *did* end up was a pauper's grave." And it hurt. All these years later, it still hurt. "She didn't love us enough to stay."

Before Lee could reply, Michael stood up, signaling the end of talk.

Lee rose as well. "Shall we join the ladies?"

"Lucky timing on your mother's part to be visiting Sanctuary today," Michael said as they headed for the guesthouse.

"Luck has nothing to do with it," Lee replied, smiling. "My mother's sense of timing is uncanny—especially if you're a young boy doing something you shouldn't be doing."

"Ah." Michael hesitated, then decided this was good timing too. "Speaking of ladies, I noticed your sister has been absent from the tour of Sanctuary."

"Something needed tending. She'll be back soon."

Where? Although unspoken, they both knew the question had been asked—and not answered. *Still an outsider,* Michael thought. *And maybe I deserve to be.*

As they approached Brighid and Nadia, he tucked that thought away in the far corner of his heart, hoping no one would be able to find it. Including himself.

"You shouldn't be poking around there," a male voice said. "The place isn't safe."

Glorianna turned and studied the man standing a few strides behind her. About Lee's age, maybe a little older. Pleasant face. Old eyes that narrowed now that he had a clear look at her.

"You came with Caitlin Marie to look at her garden," he said. He wasn't standing in the right place to see it, but he looked toward the meadow. "That strange, rust-colored sand disappeared after you were here." His eyes widened. "You're a sor—"

"Landscaper." She put enough emphasis on the word to silence him. "And a Guide of the Heart. Be careful of your words. They have more meaning than you realize."

He hesitated, then moved closer. "I'm Nathan."

Glorianna tipped her head. "You're the anchor." He frowned at her, but she smiled because there was a shimmer of recognition in his eyes.

The word itself meant nothing to him the way she was using it, but the *meaning* did. "You remember what Raven's Hill used to be."

"I'm not *that* old," he grumbled. But he also nodded. "My grandfather used to tell me stories. It was a good village, and a fairly prosperous one when the quarry was open. Fishing was better in those years. There was more game in the hills. And people were kinder."

They can be again. "It wasn't their fault," she said gently. "Michael, Caitlin, and Brighid."

"Of course it wasn't their fault," Nathan snapped. The snap was automatic—a habit established long ago—but underneath there was uneasiness and doubt. "A young girl can't turn a fountain foul beyond any hope of cleaning or ruin a vegetable garden just by looking at it. A boy can't bring someone good luck or bad just by wanting something to happen to someone. That's all a load of—"

"Truth." She watched his mouth fall open, then waited for him to regain his mental balance. He'd known it was true—had known Caitlin and Michael *were* capable of such things, but he hadn't expected anyone to acknowledge what they could do without condemning them for it. "In many ways, it was unknowingly done, unwittingly done, and the legacy of unhappiness was inherited along with this house. But Caitlin is a Landscaper who *can* alter the world to some extent, and since the village was already predisposed to brand her a sorceress, they helped shape her and, in return, she helped shape the world they had to live in. But even she couldn't influence Ephemera beyond a certain point. Because you were here."

He shook his head. "I don't have any magics."

"You love this place. Despite the troubles that plague this village, you love it. And your heart holds the memories of what this landscape used to be. You haven't let go of the memories that were passed down to you or the hope that Raven's Hill will be what it once was."

He looked sad. "So everyone was right about Michael and Caitlin?"

"Yes and no." Glorianna looked at the burned ruins of the cottage, feeling the knot of Dark currents directly under it. Why would anyone have built a home on a spot that must have made all the workers uneasy? And how much courage had it taken to live in the cottage, even if the people living there had no knowledge of the currents?

Sorrow's ground. The words came like a whispered memory. She closed her eyes against the pain of it.

"What's the matter? Are you unwell?"

A light hand on her arm. Concern in Nathan's voice.

She opened her eyes and looked into his. *He can change things.*

"If you want to help your village and your people, this is what you must do." *Ephemera, hear me.* She scuffed the ground, then picked up a palm-sized stone that matched the stone in the quarry. She made a sweeping gesture that took in the ruins of the cottage and the meadow around it. "Know the true names of things. This is Sorrow's Ground. It is not a place that should be built on or lived on. It belongs to Sorrow, to the hard feelings that plague the heart. It belongs to regrets, to disappointments, to loss. In season, pick a wildflower from the meadow or bring a flower from the home garden, or select a simple stone, and whisper what troubles you as you give your offering to Sorrow's Ground." She demonstrated by tossing the stone into the ruins of the cottage.

"All well and good if people don't think it's too daft to do," Nathan said. "But what is it supposed to accomplish?"

"It's a cleansing," Glorianna replied. "Since there are already hard feelings about this little piece of Raven's Hill, people won't find it that difficult to believe this is the village's dark place."

"If you're not careful, Sorrow could become a mysterious, black-haired sorceress who walks among the ruins or out in the meadow and listens to the grievings and regrets," Nathan said.

She heard the unspoken question, felt the yearning in his heart—and felt a moment's regret that her own yearnings pulled her toward a man whose heart was clouded enough that, even though she was drawn to Michael, might even be falling in love with him, she wasn't sure she could trust him.

"Caitlin and Michael won't come back to Raven's Hill. Neither will I. So if you think it will help your people, then tell the story of a sorceress called Sorrow who came to restore balance to this piece of the world. And when the next one like me comes to Raven's Hill, be careful what you name her. A Landscaper keeps her pieces of the world in balance. It is what we do and what we are. If you can accept her, the two of you can build something good here."

"How do you . . ." His face flushed.

"The heart has no secrets. Not from me." *Not usually.* Rising up on her toes, she kissed his cheek, then stepped back. "May your heart travel lightly."

She saw the other men approaching, some grim-faced, some concerned. Nathan heard them and looked back as he raised a hand in greeting.

They trusted him. Good. And there were enough of them to stand witness for each other. Even better.

She gave the men one long look that had them hesitating, then turned and took that step between here and there—and vanished right before their eyes.

Chapter Twenty-five

When It reached Kendall, It slipped into the seaport quickly and moved away from the docks and the delicious stew of hopes and fears—and the hearts that held a guttering Light that could be snuffed out so easily. The docks, and the streets surrounding them, belonged to the male Enemy who had been strong enough to escape being pulled into Its dark landscapes. It did not want to alert that male to Its presence, especially since It still chewed on the kernel of worry that the Enemy had found the True Enemy and had united with her against It.

So It headed away from the docks, flowed beneath the streets that belonged to the merchants and bakers and carpenters who were too stolid to be interesting prey until the mallet of fear had softened them and . . .

It turned back, intrigued by the fear pulsing from a round little man hurrying down the street, glancing over his shoulder, jumping at every noise.

It followed, lapping up the man's fear, slipping into his mind to learn the shape of the phantoms that rubbed away the satisfaction of owning a thriving business.

✻ ✻ ✻

He hurried down the street, knowing it was smarter—safer—to walk as if he were simply heading home at the end of the workday. He didn't dress in a way that shouted "prosperity"—except when his wife made him—so he looked like an employee rather than the owner of a successful business.

But business had been good, very good. Which was why he was so late closing up the shop, why he hadn't been heading home with all other merchants who had shops on Ware Street, why his footsteps were the only . . .

Another footfall. A scrape of boots on cobblestone. Something sly about the sound.

He didn't dare look around, didn't want to alert whoever was behind him that he was aware of the danger. Thieves lurked in the alleyways, waiting to strip honest men of their wages. Nervous about leaving all the day's till in the shop's safe, especially since someone had tried to break into Wagerson's shop the week before, he was carrying a thieves' bounty home with him to tuck into the house safe.

Now someone followed him, intent on robbing him. Maybe would even hit him over the head and leave him bleeding in the gutter, alone and helpless until the constables made their rounds and noticed him.

His wife scoffed when he mentioned such things, telling him fear was the only thief that visited, robbing him of his peace of mind. Then she would suggest he take a cab home if he worried about walking the streets after dark, especially on the nights when he carried a packet to put in the home safe. As if he would squander good coin for a horse and driver, except in foul weather, when only a few blocks separated shop and home.

But . . . Those footfalls. Those sly steps following him. Were they getting closer? Should he run? Only two more blocks and he would be home, safe behind his doors and locks.

Where were the constables? Shouldn't they be walking their beat? Why was he paying all those taxes for their wages if they weren't around to stop an honest man from being beaten and robbed?

And it *did* happen, despite what his wife said. It didn't matter that he didn't know anyone personally who had been robbed. He didn't want to be the first of his acquaintance to have the experience.

But he might be the first. Maybe even tonight.

His heart pounded. His breath came in pants as he rounded the corner and saw the welcoming lights of his home—and the lights in the houses of his neighbors, who would all come to the rescue of one of their fellows because, like him, they were all good, hardworking, honest people.

Those footsteps were getting closer, hurrying now as if the thief sensed how close his prey was to safety.

Emboldened by his surroundings and knowing his shouts would bring a quick response, he spun around to confront his pursuer.

And saw nothing but shadows.

A darker shadow among the shadows, It watched the little man scurry into his house, almost glowing with the Light of happiness.

Time and the repeated feeding of the same fear were required to create something like the bonelovers or the death rollers, and while It could create access points for humans to stumble into, even lethal creatures were at a disadvantage in a city.

But this delightful fear of a phantom predator. This didn't require one of Its creatures, didn't require an access point that would be noticed and, possibly, reported to whatever Landscaper provided the bedrock for this part of the city. This predator could be nurtured in dozens of hearts through the twilight of waking dreams—something that, when manifested, was nothing more than sounds and a glimpse of something lurking in the shadows, not quite seen. A phantom that did nothing more than nurture fear. Except when *It* did the hunting. Then there would be blood and pain and terror. But perhaps not death. Not always death. Because the ones who survived would be crippled by fear, would smear the streets with those feelings and help smother the Light.

A phantom predator.

Could changing this part of Kendall into a dark hunting ground really be that easy?

Yesssss.

Doreen looked out the window of her room at the boardinghouse. It was a respectable location for a single lady, the cabbie had assured her. And it *was* respectable. Gentility on a strict budget. The room was clean, as were the sheets, but the quality of the furniture and linens was little better than what she'd had at home. And she wanted more. So much more. *Deserved* more.

She'd always thought the Magician would be her meal ticket out of Foggy Downs. She'd even been willing to give him sex in exchange for taking her with him on the road. Not that the bastard had appreciated the offer.

She wouldn't have stayed with Michael. Stay with a man who didn't have two coins to rub together half the time? Oh, no. She wasn't interested in someone who couldn't buy her pretty things.

In the end, though, the Magician *had* been her meal ticket. If she'd known accusing him of being what he was would get Shaney mad enough to empty the till to pay for her coach passage out of Foggy Downs, she would have made the accusation long ago.

It had embarrassed Shaney's wife beyond shaming that everyone in the village, even the most pinchpenny among them, had tossed a coin or two into a hat to help with expenses. Some of the shops had donated toiletries or other bits and pieces for "luck on the journey."

She wasn't fooled for a tinker's minute. They'd rather be rid of her, who lived and worked among them, than chance having the *Magician* avoid the village on his wanderings.

So be it. It had gotten her here, hadn't it? A boardinghouse around the docks would have let her squeeze out her coins a bit longer, but she wouldn't find the kind of man she was looking for around the docks. She wasn't interested in humping behind the shed anymore. That had never gotten her more than winks added to a generous tip, which she'd more than earned with most of those dolts. No, she would find a gentleman who would appreciate her beauty and set her up in style with a little house of her own and fine clothes.

Before she had to pinch her pennies, she would find a man who would give her what she deserved.

Michael raised his mug and took a healthy swallow of ale. Crossing over from Sanctuary to the Den of Iniquity was a jolt for mind and heart—more so, he figured, than a person would experience coming from an ordinary place like Aurora or Kendall or even Foggy Downs. The Den and Sanctuary both made him want to take out his whistle and play along with the music he could hear in the land, but the tunes were so different.

As were the men who lived in those places. He glanced at the table where Yoshani was talking to Nadia and her husband Jeb, then looked at the man sitting at the table with him.

"So when do we have this strategy session?" Michael asked.

"When Glorianna gets done primping and decides to join us," Sebastian replied, giving him an edgy look out of those sharp green eyes.

Time to change the subject, since he really didn't want Sebastian thinking too long or too hard about why Glorianna might be primping. If primping was, indeed, the reason she'd asked Sebastian for the key to his room in the bordello.

Primping was good, wasn't it? It meant a woman wanted to attract a man. Or arouse a man. Or . . . Maybe he should borrow the room key and do a little primping himself if . . .

He looked into Sebastian's eyes and knew it was *really* time to think about something besides primping and Glorianna and what could be done behind locked doors in a bordello.

So he focused on Teaser, who seemed to be having some kind of "discussion" with Lynnea.

"What's he doing?" Michael asked, raising his chin to indicate the pair, who looked like they were going to start throwing more than words at any moment.

Sebastian glanced at his wife and friend. "He's learning how to be more human."

Michael cocked his head but he was only catching the tone and not the actual words. "Sounds like a cranky older brother to me."

Sebastian gave him a bland look. "He's learning how to be human." He waited until Michael was swallowing a mouthful of ale before adding, "He's using you as a role model."

"Ripe bastard," Michael said when he stopped choking.

Sebastian bared his teeth in an insincere smile. Then his expression froze. His eyes heated. He pushed back his chair—and Lee dropped into the other chair at the table and said, "Mother says if you do the stupid thing you're thinking of doing, you will have to apologize three times to every woman in our family—and the apologies will include flowers, candy, and groveling—before there is even a chance of you being forgiven."

"But . . ." A noise rumbled up from Sebastian's chest that didn't sound remotely human. "Did she explain—"

"She's my mother and your auntie," Lee said. "She doesn't need to explain anything."

Since Sebastian looked ready to choke, Michael focused on the street to figure out what had caused that reaction. All he saw was Glorianna.

All he saw was Glorianna.

A dark skirt and a dark jacket with embroidery at the neckline and cuffs. A light shirt. Her hair up in a simple knot. Lovely to look at on the surface. But under the lady-attending-a-luncheon clothes, she moved as Woman. Potent. Primal. Sexual.

"Lady's mercy," he whispered. Then he looked beyond her, though it pained him to take his eyes off her as she crossed the street and moved toward him—and saw what had set Sebastian on edge.

Saw the difference between human men and incubi.

The human men, coming to the Den for something more tasty than the women they knew, glanced at Glorianna and looked away, seeing someone too much like them to be of interest. The incubi stopped in their tracks, entranced by the prey. This was the kind of woman whose emotions and desires would be a feast for them, whether they were dream lovers or physical lovers.

Then she got to the edge of the courtyard and looked back at them, and they realized who—and what—she was. All of them scurried away, nervous now about showing interest in Belladonna, who might not find their interest appealing.

"What's wrong with them?" Glorianna asked, turning back to the table. The tiny frown line between her eyes deepened as she studied Sebastian. "What's wrong with you?"

"He swallowed something that didn't agree with him," Michael said, keeping his face bland but letting his voice ring with amusement. Which was a fine bit of work since just looking at her stirred up a messy stew of wants and needs that were neither bland nor amusing.

"Watch your step, Magician," Sebastian growled. "We paid the Merry Makers two goats for you, which is something we can rectify by giving you back to be the second course."

"Sebastian." Glorianna sounded shocked.

Lee popped out of his chair, slipped an arm around her waist, and herded her away from the table. "Philo set up some food inside. Thought we'd prefer to keep this discussion private. Let's round up the others."

Michael pushed his chair back, intending to follow Glorianna and Lee.

"Sit," Sebastian said quietly, watching the others head for the indoor dining room.

"But . . . ," Michael said.

"Sit."

Teaser, being the last one to reach the door, glanced back at them. Before Michael could decide if he was or wasn't going to ignore the command, he was helped to his feet by Sebastian grabbing a fistful of his shirt and hauling him up.

"Not here," Sebastian said, the threat in no way softened by the fact that it was said quietly. Especially when Michael was getting an odd, buzzy tingling in his skin where Sebastian's fist rested against his chest. "Not on my ground. Sooner or later, she'll invite you to her bed, and nothing I say will change that. But there's something about you, Magician. Threat and promise. I don't know why that's so, but it is."

"Are you saying we're enemies?" Michael asked, wondering how well ill-wishing would work on an incubus.

"Not yet," Sebastian said, releasing Michael's shirt. "Maybe we'll even end up friends."

The first thought—"not likely"—got swallowed as he listened to the music that made up Sebastian.

It's possible, Michael thought, surprised by how appealing the idea was.

A friendship between them was possible—at least until Sebastian discovered that he really was a threat.

*   *   *

As soon as they got into the dining room, Glorianna pulled Lee away from the others. "What's *wrong* with him?" She wanted to shout, so the effort to keep her voice low enough for the conversation to remain private strained her throat muscles.

"Don't know Michael well enough to say," Lee replied.

"Not Michael. *Sebastian.*" Could her brother really be that obtuse? "He just threatened to give a human to the Merry Makers to *eat.*"

Lee shrugged. "I'm sure he was just teasing."

No, he wasn't—and neither are you. Lee had gotten along with Michael during the journey to the White Isle, and had even developed a fledgling friendship. But liking a man and trusting him weren't the same thing, and there was only one reason she could think of—that Lee would know about—that would give her brother an excuse to look away if trouble started.

Since she couldn't hit him without her mother getting involved, she slapped with words. "I'm sorry if this is a shock to you, but I've had sex before. Michael wouldn't be my first lover."

He slapped back. "He's the first one you brought home."

"We're not home."

"Think again, Glorianna. The man was sitting at a table with your cousin. Your mother and brother were nearby. This place belongs to family. If that's not bringing him home, then what is?"

She didn't have an answer to that. Wasn't sure he was entitled to an answer. Wasn't even sure . . .

No, she was sure about that. Michael was an attractive man, and judging by his kisses, would be a pleasing sex partner. Then there was that blend of the wistful, stray puppy look he sometimes got in his eyes combined with a practicality born of being self-sufficient that intrigued her. He wanted love, wanted *to* love.

And he had the answer, already knew what might be done to stop the Eater of the World. But he wasn't going to tell her. Watching Michael walk into the dining room with Sebastian, she felt it in the currents of power as clearly as if he'd said the words. More to the point, he didn't *want* to tell her. Not here, where her family was a constant reminder of the hearts that might be hurt by what he offered. It would have to be on his ground.

She wanted to see him on his own ground. Here he had been a stranger stumbling over the unfamiliar. Who was Michael the Magician in the landscapes he tended? She wanted to know who he was, wanted to know if she could walk in his landscapes.

yes yes yes.

She watched him stop and cock his head. A hint of a smile curved his mouth, as if he were listening to an excited child telling him something wonderful.

The wild child. Wasn't that what he called Ephemera?

yes yes yes.

Ephemera's currents of power washed through her, resonated with her.

Michael's eyes widened as they met hers.

Not resonating just with her. He was there in the currents, with her—and she heard the feel of his heart as music.

The romance of him tugged at her, swirled around her.

"Have you heard *anything* I've said?" Lee asked, sounding exasperated.

"What? No, I wasn't listening." Ignoring his sputtered grumble, she walked over to the table where the others were filling plates and choosing seats. She pulled out a chair opposite Sebastian and Michael—and noted that Lee chose a seat that didn't put him beside Michael or her.

She filled a plate to avoid comments about her not eating, then waited until everyone had settled in their places. She looked at each of them in turn—Nadia and Jeb, Lynnea and Sebastian, Yoshani, Teaser, Lee, Michael. She didn't think anyone but the Magician was going to like what she was about to say, but she hoped some of them would support the decision.

"We need to find a way to reach Michael's landscapes," she said.

"He has a way," Lee said. "Bridge between Aurora and Darling's Harbor will get him back to Elandar. A ship will get him to his own landscapes."

"I'd like something that didn't take as much time since I'll be going with him."

Lee jumped up. "Has the thought of getting sex made you completely crazy?"

"*Lee.*" Nadia's voice cracked through the room like a whiplash.

"I, too, must protest," Yoshani said. "That comment was uncalled for—and unjust."

Teaser looked around the table. "Why can't they have sex here?"

Sebastian growled.

"Oh," Teaser said. "Yeah, being crisped by wizards' lightning *would* spoil the fun."

Protests and grumbles rolled around the table in a wave. Glorianna didn't hear any of them. She kept her eyes on Lee's.

The Warrior of Light must drink from the Dark Cup.

He'd been with her when Caitlin said those words. He'd felt the response of Ephemera's currents to those words.

He knows, Glorianna thought. *Sex is just the excuse he's using to try and push Michael away from all of us.*

"Life's journey, Bridge," she said.

"I know." He sat down and pressed his palms against his forehead. "I know."

She felt the weight of Nadia's stare and turned her head to meet her mother's dark eyes.

"I think you have some explaining to do, daughter," Nadia said quietly.

Glorianna hesitated, then nodded. "Privately."

"Very well." Nadia swept her eyes over all of them, lingering just a moment longer on Sebastian and Lee, as if warning them to behave. "Michael. You visit villages, yes? What are their names?"

He didn't turn his head, but his eyes shifted in Sebastian's direction before he answered. "Kendall, which is a seaport. Dunberry, but that's not a safe place anymore."

"Why not?" Nadia asked. "It is yours, is it not?"

"Was mine, but something happened there. The song changed, and now it's not safe to enter the village."

Sebastian swore quietly.

Ignoring that for the moment, Glorianna concentrated on Michael. "Why didn't you do something to change the song back to what it was?"

"Two boys disappeared and a young woman was murdered. They're looking for someone to blame. I can't go back."

"They're your people," Nadia said. "That landscape is your responsibility."

"The Eater of the World must have touched that landscape and poisoned the hearts of those people," Glorianna said. "You have to fix it."

"I can't go back to the village," Michael said with strained patience. *"Tch."*

Glorianna glanced at her mother and saw Nadia's lips twitch as they both realized they'd made the same sound of annoyance.

"If nothing else, you'll need to go with him to Dunberry and show him what's to be done," Nadia said.

"Agreed," Glorianna replied. "But it was a place called Foggy Downs that the Magician asked me to see."

Sebastian swore again.

She saw Michael wince and shift his weight as if he'd like to put some distance between himself and her cousin but didn't quite dare.

"It takes a couple of days to get from Dunberry to Foggy Downs," Michael said.

"No, it doesn't," Sebastian said, staring at the plate in front of him. "Not from the waterhorses' landscape."

Glorianna sat back. "So what aren't the two of you telling the rest of us?" When they didn't answer, she added, "I can send a command through the currents of power so that every time it rains you end up stepping in a puddle and getting your feet soaked."

Sebastian gave her a puzzled—and sulky—look. Michael huffed out a breath and said, "Ah, now, Glorianna. That's an unkind bit of ill-wishing."

"You can do that?" Teaser asked, looking at Michael.

"I've never done that particular thing," Michael muttered. Then added reluctantly, "Well, not often anyway."

"The point is, gentlemen, we understand each other," Glorianna said. Then she waited.

"There's a bridge outside of Dunberry," Michael said. "Most times if you cross it, you'll keep going up the road to Kendall. But sometimes when you cross the bridge, there is no road, just open country, and soon enough a pretty black horse will come trotting up to greet you. There have been enough fools who have thrown a leg over one of those pretty horses. A few have gotten no more than a dunking and found their way home. Most end up drowned. Some are never found or seen again."

"Koltak mentioned those places," Sebastian said. "Dunberry. Foggy Downs."

"Koltak?" Michael asked. "He was someone from here who crossed over to Elandar?"

"My father. Wizard Koltak." Sebastian spat out the words as if they were bitter gristle. "When he crossed over from Wizard City, intending to find me in the Den, he ended up in the waterhorses' landscape instead. A few weeks before that, when I had gone to Wizard City to report the murders in the Den, I ended up in the waterhorses' landscape too, when I crossed a bridge to get away from that thrice-cursed city. I walked a few hours before meeting a waterhorse that was willing to give me a ride without tricks."

"The Eater had killed one of them," Glorianna said. "It was scared."

Sebastian nodded. "Didn't take that long to reach the border and cross over to the Den. But Koltak wandered through that landscape for days trying to find the Den, and ended up going to Dunberry and Foggy Downs."

Michael nodded. "Would have taken him some time to go from one place to the other, even on horseback."

"The point is, he was able to reach both from the waterhorses' landscape."

"Are there waterhorses around Foggy Downs?" Glorianna asked Michael.

"Sometimes," he said. He looked at Sebastian. "You're thinking going through the waterhorses' landscape would be a shortcut to Dunberry and Foggy Downs?"

"Maybe," Sebastian replied. "I just know Koltak ended up in those places while he was looking for the Den."

"The Eater of the World is out there in Elandar," Lee said, bracing his hands on either side of his plate. "We know that. Creating the bridge between Aurora and Darling's Harbor was risky enough since that provides a way in to both your landscapes." He tipped his head to indicate Nadia and Glorianna. "Creating a bridge between—"

"A resonating bridge," Glorianna said, interrupting him. "In the waterhorses' landscape. And you could create a couple of one-shot bridges Michael could carry with him that would get him back—"

"Here," Sebastian said, interrupting her. "That would get him back to the Den."

"A wise choice," Yoshani said. "I agree."

"All right," Glorianna said. "One-shot bridges that would get Michael back to the Den if I need to return to my island."

Lee didn't look happy, but he nodded.

Jeb pulled out a pocket watch and studied the time. "Still the shank of the evening in Aurora. Barely past dinnertime."

"In that case, let's enjoy the food Philo provided," Nadia said.

Meeting adjourned, Glorianna thought as she picked at her food. Discussion ended. She would need to pack tonight, would need to consider what to carry.

Tomorrow she would begin another stage of her journey.

She tried not to wonder if she would ever return home.

Chapter Twenty-six

Michael stared at the sand and stone that scarred the rolling green land. "That isn't right. That doesn't belong here. Did that . . . *Eater* . . . do this?"

"No," Glorianna said, her voice as dry as the sand. "I did." She swung off the demon cycle, then shrugged out of her pack and set it on the ground before moving closer to the sand.

"Why?" Michael asked. Either she didn't hear him or chose to ignore him, so he swung off the demon cycle he was riding and shrugged out of his pack too. Since he had his full pack with all his gear, he didn't see any reason to be clanking and clanging while he tried to talk to the woman.

"Careful," Sebastian warned.

Not sure if the warning was meant as a caution about approaching the sand or Glorianna, Michael took care as he got closer to both.

"So," Michael said. "Is this like the sandbox?"

"No, this is a desert." She studied the sand and stones, then nodded as if satisfied.

"So if someone steps onto the sand . . ."

"They cross over to that landscape."

Wasn't much of a landscape, Michael thought as he took a step closer. Some stones and sand and . . . Was that the remains of a horse's head?

"So you step over the stones and end up in a desert. Then you step back over to this . . ." *Part of the world*, he finished silently as it occurred to him that he was looking at a piece of the world far away from anything he knew.

"The stones form the border here in the waterhorses' landscape," Glorianna said. "They don't exist in the desert landscape."

Michael frowned. "Then how do you know where to cross over to get back here?"

"You don't get back here, Magician. That was the point of altering the landscape."

He stared at her.

Glorianna huffed out a breath. "The Eater had formed an access point for the death rollers in the pond that existed here. I closed it once after Sebastian told me about the waterhorse being killed, but a dark heart passed this place often enough to allow the Eater to restore the access point. So I altered the landscape, changing the pond and the surrounding land to desert and stone. Even if the Eater manages to keep the access point open from Its landscape, the death rollers will cross over into a desert where they can't survive." She turned back toward the demon cycles.

Michael looked at Sebastian and Lee, then at Glorianna. "Did none of you think to post a sign?"

She spun back to face him and threw her hands up. "To say what? 'Dangerous landscape, do not cross over'?"

"Why not?"

"For one thing," Lee said, "would anyone in your part of the world understand what that meant? Or pay attention even if they did?"

Lee had a point. If a man landed himself in this part of Elandar and was dumb enough to ride a waterhorse, he was dumb enough to ignore a sign and end up in a desert with no food or water—and no way back.

"For another," Glorianna said, "waterhorses can't read, so there's no point posting a sign for *them*, and it's unlikely anyone will get this far into their landscape without encountering one of them."

As if her words were a signal, four waterhorses came over a low rise and headed toward them. Their black coats shone in the morning sunlight and their manes lifted with the air stirred by their movement. Trotting in unison, they were gorgeous, and even though he knew better, he felt a keen desire to ride one.

They stopped. No words were spoken, but Michael heard the message just the same. *Come with us. We'll give you a better ride. And we're prettier.*

He glanced at the demon cycles. One of them was licking its lips as it stared at the waterhorses.

"No," Glorianna said.

He wasn't sure who the "no" was meant for, but all the demons—horse and cycle—were suddenly doing the equivalent of scratching an elbow and trying to look innocent.

"You four," Gloriana said, pointing to the waterhorses. "Would you go into that?" She pointed at the sand.

They shook their heads.

"See?" she said to Michael. "They know better. Are you saying humans are dumber than waterhorses?"

Out of the corner of his eye, he saw four black heads bob up and down.

Sebastian and Lee started coughing. Glorianna's face turned red with the effort not to laugh. He stared at the ground, not wanting to be the one who had to explain to demons that he wasn't laughing *at* them. Of course, he couldn't say he was laughing *with* them either.

"Where is the closest place to find humans?" Glorianna asked.

The four waterhorses looked at Sebastian.

"Besides the Den," she added.

They turned and trotted back up the rise in the direction they had come from.

Glorianna hurried over to her pack and slipped into the straps before swinging a leg over her demon cycle. She and Lee headed after the waterhorses. Michael was a little slower since he needed a few moments longer to get his pack settled. When he was ready, he looked at Sebastian, who just looked back at him.

"Magician, I think it's time you educated the people in your landscapes about the nature of Ephemera."

Michael looked at the sand and stone that scarred the rolling green, then looked at Sebastian. "Won't that be fun?"

The smile came first. Then the laughter. He didn't mind the laughter. It was a sympathetic sound.

Glorianna and Lee studied the bridge that crossed a stream. There was something nearby she didn't like. Something that made her edgy, uneasy. But not here. That, too, made her uneasy. Unless she discovered another landscape that belonged to her on the other side of that bridge, she shouldn't have felt any resonance or dissonance. Except she *had* been aware of the currents flowing through the White Isle until Caitlin broke the connection between their two landscapes. And Michael . . .

She suddenly had an image of walking through a garden—her garden?—and hearing the clear notes of his whistle drifting through the air, calling her home.

Why would that image make her heart ache?

"Looks like I don't have to make a resonating bridge after all," Lee said, rubbing his chin. "That's a stationary bridge. Crosses over to one—maybe two—other landscapes. I can tell that much from the resonance of it."

"So my landscapes aren't as closed off as I'd thought," Glorianna said.

"Going out isn't the same as coming back in," Lee pointed out.

"Koltak got in. And the Eater must have used the waterhorses' landscape as Its entry to Elandar."

"You don't know that, Glorianna." He sounded annoyed, but she wondered if he privately agreed with her. "Other Landscapers could have had landscapes in Elandar. The Eater could have gotten here through one of the gardens at the school."

She heard the clank and clatter of the pots and pans hung on Michael's pack before she saw him and Sebastian. They dismounted, but this time Michael didn't shrug off the pack.

"You said the feel of Dunberry turned dark," she said when Michael got close enough.

He nodded. "Two boys have gone missing, and a young woman was brutally murdered."

"After the Eater disappeared into the landscapes, two females were murdered in the Den," Sebastian said. "A succubus and a human. Those killings were brutal."

"Is there a pond or river close to where those boys were last seen?" Glorianna asked.

"Pond," Michael replied.

She watched his expression harden as he began putting the pieces together.

"The Eater of the World was hunting in Dunberry," she said quietly.

"It brought those death roller things into that pond?" He sounded outraged.

She shook her head. "Possible, but just as likely It took the form of a death roller and did the hunting. Just like It would have assumed a form that made It the best predator for killing that woman."

"And the lamplighter," Michael said. "I forgot about the lamplighter. Killed the same night. Some of his bones were crushed and there were other . . . odd . . . things about the way he died. Or so I was told."

"When Lynnea and I were escaping from the Landscapers' School, we saw creatures that could have crushed bone," Sebastian said.

Michael shuddered. Then his eyes filled with a mixture of anger and shock as he pointed at her. "No. I'll not have it. You will *not* take this on your shoulders, Glorianna Belladonna. If a man bolts the door against a beast trying to attack his family, do you blame him for protecting his own? And if the beast turns away from his door to attack another's that is less well defended, is that his fault because he didn't step aside and let it attack what he loved? You bolted your own door, but you didn't aim that beast at a neighbor."

What was he hearing in her "music" that revealed so much of what she was thinking—and feeling? She *wasn't* to blame for where the Eater chose to hide after she had altered the landscapes and closed Wizard City away from the rest of the world, but she didn't like feeling this exposed and wasn't used to someone who wasn't family reading her so clearly.

"If the borders in this part of Ephemera are as fluid as they seem, the Eater could have gotten here from Wizard City before I broke that bridge," Lee said. "Might have avoided your landscapes altogether."

"Maybe." If Michael and Caitlin hadn't stumbled into her life, she wouldn't have known where the Eater had gone, would have had no hope of finding It. Or stopping It.

"This is it then," Michael said, lifting a hand to indicate the bridge. "Either the road leading into Dunberry starts when we cross the bridge, or we'll be standing on the other side of the stream waving at your brother and cousin. Coming back across the bridge in the other direction should show us the road leading to Kendall. There's a posting house about halfway, where coaches change horses and such. The road that turns off the main one leads to Foggy Downs."

No matter what she found on the other side of the bridge, taking that step between here and there was all she needed to do in order to go home. No matter what they found when they crossed over, she could get them to a safe landscape in a heartbeat.

But the prospect of crossing over to a landscape that wasn't hers was exciting and scary—and made her feel adventurous and foolishly young. Had Michael's mother felt like this the first time she had begun a journey with his father? Had she felt this excitement for the adventure—and for the man? And look how *that* had ended. Maybe . . .

She took a step back. Shook her head violently.

"Glorianna!"

Whose voice? She couldn't tell, didn't know. All three of them were around her. Then she felt his hands on her shoulders, felt the warmth of him. Heard the music in him.

She'd never thought of people as songs before she met him. Still didn't for most. Lee and Sebastian were a resonance. Michael was different. Michael was unlike anyone she had known before.

"It's sly," she said, pushing back her hair as she concentrated on taking steady breaths.

"It's *here*?"

She paused a moment, thinking something was wrong with her hearing. Then she realized all three of them *had* asked the same question.

"No." She paused again. "My head hurts."

She felt Michael's lips against her ear. Felt those lips curve into a smile.

"Then stop pulling on your hair," he whispered.

She put her hands down—and looked at two pairs of green eyes that were sharp with worry.

"I'm all right," she said.

"You're going back to the Den," Sebastian said.

"No, I'm not."

"Leave the woman be," Michael said. "The land is sour here, and I'm thinking the badness that changed Dunberry spilled over a bit."

"This has happened before," Glorianna said, knowing by the way Lee sucked in a breath that he wouldn't keep that bit of information to himself and that she could look forward to one of Nadia's rare, full-tempered scolds when she got home. "The Eater tried to turn me away when I altered the pond to shut off the death rollers' access to this landscape. Now Its resonance in the Dark currents around the bridge brushed against me, tried to turn me away from crossing the bridge with you." She looked over her shoulder at Michael.

"Will crossing that bridge put you in danger?" Michael asked.

She gave the question serious consideration before shaking her head. She slipped out of their protective circle and retrieved her pack. Clothes, toiletries, some gold and silver coins, since those were acceptable tender in any landscape. Pencils and some folded sheets of paper to make notes of what she saw and how landscapes connected. A canteen clipped to the outside. Michael carried a bit of food, along with all his belongings—enough to get them through a lean meal or two if Dunberry turned elusive.

She had traveled farther with less fuss simply by crossing over to one of her distant landscapes. Wasn't the same.

She hugged Lee, an awkward business since the pack got in the way.

"We'll be back in a few days," she whispered in her brother's ear.

He kissed her cheek and whispered back, "Travel lightly."

Sebastian next, and just as hard to say good-bye. Harder in some ways.

Don't get maudlin, she thought. *Don't feed the Dark currents. You could get back to the Den faster than they can.*

"Travel lightly," Sebastian said, looking at Michael.

"And you," Michael replied softly. Then he held out his hand to her, linked his fingers with hers.

Together, they walked across the bridge.

✳   ✳   ✳

A familiar road. Familiar land in terms of the looks of it. But a terrible, sour music that ripped at the heart. When he'd last been in Dunberry, he hadn't known what had caused the change in the village. Now his stomach churned with the knowledge of what had come to this place and what the Eater of the World had done to these people.

"Do you feel it?" Glorianna asked, looking around.

"Darling, the only *good* thing I'm feeling is your hand in mine," he replied.

"There's an access point nearby." She moved toward the stream's bank, tugging him with her.

He'd known the world had done one of its little shifts—no, that *they* had crossed over to another landscape—the moment his foot had touched the road, but he still looked across the stream to confirm Lee and Sebastian weren't there.

"This is the spot," she said, crouching down.

Since he wasn't about to let go of her hand, he crouched with her. "I don't see anything."

"What do you hear?"

A dark song, but faint and scratchy. What he heard clearly was her—the light tones as well as the dark.

"It can't touch me," he said, staring at her as the wonder of that truth filled him. "When I fought It, I was being pulled into darkness—and I chose what darkness would be my fate. So I can hear what It has done to Dunberry, but *Its* song is nothing more than a scratchy annoyance.

"Then what *do* you hear?"

"You." He watched her eyes widen. " 'Her darkness is my fate.' That was the choice I made. And that choice has made me tone-deaf to the Eater." He waited a beat, then tipped his head to indicate the stream. "So what is it you're feeling here, Glorianna Belladonna?"

"This is the Eater's point of entry when It comes to this landscape," she said.

"Like those bits you have in your garden?" He waited for her nod. "So It's made a garden?"

The arrested, thoughtful look on her face kept him silent.

"It turned the school into Its garden," she finally said. "The school is now full of Its creatures, so that would be the safest place to maintain Its own dark landscapes."

"Is that what Dunberry has become? One of Its dark landscapes?"

"A lot of Dark currents here, more than is natural for this place. But despite those currents, I don't think it's changed into one of the Eater's landscapes. Not yet." Glorianna rose to her feet and stepped away from the bank, her hand still linked with his. "Landscapes, like people, can change, Magician. This place didn't start out this way. It doesn't have to stay this way."

"What about that?" He used their linked hands to point toward the stream.

She smiled. "Ask the wild child."

He studied her a moment and decided she wasn't teasing. Ask the wild child. Ask Ephemera. Lady's mercy, hadn't he seen what *she* could do by asking the world to make—or remake—itself?

"This feels foolish."

"Then foolishness is all that will come of it," Glorianna replied. "You are still the bedrock here. The connection hasn't been completely severed. Ephemera will give you what your heart tells it to give you. If you believe you will fail, then that is what you will do—because that is your truth in this moment. That you want to fail. Maybe even need to fail because you're not ready for the next stage of your journey."

He couldn't deny the truth of her words, even if he didn't like the sound of them. "Would you mind standing over there, then? This is a private conversation."

She looked at their linked hands, then up at him—and he realized he'd been the one holding on, reluctant to let go. He released her hand and watched her walk a couple of man-lengths away, the polite distance someone would give people who needed a moment of privacy. It felt too far. Much too far. Because he knew if she were standing no farther away from him than she was now but was in a different landscape, he wouldn't be able to see her, or even know she was there.

Shaking his head to dislodge that thought, he went back to the stream and crouched on the bank.

"Wild child," he called softly. "Can you hear me?"

He waited, almost called again. Then he felt it—that same sensation he had in the pubs sometimes, of a child hiding in a corner, listening to the music. But now the sensation was more like a child hiding behind *him* in order to escape being seen by something that frightened it.

"This access point," he said, pointing toward the stream and wishing he'd asked Glorianna to show him the exact spot. "It's a bad thing."

No disagreement about that.

"Can you get rid of it?"

Hesitation. Confusion. Even a little fear? Well, the enemy *was* called the Eater of the World.

Still crouched, he pivoted on the balls of his feet until he could see Glorianna. "What happens if we don't remove the access point, just try to change Dunberry?"

She walked back to him. "Depending on how often the Eater checks the daylight landscapes It is changing into dark landscapes, It will sense a dissonance and come back to restore the balance in Its favor."

Meaning anything he did wouldn't help the people in the village.

"Removing the access point removes Its shortcut to this place," Glorianna said. "It could still return, but It would have to travel overland to reach the village."

"It would know someone got rid of Its shortcut?"

She nodded. "It would know the Landscaper who held this village had reclaimed the landscape. That may make It reluctant to return—

especially if It wants to avoid you." She crouched beside him. "The core of your gift is the same as other Landscapers', I think—to be the bedrock through which Ephemera interacts with human hearts—but how that gift manifested is different. I wonder if that's true in other parts of the world."

"Like a story, you mean?" She didn't understand him, but she was listening, learning the language of how he saw the world. "Stories change from place to place. The bones of them stay the same, but they're clothed a little differently, and that reflects how the people dress them up to fit themselves."

"Yes," she said thoughtfully. "Yes. Guardians. Guides. All the survivors went into hiding in one way or another after Ephemera shattered and the Eater was caged. They called themselves by other names, and those names took on different meanings. But the core of what they were meant to be and meant to do didn't change."

"The perception of the people around them did," Michael said.

"Yes." She gave him a look that made him nervous. "It's time to change that perception again, Magician, for your sake and the sake of the people who need you and the others like you to keep the currents of Light and Dark balanced in the landscapes that resonate with your heart."

Michael took a deep breath, then puffed out his cheeks as he blew the air out. "All right, then. Let's start with this. How do we get rid of it?"

Glorianna pursed her lips. "The stream was already here and is part of this land, so we can't tell Ephemera the stream doesn't belong here, because it does. So it would be easier to change where the access point leads to."

No point telling her she had switched to that way of speaking where the words had no meaning. At least, for him. "What happens when we move it?"

She made a circle out of her arms, fingertips touching fingertips.

"You'll have a piece of stream about this big plopped into a different landscape."

"Into the sea?" he asked, thinking of that mist-filled, haunted piece of water.

"Stone is stone. It won't float. So this access point would settle at the bottom of the sea. It would still be a circle of fresh water running over those stones just as it is now."

"Well, that would be a bite in the ass, now wouldn't it?"

"I wouldn't know."

Her dry tone had him grinning. Then he held out a hand. "Show me how to mend the world."

Her hand slipped into his. "Ephemera, hear me."

He felt the currents of power, felt the world changing around him. Not as music this time, which he found interesting. No, this was more like a tuning fork being struck, and he was using himself to tune the world to match that resonance. He knew the moment it was done, the moment that resonance was tuned just the right way so that it no longer belonged in a piece of the world that could hear his music.

"Now what?" He felt his knees pop as he stood up—a reminder that a dozen years on the road could make parts of a man feel older than his years. He wasn't sure he wanted to tend a garden like Caitlin did, but he wondered if there wasn't a compromise that would let him look after his places without being on the road so much. Because, truth to tell, he'd lost the taste for traveling. Wouldn't have lost it if he hadn't been thrown beyond the world he knew. He couldn't see himself settling down in any of his "ports of call," as Kenneday put it, but he could see himself making a life and a home in Aurora—or on the Island in the Mist. Could see himself spending time with Jeb and Lee and, Lady of Light have mercy on him, even Sebastian.

He wondered if any of them would have anything to do with him when all was said and done.

"What would you usually do when a village was out of tune?" Glorianna asked.

"Play some music to help folks get back in tune. But we can't go down into the village. I'm not ashamed to say I snuck out the back way last time I was here, and I don't fancy going down there now." *Especially if it might put you in danger.*

"Where does the landscape begin for you?"

"Here. The land always has a slightly different feel as soon as I cross the bridge."

"Then we don't need to go into the village. You're playing for the wild child now, to help balance the currents. If you help the Light shine a little, a heart will warm and shine a little in response."

"Like candles. Light one and more can be lit from it."

She smiled at him. "Yes. Like candles." She shrugged out of her pack and sat by the side of the road.

He shrugged out of his pack and opened the flap just enough to pull out the whistle. He stood for a moment, with his feet planted for balance and the sun warm on his face, aware of the woman as much as the land.

He wouldn't be playing just for the wild child.

The notes flowed through the air, bright threads of sound. Hope. Happiness. The contented fatigue of a good day's work. Laughter. Romance. The pleasure of a satisfying meal. The warmth of friends.

He didn't know how long he had played, with the music flowing through him, before he became aware of the sound of hand against leg, of her setting a rhythm using her body as a drum.

Did she play an instrument? She hadn't mentioned it; he hadn't asked. Or was she simply responding the way folks in a pub would, beating out the rhythm of a tune? Would she like the sound of an Elandar drum?

His mind wasn't on the land or the music anymore, so he finished up the tune, letting the last note linger.

"That's it, then," he said, tucking the whistle back in the pack and unhooking the canteen for a long drink.

"We've got company," Glorianna said quietly, getting to her feet.

"I see it. If need be, you take that step back to your own ground."

She gave him a long look that didn't tell him anything, so he concentrated on the horse and cart coming toward them—and the man driving.

He opened the canteen and took a drink, all the while watching the man, whose hands tightened on the reins when he realized who was standing by the road.

"Whoa." The man glanced at Glorianna, then looked away. "Good day to you, Michael."

"And to you, Torry," Grief-dulled eyes. Troubled heart. "What brings you out this way?"

"Needed to get away for a few days. Just . . . away. Borrowed the rig, figured I'd go up to Kendall."

A man who looked that broken and empty, walking down the wrong streets, could find himself beaten and robbed, if not dead.

Which is why he's going.

"You didn't kill her," Glorianna said quietly. "It wasn't your fault."

Anger darkened Torry's face as he twisted in the seat. "And what would you be knowing about it?" He twisted around back to Michael. "Have you started bringing your whore with you, Magician?"

"That's enough!" Michael roared.

"You didn't kill her," Glorianna said again, her voice still quiet. "That voice whispering to your heart is a liar. That whisper belongs to a thing that devours Light and heart and hope. It killed her, Torry. Not you."

The anger faded from Torry's face, leaving a wasteland of despair. "She wouldn't have been in that alley if not for me."

"Was she waiting to meet you?" Glorianna asked.

"No! She wasn't that kind of girl to be meeting me—or anyone—in an alley."

"Were you supposed to walk her home? Were you late?"

"No. She was at her friend Kaelie's house. Went over to talk about wedding things. Our wedding. I went to the pub with a few of the lads. Just to have a drink or two, play some darts. Nothing more."

Michael stepped up and took hold of the horse's bridle since Torry had let the reins slip from his hands.

"I'm sorry for your grief, Torry," Michael said. "And I'm sorry for Erinn. I am. But Glorianna is right. Evil killed your girl and the lamplighter and the two boys. And Evil has tried to break you by heaping blame on your shoulders as well as grief."

Suspicion filled Torry's eyes. He gathered the reins. "No one has said those boys are dead. But they went off with someone. A familiar stranger."

"I heard the same thing when I was here last—and more," Michael said. "Who saw the boys go off with this stranger? Who came forward as witness?"

Torry opened his mouth. Closed it. Looked thoughtful.

"Whispers in the dark," Glorianna said. "Everyone has heard a 'something.' No one knows where it started or who first said it."

"The Destroyer of Light is among us, Torry," Michael said.

"The Destroyer is just a story," Torry protested.

Michael shook his head. "No. It's not." He gave the horse a pat and stepped back. "You need to get away for a few days. I understand that. Sometimes you need to see the same stars from a different place to help your heart settle when it's hurting. But don't go to Kendall. There's been some . . . darkness . . . there too."

He's a good man, Michael thought. *Come on, wild child, give him a bit of luck to help ease his heart.*

"You heading down to the village?" Torry asked after a long moment.

"No," Michael said. "We just stopped for a rest and a bit of music. We're headed for the posting house and then on to Foggy Downs tomorrow."

A blush stained Torry's cheeks. "Bit of a walk for a lady, isn't it?"

He hadn't called Glorianna a lady a few minutes ago.

The music is changing in the lad, Michael realized, feeling his own heart lighten.

"They'd have a pub there, wouldn't they?"

Michael nodded. "Shaney's. Food, drink, a few rooms to rent upstairs."

"Music?"

"There will be tomorrow night." Michael gave Torry a man-to-man smile. "Might even teach the woman how to play the drum."

"What?" Glorianna yipped.

"That little bit of hand-slapping was fine out here," Michael said, making his voice a blend of soothing and condescending, a blend that was guaranteed to put—yes, *that* was the look—fire in a woman's eyes. "But no one will hear it over the dancing."

"And you won't hear anything over the ringing in your ears once I'm done whacking you upside the head."

Lady's mercy, she just might mean it.

But Torry burst out laughing, and the sound made her narrow her eyes at Michael.

"Peace, lady," Torry said. "He'll play better if he can hear the tune." He paused, then added shyly, "There's room in the rig. I could take you as far as the posting house. Save you that much of a walk."

"In return for me not whacking him upside the head?" Glorianna asked in a voice women perfect to scrape a layer of skin off a man's hide.

"My mother always says kindness begets kindness," Torry said meekly.

Glorianna stared at him. Then she sighed and picked up her pack. "Your mother is right. Mothers always are."

Doreen walked toward the boardinghouse, too tired to feel discouraged. She'd been out and about since morning, doing what she could to meet the right sort of gentlemen, and here it was suppertime and not even a flirtation to show for the effort. But how was she supposed to be seen when she couldn't afford to be *seen*? Her best outfits were out of fashion, and there was no chance of doing anything about that because everything cost more than she'd expected.

Maybe she should have gone a little farther and stopped at another excuse for a village like Foggy Downs. She could have lived pretty for a month on what wouldn't last more than a week here in Kendall. Or maybe she should have gotten passage on a ship heading north. Or even taken a walk through a pair of Sentinel Stones to see if she would end up in another part of Elandar that would be more to her liking.

She'd find someone. She had to. She *wasn't* going back to Foggy Downs. She was going to find . . .

Someone like him—that middle-aged, elegant gentleman walking toward her with his lips curved in a hint of a mysterious smile. He looked like he would know what to do with a woman.

"I beg your pardon," he said. "I noticed you earlier today, but could not find anyone to introduce me."

She lowered her eyes, then gave him a flirtatious look through her lashes. "I've just recently come to town and don't, as yet, have any particular friends." But if his purse matched the quality of his suit, he might become a *very* special friend.

"Then, please. Allow me to escort you back to your lodgings. A lady should not be walking alone after dark."

It seemed a bit odd that, having mentioned a lack of introductions, he hadn't offered his name or asked for hers. But she pushed that thought aside. He was the first man who had shown interest in her, and he looked like he could afford to be generous.

"Maybe we could go somewhere first since it's such a pleasant evening. I would like to get to know you better," Doreen said, smiling. If she could talk him into buying dinner, she'd save a little off her room and board.

"Yes," he said, returning the smile. "I think we could do that."

Another footfall. A scrape of boots on cobblestone. Something sly about the sound.

The round little merchant tightened his hand on his walking stick. He didn't have a packet for the home safe tonight. Didn't even have enough coin to stop in a tavern and have a pint. Not that he would since that would make him late for dinner, and his wife had told him in no uncertain terms that she wasn't waiting dinner for him again. If he was late, he could eat what was left and eat it cold.

So he was going home at the proper time. Plenty of people on the street. But . . .

That sly sound. A heavy footfall trying to stay quiet.

Plenty of people about. Plenty of carriages on the streets, taking people home or taking them to some evening social engagement.

Nothing to worry about. Nothing to fear. Nothing . . .

The footsteps stopped. Vanished. Then *something* laughed.

He stood frozen as the sound crawled over him. As the light from the streetlamps became oddly veiled. As the sounds of carriages and ordinary life faded.

Then he heard another sound, more an exhalation than a word.

"Pleeeease."

Turning slowly, his leg muscles protesting the effort, he realized he had stopped at the mouth of an alley. There was something in the alley, just beyond the light thrown by the streetlamp.

Was that a woman's *arm?* Perhaps one of those mannequins that some of the clothing stores had imported from another country. The wife and some of her lady friends were talking about setting up a committee to protest the use of such things in store windows, claiming the sight of limbs caused unseemly thoughts in young men.

He didn't think all the young men in Kendall had two thoughts between them when it came to artificial limbs, female or otherwise, but saying that to his wife might make it sound as if *he'd* had a thought or two about the matter. Which he didn't. Except to envy the merchants who could afford such an extravagance.

Yes, it was probably a mannequin's arm, left here as a schoolboy prank.

Nothing artificial about the sound, something whispered. *Someone could need help.*

He shuffled his feet, uncertain about what he should do. Then he looked down as the toe of one shoe tapped an object and made it rattle.

A box of matches. And a candle stub lying next to the corner of the building. Wouldn't provide much light, but it would be enough to see if there was reason to shout for the constables.

He crouched down, puffing a bit as his belly got squeezed but unwilling to get his trousers dirty by kneeling on the cobblestones. He used up three matches—and there were only five in the box to start with—before he got the candle lit. With his walking stick tucked under one arm and a hand shielding the flame, he walked into the alley.

A filthy trick! A filthy, dirty, awful trick to play on people, leaving something like that for an innocent man to find. Why, he almost soiled himself from the fright of seeing such a . . .

"Pleeeease."

He stood there, staring stupidly, while his mind accepted the horrible truth: Not a trick. Not a mannequin. Not red wine or red paint staining the alleyway. The severed leg, the bone stabbing out from the flesh looking too jagged to be the work of an ax or saw. And the torso. Cut up. Torn up. Wounds too desperate for any surgeon to heal. It was a wonder the woman was still alive.

"There there, my dear," he said, going down on one knee in the blood and the dirt, tears running down his face unnoticed. "Everything will . . ." Be what? Not all right. Never all right. This was even worse than those killings that had occurred around the docks not long ago. But this wasn't a prostitute, just a young woman.

"Doooooreeen." Her voice sounded thick, clotted. "Fooooggy Doooowns."

"Doreen from Foggy Downs," he repeated. "Yes, I'll tell your people. I'll send a letter out, express. You won't be left to strangers, my dear. I'll see that you get home. I promise."

No more words. No more breath.

As he stumbled out of the alleyway, calling for help, he heard the jagged sound of soft, inhuman laughter.

Chapter Twenty-seven

"Stop here," Michael said to Torry. Then he turned in the seat to look at Glorianna. "What do you think?"

There was a look on her face. Pleasure? Pride? He couldn't tell.

"It was a dark landscape," she said softly. "Fog obscures."

"I remember," he said just as softly, ignoring the amused yet confused look Torry was giving both of them.

"Left to itself, this place would have attracted dark hearts or dark natures—maybe even a demon race."

"What?" Torry said.

"Hush," Michael said, laying a hand on the younger man's arm.

"They made a choice, those people who first settled in this place," Glorianna continued. "Maybe there was a Guide with them originally. The people might have stories about their ancestors that could provide a clue. Those original settlers chose to quiet the Dark and feed the Light. They brought love and laughter and anger and sorrow and all the messy tangles that make up a human life. And they kept this a daylight landscape that leans toward, but never surrenders to, the Dark. Every day, simply by living here as they do, they make the choice to hold on to the Light."

He looked at the village of Foggy Downs spread out below them. Good people with heart. That's why he'd wanted her to see this place. He'd thought, hoped, she could help them. Do something with this landscape he couldn't do. But he understood now her pleasure and pride as she looked down at the village and considered the people who lived there. As she looked at him.

"So the music does make a difference here," he said, not sure if he was making a statement or asking a question.

"It makes a difference in all your landscapes, Magician," Glorianna replied. "Our connection to Ephemera is the reason our ancestors were shaped to walk in the world." She looked at the land spreading out before them. Then she smiled and sat back. "Let's go down and meet your people."

"She called you a Magician," Torry said out of the side of his mouth after giving the horse the signal to move forward. "You feel easy about that?"

"Yes, she did," Michael said, smiling. "And yes, I do." Because something about the way she said the word sang for him right down to the marrow in his bones, he focused all the luck-bringing skill he had into a single wish: *Let her have a day of light and laughter, a day of simple pleasures. Let her have a day to be a woman instead of a warrior. Let her have a day when Glorianna can dance.*

Michael brushed his hair, then straightened the vest. Good shirt, embroidered vest, good trousers. Yes, he did clean up well and would turn a few female heads.

But was it enough to turn Glorianna's head? They had the bed and the candlelight he wanted for their first lovemaking.

He sighed. And they had a village full of chaperones. Added to that, Shaney's wife had put Glorianna in the room that had the squeaky floor, so a man couldn't even approach the door of the damn room without everyone in the main room below knowing about it. Hadn't he learned that for himself when he'd knocked on the door to see if Glorianna had everything she needed? There was no harm in a man enjoying a kiss, especially when he had sense enough to stay in the doorway. But Maeve, the postmistress, had come puffing up the stairs, then stood there and told him to get on with it so the girl could close her door and get a bit of rest before the evening's dancing.

How did she expect him to get on with it, with her standing there tapping one foot and looking stern?

Sebastian probably could have gotten on with it.

"Put the ripe bastard right out of your head," Michael muttered to himself. "He didn't fare so well against his own auntie, now did he?"

Cheered by that thought, he left his room, considered tapping on Glorianna's door, then went down to the main room to spare Maeve another run up the stairs since she seemed to be the one keeping guard.

A day of simple pleasures, of light and laughter. A day when Glorianna could dance.

So far, she'd had the light and the laughter. Now he'd give Glorianna Belladonna the music for the dance.

"You shouldn't have gone to so much trouble," Glorianna said as she helped set the tables.

The Missus, as everyone seemed to call Shaney's wife, just *tsked*. "It's no trouble. Besides, we probably won't see either of you again until after the wedding."

Glorianna bobbled a dish and decided she'd helped enough. Besides, her knees had gone weak. "Wedding?"

Maeve glanced at the Missus, and they both gave a sharp head bob.

"Liked his kisses well enough, didn't you?" Maeve said. "He's never been careless when it comes to the girls, but you have to figure a man like that has learned enough to know what to do when he's between the sheets."

They were both looking at her expectantly. "Ah . . ."

"Where did you say you were from?" Maeve asked. "Aurora, wasn't it? A fair piece from here would you say?"

"Um . . ." Most likely it *was* a fair piece from here. Or as close as crossing a bridge. She just wasn't sure she should be the one to try to explain that. Especially now that she realized all the little comments about Michael that Maeve and the Missus had been tossing at her since she came downstairs weren't just little comments. More like what she'd expect doting aunts—or horse traders—to say when they were trying to sell a favorite nephew to a potential wife.

Which was exactly what they were trying to do.

Then she caught a movement on the stairs that led up to the rooms. Her legs folded, and it was sheer luck that she ended up halfway on a chair. "Oh, Guardians and Guides."

No, she hadn't seen him to advantage. Even during the evening they'd all spent in the Den, she hadn't seen him for who he truly was.

He'd shed the scruffy, friendly stranger along with the worn shirt and trousers he wore for traveling. He'd shed Michael in the same way she sometimes shed Glorianna, the part of her that had family and friends.

The man who slowly walked toward her wasn't Michael. This was the ill-wisher, the luck-bringer who could command the currents of power that flowed through Ephemera. The Magician.

The voices around them faded. Or maybe she just stopped paying attention to anything but him.

I did this, she realized as she looked into his blue-gray eyes. *I uncovered a veiled mirror and gave him a clear look at what he was, at who he could be. Guide of the Heart. I showed him the path. Now it's up to him to move on to the next stage of his journey.*

She stood to meet him. "Magician."

People around them sucked in a breath, but he nodded. "That is what I am. Ill-wisher. Luck-bringer."

"The one who keeps the currents of power balanced in your pieces of the world. The spirit who opens the Door of Locks. That's who we are, Michael. That's who we came from—and that's why we are still here, walking in the world."

A tingle in the air between them, as if something was trying to get in.

"It's time," Glorianna said softly.

"It's time," she said, and her music was so beautiful and so bittersweet that it broke his heart.

It *was* time but . . . Not yet. A few more hours. Just a few more hours.

He shook his head. "First there's the music—and the dancing. You'll dance with me, Glorianna Belladonna." He raised a hand, brushed a finger down her cheek. "You'll dance with me."

Shaney—or maybe it was the Missus who had made the decision—closed the tavern, shooing the last man out as the families who had been invited to the covered-dish dinner began coming in. The others would be back in an hour or two, when Shaney opened the doors again. Then the room would be packed. Not for the music or the dancing. Not tonight, although they would get both. No, tonight they wanted a better look at the woman who had walked into Shaney's with him, the woman who came from a distant land. The woman who had called him "Magician" in front of them and had given the word a different meaning. Magician. The one who helped maintain the balance between Light and Dark *for the sake of the world*. The one who, by helping one heart open a door, might help so many.

The one who, by helping that particular heart, would burn the budding promise of his own life to ash.

So he held on to everything that was her. The sound of her voice, both amused and puzzled, as she gave Maeve straightforward answers about home and family that made no sense unless a person had seen Glorianna's part of the world. The scent of her beneath the milled soap the Missus only put out for special guests—a ripe scent that could get a man drunk before he'd gotten a good taste of her. The way her green eyes filled with a child's glee when she'd gotten her first look at an Elandar drum—and the way she'd looked when she'd been taught a simple rhythm and had played a song with him, just him, while the other musicians sat quietly and smiled or winked at him.

He held on to the way it felt to dance with her, both of them laughing as she learned the steps, both breathless with desire as they circled, their eyes seeing nothing but each other. Then he kissed her, long and slow and sweet, lifted up by the laughter and applause of the people around them . . .

. . . until the tavern door crashed open.

"Lady's mercy!" the man said, swaying in the doorway. "Almost had to give it up. I'd swear the road kept disappearing on me, or I would have been here hours ago."

A chill ran down Michael's spine as he watched the exhausted man stagger toward the bar. He recognized the badge on the man's coat. Express rider.

He'd asked for a day—and Ephemera, the wild child who liked his music, had done its best to give him that day. So a road had turned elusive in order to delay a message.

"Have a seat, man," Shaney said, hurrying behind the bar. "You're done in."

The man shook his head. "Horse could use some care. Poor beast is almost run off his legs."

"I'll see to the horse," one of the men called.

"There now," the Missus said. "Sit on that stool there and we'll get you fixed up with a bit of food and drink."

Michael slipped an arm around Glorianna's waist and waited.

Then Shaney finally recognized the badge as he set a glass of ale in front of the rider. "Who would you be looking for?"

"Don't rightly know. Anyone here know a woman named Doreen?"

A shudder went through him for no reason he could explain. He wasn't going to hide what he was anymore, so Doreen couldn't do him any harm no matter whom she chose to tell.

"She used to work here," Shaney said warily.

The man drew the letter out of his pouch and handed it to Shaney. "Then this is for you."

Shaney stepped aside as the Missus put a bowl of stew and a plate of cheese and buttered bread in front of the rider.

No one spoke as Shaney broke the seal and read the message.

A broken song of pain and grief—and a little guilt.

"She's dead," Shaney said. He looked at Maeve, not his wife, when he said it. "Murdered."

"Lady of Light, have mercy," Maeve murmured, sitting down heavily. "We'd had enough of her and wanted her gone, but no one wanted this."

The Missus burst into tears. Shaney wrapped his arms around her and swayed.

"Where?" Glorianna asked, looking at the rider.

"Kendall," he replied. "Started out from Kendall late last night with several express letters. Would've been here sooner, but I couldn't find the damned road."

Michael bent his head and whispered in Glorianna's ear, "Wait for me by the stairs."

It's time.

Yes, he thought as he moved through the crowd to have a word with Shaney. It was time.

*　　*　　*

Had they been lovers? Glorianna wondered as she waited by the stairs and watched Michael talk to Shaney and Maeve. No, not lovers. Not even friends. But there had been something between them.

The party was breaking up. Families were gathering up their children and going home. No more music, no more laughter. Not tonight.

It's time.

He came toward her, his face tight with grim sorrow—and resignation. She'd seen that look on her mother's face. Had seen it in a mirror often enough over the years.

Landscaper, Guide, Guardian, Magician, Shaman, Heart-walker, Heart Seer, Spirit. What difference did the name make? The feeling was the same. Sometimes you opened a door, revealed a path, provided that moment of opportunity and choice—and that choice, despite all its promise, turned bitter, turned tragic. Turned to sorrow.

"Michael?"

He shook his head, cupped his hand under her elbow, and guided her up the stairs. When they reached the door of his room, he stopped. "We need to talk."

"About Doreen."

"Not so much."

He opened the door, then stepped aside, letting her enter first. When he came in, he locked the door. The sound scraped her nerves.

"I think that monster is back in Kendall," Michael said. "The letter . . . It was a hard death, Glorianna. Doreen wasn't a kind person, but no one deserves that kind of death."

She turned to face him. "What does that have to do with you?"

"Shaney emptied the till, bought her passage to Kendall." He hesitated. "Being a Magician . . . It's not talked about, you understand. It needs to be talked about. I've learned that much from you and your mother—and from seeing the people in Darling's Harbor. Anyway, she tried to cause trouble for me after I left here because I wouldn't . . ."

He glanced at the bed. "She didn't belong here. Didn't fit the music of Foggy Downs anymore."

"So she used a dark way of achieving her goal of leaving this landscape, and that attracted more darkness." Glorianna sighed, then sat in the chair. "And her choices in that time and place put her in the path of the Eater of the World."

"Kendall is a seaport. Ships come in from all over the world. It could slip aboard a ship and end up in some part of the world I've barely heard of and you never have. And if It does that, It will keep killing, keep tormenting."

"Yes," she replied, keeping her eyes on his. "That is Its nature."

He swallowed hard. Seemed to brace for a blow.

She could feel his heart crying out in pain.

"I need your word, Glorianna Belladonna," he said softly. "I need a promise that will not be broken."

"I don't give my word if I can't keep it," she said just as softly.

"I need your word that you won't leave without me. I need your promise that when you go, you'll tell me where you're going. *Exactly* where you're going."

"And if I don't promise?"

"Then I'll bid you good night."

"And what is left unsaid will remain unsaid?"

Another hard swallow. "Yes."

He meant it.

She felt the currents of power flow through the room, flow through her. Felt them brush against her skin.

When she had performed Heart's Justice to take the Dark Guides away from the Eater of the World, she had depended on Lynnea's love and courage to hold Sebastian's heart and keep him safe. She had come to that same moment, here and now, with the Magician.

Opportunities and choices. She could turn away, keep her own landscapes safe, and try to build a life with a man she suspected she could truly love—even though they would always wonder what their life together had cost another part of the world. Or she could have the courage to accept the key Michael held inside himself and open a door that would take her to the next stage of her journey.

"I give you my word," she said.

He crossed the room, knelt in front of the chair, and took her hands in his.

"In that case, I need to tell you the story about the Warrior of Light."

Chapter Twenty-eight

Glorianna walked the paths inside her walled garden on the Island in the Mist, wandering without destination. Despite being out there in the cold hours of the night, the lantern she carried remained unlit, the matches in her coat pocket untouched. She didn't need those things when she walked these paths.

I want to go home. I need to go home.

After he'd told her the story about the Warrior of Light, Michael hadn't questioned her need to return to her island, hadn't argued about the lateness of the hour. She didn't know what explanation he had given to Shaney and the others. And she didn't know what any of them had thought when she and Michael walked out of the tavern and vanished as they took the step between here and there.

He hadn't argued about being given a guest room instead of being invited to her bed. But she couldn't have him there, not yet. Not quite yet.

The Warrior of Light must drink from the Dark Cup.

Listening to him tell the story had been like having a memory rise up through her skin. She'd heard the echo of his words in her blood and bone.

The Guardians of the Light had kept themselves apart from the everyday life of humans, devoting themselves to nurturing the Light so that it would always shine in the world. But the Guides of the Heart had walked in the world. Had fought for the world.

Had died for the world.

She had come from them. She was one of them. She would follow their path.

But this . . . This would be worse than dying.

She knew how to build the cage. Had known for sixteen years without realizing it. And because this would be her choice, she knew how to lock the door of that cage and seal it tight. So tight.

Maybe it was just as well she hadn't met the Magician earlier in her life. That much less to remember. That much less to regret leaving behind.

Ephemera, hear me.

Questions asked. Answers given. It would be all right. She could give him this much. And he would be the Guide he was meant to be.

The Light called.

She smiled when she saw where her wandering had ended. Even as her eyes filled with tears, she smiled.

And took the step between here and there.

"Glorianna? Glorianna!"

Michael held the lantern up and looked around. A waste of breath to swear, but he swore anyway. Without heat, but with a great deal of creativity. The woman may have followed the literal meaning of her promise but she'd fallen short of the spirit of that promise. Which was something they were going to discuss when he found her.

If he could find her.

He *would* find her. Oh, he would. A note slipped under his door wasn't what he'd had in mind when he said he wanted to know where she was going.

Magician, I'm taking a walk in the garden. If I cross over, it will be to a Place of Light. And I will be back.

Well, good. Fine. *When?*

The wild child circled round him, anxious and confused. Did he want something? Should it make something? What? *What?*

He paused long enough to grab hold of his own emotions and consider where he was—and what might happen if he got careless about how he expressed his feelings.

"Nothing," he muttered. "It's nothing. Well . . ." He paused. Considered. Surely that couldn't hurt her landscapes, and it would certainly help him and the wild child calm down. "Maybe we could find a place to play a little music while we're waiting for her to come back."

Here here here. This way.

He followed the "tug" in the currents of power, not exactly sure where he was going, but since he was still within the walled garden, he wasn't worried. He had acquired a heavy coat before he and Glorianna had crossed over to Dunberry—this one a loan from Jeb—so he was warm enough despite the chilly autumn night. If worse came to worst, he would simply wait for sunrise before looking for the gate that led back to the house.

But as he stepped off one path and onto another, the change in the feel of things was enough of a jolt to make him stop.

This part of the garden didn't feel like Glorianna.

The buzz of the land flowed through him, making him want to scratch an itch he knew wasn't physical.

Potential. Possibility. Change.

He set the lantern down, then spread his arms, raising his hands up shoulder-high. He closed his eyes and lifted his face to the night sky.

A month ago he would have felt foolish standing like this. Now he felt the power and duty and joy of what he was.

"Ephemera, hear me," he said softly. "It is Michael. The Magician."

He was a tone that flowed through the currents of the world, both

Light and Dark. He was a clear, powerful song. He was a Magician, and he heard the music of the world.

The buzz of the land kept shifting until it fit the tone that was him, became part of the song that was him.

Most important, this odd place, while it didn't have quite the same feel as the rest, now belonged in Glorianna's garden.

Then he opened his eyes and looked at the ground in front of him.

"Lady's mercy," he whispered. "What have I done?"

"You're up early," Glorianna said as she stepped into the kitchen of Sanctuary's guesthouse. She saw the woman stiffen, saw the wariness in the eyes before Brighid recognized her and relaxed.

"I'm thinking the sun has been up quite some time in Elandar, and my body still answers to that sunrise instead of when the sun awakes here," Brighid replied as her hands worked a mound of dough.

"Yes, the sun is on the other side of dawn over there."

"I missed the songs," Brighid said quietly. "Lighthaven is a beautiful place, but the only thing I truly missed was the songs that marked the points of the day, the cycle of the moon, the turning of the seasons."

"What kind of songs?" Glorianna asked, slipping into a chair by the table where Brighid worked.

"Chants, mostly. Not what most people would consider singing."

"What kind of chants?"

Brighid hesitated, then sang very softly:

> *"We lift our voices to the Light.*
> *We lift our faces to the Light.*
> *We give our spirits to the Light,*
> *To shine in us forever."*

"You don't sing those songs anymore?" Glorianna asked.

Brighid shrugged. She set the dough in a bowl and covered it with a cloth to let it rise. "Tried for a while when I first went to live in Raven's Hill. But it made me sad to sing them there, so I stopped. At Lighthaven, even if you were alone when it was time to call that part of the day, you knew other voices were rising with yours, saying the same words. Even if you couldn't hear them, you knew. There was comfort in that, peace in that."

"You can sing them here," Glorianna said.

"They aren't a tradition here."

"If you don't share them, how can another heart embrace them?"

Brighid looked at her for a long moment, then said, "A Guide of the Heart even for a Guardian of the Light?"

Glorianna smiled. "Why not?"

Brighid walked over to the counter. "Would you be wanting some of this koffee, or has Michael enlightened your palate with a good cup of tea?"

Tears stung her eyes. Emotions stormed through her. Just hearing his name rubbed her heart raw.

"Ah, now. You've not had a parting of the ways, have you?" Brighid pulled up another chair, sat down, and took Glorianna's hands in hers.

Not yet, she thought. *Not quite yet.*

"He's a good man, Glorianna," Brighid said, her voice filled with earnest conviction. "I couldn't see it when I lived in Raven's Hill, and I'm sorry for that. I'm not saying there isn't a bit of Dark in him, because there is. Has to be with him being a Magician. But he has a good heart."

"I don't want to love him," Glorianna whispered. "I think I do, am almost sure I do. But I don't want to."

"Why ever not?"

"Because there has to be a parting of the ways."

"You don't think he could fit into your life?"

"He could, yes." He already fit so well it was as if he'd always been there. And yet everything was new with him, and there was so much they didn't know about each other, about how it might be *with* each other.

She didn't want to talk about Michael—didn't want to think about Michael. So she pulled her hands out of Brighid's and wiped away the tear that had dared spill over. "I know why the Places of Light need currents of Dark. Why do dark landscapes need currents of Light?"

"For hope," Brighid said with such certainty Glorianna just stared at her. "Even a dark heart hopes its plans will succeed, that it will be the victor in the struggle against its adversaries. More than any other reason, that is why the Places of Light exist. Love, laughter, kindness, compassion. These feelings will take root in a heart on their own. But it is hope that flows through the currents of Light. Because without hope, those other seeds will never find fertile ground."

"There are people who have no hope but are still able to love, to offer kindness and compassion."

"A heart that stands deep in the Light can give those. And when it does, what is the seed that is planted in other hearts called?"

"Hope," Glorianna whispered. "The seed is called hope."

"Glorianna . . ."

She shook her head. Pushed her chair back. "I have to go." She pulled a folded, wax-sealed paper from her pocket. "Would you see that Yoshani gets that?" She waited for Brighid's nod, then hurried to the kitchen door. As she reached for the knob, she paused and looked back. "Travel lightly, Brighid."

She hurried away from the guesthouse. There was only one person she wanted to see. Then she wanted the rest of the day to herself. With Michael.

Surely one day wasn't too much to ask. Not when she was about to sacrifice the rest of her life.

*　　*　　*

Brighid stood at the kitchen window for a long time. Still too dark to see outside, but that didn't matter.

A parting of the ways. Why? There was a spark between Glorianna and Michael. She'd seen that for herself when they'd all sailed to the White Isle. If there was more interest on Michael's side and wariness on Glorianna's, well, so be it. A woman was entitled to be wary about where she gave her heart, wasn't she? And with the bridges these folks knew how to make, neither of them would have to sacrifice their pieces . . . of the . . . world . . .

She stared at her reflection in the window.

She'd forgotten. Or hadn't wanted to remember. A riddle. An answer. And a story about love—and sacrifice.

She went back to her work, doing her share to provide food for the guests and residents of this house in Sanctuary. But even as her hands performed familiar tasks, nothing was quite the same. Would never be the same again.

Travel lightly, Brighid.

Advice and blessing from a Guide of the Heart. She would heed that advice, honor that blessing. And when the sky began to lighten, she would walk out to the koi pond and, for the first time in many years, lift her voice in celebration of the dawn.

"Is there a reason you're here at this hour, emptying my pantry?" Nadia asked, pushing her sleep-mussed hair away from her face as she eyed the supplies spread out on the kitchen table.

"Just need a few things," Glorianna muttered as she packed a couple of items into one of the two market baskets. "Michael will be awake soon and I didn't think about getting supplies on the way back to the island."

Nadia tightened the belt of the robe she'd thrown on over her nightgown. "You could always just bring him around for breakfast and then do some marketing on your own."

Too many people. Too many distractions.

"Glorianna?"

"I want a day with the Magician. Alone. On the island," Glorianna said softly.

"Well, that's fine, but that's no reason to be taking all my eggs."

"I know how to stop the Eater of the World. I know what to do."

"Glorianna?"

The sharpness in Nadia's voice warned her that her mother had heard what was under the words.

She raised her head and met Nadia's eyes. "I know what to do."

"Then we'll talk about it. All of us. Jeb can fetch Lee and Sebas—"

"No." She couldn't have all of them around her. Not today. Maybe that was selfish—it was certainly unfair—but she couldn't face all of them. And she couldn't stand the thought that her last feelings for all of them would carry the resonance of an argument.

She walked around the table and put her arms around Nadia. Felt her mother's arms tighten around her in response.

"He'll be angry and he won't want to do it, so lean hard on Lee to make the new bridges that will be needed. And don't turn your heart away from the Magician. It's not his fault. Opportunities and choices, Mother. He provided the opportunity, but the choice is mine."

"Glorianna."

She heard the tears.

"I love you," Glorianna whispered. "When you think of me, remember that. I love you."

They finished packing the baskets in a silence that held too many things that were said without words.

Then Glorianna walked out of her mother's house, walked into the dawn's light, and took the step between here and there.

*   *   *

Glorianna had called it virgin ground. He remembered that much now that his brain started thinking again. She just hadn't explained the *significance* of virgin ground, which was going on the list of things he intended to discuss with her.

"You've had a busy time, haven't you?"

Michael whirled around and saw Glorianna standing nearby, holding two market baskets. Since he didn't think the Places of Light had markets, that meant she'd gone somewhere besides where she said she was going. And that was another something to discuss. They were going to have a plentiful amount to discuss, and to his way of thinking, that discussion would be held at full volume. The fact that she seemed amused by what she was looking at wasn't doing anything for him either.

What what what?

And now the wild child was upset again.

He pointed to the ground in front of the new two-stone-high wall that formed a border around the virgin ground. If it could still be called virgin ground. "We need some stone there. A nice thick layer of pebbles, I'm thinking. In different colors."

There. That should keep Ephemera busy for a while.

He watched the ground change with a speed that staggered him. And right before he closed his eyes to shut it all out, he saw Glorianna set the baskets on the ground, cross her arms, and tip her head to one side as she studied the addition to her garden.

A lesson to him. That's what this was. If he ever had the luck to become a father, he would never ever give a flippant response to a child without considering the consequences of the child's taking him at his word. No, he would never ever give a flippant response.

Especially when the wife was standing right there and could hear him.

He listened to Glorianna move over to the changed ground, heard her sift through the pebbles.

"Well," she said. "I'm not good at identifying uncut stones, but I think you have some precious gems in here, along with a good haul of semiprecious stones."

His eyes popped open. "Huh?"

She scooped up a handful of stones. "You asked for different colors. Here's garnet and malachite. Lapis and citrine. Topaz. Oh, and here's a lovely amethyst. And this might be an emerald."

He crouched beside her. "I was just trying to distract the world, give it something safe to do."

"And you did a fine job. We can pick through these later. If you take them to a gem dealer, you could get a good price for them."

"I didn't do this to line my pockets."

Her free hand brushed his hair back, stroked his head. "Magician, how do you think we get by most of the time? Landscapers don't get paid directly for what they do, so most gardens have a little 'treasure spot'—a place where you can turn the earth and come up with the coins that were tossed in wish wells, or gold or silver nuggets—or gems—that come from Ephemera."

So the story about a treasure hidden in Darling's Garden wasn't just a story. Did Caitlin know about having a treasure spot? "Is it always this easy?"

"Well, for most it's not quite this simple. But the wild child is very responsive to you."

Her lips touched his. Warmth rather than heat. Affection rather than lust. And yet the promise of heat was there, simmering between them.

Friend. Lover. Both.

"Show me what you've done," Glorianna said. "Then let's get some breakfast and put the rest of the food away."

"Ah." He cupped a hand under her elbow, helping her to her feet as he rose to his. "Didn't know what I was doing. Still not sure what I did."

"You made a garden, Magician."

"I don't know anything about tending posies." And whether he was keen on it or not, he had a feeling he was about to learn.

"Then let's see if you have any to tend."

For a man who didn't know what he was doing, he'd done well enough, Glorianna decided as she studied the newly made garden within her garden. All right, two rows of rectangles weren't the most interesting configuration, but he wasn't a Landscaper as such, so all he really needed was a basic garden that provided access points to his landscapes.

He had those. One rectangle was covered with fog over grass. Another looked like ordinary grass but she recognized the resonance of Dunberry. Another was cobblestones, but when she leaned in and sniffed the air, she smelled the sea. He confirmed Foggy Downs, Dunberry, and Kendall, along with three other places in Elandar that had made up his circuit of landscapes.

She pointed to the last two rectangles. "What are those?"

Michael shoved his hands in his pockets and mumbled, "Don't know their songs."

"I beg your pardon?"

He winced. "Don't know those places. Never heard their songs before."

She stared at him as she considered a possibility. "But you hear their songs now?"

He nodded warily.

"Can you play those songs?"

Another wary nod. Then he pulled his whistle out of an inside coat pocket, pointed to one rectangle, and began to play. After a minute, he pointed to the other rectangle and played a different tune.

Not Elandar. It took on a little of the flavor of that land because he was playing the tune, but those new landscapes weren't in the part of the world he had known.

"Looks like Lee is going to have to create a couple of bridges," Glorianna said.

Michael tucked the whistle back in his pocket. "Why?"

"A lot of Landscapers were lost when the Eater attacked the school. The bedrock in the landscapes they tended has been crumbling. Those *landscapes* have been crumbling, becoming mired in the manifestation of emotions without any guidance. But Ephemera wants guidance, and landscapes, like people, change. Some landscapes that were mine when I was sixteen were no longer mine when I was twenty-six. I let them go so that someone else would respond to their resonance. You opened yourself to the world, Magician, and Ephemera found two other places that need your music."

He paled. "But . . . *where?* Am I adding another day or two on the circuit to get to these places or . . ." A little more color drained out of his face. "They aren't in Elandar, are they?"

"No, they aren't in Elandar."

"Then how . . ." He put it together, piece by piece. "Bridges. You said Lee would need to create bridges."

She nodded. "I recognize the tunes. At least, a similarity between what I've heard and what you just played. Lee could tell you better than I, but I think these new landscapes of yours are close to places Mother or I hold. Stationary bridges would let people cross over between the landscapes."

"If those places had been connected to the school, won't the Eater find Its way here?"

"No," she said softly. "Different bedrock now, different resonance. The access point that was at the school no longer matches that place. But if the Eater has established any of Its dark landscapes in those places, you'll have to deal with them, eliminate them. Anything that isn't part of your song doesn't belong in your landscapes," she added when he started to protest. "I—Nadia can teach you how to cross over to your landscapes, and you talk to Ephemera as easily as I do—better than anyone else I've known, including my mother—so asking it to take away what the Eater brought in won't be a problem for you. But don't go into those new landscapes alone the first few times. Have Nadia or Lee or Sebastian go with you. There are still wizards and Dark Guides roaming the landscapes. Not all of them were trapped in Wizard City. They could hurt you before you realized you were in danger. So take someone with you who can show you what you need to know."

"You'll show me," he said. "You'll teach me."

You know better, Magician.

She wanted to throw herself into his arms and hold on, but if she allowed herself to feel weak, she wouldn't find the courage to take the next step of the journey. So she looked at the grassy space behind Michael's garden, and at the young tree, its branches bare of leaves now, that would provide shade in the summertime. Did she have any bulbs? Maybe she could plant a few crocuses around the tree. That would be a cheery welcome when he walked there in the early days of spring.

"It would be nice to have a chair or a bench there," she said, tipping her chin to indicate the grassy space. "You could sit and play your music. Jeb could make you a bench."

He gave her a Patient Look. "Aye. Well, as soon as I have a diamond I can spare, I'll be seeing about a bench—and a birdbath as well, so the fluffy things can have a splash and twitter."

They heard the *pop*, like a kernel of corn in a hot pan.

He just closed his eyes. She pressed a hand against her mouth to keep from laughing.

"Haven't learned yet, have you, Magician?" she asked when she could speak.

"Apparently not."

"Then let's gather up your diamond and go up to the house to make breakfast."

* * *

She planted bulbs beneath the tree near his garden. Crocus, she said. He knew what those were. Maybe.

They didn't speak much throughout the morning. What was there to say? So he helped her in the garden and did his best to soothe the wild child.

That was something whoever had first shaped the story about the Warrior of Light hadn't mentioned—or hadn't understood.

She was going to scare the shit out of the world.

"Where is the heart's hope?" Glorianna asked.

The words stabbed him in the gut, in the heart, but he kept his voice easy. "Which bit? There were several I saw in the garden."

"Yours. The plant you wanted to keep when . . ."

When I revealed my heart.

He stopped and listened to the island. "Over here."

"Should be in the garden," she said as she fell into step beside him. They left the walled garden and headed for the house. "It should have anchored in a bed that represents your home landscape." Her voice trailed away as they stopped in front of an oval of recently turned earth.

He didn't need to ask if it was a new bit of garden. He could tell by the look on her face she hadn't created this new bed near the house.

His home landscape. Not in the walled garden. Not in the landscapes. But here, where it was personal. Where it was just between the two of them. Because that was what he saw—the stone, the grass, the heart's hope. The things that had represented home and were native to Elandar. And behind the stone, forming a protective half circle, was belladonna.

My heart's hope lies with Belladonna.

That truth had brought him to the Island in the Mist. That truth was now manifested in plants and stone.

"This is your home landscape," Glorianna said quietly.

"I know," Michael replied. "I knew from the moment I set foot here."

"I left a note for Yoshani, telling him I was leaving the garden in your care because you can keep the landscapes balanced until they resonate with someone else. And I told him I was giving you the Island in the Mist and the house here. You'll take care of it, won't you?"

"I'll tend to all of it. That's a promise."

He stepped behind her, put his arms around her, drew her back against his chest.

Her breath caught as her hands settled over his.

"When?" he asked.

"With the dawn."

He rested his cheek against her hair. "Then I want this evening. Invite me to your bed, Glorianna Belladonna. Let me love you tonight with all my heart."

"I won't remember you," she whispered.

The pain cut deep. "I know. I'll remember for both of us."

She turned in his arms and rested her hands on his chest as she looked into his eyes. Her lips brushed his once, twice.

"Come to my bed, Magician. Show me the magic of love."

Chapter Twenty-nine

I n the pale gray light, that herald of the dawn, Michael reached for the woman who filled his heart and his dreams—and woke up, alone.

He lit the lamp on the bedside table, plumped up the pillows behind him, then looked at the painting on the wall near the bed.

Sebastian painted that for me, Glorianna had said.

Quite a jolt to see himself in a painting that came from an incubus's imagination—and to wonder if his dreams had influenced the image Sebastian had chosen for Glorianna's moonlight lover or if the painting had, somehow, been the source of his own dreams and yearnings. Just as much of a jolt to look past the romantic costumes and realize he and Glorianna had stood exactly that way in the garden yesterday after discovering the new bed that represented his home landscape.

They'd had their night of lovemaking, and he'd taken extra care to please her, to pleasure her. He had wanted to absorb the music of their lovemaking, had needed to fill his heart with the song of her when passion and love climaxed and shone with a fierce Light.

Now . . .

He pushed back the covers, went into the bathroom, and ran water for a bath. As he waited for the tub to fill, he closed his eyes, turned his head toward his shoulder, and breathed in the scent of her on his skin. He didn't want to wash off that mingling of scents, but there was no telling what was going to happen in the days ahead or when he'd have another chance at taking a full bath.

So he soaked in the hot water and tried not to think about what was to come.

She'd been hesitant at first, almost shy when she brought him to her bedroom last night. It made him wonder how long it had been since she'd had a lover. Then he'd stopped wondering and just enjoyed the way her mouth had opened for him, the butterfly touch of her tongue against his. The feel of her skin beneath his hands. Her moan of pleasure when he'd suckled her breasts. The way her strong fingers had gripped his shoulders the first time he'd stroked her body over the edge of pleasure. And the way . . .

Michael blew out a breath and sat up in the cooling water.

"Maybe you don't need to be remembering quite so much right now," he muttered as he picked up soap and washcloth.

Keeping his mind on the mechanics of what he was doing, he got washed and dressed, and walked into the kitchen. That's when his heart got the first of what, he knew, would be many bruises.

His pack was still by the door. He'd removed his clothing and personal gear last evening while she'd been putting together a bit of dinner for the two of them. The pack was too big and heavy for a woman to carry for long, but it had everything she would need to set up a camp—sleeping bag, pots and pans, candles, matches, lantern. Plenty of room for her clothing and female things. A camp, that's what he'd been thinking. And she hadn't argued with him, hadn't disagreed.

But she hadn't taken it with her, had turned away from even that much comfort. Had turned away from even that much of a reminder of him.

The perk pot still held koffee, so he heated that up instead of making the tea he would have preferred.

He didn't have an appetite, and lost most of his interest in food when he realized she hadn't taken any of *that* with her either, but he ate one of the eggs she had hard-boiled yesterday, then took his cup of koffee and a thick slice of bread and butter out with him. He didn't look at the walled garden, didn't even consider going in. Not yet. Instead, he went to the new bed that held his heart's hope and the belladonna.

"Wild child," he called softly. "Ephemera, can you hear me?"

It heard him, but he sensed a resistance, almost as if it feared what he might ask of it. Did the world know what she intended to do?

"Listen to me, wild child. Don't let her Light scatter. Find a place for it where it can be cherished and kept safe."

Ephemera didn't understand. Not yet.

Door of Locks. Stories and spirits and keys. He'd chosen a lock, based on dreams of a black-haired woman he'd fallen in love with before he'd truly seen her face or heard her voice—or known her heart. But she, as Guide and spirit, had used that key in his heart to open the door and show him a life he couldn't have imagined. Because he hadn't known the possibility of being accepted for what he was had existed.

He ate the bread and drank the koffee. He washed the dishes and the perk pot. He repacked his clothes into the big pack, then took them out and put them in the smaller travel pack. A change of clothes, a canteen, and his whistle were all he needed right now. He slipped one of the one-shot bridges Lee had made for him into his coat pocket. The others, wrapped in scraps of cloth and stored in a drawstring pouch, he tucked into the pack.

Give me enough time, Magician, she had said. *I couldn't bear it if someone else was caught when I altered the landscapes.*

He waited while the minutes crawled by. When the sun had risen high enough that he could be reasonably sure that the folks in Aurora would be up and about, once he actually got there, he picked up the travel pack and left the house.

As he followed the path that would lead him to the river, he slipped his hand in his pocket, wrapped his fingers around the one-shot bridge—and crossed over to the Den of Iniquity.

An abandoned garden. A small plot of ground compared to what she had ended up creating on the Island in the Mist, but it had been hers once, and there was just enough of her resonance left for her to take the step between here and there, to cross over to this enclosed piece of ground.

Safety first. It would all be for nothing if the Eater's creatures killed her before she finished her task. Afterward . . . Maybe it would be a blessing afterward.

Sixteen years ago, the Dark Guides had tried to seal her in by poisoning her mind. If they had succeeded, she would have altered the landscapes to create a smothering cage, and never would have realized she had been the instrument they had used to destroy her, never would have realized it was her power and not theirs that had chained her to a barren existence.

Now she was going to do what the Dark Guides had failed to do. Now she was going to do much more than they had intended to do.

Much more.

"Ephemera," Glorianna Belladonna said softly, "hear me."

The Eater of the World, in the form of an elegantly dressed, middle-aged gentleman, stepped onto the rust-colored sand that spilled out of the back of a smelly alley. Its mouth fell open in astonishment. Its eyes widened in shock.

A dissonance in Its landscapes! New, strange flavors of Dark—and delicious ripples of Light that winked out. Then It felt Ephemera manifest a will, obey a heart. It felt the ripples of that command in the currents of power that flowed through the world. Then It felt . . .

It looked down at the sand beneath Its feet. "No," It whispered. "The bonelovers are mine. That landscape is *mine.*"

But some sly, dark heart had slipped into Its landscapes and *stolen* the bonelovers' landscape by altering the resonance just enough to shut It out. Something had shut It out of a landscape *It had made.*

Thief!

It staggered back a step, braced a hand against a dirty wall.

She walks in the gardens, a voice, harsh yet oddly melodious, whispered through the currents of the world. *She walks in the gardens, stealing all your work, all your creations. All your puny little creations. Boo, hoo. Boo, hoo. Poor little Eater, not brave enough to do anything but hide. She already controls the Light. Where will you go, little Eater, when she rules the Dark?*

Ragged breaths as the body trembled. Fear and rage as It considered the message in those whispers.

The True Enemy had come to the Landscapers' School. Was *in* the Landscapers' School, taking Its dark landscapes and making them her own.

Not fair! *Not fair!*

Coward, the voice whispered. *Even the Dark Guides have come to play.*

It wasn't a coward. It wasn't afraid. It was the Eater of the World. It was *feared.* Even the *world* feared It.

Laughter whispered through the currents of the world. Cruel, mocking laughter.

We're connected with the world again, another voice whispered through the currents. *We're connected to the school!*

It remembered that voice. Harland. The head of the Wizards' Council. The leader of the Dark Guides.

Our own magic wasn't enough to seal her in, Harland's voice whispered. *And we didn't know the bitch could use Heart's Justice the way she did. But we can use the creatures the Eater has at the school. Use them up to wear her down. And then . . . DESTROY HER!*

Laughter whispered through the currents of the world. Cruel, mocking laughter.

Were there ripples of fear beneath that laughter?

She wasn't as strong as she wanted them all to believe. Had *never* been as strong as she wanted them to believe. She was on *Its* ground, where It had slaughtered so many of her kind.

It would have her. In the end, It would have her. Its creatures would attack her body. The Dark Guides would attack her mind. The Light inside her would beckon all the dark things.

In the end, It would have her. It would peel off her skin. It would crack open her bones like the shell of a nut and pick out all the delicious meat. It would feast on her screams and her cries and her misery. And then, when the True Enemy was nothing more than scattered garbage, It would break open another shell—and feast on the Places of Light.

It stepped back onto the sand, forcing the resonance of Its darkness upon the landscape that held Its first creation. Forced Ephemera to accept Its dominance, Its resonance, until the bonelovers' landscape once more belonged to It. Then It changed to Its natural form, a rippling shadow beneath the skin of the world, and flowed as fast as It could to the access point that would take It to the school.

It was coming.

Fear shivered through her, but Glorianna kept at her task of shifting the resonance of the currents of Light that flowed through the school—and through the dark landscapes that belonged to the Eater of the World. She'd set the trap and had sent the bait flowing out into the currents of the world.

Borders and boundaries. She had brought Wizard City back into the world, and that landscape was now connected by a border with the gate that had opened to the Bridges' part of the school. If the Dark Guides tried to come after her, they would have to cross more ground, take more risks against the Eater's creatures.

The cage was almost closed. The Eater had touched less of the world than she had expected. Not surprising, now that she considered it. There were hundreds of landscapes held in the walled gardens at the school. The surviving Landscapers would reclaim their pieces of the world and take on the responsibility of being the bedrock for others. Ephemera would survive.

The landscapes she was leaving behind would be cared for.

It's not a feather bed, but the nights are cold this time of year, and the sleeping bag will keep you warm.

She'd left it behind. Had to leave it behind, along with everything else Michael had wanted to give her.

Because kindness would kill her.

As she pushed the image of Michael's face out of her mind, another face took its place. Dark eyes that held deep pools of wisdom. A hand holding out a white stone.

That day, when Yoshani had told her about the magic of his people in using the jar of sorrows, he had offered her a white stone as a way to cleanse her heart and let go of the hurts of the past. She had refused his offer, had refused that kindness because she had known, on some level, that she would need those kernels of remembered pain.

For this place. For this task.

Yes. She would need her sorrows.

She looked at the sky, at the daylight growing stronger.

The Eater of the World was coming. When It was inside the school, she would lock the last door, seal the last gate.

Then there would be just one more thing left to do.

The Warrior of Light must drink from the Dark Cup.

Hold them off a little longer, Magician. Just a little longer. After that, it will be too late—and they'll be safe.

Teaser saw him first.

Michael had a moment to feel grateful that Lee wasn't at Philo's place with the two incubi. That would buy her a little more time. Besides, he wasn't looking forward to facing Glorianna's brother.

Then Sebastian turned around, and those sharp green eyes looked right at him. Right through him.

He kept walking toward the courtyard. Sebastian stepped away from the tables and chairs, meeting him on the cobblestone street. They stopped just out of reach of each other.

"Threat and promise is what you called me," Michael said quietly. "I've made good on the threat, for the sake of the world."

"What have you done?" Sebastian asked, his voice rough with restrained, but rising, anger.

"Told a story. Provided a key to a locked door."

"In clear words, Magician."

"I told Glorianna how to stop the Eater of the World. She's gone to the Landscapers' School."

Chapter Thirty

They couldn't reach Lee, who had used his little island to go to the Island in the Mist, and Michael thanked the Lady of Light for that blessing. The timing had been a little off. Just enough. Based on what Yoshani had told them, Lee must have gone to Glorianna's island within minutes of Michael crossing over to the Den.

So Lee was wasting time checking the house and the walled garden, while Glorianna . . .

They were all at Nadia's house now, waiting for Lee because his island was the best chance of reaching the landscape that held the school. Nadia couldn't cross over from any of her landscapes. Yoshani and Teaser, as unlikely a pair to become friends as he'd ever seen, had tried, separately, to cross over to the school by using the resonating bridge near Nadia's house. But the bridge no longer worked. At all.

Ephemera was frightened. It wasn't words he was picking up from the world, it was story-songs. Mood-songs. It was being asked to do things it didn't want to do—was afraid to do. Asked by a heart it trusted. Commanded by a will so strong it couldn't disobey.

Hearts had no secrets from Glorianna Belladonna. She understood the people who loved her all too well.

And they were all here now. Teaser and Yoshani. Lynnea and Sebastian. Nadia and Jeb. Even Caitlin Marie and his aunt Brighid.

It felt like a deathbed vigil—the women talking in the kitchen while they made mountains of food no one wanted to eat; the men in another room, talking in hushed voices, trying to fill time with words while they all waited for the transportation that would take them to the site of the grave.

Not enough room in the house. Not enough air in the house.

He was outside, staring at a flower bed in Nadia's personal garden, with no clear memory of how he'd gotten there. He didn't turn around to see who had followed him out of the house. Didn't have to. Even lowered by sorrow, the music of Yoshani's heart was a clear song.

"What brought you here this morning?" Michael asked.

"Your aunt," Yoshani replied. "All day yesterday, she had been quiet, thoughtful. Except when she would go to the koi pond and 'sing the day' as she called it. There was a radiance in the air around her in those moments, and what flowed through Sanctuary made a person want to weep and smile at the same time. This morning she gave me a letter Glorianna had left for me and said she needed to speak with Nadia. She asked me to come with her."

"And Caitlin Marie came this morning for her lesson."

"Yes. So you, too, have your family around you during a difficult time." Yoshani paused. "This story you told Glorianna Dark and Wise. Would you tell it to me?"

Michael shook his head. "Maybe sometime, but not now."

For a moment, he thought Yoshani would argue, but the man simply bowed his head.

"It took courage to let her go, Michael the Magician," Yoshani said gently.

Before Michael could think of a reply, Lee hopped over a broken part of the wall. Looking toward the house, he hollered, "Hey-a, what's going on? The resonating bridge near the house is gone, just gone, and I can't find . . ."

Lee saw him and stopped. Stared.

Words had not been spoken yet, so Lee's mind didn't understand what his heart already knew.

His expression turned grim. He took a step toward Michael.

And Sebastian was suddenly out the kitchen door, both distraction and threat. The Justice Maker flicked a glance at Michael, then focused on his cousin.

"Lee," Sebastian said. "We need to talk."

It tasted her fear in the currents that flowed through the school. It tasted her doubts. And It lapped at the Light as It flowed beneath the paths of the school, easily evading the silly traps the True Enemy had set to capture It.

The Dark Guides had succeeded in trapping the True Enemy in a landscape where she could be destroyed! They had finally succeeded! She was tangled up in Its landscapes at the school, unable to cross over to any place that didn't resonate with It. When she realized she was trapped, she had tried to change Its landscapes and make them hers, but It had been too strong, too powerful, and It had reclaimed what belonged to It. Now she was drawing in all the Light, trying to make a *Place of Light*, thinking that, somehow, she would be safe and beyond Its reach. How delicious! How wonderful! How tasty!

It couldn't wait to feast on the heart of Belladonna.

She listened to the Dark Guides' whispers, let their verbal rape wash through her heart, while building walls that would stand far longer than stone.

And while she listened, while she waited for the right moment, she gathered the Light. She wasn't able to destroy all the currents of Light completely, so she sucked them dry until the threads that were left were so weak and thin that they couldn't support the smallest seed of hope.

The Eater of the World was in the school. Was coming toward her.

She altered the landscapes and closed the last door. Turned the key in the last lock. When she destroyed the key, there would be no getting out, no turning back. When she destroyed the key, she and the Dark Guides and the Eater of the World would be locked in this landscape forever.

She closed her eyes, denying the tears that wanted to fall.

"I am the Warrior of Light," she whispered. "It's time to drink from the Dark Cup." Her voice broke. She paused to steady herself. Then she added, "Ephemera, hear me."

"Daylight!" Sebastian said as he stepped off Lee's island. "Why does the school look like that? Why is it *doing* that?"

Michael didn't answer. Lee swore. Caitlin gasped.

The school faded a little more, just as the White Isle had faded when Kenneday's ship approached it. It wasn't quite in the world anymore, but it wasn't completely beyond reach yet.

Michael watched as the rest of his companions stepped off of Lee's little island. He listened to their music and assessed what he heard in each of their hearts.

Wild child, he called. *We need to do a bit of ill-wishing.*

She felt their resonance through the currents that flowed through the world. Sealing this cage hadn't severed this landscape's connection to the world quite enough. It wouldn't be possible to get out, but it was still possible to get in.

She couldn't let that happen.

Not your part of the task anymore, she thought. *The Magician will look after the others.*

Despite the risk that one of them might figure out how to cross over and become trapped in this landscape, she gave herself a moment to picture each of them, and let her affection for each one flow through her.

Caitlin and Brighid. They were finding their true places in the world, and their joy would feed the Light.

Teaser. Cocky grin and swagger—and a vulnerability and yearning to be more that was being answered by his friendship with Lynnea.

Lynnea, who bloomed into a strong woman with a loving heart a little more each day.

Jeb, a man of earthy practicality who was still fumbling a bit as he tried to be a stepfather to grown children.

Yoshani, who had loved her in ways and for reasons she hadn't known until recently.

Nadia, who had a mother's courage and a Landscaper's understanding of what it sometimes cost to take care of the world.

Lee. Brother and friend—and partner in the care of Ephemera. She wished they could have had one more squabble over something that would make him smile in the years to come.

Sebastian. Even more than her mother and brother, she was going to miss Sebastian because he had been the one closest to her heart.

And Michael. He was just emerging from the tight cocoon of who he had been, was just making the transition into who he would become.

For a moment, she let the memory of his arms around her take on physical weight. Comfort. And love. They could have had both, could have offered so much to the world—and each other.

Glorianna shook her head. *Let them go.*

She took a deep breath, then exhaled slowly.

Ephemera, hear me.

"I cast out the Light from this land that is bound to me. I cast out the Light from my heart. I deny all things that come from the Light. I repel all feelings that come from the Light. They have no place in this landscape. They have no place in this heart. I cast out the Light."

"Something's happening," Lee said as he stared at the outside walls of the school. "The resonance is changing, but . . ."

Michael watched Lee. Drifted a little closer. Yoshani and Jeb probably wouldn't act fast enough. Sebastian and Teaser would.

"Guardians and Guides," Lee gasped. "The landscape is getting darker. It's getting *darker.*"

The Warrior of Light must drink from the Dark Cup, Michael thought, feeling his heart ache as he drifted a little closer to Lee.

"I cast out the Light from this land that is bound to me. I cast out the Light from my heart."

Ephemera, obey me!

"I can feel her resonance," Lee said, turning back toward his island. "I think I can still get in, still get her out."

No, you can't, Michael thought.

He threw himself on Lee, ramming into Sebastian as he and Lee hit the ground. They rolled, scrabbled, kicked. He'd gotten his arms around Lee and was holding on since he didn't want this to turn into a vicious brawl, and there was no question that it would turn vicious if Lee managed to shake him off.

Teaser jumped into it and got his legs knocked out from under him, half landing on both of them as they continued to roll and getting elbowed in the head with enough force to take him out of the fight.

Michael kicked out at someone and heard an angry female squeal in response. He'd pay for that kick. He surely would. He couldn't keep this up much longer. The surprise of the attack had worked in his favor, but all Sebastian needed to do was grab hold long enough to use that wizard magic and the fight would end.

More than the fight would end.

Wild child! he called. *Now. Now!*

"I cast out the Light from this land that is bound to me. I cast out the Light from my heart."

Ephemera, obey me! Do this for me and for everyone I love! Now. Now!

Something happening. Strange resonances in the currents. What was *she* doing to Its landscapes?

The ground thickened until It couldn't flow through It in Its natural form. So It changed into the middle-aged gentleman and began to run toward the part of the school that now pulsed with potential, possibility, *change*.

Lee got one arm free, flailed a moment, then reached back and grabbed Michael's hair, yanking hard enough to tear scalp. Sebastian grabbed at both of them but lost his balance when the ground suddenly crested like a wave beneath his feet. Michael rolled, bringing Lee partway under him, pressing Lee's left forearm to the ground at the same moment a rib of stone pushed up from the earth—and Sebastian fell on top of them.

Bone snapped. Lee cried out.

"I cast out the Light!" Glorianna shouted. "I cast out the Light! *I cast out the Light!*"

A tearing inside her. A pain beyond anything she could have imagined. Dark and Light. Two halves of a whole. One could not exist without the other.

But it could. And it did.

She roared through the landscape that had once been the Landscapers' School, changing it. Twisting it until the place reflected the resonance that was her. Until it reflected nothing but her sublime cruelty and held nothing but the Dark.

"It's gone!" Lynnea shouted. "The school is gone!"

Michael shuddered. He'd heard the music. Beautifully twisted. Vibrantly terrible. A glorious song of malevolence.

Travel lightly, Glorianna Belladonna.

He had kept his promises to her, had fulfilled his duties to the world. Because of that, the woman he loved no longer existed.

It was Jeb who pulled him to his feet and looked ready to beat him half to death. And it was Nadia who stepped between them and just stared at him, silently asking for an explanation he didn't want to give.

"She cast out the Light," he said, speaking to Nadia, although he knew the rest of them were listening. "In the story, in order to save the world and everything she loves, the Warrior casts out the Light and embraces the Dark."

"What does she become?" Nadia asked.

He didn't want to tell her. Vowed, in that moment, that he never *would* tell her the story, that he would hide the book and keep it hidden until the day came when the story was, once again, nothing more than a story.

"What does she become?" Nadia asked again.

"She becomes a monster," he said, his voice dulled by sorrow. "She becomes the thing that Evil fears."

There was a time, in the days of old, when Evil walked in the world.

When Evil ruled the world.

One by one, It destroyed the Light in people's hearts, making them slaves to the Dark.

The people who eluded It cried out in fearful desperation. "A champion," they cried. "We need a champion to save the Light."

Now, there was one among them who saw what could be done. Might be done. Must be done. So she commanded the people to build a huge maze, a labyrinth, a tangle of paths and hiding places. And then, when they had done all she had commanded them to do, they built a wall around the place—a wall so high and jagged that nothing could climb it and escape.

When all the preparations were done and everything was ready, the woman slipped into the maze and challenged Evil. "I am the warrior who defends the Light, and I will free the people enslaved in the Dark."

Evil, hearing the challenge, followed the woman into the maze, followed her through the secrets of the labyrinth, searched for her along the tangled paths and in the hiding places. And while Evil followed the Warrior of Light, the people sealed the entrance so that nothing could escape.

When the last stone was in place and the wall was unbroken, the woman faced her enemy and said, "Because I love, I stand here. Because I love, I will stay here. I cast out the Light and bind you to me. I cast out the Light and become your dwelling place. I cast out the Light that lives within me and will walk in this Dark place forever!"

The woman's heart ripped in two. The Light burst out of the maze and flowed through the world, freeing the people who had been enslaved in the Dark.

Seeing the Light and knowing Evil had been defeated, the people who had followed the woman stood outside the high, jagged wall and cheered and cheered.

Then they realized the terrible truth.

By casting out the half of her heart that held the Light, the woman had become something worse than the Evil that had plagued them. She had become a monster that Evil feared. And the people understood then that the walls had been built so jagged and so high because the woman, who had been Light's Warrior, had become something too fearsome to live among them.

So they wept for the loss of the Warrior, and they cherished the Light to the end of their days. But even though they never forgot her, no one went back to that walled-in maze to offer company or comfort to the monster that Evil feared.

—*Elandar story*

Chapter Thirty-one

R age stormed through her landscapes. Raindrops, thick as pus
and stinking of decayed dreams, splatted on ground cracked
by desperation. Death rollers choked and drowned when
freshwater ponds suddenly changed to the boiling mud of fury—or
were frozen by bone-chilling indifference. Bonelovers, pouring out of
their mounds in search of prey, found themselves swimming in the acid
of disappointment, and even as they climbed over each other in their
desperation to get back to safety, the acid ate through their carapaces,
dissolving their bodies as they crawled. The Wizards' Hall was now an
island trapped by a piece of sea, and the Dark Guides, who had rel-
ished being the whispers that had dimmed the Light in people's hearts,
now prowled the corridors throughout the nights, haunted by the
voices of men calling for help, calling for mercy. Just calling. The voices
of doomed men, already dead. And in the morning, when there was a
morning, the Dark Guides would gather and look at the empty places
at the tables. When they checked the rooms of those missing companions, they would find the carpets soaked with seawater—and there
would be more voices in the night, calling. Just calling.

She walked these landscapes, folding them into each other, turning them into mazes that celebrated her Dark purity, altering them into labyrinths that offered no peace, no comfort. Those things did not exist in her world. She created out of the brutal beauty that came from the undiluted feelings that lived in the dark side of the human heart. She was sublime madness, magnificent rage, divine indifference.

As the weeks passed, the Light, that part of herself that had been called Glorianna, became nothing more than a wispy dream of a fading memory, a sometimes-aching scar.

Here, now, there was Belladonna.

Only Belladonna.

Chapter Thirty-two

The land bloomed with the promise of spring, but winter still lived in Michael's heart.

He'd kept his promise—for the most part. He'd learned from Nadia how to take that step between here and there so that he could use the access points in his little piece of the garden to reach his landscapes instead of traveling like he used to. He considered the rest of the walled garden on the Island in the Mist another place in his circuit and wandered the paths, playing the songs he heard in each access point to a landscape. Shoring up the bedrock, that's all he was doing, but the tunes were starting to shift nonetheless. Maybe they were meant to, but he would hold on to them for as long as he could.

He spent a day on each circuit within the walled garden. But he never stepped beyond that. Never went past the gate and up to the house that was now his—the home he had yearned for. Still yearned for. Nadia grew impatient with him sometimes because of it, but his self-imposed exile was the only reason Lee could tolerate dealing with him when they had to meet for business.

Since the Eater of the World was caged again, and it was safe once more to connect landscapes, Lee had done his duty as Bridge and created a stationary bridge that connected the Island in the Mist to Sanctuary. From Sanctuary, another stationary bridge connected to Aurora, the Den, and Darling's Harbor, giving him easy access to his family and the places Glorianna would have wanted him to be able to visit.

Not that he ever used the bridge that led to Sanctuary. It was within sight of the house—and within sight of the bed of turned earth that held the piece of granite and the heart's hope that was his heart's symbol for home.

Putting the bridge there, where he would be reminded of what Glorianna had given him every time he used it, was a piece of calculated cruelty on Lee's part—payback for a broken arm and a lost sister. He understood that well enough.

So he did his duty to the world and played his tunes while his heart froze in a winter that would never end.

There was no Light.

At first, It had felt gleeful that the surviving currents of Light within the school had been so diminished that they were little more than starved threads, easily snuffed out. It had reveled in the despair and anger that had flowed from the surviving humans in Wizard City, as well as gulping down the fear that had flowed from the Dark Guides.

But the glee had faded with the Light's currents. It found no pleasure in the dark landscapes. It took no satisfaction from the knowledge that the True Enemy was trapped within Its landscapes. It had come to realize that It, too, was trapped. With *her*.

So It felt no glee, no pleasure, no satisfaction. The feelings that fed, and were fed by, the Light were snuffed out almost before they could form.

But It did know fear. It crossed the rust-colored sand of the bone-lovers' landscape and found mounds of half-dissolved carcasses. It discovered death rollers impaled on the branches of thorn trees, hanging in the sun like some obscene, rotting fruit. And It watched humans, gathered in hunting parties for safety, grimly butchering one of those death rollers before the meat spoiled.

When It rested, images crept into Its mind. Nasty dreams about Its fluid, natural form becoming stiff as leather; no longer able to flow beneath the skin of the world; just barely able to hump over the surface, defenseless and exposed. Or It would get stuck in the transformation between one shape and the other, stuck between a land creature and a sea creature, unable to live in either landscape, gasping to survive. Or It would change into the middle-aged gentleman, but the body would divide at the waist, becoming the gentleman and one of the female prey. Sometimes the gentleman had a knife, sometimes claws. Either way It would rip and tear Its prey, screaming in pain because It ripped and tore into Itself.

This was Its purpose. This was why the Dark Guides long ago had shaped It from the darkest desires of the human heart and brought It into the world: to destroy the Light. But . . .

It didn't like the Dark. Not *this* much Dark, where there was no hope of a successful hunt, where the human hearts were already so dulled by despair they couldn't hear It—and didn't care when they did.

The Light was gone. It should be happy. But happy belonged to the Light, so the feeling withered before it bloomed.

It didn't like this landscape. And It was afraid of the thing that walked in the Dark because she could sense Its wishes as swiftly as It could make the wish—and destroyed the manifestation of that wish the moment after It realized It had gotten what It had asked for.

No, It didn't like this much Dark. This *wasn't* what It wanted. This place was too cold, too barren, too bitter. Too lonely.

World? It whispered. *Ephemera? Where is the Light?*

Its only answer was Belladonna's cruel, mocking laughter.

☼   ☼   ☼

The Eater of the World craved Light. Wasn't that delicious?

She could feel those tiny threads inside It. A flaw on the part of the Dark Guides who had brought It into being so long ago. It enjoyed snuffing out the feelings that came from the Light, but It also *needed* those feelings for Itself.

The Eater of the World was a flawed creation. Unlike her, who walked pure and undiminished in the Dark.

And if her chest ached so fiercely at times that she wondered why there was no deep, violent scar carved in her flesh, well, that didn't matter because she no longer remembered what she had lost.

You won't find the answer to whatever pains your heart at the bottom of a bottle, Michael, Shaney had said.

You're not doing yourself or the world any good, Magician, Kenneday had said. *Go somewhere your heart can find peace.*

Michael sat on a stone bench and watched the koi in their pond. Find peace. Well, there was no better place to find it than Sanctuary, was there?

It always came as a jolt to realize he had known her for no more than a double handful of days. Oh, he dreamed of her for longer than that, but he hadn't known the woman for more than that short span of time.

So much had happened in those too few days.

My heart's hope lies with Belladonna. Her darkness is my fate.

Too few days. But he would spend the rest of his life living in her shadow.

"It has been quite some time since you visited here," Yoshani said, sitting down on the bench.

"Haven't been in tune with the place, have I?" Michael replied, not caring about the bitterness that flowed through his words.

"Perhaps you haven't wanted to be in tune with the place," Yoshani said gently. "Perhaps now you are starting to heal." He paused, then added, "They understand, Michael. It hurt them—hurt all of us—but we had known Glorianna would stand against the Eater of the World and, most likely, not survive."

"They don't understand—and they haven't forgiven." Michael turned his head and looked at Yoshani. "Nadia has forgiven, as much as she can, but not Lee. Not Sebastian. What happened to Glorianna was no clean death, no peaceful ending. She cast out all the things that belong to the Light—joy and kindness, compassion and love. Hope. She wears a coat of misery, makes a bed out of despair, and drinks sorrow. And the forces of darkness must sit at the table she has made from the bones of their kin and weep bitter tears over the banquet she has set before them."

A long pause. Then Yoshani said, "Those words do not come from the story about the Warrior of Light." He smiled when Michael narrowed his eyes. "You left the box of books with Caitlin Marie. She showed me the story. Your words tell me you have given that dark place, and the woman who walks there, much thought."

"So what if I have?" He hadn't dreamed about her once since she disappeared into that dark place. Some mornings he woke up weeping because he didn't even have that much of her anymore.

"There is something I have wondered."

Yoshani fixed his gaze on the koi pond. That avoidance of meeting another person's eyes caught Michael's attention as nothing else could.

"What happened to the Light?" Yoshani asked softly. "In the story, it is dispersed through the world. But I have also heard about the dark landscape that was created when the Dark was cast out of Lighthaven. So I wondered what happened to the other half of Glorianna's heart. Was her Light dispersed through her landscapes or is it—"

Michael sprang to his feet and took a few steps before realizing he had moved.

He'd asked Ephemera to keep the Light safe. Hadn't he? He couldn't remember. He had accepted the tragic ending of the Warrior of Light. Why hadn't it occurred to him that it was *just a story*? And stories could be changed.

Wild child? he called, hardly daring to breathe. *Wild child? Do you know how to find Glorianna's Light?*

yes yes yes

Faint notes carried on the air. A song he thought he would never hear again—the bright part of the music that was Glorianna Belladonna.

Happiness flowed in the currents around him. As if Ephemera had been waiting for him to ask the question. Or discover for himself where it had put the Light half of Glorianna's heart.

Fool. The world *had* been waiting for him to ask the question.

"I have to go back to the Island in the Mist." He spun around to face Yoshani. If he was wrong, he wanted someone with him because the despair would crush him. If he was right, he wanted to share the joy. "Come with me?"

The bridge that led to the Island in the Mist was on one of the little islands that dotted Sanctuary's small lake. It was separate from the other little islands and not easily accessible, but flat stepping stones rose above the lake's surface as he and Yoshani approached the shore, giving them a slippery path.

Michael trembled as he crossed over to the Island in the Mist. Not to the walled garden this time, but to the part of the island that would have been his home with Glorianna. The part that would have nurtured their life together.

The music rang in the air, calling him.

He ran, knowing exactly where to look, with Yoshani right behind him.

Had it been there all these months, waiting for him to find it? He hadn't heard a single note of this when he was in the walled garden. Hadn't suspected it was here.

He skidded to a stop in front of a bed near the house. His heart's hope plant looked brittle. Dead. But there was one little patch of new, green leaves. And one tiny bud struggling to bloom.

Beside his little plant was a glory of Light. A heart's hope bigger than any he'd seen and covered with buds.

"Michael?" Yoshani asked, looking at him, then at the bed, then back again.

He pointed to the heart's hope. "Her Light."

Yoshani frowned. "Nadia, Lynnea, and Caitlin have all been here to tend the gardens and do the mundane work. Lee was here to make the bridge. Even Sebastian has been here. They said nothing."

"They don't know," he said softly, as stories and memories and all the things Glorianna had told him about the connection of Dark and Light spun through his mind.

My heart's hope lies with Belladonna. Her darkness is my fate.

The key had been inside him all the time. Had he realized the answer too late, or would he be able to open that locked door?

"Forgive my doubt, Michael, but how do *you* know?"

He gave Yoshani a brilliant smile. "I can hear the music of her heart."

Chapter Thirty-three

The sand in the box Glorianna had referred to as a playground didn't change. Hadn't changed in the handful of days since this idea had taken root. He hadn't been rewarded with a pebble or a weed or even a tiny patch of bog. Nothing. He had hoped that music could be a bridge between landscapes, could touch what, otherwise, couldn't be reached. But there had been no indication, not the slightest, that his music was reaching the woman he played for.

Discouraged, he tucked the whistle in his pocket, then let his hands fall into his lap.

"I don't know, wild child," he said. "Maybe I left it too late, didn't figure things out fast enough." It had occurred to him, while he was doing the washing up after dinner last night, that time was a factor. Every day Glorianna Belladonna remained a heart divided was another day she would change a little more, become someone different from the woman he'd known—and the song he remembered would no longer be the song that matched the whole of her heart. Months had already gone by since she'd taken the Eater and Its landscapes out of the world. Who was she now? Did she remember anything about her family, about him?

He'd played the music that was Glorianna Belladonna. And he'd played the music that was Michael the Magician, hoping the memory of being with him would stir something in the currents of the world.

The only thing it had stirred up was his longing for her.

As he sat there, staring at the unchanging sand in the box, his mind drifted, and an image from a story floated up to the surface of memory.

A door with a hundred locks. A key that came from the heart.

His breath caught. He sat up straight, his blood pounding in his veins.

"One lock this time," he whispered. "And only one key that will open it." Then he felt a stab of sorrow so fierce that he bent over, pressing his forehead to his knees to try to ease the pain of it.

Only one would open that lock. And he wasn't the right key.

"Well, look who's here."

It wasn't the warmest welcome, Michael thought as he stepped into Philo's courtyard, but at least Teaser wasn't hurling threats at him—or stones.

"Michael!" Lynnea hurried over. "It's been so long since we've seen you. Where have you been? Have you eaten? You haven't eaten, have you? Sit down right there, and I'll bring you something. Teaser, you keep him company."

"You don't have to be fussing over me," Michael protested. "I just . . . Is Sebastian around?"

"You're nothing but skin and bones," Lynnea said.

A little worse for wear, maybe, but hardly skin and bones.

"You will sit, and you will eat."

She suddenly sounded like a younger version of his aunt Brighid, which scared him enough to make him keep quiet and pull out a chair at a table. When she swung into the building to place his order, he looked at Teaser, who shrugged.

"She's practicing to be a mommy," Teaser said, dropping into the opposite chair.

"She's pregnant?" That would be good news for the family, wouldn't it?

"They're working on getting her that way."

Michael scratched his chin. "They weren't working on it before?" He couldn't picture Sebastian abstaining from sex.

"Nah," Teaser said. "Before, if it happened, it would have been an accident. Now it's deliberate. Don't ask me what the difference is. I'm just an incubus, and from where I'm standing, it looks the same to me."

He smiled, finding comfort in the ordinary. And he could admit to himself that that was the reason he'd avoided the Den over these past few months—he hadn't felt he deserved the comfort he'd found in this landscape, with these people.

Then he heard the song, before he turned his head and saw the man. A dark song, full of power, threaded with Light.

"Word has it that you've settled into the house on the Island in the Mist," Sebastian said as he joined them.

"I have, yes."

Lynnea came back and set a plate in front of him piled with roast beef, potatoes, and some kind of casserole. She placed a bowl of melted cheese and a basket of Phallic Delights between Sebastian and Teaser.

"The man isn't taking care of himself," she said, glaring at Sebastian. "Don't let him leave the table until he eats."

"What's he supposed to do?" Teaser asked, reaching for a Phallic Delight. "Give Michael a bit of a sizzle?"

Lynnea whacked the incubus on the shoulder and huffed off to a table full of visitors, who cowered at her approach.

"She tangled with Lee over something this morning and has been a bit pissy ever since," Sebastian said, swirling a Delight in the melted cheese.

"Over me, is what you're not saying." Michael started to push the plate of food away, then glanced up and saw Lynnea glaring at him, so he picked up a fork and stabbed a piece of potato.

"Good choice," Sebastian said. "Anyone who tangles with her today is on his own."

The first few bites didn't go down easily, but as he listened to Teaser and Sebastian talking about the Den, he began to relax and enjoy the meal.

Lynnea returned, declared herself satisfied that he'd eaten enough, and removed the dishes.

"Well," Teaser said, looking from him to Sebastian. "I'll just take myself off and do . . . something."

When they were alone, Michael could feel those sharp green eyes staring at him, so he lifted his head and met Sebastian, look for look.

"Threat and promise is what you called me," Michael said quietly. "I made good on the threat by helping Glorianna cage the Eater of the World—and cage herself in the process. Now I'm asking for your help, Justice Maker, in order to make good on the promise."

"In clear words, Magician," Sebastian said.

"I think there's a way to get her back. And I think you're the key to doing it."

Sebastian stared at him for a long time. Then, softly, "What do you want me to do?"

"It might not work," Michael said as he and Sebastian walked over to the sandbox.

"You said that."

"I don't really know what I'm doing."

"You said that too."

"I just don't want you to hope for too much."

Sebastian stopped. "Magician. Isn't that the whole point? To hope?"

Michael swayed with the force of those words flowing through the currents on the island. "It is. Yes, it is."

They stepped into the gravel side of the box and sat down on the bench.

"What do you want me to do?" Sebastian asked.

Michael took out his whistle. "I'm not sure how this reaching through the twilight of waking dreams works, but you were able to reach my aunt and the Ladies of Light on the White Isle when you sent that riddle, so I'm thinking you could reach Glorianna in this other landscape."

Sebastian looked at the tip of his boot. "I've already tried that. It didn't work."

Michael nodded. "And I've tried what I could do. I'm thinking neither is enough by itself, but together . . . All we need is a crack, a way to send a little something to help her remember who she was. She divided her heart and built a wall to keep them separated, but given a chance, they'll come back together. We're trying to create just enough of a chink in that wall for her to feel the other half of her heart."

It was tempting to play the love inside himself, but while Sebastian unfurled the power of the incubus and moved through the twilight of waking dreams, Michael played the music he heard in the incubus's heart.

A beautiful bed in a garden. A piece of granite, the stone of strength, with veins of quartz that sparkled in sunlight. Rich earth. And flowers that rose out of the ground in a dazzle of colors that delighted the eye—and made the scar in her chest ache and ache and ache until . . .

That was better. Much better. Those beautiful flowers were nothing more than a lure. As they bloomed, the nectar dripped down the petals and poisoned the rich earth, killing the beauty.

And despair moaned through the dying trees, and sorrow was a bed of stones.

And somewhere, just out of sight, a boy laughed, his delight at being included, at being accepted, producing a shimmer of Light.

She woke, her hand pressed against her chest to ease the terrible ache.

Something stirred in her landscape. Something that didn't belong here.

Something she couldn't want here.

She rose, feeling stiff, feeling achy, feeling angry. She would strip away any pretties that had crept into her landscape. She would crush anything that fed the weeds of Light, those damned currents she couldn't eliminate completely, no matter how often she tore at the roots.

Time to find the Eater again. It gave her a savage pleasure to use those remaining flickers of Light to manifest something desirable and watch It try to belong, to fit in with the very creatures It had once wanted to destroy.

Boo, hoo, boo, hoo, little Eater. Belladonna has a treat for you. Poison in the pretties.

Or maybe just a pretty. The hearts in this landscape would tear each other apart to possess something truly pretty. Or tasty. Or desirable.

She laughed, and the sound was a blight on the land.

But as she prepared to leave the lair she had created from a garden a girl had abandoned long ago, she stopped and listened.

For a moment, she thought she heard music. And then there was only the wind.

Sebastian rubbed the back of his neck to ease the ache.

Michael tucked his whistle in his pocket and ignored the stiffness in his hands—and wondered how long they'd been at this before neither had been able to sustain the effort.

"What do you think?" Sebastian finally asked. "Did anything happen?"

"I don't know," Michael replied wearily. "I don't know."

Sebastian stood up and stretched. Then he looked at Michael. "Then I guess we do this again tomorrow."

"I guess we do."

He walked with Sebastian to the stationary bridge that would take the incubus to Sanctuary and the first step on the journey home. Alone again, he stopped at the bed near the house—and smiled.

"Something happened," he whispered. "Something did."

The bud on his little heart's hope plant had bloomed, and another bud was starting to grow.

Chapter Thirty-four

Michael half turned when he heard the brisk knock on the kitchen door, but before he could step away from the stove, Sebastian was inside, closing the door against the wind and the wet weather.

"You got rain." Sebastian set the market basket on the table, then stripped off his coat and hung it on a peg by the door.

"Not the best of days to be trying the music," Michael said, "but there's an umbrella here. We can stuff ourselves under it for a little while."

"Won't that be cozy?" Sebastian rubbed his hands as if he were trying to warm them up. "It's not raining in Aurora."

There was a message in those words. "I'm making tea," Michael said. "If you want koffee . . ."

"I'll make it myself," Sebastian finished, taking a few things out of the market basket.

"I can make it," Michael said, feeling as if his hospitality had been called into question.

"No," Sebastian said firmly. "You can't."

Ah. So it wasn't his hospitality that was being called into question but his ability to make an acceptable—according to Sebastian—cup of koffee.

"Fine then," Michael grumbled. "Make it yourself."

"I've got two jars of Aunt Nadia's soup, and Lynnea made a couple of beef sandwiches."

Bribery. And since that would make a far better meal than anything he would have scrounged for himself, he got a pot out of the cupboard to heat up one jar of soup, then set two places at the table.

"It's been a few days now, Michael," Sebastian said after he ground the koffea beans and got the brew started. "I couldn't keep sliding around the question of where I was going each day. So I told Lynnea where I've been going—and that led to telling her why."

Michael ladled the soup into bowls while Sebastian put the sandwiches on plates. "And she told Nadia." Which explained the food.

"It's made them hopeful—and that has given them all a lot of energy."

The way Sebastian smiled gave him a very bad feeling.

"So who else knows?"

"Just the people you'd expect. Family—and close friends."

Lady's mercy. That wasn't all of it. He sensed there was more, but whatever else Sebastian wanted to tell him was something he really didn't want to know.

When they were halfway through the soup, Sebastian said, "It's spring. I was told it's time to tidy up the gardens."

"What's that mean?"

"That means it's not going to rain here tomorrow, Magician, so you'd better be home and you'd better be prepared."

Michael blinked. "For what?"

Sebastian shook his head and sighed. "Four women, which includes your aunt Brighid, who like to play in the dirt and grow green things."

"Uh-huh."

"They will be here tomorrow—along with me, Teaser, Jeb, Yoshani, and Lee—to help you tidy up the walled garden, and plant a few flowers in the personal garden."

Michael plopped his spoon in the bowl, slumped in his chair, and stared at Sebastian. "There's close to two acres of land in the walled garden, and that much or more that could be considered the formal grounds around the house."

"Uh-huh."

"All of it? We're going to tidy up *all* of it?"

"Uh-huh."

He felt the blood draining out of his head. But maybe it wouldn't be so bad. He wasn't a gardener, and didn't pretend to be, but the gardens didn't look too bad to his untrained eye. "So what's to be done then?"

Sebastian held up a hand and began ticking items off with his fingers. "Weeding, mulching, raking the leaves that were neglected last fall—"

"Raking *leaves*? Why?"

"Because they fell off the trees and are now on the ground. We can rake them up or we can tack them back onto the trees, every single one of them. That's a direct quote."

Michael braced his head in his hands. "Lee doesn't want to come here. His arm has been out of the plaster for a while now, but I'd think he'd use the excuse of a healing bone to get out of coming here."

"He tried," Sebastian replied dryly. "He was told, and I quote, 'You don't need two hands to pull up weeds.' "

"Lady of Light, have mercy on us."

"Well, I hope someone does, because Aunt Nadia is pretty ruthless when it comes to cleaning up the garden. And Lynnea isn't much better," Sebastian added under his breath.

Michael fiddled with the spoon for a moment, then pushed the bowl aside. "If you could go back and make that choice again, the one that has you tidying up gardens because a particular woman wants it of you . . ."

"I'd make the same choice," Sebastian said. "I chose love, Magician. Just like you. Isn't that why you're here?"

He nodded. "That's why I'm here." He studied what was left of the soup in his bowl. "Did Glorianna like this soup?"

"It was her favorite. Aunt Nadia calls it comfort soup." Sebastian looked at the other jar of soup on the counter and then looked at Michael. "Magician, I have an idea."

Crying softly, the Eater of the World wrapped the tatters of Its shirt around Its wounded arm.

There had been bushes of ripe berries. Succulent. Sweet. It hadn't wanted many, just a few. Just a taste of something good.

But the humans had found the berries too, and their minds had been too clotted with greed and viciousness to hear anything else. They trampled each other and tore at each other in order to get to the berries. They stabbed at each other and stoned each other as they fought to stuff handfuls of the ripe fruit in their mouths. They destroyed the bushes and mashed half the berries underfoot in their efforts to have as much as they could—more than anyone else.

And when It had tried to move among them and get Its own small share of the berries, they had turned on It, attacked It, ripped at Its clothes, and driven It away.

They had hurt It. And there was no one—*no one*—in this landscape who had the kind of heart that would have taken It in to tend the wounds and look after It.

Well, there *were* hearts in this landscape that were able to feel kindness and compassion, even if only a little, but those feelings just withered without . . .

World? It whimpered. *World? Where is the Light?*

"Come on, wild child, you can do this," Michael said as he set the basket on the sand in the box. "You brought Caitlin's hair to Aurora to help her, remember? This is the same thing. We just want you to take this basket to Belladonna. Just leave it where she'll find it. It's important. You can do this. We know you can." Michael looked over his shoulder and made a circling "say something" gesture.

"If you could do this, it would mean a lot to the people who love her," Sebastian said. He didn't sound confident, even though this had been his idea, but at least the Justice Maker wasn't trying to fool the world with false heartiness.

Stepping back, Michael tucked himself under the umbrella Sebastian held and gave the other man a minute to unfurl the power of the incubus. Then he pulled out his whistle and began to play.

There was a basket on the ground by the fountain, and a resonance flowing through the currents of this old garden.

She moved cautiously toward the basket, expecting some kind of trap, obscenely angry that anything would dare enter her lair. But there was nothing in the basket except a bowl, a spoon, and a jar of . . . soup.

Something prickled the edges of her memory, a painful tingle like a limb waking up. And that resonance. She felt it hook into the scar in her chest, felt it dig in and set. And from that hook the thinnest thread of Light flowed out to someplace beyond her landscapes. She should pull it out. *Would* pull it out. Except the thread flowed with that resonance.

She looked at the jar of food—and her belly growled, so she poured some of the soup into the bowl, then sealed up the jar before she picked up the spoon and took a taste.

The sound of chattering birds coming from the room beside the kitchen. Two boys at the table. Her brother Lee and . . .

So watchful, so wary, so wanting to belong. She felt a connection between his heart and hers, knew this now-stranger would resonate through her life.

Sebastian.

Watching him eat the soup her mother had made. Watching him savor the taste of it, the sensuality of soup and bread eaten at a table where love was served along with the food.

Lee. Sebastian. Nadia.

She flung the bowl away from her. Tried to fling the memory with it. But the memory was more tenacious, had already hooked into the scarred part of her.

"Mother."

Nadia wasn't here. *Couldn't* be here. Nor Lee. Nor Sebastian. But the basket . . .

She heard it then. The music that matched the resonance of a boy who had sunk a hook into her heart so many years ago. Too late now. Too late. She had managed to tear that resonance out of her heart once before, but she couldn't do it again. Not again.

In that moment, suspended between the Dark she could feel and that resonance called Sebastian that made her yearn for *something*, another resonance rippled through her. The faintest whisper, the merest tug.

A promise.

Chapter Thirty-five

The next morning, Michael stepped outside and looked at the two men waiting for him.

"You here already?" he asked.

Teaser grinned. "You are a lollygagger, a layabout, and a . . . What was the other word?" He raised his eyebrows at Sebastian.

"I think Michael gets the idea," Sebastian said. "We've been here long enough for the ladies to have made an assessment of people's gardening skills." He handed Michael a rake. "They have taken the sensible men and are working in the walled garden. We—"

"The garden idiots," Teaser said gleefully.

"—get to rake the leaves around the house and do the weeding in the flower beds where our efforts will cause the least harm," Sebastian finished. "Unsupervised."

Michael looked at the two incubi, who looked extraordinarily pleased about this arrangement. And he was beginning to understand the gleam in Sebastian's eyes. "Well, I guess that tells us our place in the pecking order, doesn't it?"

"You do some luck-wishing for us this morning, Magician?" Sebastian asked.

"Maybe a little." Michael grinned. "Maybe just a little."

She shivered in the chilly air. Because being cold and unhappy made her vengeful, the deserts within her landscape baked under a merciless sun, and the surviving bonelovers couldn't cross the burning sand. The river in the death rollers' landscape got so hot fish cooked in the water—and even the death rollers were driven out of the water by the heat. But fog shrouded the plateau where the Wizards' Hall stood, and fog filled the corridors, brushing against the Dark Guides' skins like damp, clingy fingers. And rain, tasting like bitter tears, poured down on the rest of Wizard City.

She walked beneath the merciless sun, walked along the banks of that simmering river, walked through the fog and the bitter rain. Her heart poured out Dark purity, and Ephemera manifested everything that came from that heart.

And all the dark things that had once wanted nothing more than to chew up the Light and spit it out now huddled in their mounds, in their caves, in their houses—and shivered in fear.

"They went home," Michael muttered as he made his way down to the sandbox. "They all went home. Lady of Light, my thanks for small favors." And it was a *small* favor, since they were all coming back tomorrow to finish the work.

He stepped into the part of the box that held the gravel, set a little clutch of violets on the sand, then sat down on the bench.

Those women were ferocious when they set their minds to a task. It scared him a little to see how well Caitlin Marie fit in with Nadia and Lynnea. And Aunt Brighid, whom he'd always thought of as a formidable woman, didn't seem intimidating at all compared with *those* two.

"They mean well. It's a small comfort to my aching body, but they mean well." He took out his whistle and sighed. "Just you and me tonight, wild child. Sebastian is done in, so I sent him on home." And part of that decision was the growing doubt that their efforts were making any difference. "If you could take that little clutch of flowers to the same place you took the basket, I'll play a little while and then we'll all get some rest."

He waited. Felt nothing.

"Wild child?"

Ephemera finally answered his call, but the world wasn't happy. He couldn't prove it, but he suspected that the Dark currents in all parts of the world were a little swollen, and little bits of unhappiness were occurring to a lot of people—a lost brooch, a broken dish, a missing toy. Each thing wasn't more than an extra drop of unhappiness, but all those extra drops eventually could change the tone of a family or a village.

"You can do this, wild child. I know you can."

Gone. A flurry of notes that sounded in his mind like a child blaming him for some unhappiness, and Ephemera was gone.

He could think of one reason why the world would be unhappy with him. "Did something happen when you took the basket?"

No response. He couldn't even do that much.

The violets looked sad in the waning light. A lover's token, rejected before it was received.

Since he was playing for no one but himself, he played the music he called "Glorianna's Light." Then he played the music of love. The music that remembered the touch of her hand, the feel of her lips, the wonder of being inside her.

Tears slipped down his face, and his heart ached with the remembering, but he kept playing.

And never noticed when the little clutch of violets disappeared.

She picked up the little clutch of violets and felt the resonances that had names, faces, memories. Pretty little flowers with savage hooks that dug in and dug in until she wept from the pain of remembering those names, those faces. Screamed out the agony of wanting to touch those names, those faces.

Don't belong there. Not anymore.

But the hooks dug in, dug in, dug in. And from the thin threads that were anchored in another landscape, Light flowed.

World? It whispered. *World? Is there Light?*

Chapter Thirty-six

W *orld?* It whispered. *World? Is there Light?*

Ephemera flowed through the currents of the Island in the Mist. It did not listen to the Eater of the World. *Would* not listen. But the question, flowing from the currents in the forbidden part of itself, brought it back to the sandbox where the Music played with it every day.

A heart wish had flowed out of the forbidden place. *Her* heart wish. But the Music did not answer, did not ask the world to send the proper answer. The Music was still learning to be Guide. Maybe the Music did not know?

She had been the last one at the school who had talked to it, had played with it and helped it shape itself. Who had understood how to be Guide to the World. Unlike the others before her, when the Dark

Ones had come, she had listened to it when it tried to save her. It had found Light, and she had followed.

It had found Light. And she had followed.

A break in the trees where a person could stand and see the moon shining over the lake. And there was the resonance called Sebastian painting a dark-haired woman who wore a gown that looked as substantial as moonbeams.

"This is where you belong," he said. "This is where you should be."

"I can't."

"You can," the lover said as his arms wrapped protectively around her. "I traveled a long way to find the treasure in my heart. Don't ask me to let it go."

She felt him fade away, but the resonance that was Sebastian was still there, as strong as memories, as full of promise as a sunrise. And then . . .

Mist. And music. The bright notes of the whistle made her smile, and the drum heated her blood until her heart pounded with the rhythm.

The music dimmed, as if someone had shut a door, and she stood outside in the mist. His arms closed around her, pulling her back against the warmth of his chest.

She heard the drum in the beat of his heart, knew the bright notes of the whistle would be in his voice, in his laugh.

"I can hear the music," she said. "I can hear the music inside you."

The music flowed over her skin, sang in her blood, rang in the scarred hollow of her chest. She swallowed and tasted tears—and didn't know if they were her own or someone else's.

Better to sleep. Just sleep. The music was a good dream. She could follow that dream and slip away forever.

Except the Light was pouring out of the music, feeding the starved currents of this landscape. Waking the predators.

She rolled onto her side and forced gummy eyes open to look in the direction of the fountain.

Then she scrambled to her feet and stumbled toward the fountain and the patch of ground *glowing* with Light.

"No," she moaned when she saw the heart's hope growing out of the sand. "Oh, no."

The size of the plant was stunning enough, but it was the flowers that made the heart ache in wonder. They ranged from white as pure as hope to the deep red of passion.

The Warrior of Light must drink from the Dark Cup. She remembered that now—remembered what she had done. The Warrior of Light must drink from the Dark Cup, and turn away from the Light forever. But the Light rang in her now. Rang, sang, *pulled* with the need to put two halves back together to make a whole.

Here here here, Ephemera called. This way.

She looked around. Her old garden. At the school. The one she had escaped from when the Dark Guides had tried to seal her in. Ephemera had come to her that day, too.

Heart's wish! This way!

"Pushy little world," she muttered.

She felt the change inside her. Had felt it starting when the resonances and memories set their hooks into her savaged heart. A tiny flicker of Light that held a promise. And music.

Just a step would take her between here and there. But . . . where? She was no longer sure who she was or where she truly belonged.

She stared at the heart's hope—and remembered two men in a dream.

"Take it back," she said firmly. "Take the heart's hope back where you found it."

Heart's wish. Ephemera sounded wistful.

"When the heart's hope is back where it belongs, I'll go where you need me to go."

Yes yes yes!

The heart's hope disappeared, leaving only a square of sand in a nimbus of Light.

Something tugged at her from the access point Ephemera had created. *Pulled* at her.

She had a sudden image of a stretchy band pulled to its fullest. A big ball of Light was at one end; she was at the other. When the band snapped back . . .

"Guardians and Guides, this is going to hurt."

She hesitated. Pain in staying, pain in going.

But something made her hesitate.

In Ephemera, there were few secrets of the heart. And even that heart couldn't remain hidden now. Not from her.

She walked back to the ragged blanket she had found somewhere, then pressed her fingers against the ground beneath one corner.

Ephemera, hear me.

Assured that the world would obey, she walked back to the square of sand and took the step between here and there.

Light!

Barely more than a flicker now, but reason enough to race ahead of whatever else might want to destroy that flicker.

Then It hesitated. There had been a place in the landscape that had been so Dark it had not quite existed with the rest of the school. *Her* lair.

But It did not feel that Dark anymore, and when It approached, It discovered the walls had been torn down, the fountain shattered. Nothing there now but an empty, broken place.

Changing back to human form, It approached the only thing of interest that had been left behind: a ragged blanket. Crouching, It fingered the material. Scratchy but warm—and more than It had now.

It started to grab the blanket, then froze as It felt the resonance beneath the material.

It lifted the corner—and stared for a long time. Then It scooped up the prize and the blanket, and hurried back to the walled garden It had made into a lair. There, It carefully unwrapped the prize and stared at it some more.

What had been in Belladonna's heart when she had commanded the world to do this? Had this been left as a punishment—or a gift?

Didn't matter. What mattered was that she had left behind a flicker that could feed the Light.

After selecting the most protected spot in Its garden, the Eater of the World planted the tiny heart's hope.

They stood outside Shaney's Tavern, the music pouring out of the open doors behind them. He wrapped his arms around her and held her against his chest.

"Stay with me," he said. "My heart's hope lies with you, Glorianna Belladonna. Stay—"

A scuffling sound in his bedroom broke the dream. He lay awake, alert. Then he almost drowned in the sound that flooded through him.

"Magician?"

A rough, rusty voice. He barely heard it above the jagged pieces of song trying to fit together. Crashing. Screaming. Dark tones and Light. A song of terrible beauty grating against so much hope.

He pushed himself up on one elbow and stared at the shadowy figure standing at the foot of his bed. "Glorianna?"

"I heard the music. I heard the music in your heart."

Then she swooned, and he leaped out of bed to catch her, to hold her as he sank to his knees. Even in the moonlight coming in the window, she looked dirty and bruised and half starved. And she was the most wonderful thing he had ever seen.

"You'll be all right, darling," he said, rocking her. "You're home now. You'll be all right."

She stirred a little.

"Glorianna? Come on now, darling. Don't be doing this to me."

"Don't tell Lee," she mumbled.

"What?" He stopped rocking and looked down at her.

"He gets upset when I faint. Don't tell him."

He laughed—and then he cried. Then he picked her up and tucked her into bed with him. And hoped he wasn't dreaming.

Chapter Thirty-seven

Sebastian burst into the kitchen, jolting Michael's groggy wakefulness.

Despite waking up again and again to reassure himself that he hadn't been dreaming, he hadn't wanted to sleep a minute longer this morning. On the other hand, he wanted to sleep for a week.

"What happened?" Sebastian asked, his voice as tense as his body. "The heart's hope is gone. Glorianna's Light is gone!"

"Not gone, exactly," Michael said, trying to get his eyes to focus. "Just transplanted, in a manner of speaking. Want some koffee?"

"Not if you're making it."

"Fine, then. Do it yourself." Which, all things considered, was a better idea.

Wishing he'd had a little more time to prepare for this, he leaned against the kitchen table and scrubbed his hands over his face. Once Sebastian got the koffee started, he said, "It's good you're here today."

"I've been here every day, Magician," Sebastian replied, still sounding tense.

"I know you have. I know." He paused, needing to get the words right. "There's always one that's harder than the rest when they're taken from you. One that has meant more to your hopes and dreams. One you love just a little more."

Sebastian watched him and said nothing.

"Let me show you Glorianna's Light."

They left the kitchen and went around the side of the house. And saw her walking back from the walled garden. She hadn't been ready to go inside, but she had wanted to stand at the gate. So he'd gone inside to start breakfast—and hoped she would still be on the island when he put the meal on the table.

Sebastian stood there, frozen, just staring at her.

"Threat and promise is what you called me," Michael said quietly. "I made good on the threat. Together, Justice Maker, we made good on the promise." He watched her move toward them. Saw her hesitate. "She took back her Light, and she came back to us. But she's two halves of a whole, and it's not a smooth fit anymore."

"Glorianna," Sebastian whispered. "Glorianna."

"She might always be two halves that don't quite fit together to make a whole."

He watched the words finally take hold. Those sharp green eyes studied him. "In clear words, Magician."

"Love isn't just something you feel. It's something you do. I love her, so I'm staying." Michael smiled. "After all, my heart's hope lies with Glorianna Belladonna. But she's changed, Sebastian. Nothing will be the same as it was."

Now Sebastian smiled. "This is Ephemera, Magician. Nothing is ever the same as it was."

Michael watched Sebastian race across the lawn and sweep his cousin into his arms. Good music. Strong music. And one or two of those jagged edges inside Glorianna were smoothed out a little more just by Sebastian's presence.

It would be all right. *She* would be all right.

As he turned to go back inside to make breakfast for the three of them, a movement caught his eye.

There, sheltered by the quartz-veined granite that stood for his home landscape, was a clutch of violets.

"Thanks, wild child."

He grinned as he went back in the house. Then he sang as he worked. And he heard the music of her—the dark tones and the light—ring out over the island.

They would be all right, he thought as he put the meal on the table a moment before Glorianna and Sebastian walked through the door. It would take time, but they would be all right.